Better Than

Chocolate

Book Two in the Serendipity Series

Brieanna Robertson

Whimsical Publications, LLC

Florida

Published in the United States by
Whimsical Publications, LLC
Florida

www.whimsicalpublications.com

Cover art by Traci Markou

ISBN-13: 978-0-9787738-6-1

Printed in the United States of America

He reached over to a bowl that was on the floor next to the couch and he offered it to her. "Chocolate?"

Kat looked at the chocolates and picked one out, smiling to herself. "I have very good memories of these," she murmured.

Van watched her with a soft smile on his sensual lips. "Want to share?"

She frowned. "My chocolate?"

"No. Your memory."

She looked away sadly and the deepest kind of sorrow welled up inside of her. Tears stung her eyes and she swallowed. "It was a long time ago," she whispered.

He gave her a look of concern, as if wondering why the memory should cause her such sadness. "Are you all right?"

She tried to mask her grief with a fake smile and nodded. "There's nothing better than chocolate," she said, trying to change the subject.

He regarded her with an expression that was solemn, but exuded warmth. It was one of those unnerving looks that made it seem like he was looking straight into her soul. It made her squirm and her pulse accelerate in a way that was extremely abnormal for her.

"Some things are," he said, his eyes holding hers.

Kat's heart lurched and she felt sick to her stomach. She looked away and pretended to be interested in a thread on the couch.

"Van!" Lance cried. "Dude! This girl's whipping us all! I'm gonna be naked soon!"

Kat and Van both looked over to see Lance sitting only in his boxers and one sock. Van laughed and Kat took the opportunity. She snapped her book open again and pretended to read, sticking her nose further into it than she needed to, trying to escape. She glanced at Van out of the corner of her eye. He looked at her and smiled knowingly, then stood and went over to Lance. She let out a relieved sigh and didn't move for the rest of the trip. She had never been so happy to see a hotel in all her life.

Hank helped Rochelle and Kat with their luggage and got them checked in. Kat listened to Rochelle go on and on *and on* about Lance's chest, Lance's torso, Lance's tattooed arms and rippling biceps, etc., etc., etc. as she put her pajamas on, glad to be in her own room and away from Van. Though she had refused to show any sign of life for the last leg of the journey, she noticed his continued quiet watching of her. He kept to himself, but she could feel his eyes burning into her. It had been the longest ride of her life.

"So I saw you talking to Van," Rochelle said.

Kat sighed as she set her suitcase inside the closet. "Yeah."

"What did you talk about? Did he hit on you?"

Kat rolled her eyes. "No, we talked about work and he gave me a chocolate. Big whoop. I'm gonna go find the ice machine." She left the room and wandered through the halls for awhile, trying to regain her usual composure. Van had rattled her much more than she would have liked. She was always in control, always cool and collected and reserved, but he had made her feel completely neurotic. The things he had said. The way he had looked at her. It was freaky. He made her remember things she had tried to forget a long time ago. Things that still hurt like they had happened yesterday.

She paced restlessly for awhile longer, until she felt like she had control over herself again, then meandered back to the room, never actually having located the ice machine. She stopped in the doorway and frowned when she saw a folded piece of paper on the floor. She picked it up and stared at it for a moment. Her name was written on the outside of it. She felt instant dread. This was something else that was going to freak her out. She could feel it. She opened it reluctantly.

This story is well written, and from an editor's point of view, an absolute joy to read. I recommend it to anyone that wants a sweet romance, that remembers those shy, gawky, awkward high school years, and the spark in your gut the first time you knew you were in love.

-Traci Markou
Forbidden Publications Editor

ACKNOWLEDGEMENTS

I do not know, nor have I ever met, Bam Margera or Ville Valo. The references to them in this story are purely fictional and an homage to the inspiration they provided.

I don't think that this book would have even been what it is if not for their influence. I was writing "Better Than Chocolate" during a dark time in my life. Halfway through the story, I got terrible writer's block. HIM's amazing music became my muse, and *Viva La Bam* was the only thing that made me laugh. These things got me through a tough time, enabled me to finish my story, and made it a better work of fiction in the process.

My thanks goes out to them from the very bottom of my heart.

Thank you, thank you, thank you, as well, to my beautiful friends Jimmy and Phil for helping me write Van's song. You are amazing poets.

To everyone who dances to the beat of their own drum.
The artists, the musicians, the eccentrics.
You are the beauty of the world. Sing your song proudly.

Prologue

Los Angeles, CA

Kat checked her watch, then glanced down at the list of contestants on her lap. One more to go. She swallowed uncomfortably. She didn't want to go home. She hated home. She looked over at her friend Rochelle, who was tapping her pen against the seat in front of her as she read down the list also, making a note here and there. "One left," Kat remarked.

Rochelle looked at Kat and rolled her bright blue eyes. "Let's just hope he's better than the last three," she muttered.

They were hosting the auditions for the Senior Show in the Little Theatre, and Kat was beginning to lose faith that her classmates possessed any talent at all. She had seen four different groups do a dance routine to the same NSYNC song, and if she heard it one more time, she was going to shoot herself. Did no one have originality anymore?

She sighed. "Next!"

There was a pause, and then a skinny young man walked slowly out onto the stage. He was tall, but hunched, like he had grown too quickly and was uncomfortable with his height. His black hair was disheveled with red streaks running through it, and his fingernails were painted black. Actually, his entire ensemble was black, and his pants had chains and zippers all over them. He had equally as dark eyeliner and he carried a beautiful red electric guitar.

Kat's lips turned up slightly at the corners. She heard snickers behind her from the empty-headed football players that had insisted on sitting in.

"Look, it's Freak Boy!" one of them shouted.

The other laughed. "What are you doing here, loser? The funeral home's down the street!"

Kat turned and gave them an icy scowl. They looked sheepish and grinned at her.

"Who's that?" Rochelle whispered. "I don't think I've ever even seen that guy before. Is he a freshman? Freshmen can't try out for the Senior Show."

Kat shook her head. "No, he's in our class. That's Jake Marsallis. You've seen him around. He always eats lunch by himself in the quad."

Rochelle frowned thoughtfully, then her eyes widened as she seemed to remember something. "Oh! The guy in your art class who freaked out on everyone?"

She nodded, taking another glance back up at the boy on the stage. She remembered that day all too well. It came into her mind every time she looked at him.

They'd all been in art class, working quietly on their own projects, when a huge crash had directed everyone's attention to the far corner of the room where Jake huddled, shaking violently and clutching at his chest. Everyone panicked because he'd overturned a supply cart and red paint had gone everywhere, making it look at first glance like he was bleeding all over the place. He screamed if anyone tried to get near him, and the teacher had called the nurse, afraid something was horribly wrong.

What stuck out in Kat's mind was how terrified and lost he'd looked. It had made her heart ache so badly that she'd found herself propelled forward against her better judgment and against the teacher's orders for everyone to stay put. She ignored the way Jake had screamed and tried to push himself further into the corner as she approached. She'd knelt down next to him fearlessly, touching his shoulder in an effort to ease whatever kind of suffering he was going through. She knew he wasn't physically hurt. Whatever turmoil he suffered was internal. She didn't know if he was on some kind of drugs and hallucinating or what. She didn't really care. All she knew was that she couldn't stand the look of horror on his face.

He'd grabbed hold of her shirtsleeve, gripping onto it like it was some kind of link to reality, and she'd touched the back of his neck in an instinctual effort to soothe him. Speaking to him in a way that one might speak to a frightened animal, she assured him that he was all right, that everything was going to be okay. She didn't know if he'd actually responded to her, or if whatever kind of fit he'd had just passed, but his grip had loosened on her sleeve, and slowly, he had gone from taking in great, gasping, ragged breaths of air to breathing more evenly. When the nurse showed up, he'd still been trembling, tears coursing silently down his cheeks, but he'd been calmer. Kat would never forget that day. She'd often wanted to talk to him after that, see what he was like. His art projects were always beautiful, if somewhat dark and bizarre.

She shook her head, dispelling the memory, and turned back to Jake. "Whenever you're ready," she said with a smile.

He glanced at her and let out a visible, calming breath. He pulled a chair from the wings of the stage, plugged his guitar into a small, portable amp he had brought, and sat down. He hunched over his instrument and closed his eyes, bunching his hands into fists a few times to try and stop their shaking. There was a brief moment of complete silence from everyone before he launched into a hauntingly beautiful melody that made Kat stop all activity and stare at him in awe. The mournful chords were so pure that it was almost painful. They wound their way around her heart, making her want to weep. She glanced at Rochelle to see that she had the same amazed expression on her own face.More snickers sounded from the peanut gallery before they progressed to all out guffaws. "What is this?" one guy cackled. "Whales mating? Gimme a break." He stood and started for the stage. "You call that talent? I've seen more talent in my little sister's poodle."

"Greg!" Kat shouted. "Sit down! You're messing up the audition! How would you like it if someone did that to you?"

He snorted and snatched the guitar out of Jake's hands. "Like he has feelings," he spat. "Freaks don't feel." He grabbed the strings on the guitar and gave them a mighty yank, pulling them off and breaking them. The guy still sitting behind Kat roared with laughter.

Kat's eyes bulged in horror and she heard Rochelle gasp.

Greg thrust the guitar back into the bewildered boy's hands with a mean chuckle. "Play it now, freak." He turned back to the girls and grinned. "Finally, no more lame auditions. We can all go home." He leered at Kat. "You want to come over to my place? I'll show you real talent."

Kat felt sick and wanted to punch him in his squinty eye. She stood and glowered at him. "I wouldn't go anywhere with you if you paid me to, you childish moron. That was something only jealous little boys do. Why don't you go home and have Mommy change your diaper?"

Rochelle giggled, and Greg stared at her in bafflement.

"Idiot," Kat snarled. She jumped up on the stage and ran back behind the curtains to where Jake was putting his guitar in its case. "Hey," she called.

He looked over at her sadly and sighed. "I guess that means I won't be playing in the show." His voice had a bitter edge to it.

She shook her head. "No, I want you to play in the show. That was beautiful! I've never heard anything like it!"

"Like whales mating," he grumbled. He picked up his case and his amp and turned. "Excuse me," he said, trying to get past her. "In case you didn't notice, I have to go buy new strings now."

"Listen, Jake, I'm really sorry about that. I thought your song was incredible. Greg's an idiot."

He glanced up at her and frowned. "You know my name?"

"Yeah. Jake Marsallis. You sit in front of me in art. You drew that picture of the dragon burning down the school."

He raised an eyebrow. "I was in the counselor's office for a week because of that drawing."

"Well, I thought it was awesome." She smiled. "The counselor should have taken a closer look at it. If she had, she would have seen that the dragon's shadow was in the shape of a man, and it disappeared up into the clouds that were raining down to put out the fire. She would have seen that the man in you overpowered the beast of rage and you didn't want to destroy. You just wanted recognition." The bewildered look fo shock and awe on his face made her grin. "I thought it was very poetic."

He looked down and shifted uncomfortably. "Why are you talking to me? You're the most popular girl in school. Shouldn't you be off with your jock friends or something?"

Kat frowned and folded her arms in irritation. "You insult me. You don't like people making assumptions about you so why would you make them about me?"

His face reddened. "Sorry," he muttered.

Kat glanced at her watch and sighed. Her stomach lurched. Auditions hadn't taken as long as she'd expected. "Hey, why don't you let me pay for your new strings?" she blurted. "It's the least I can do."

He shook his head. "It's fine."

"Come on," she urged. "Just take me to wherever you buy them and I'll pay."

He looked up at her with a genuinely confused expression. "You want to go *with* me?"

"Well, yeah. I wouldn't know what to buy otherwise. Wanna go?"

Jake blinked. "Uh... O-okay, I guess."

"Great. Let me just tell Rochelle. And I have to find Mr. Cunningham since he disappeared into his office about an hour through auditions. I have to give him the list of participants. Don't leave without me."

Jake watched her go, her long brown hair shining, her perfect body teasing and taunting. Anyone with half a sex drive wanted Kat. She was beautiful. She and Rochelle both. Rochelle was the blonde bombshell while Kat was the dark temptress. They ruled the hallways with their amazing, goddess-like presence and participation in nine out of ten school functions and extracurricular activities. They were the elite...and one of them was going with him to get his guitar re-strung.

The one he had been enamored with since freshman year.

He shook his head, still not fully comprehending what was going on. He would probably wake up in his bed at any given moment to find all of this a horribly tortuous dream.

One he wouldn't trade for anything.

* * * *

"I really like your guitar," Kat said as she watched Jake re-string it at the music store. "It's a beautiful color."

He gave a bashful smile, but said nothing.

She sighed. He had hardly said anything since they'd left school. She watched his fingers deftly attach the strings, touching the instrument lovingly.

"My father bought it for me," he finally murmured. "He said it would match the red in my hair." He smiled, running his hand down the neck of the guitar in one final caress before placing it back in its case. "Thanks for buying those."

"It was no problem." She glanced down at her watch and frowned as her stomach churned. "What-uh-what are you going to do now?" she stammered.

He looked up at her with a puzzled frown. "Go home."

"Can I come?" she spat out without thinking.

He raised an eyebrow. "Are you insane?"

She looked down and bit her bottom lip in embarrassment. "No," she murmured. She couldn't go home. Not yet. Not until *he* went to work, and *he* didn't go to work until seven. She usually went to Rochelle's, but Rochelle had gone to a family event. She had to stay away until seven. She imagiend she could go to the library or wander around the mall or something.

Jake frowned as Kat twisted her fingers and stared down at the carpet. "Sorry, I didn't mean to sound harsh, and I didn't mean that you're insane to think I would want to hang out with you. I just meant, why would someone like you even want to be anywhere around someone like me? We're from two completely different worlds."

"How do you know what world I'm from?" Her gaze jumped up to meet his. "You don't know me at all. You, of all people, should know what it's like to be judged unfairly. You, the one who flips out and has spaz attacks in the middle of class."

He flinched at her acidic comment and looked down in abject humiliation.

"Yeah, I remember that day in art," she continued. "Everybody remembers that day in art. Thought you would too considering I was the only one brave enough to come near you when everyone else was terrified because they all thought you were on some kind of trip."

His head snapped up and he stared at her. "That was you?" He hadn't been able to remember who it was who'd helped him, who'd so lovingly and selflessly come forward and touched him, soothed him, stood by him during the worst moment of his entire life. The moment that had ensured social suicide as a high school student who was a weirdo. He hadn't paid attention to the person. All he remembered was the presence, and the way the fingers had felt on the back of his neck, a gentle caress, an anchor of light in a world of blackness. To know it had been her...

She snorted. "Yeah, that was me. But apparently you still feel like lumping me in with all the other stereotypical popular girls out there. Well, whatever. If you want to judge me without even knowing me, you deserve to be treated the way you are." She spun and headed for the door.

Jake's eyes widened. "Whoa, wait a second!" he called. "Geez." He ran his hand through his hair, still trying to wrap his mind around the fact that the person who had consoled him had been the most sought-after girl in school. "I didn't know, okay? I didn't know that was you. You can come over. Just don't yell at me anymore. Your fire hurts my eyes." When she looked at him with narrowed eyes, as if trying to assess whether or not he was being genuine, he grinned for the first time all day. Some strange part of him warmed at knowing she was just as skeptical about him as he was of her. Maybe they really weren't all that different after all.

Kat smiled and averted her gaze as a slight touch of color came into her cheeks. "I don't like assumptions either."He chuckled. "I guess." He picked up his case and started for the door, but stopped before he opened it. He took a deep breath and turned to face her. "Hey, thanks."

"For what?"

"For what you did in art. It...it meant more to me than I could ever express."

He liked the warmth in her eyes as she answered him. "It's fine. Just repay me by letting me come over and, for goodness sake, let me eat something." She rubbed her hand over her growling stomach.

He gave a nervous laugh. "I don't exactly know what to do to entertain you."

"Finish playing your song," she urged. "I never got to hear the rest of it."

* * * *

Kat popped another chocolate into her mouth as she continued to watch Jake. He had played her his audition song, as well as some others he had written. They were all equally beautiful, and Kat was amazed. She'd had no idea that he was so talented, but then again, no one did. Everyone just assumed he was one of those goth freaks who dreamed of shooting the school up. People avoided him like the plague. She'd always thought it was unfair.

Jake sighed as he finished up the last song and set his guitar aside. "That's all I have," he said.

She grinned and clapped. "Your music is wonderful. Are you going to pursue it after high school?"

He shrugged.

"You should. You have so much talent. I bet you could be famous."

He looked up at her with a shy smile. He moved from where he had been sitting on his bed down to the floor next to Kat. He picked up a chocolate and played with the wrapper.

She looked around his room, which was currently only lit by about ten candles. He'd said he liked candlelight because he found it more soothing. She didn't mind. Between that and the incense he was burning, she was more relaxed than she had been in ages. She glanced up at several posters he had on the wall next to his bed and frowned in curiosity. One of them had a bright, hot pink-colored background with a man standing shirtless in a black, fur-collared coat smoking a cigarette. It said HIM in large capital letters across it. She pointed over at it. "Who's that?"

"HIM," he replied vaguely.

She rolled her eyes. "Well, obviously."

He smirked.

"I mean, I've never heard of them before."

"They're a European band, from Finland. A friend of mine heard of them somehow and bought an import CD online. I love them. The music is incredible, so poetic, full of metaphor."

Her eyes wandered to the poster next to it, which was of a band called Type-O-Negative, another group she'd never heard of before. He had a poster of a guitar player named Steve Vai, and one of Jim Morrison. She pointed to a smaller poster above his desk. "Isn't that Bam Margera?"

He nodded with a smile.

She raised an eyebrow. "I wouldn't figure you would be much into pro skating."

"My friend Lance is. I like Bam...in a strictly heterosexual way, of course."

She laughed and unwrapped another chocolate. "So, you're in a band, right?"

He nodded, but looked at her with a quizzical expression. "With Toby Johnson and Aaron Frome?"

"How do you know that?"

"You all sit together in a pod in band." She glanced at him. "I *am* in band, you know. I play clarinet. Do you ever notice me at all?" She flashed him a teasing smile.

He rolled his eyes. "I notice you. Everyone notices you, Kat. You're the most popular girl in school."

She wrinkled her nose. "I don't get why everyone thinks I'm so popular."

"Well, you're in everything. You're in media production, you're on the debate team, you're on student council. You help organize the assemblies and the pep rallies. You're in band. Should I go on? You have enough extracurricular activities to get into any college you want."

She averted her gaze to the floor. "I don't do them for college reasons. I mean, media production I do because that's kind of where I want to go for a career, but the other things I do just to take up time." She mumbled the words, shying away from the subject.

"How come?" he prodded gently.

She swallowed uncomfortably and sighed. "My parents aren't home until after seven and my uncle is the only one home. He—" She contemplated on whether or not she should actually tell him what only Rochelle knew. For some reason that she couldn't explain, she felt very comfortable around him. He had gradually loosened up and they had been sharing good conversation, conversation that had substance. He listened to her, *really* listened to her, like what she had to say mattered to him. He didn't seem to want or expect anything out of her. He was okay just sharing his time with her. The guard she always had up felt like it had slipped down a bit.

She sighed. "He tries to touch me while they're gone. They don't believe me, though." She glanced over at him. "I don't like to go home. I'm always running like a scared little rabbit, trying to avoid him."

He had concern mirrored in his gray eyes. "Has he ever...you know?"

She shook her head. "No, he's never actually succeeded, but he makes gross comments and threats, and one time I'm sure he would have made good on them if I hadn't slapped him hard enough to stun him for a second."

"Well, if you ever need anywhere to go, you can come here." He blushed and tugged on his bottom lip with his teeth. "I mean, if you can't go to Rochelle's. My parents won't mind. My mom will be excited to finally see a girl over here. As you could probably tell when she came up here with every appetizer in our freezer for you to eat."

Kat smiled. "Thanks, Jake..." She played with a piece of her hair, focusing her attention on it instead of him. "You're really sweet, you know?" He smiled in his bashful way, and it warmed her heart. His smile absolutely lit up his otherwise somber face. "Why do you shut yourself off from people?"

He gave a slight shrug. "People think I'm weird because I dress gothic and wear eyeliner. You know how it goes. I just keep my distance from them. Plus, I have an anxiety problem. I can't handle being around a lot of people sometimes. I have bad panic attacks."

She blinked as everything suddenly made sense. "Oh, you mean..." Her heart squeezed painfully as she realized what had happened in art. "In class...that was a panic attack?"

He nodded solemnly. "They just come out of nowhere, for no reason. I don't know why. Sometimes they're not so bad. Other times, I feel like I'm having a heart attack. That time in class was probably the worst one I've ever had. It felt like someone had sucked all the air out of the room and the walls were closing in on me."

"That's awful. I'm so sorry."

He shrugged, then looked up at her. "It's all right. You made it better." He blushed and glanced down again. "I take pills, but they don't always help."

"If you have such bad anxiety, how can you audition for the Senior Show and play in a band?"

He chuckled. "Well, I don't think performing in the garage in front of Lance's girlfriend and a bunch of trash cans counts as being in a big group of people. As far as the Senior Show goes..." He shrugged. "It's different when I play. It's like the whole world disappears. Everything just fades away but the music. It's like I'm floating on the notes." He smiled and met her eyes, staring at her for a long, quiet moment. "You know, you're also beautiful," he murmured. "That helps your social status a lot." He averted his gaze to the carpet.

Kat found his shyness endearing, and something about him tugged at her heart. He was real, and so many people in her world lived behind fake fronts. "In that case, you should be popular too."

He looked back up at her and his heart started beating way too fast. She had just told him that he was beautiful. No one but his mother had ever told him that. Suddenly, he didn't know what he was doing. His body moved of its own volition and he found his lips pressing against hers. He pulled away quickly, wondering if he'd lost his mind. "I'm sorry," he whispered.

Kat shook her head. "It's okay." She giggled nervously. "You know, I've never been kissed before." Her voice was breathy, and it wavered slightly.

"You're kidding me."

She shook her head.

"But everyone wants you."

She raised an eyebrow. "Well, they can want as much as they like. Doesn't mean they're going to get anything."

He smiled. "I've never been kissed before either," he admitted. He played with the ends of his sleeves nervously, wondering what in the world was wrong with him. He didn't do stuff like that... Ever. His head was still spinning.

She reached out and touched his bottom lip with her finger. "You have really nice lips," she murmured. "Soft..." She bit her bottom lip self-consciously. "This is strange, Jake. You're the only boy I've ever wanted to share affection with. I've had lots of guys try to date me, but I've never been interested in even going to a movie with them much less kiss them."

He met her eyes and gently took her hand in his. "Why are you doing this?" he asked, playing with her fingers. "I mean, why me? Why now?"

"Maybe I just realized that something beautiful can be sitting in a corner, but you never notice because you're too busy to pay attention." She shrugged. "Until it glints and catches your eye."

He studied her for a moment and a slow smile spread across his lips. This girl was going to kill him. He was in great danger of just falling in love with her right there. No one had ever gotten to know him before. No one had ever given him a chance. No one except for the two friends he had in school that he played in a band with, and no one liked them either. Aaron looked like he came to school in the clothes he'd slept in for the last three days, and Toby scared people because he looked like he was constantly pissed off and about to blow his top. Jake never would have thought that the most popular, beautiful girl in school would even glance his way, let alone spend the afternoon with him, talk to him, touch him...kiss him.

He reached his hand out and caressed her cheek with the back of his knucles. His heart ached in his chest, ached with longing and devotion. She would probably never really know how much of him would always belong to her from that moment on. She had stepped forward when no one else would. Even if she never spoke to him again, the fact that she had taken the time to know him for one second of her life would make him her slave forever.

Kat's eyes closed at his tender touch and her breath caught as his lips touched hers again, timid at first, then bolder as he gained confidence. She returned the kiss, opening her mouth for him so he could deepen it and explore further. When he pulled away, they were both trembling.

"You taste good," he whispered.

She gave a nervous laugh. "Like chocolate."

He shook his head and touched her face again. "Like something wonderful."

"Better than chocolate?"

He smiled. "Much better."

Kat placed her palm over her heart, almost as if she was trying to stop its pounding. "Today has been really nice," she murmured. "Thank you."

"Do you want to stay for dinner? I think my mom's making lasagna."

She grinned and nodded.

He reached over and turned on the radio, suddenly finding the silence too quiet to suit him. He needed to distract himself or else he would spend the rest of the night kissing her, and he had a feeling that it would be bad to push too much physical affection on her. Just because he was starving for it didn't mean he needed to scare her to death and chase her away. He wanted to keep Kat around. *Who am I kidding? I want to keep Kat forever.* He refused to do anything that might jeopardize their budding...thing. What was it exactly?

Friendship? Relationship? That was probably way too much to hope for.

"It's Been Awhile" by Staind started playing, and Kat smiled. "I love this song," she said absently, closing her eyes. "I love the lyrics. I wish one day someone would say romantic stuff like that to me. All I ever get is Greg friggin' Carlyle going, 'hey baby, why don't you come back to my place?'" She shuddered and made a face.

He smiled and watched as she lay down on her back and crossed her legs, swinging her foot to the rhythm of the music.

* * * *

One month later

Kat grinned at Rochelle and clapped as several of their friends finished up their number in the Senior Show. Jake had already done his number, and Kat had cheered rather loudly. Because Kat had cheered, a lot of other people had also.

"That was a great show," Rochelle said. "We did an awesome job, if you ask me."

"Well, we make a good team."

"Jake did great."

Kat nodded.

"Have you seen him lately?" Rochelle prodded.

"Not much. It's been difficult since I've been working so much on the prom committee, and then with all the graduation stuff going on. I usually only see him in class. He's been practicing with his band a lot, too. I asked him to go to prom with me, but I don't think he can handle it. You know, the crowd and all." She shrugged.

"That's okay. We can just go together. Forget boys. I'm over them right now since Zach dumped me for Anna Smith. She smells like bologna."

Kat giggled, but was still disheartened that Jake wouldn't go with her. They'd grown to be close since that day in his bedroom. When she wasn't insanely busy with school stuff, they would hang out whenever they could. They shared good conversation and she liked how creative he was. Sometimes she would just go to his house and do her homework while he played his guitar. She loved being there in his musical lair. It was peaceful, and so much better than being home, watching the shadows under her door, terrified that when her parents weren't paying attention, her uncle would try to come in.

Everyone thought she'd lost her mind because she insisted that Jake eat with her at lunch, but she didn't care. No one had the right to dictate who her friends were, and she cared about Jake. She hoped that they could stay friends through college. She was going to UCLA and he was going to some school in Washington. She didn't want to lose contact with him. He meant so much to her, more than he probably knew. More than she was really willing to admit at the moment because it frightened her.

Suddenly, the microphone on the stage squealed horribly and Kat and Rochelle winced.

"Sorry," Jake's voice came. He looked down at them. "I have one more, okay?"

They exchanged confused glances, but motioned for him to continue.

He smiled and plugged his guitar into his amp. He took a deep breath and closed his eyes.

"What's he doing?" Rochelle whispered.

Kat shrugged.

He cleared his throat. "This is a song I wrote," he said softly, "for someone who means a great deal to me." He took another deep breath and started to sing.

"Dulled senses, apathetic heart
I know I should feel, I know I should hurt
I want to know how to get back
To that genuine, fulfilling happiness I lack
It's known to the past, I remember vaguely
Shadows, silhouettes of a life long lost
To the pills that steady me

So as I lay here so restlessly,
Begging the silent night to comfort me,
My final thought, that peaceful place,
As I close my eyes, I still see your face
And my lips still linger of your taste.

The exhilaration of emotions that came
With a touch of minds that shared the same plane
Delight higher than angels could dream
Stifling my persistent, silent scream
I was awakened by dawn, by the fire inside,
With the touch of your lips I burned alive
I would trade all, endure more, and carry on
Just to keep singing your radiant song
I belong to you and this night is my witness,
You provided my heart and life with a purpose.

So as I lay here so restlessly,
Begging the silent night to comfort me,
My final thought, that peaceful place,
As I close my eyes, I still see your face
And my lips still linger of your taste
My lips still linger of your taste...."

Jake's eyes riveted on Kat's as he sang the last chorus, and she felt lightheaded, her heart thudding in her chest.

"Oh man," Rochelle breathed, "he's singing straight to you!"

Kat nodded, numb. She watched him finish the song, and he held her eyes all the way through the end. When he had finished and walked off stage, Kat sat back in her chair, dumbfounded. She felt breathless and giddy, and she wasn't exactly sure what to do with that feeling.

"That was amazing!" Rochelle cried as people started to file out of the theatre. "Did you hear him? Dang! I didn't know he could sing like that!"

Kat tried to regain her senses, but his deep, melodic voice was still ringing through her ears.

"What did that freak think he was doing?" Kat overheard a girl behind her saying. "This isn't a concert."

"He's so stupid," her friend replied. "He wears makeup all the time. I think he's gay."

Kat felt fury well up inside of her. She stood and scowled at the two girls. "Is Robert Smith from The Cure gay? Are half the musicians on the planet gay? Jake's *not* gay and he's *not* a freak! Back off!" She ran backstage and caught Jake just as he was heading for the stage door. "Jake!"

He stopped and turned to face her with a smile.

"Why did you do that?" she asked breathlessly.

His smile faded. "It was for you. Didn't you like it?"

"I loved it! You are amazing! Your voice…" She shook her head, unable to find words. "Your lyrics, I.…." She felt so confused all of a sudden. She wanted to cry and she wasn't sure why. Maybe because she never thought she'd ever mean that much to someone, never thought she'd ever affect anyone the way Jake claimed she affected him.

He smiled and reached out to caress her cheek with his knucles. "I'm glad you liked it. It was all for you. Straight from my heart."

She looked up at him, tears hovering just behind her eyelids. She wrapped her arms around him and held on tight. "Thank you," she whispered. She loved his beautiful heart, and she loved his touch. He didn't touch her like she was a thing. He didn't touch her like he was lusting after her. He touched her like she was revered, treasured. He touched her like she mattered to him. Like *she* mattered to him. Kat. The person. Not the Kat everyone thought she was, or thought she should be.

He ran his hand slowly through her hair with a sigh. "You're more than welcome." For a moment, his fingers tightened for a moment in her hair and it seemed like he was holding his breath. She could hear his heartbeat pick up pace, and she thought he was going to say something, but then his shoulders slumped in a defeated way, and his breath left him in a rush. "I-I have to get going," he stammered. "I have a huge chemistry test tomorrow that is pretty much determining whether or not I graduate. I'll see you in band, though."

She nodded and pressed a kiss to his cheek, hugging him again. "Thank you so much, Jake."

He smiled shyly.

Kat watched him disappear out the door, her heart aching in a peculiar way at his absence.

* * * *

Two and a half months after graduation

Jake frowned and turned from where he had been packing a box of his favorite CDs. He heard a soft knocking on his window and he went to it, perplexed. He pulled back the curtain and his eyes widened as he saw Kat perched precariously on the ledge. He opened the window quickly and grabbed a hold of her, terrified that she would fall at any second and break her neck. "Kat!" he cried as he pulled her inside. "What are you doing out there?"

"I thought it was probably too late to ring the bell. I didn't want to wake your parents up." Her foot caught on the ledge and caused Jake to stumble backwards and fall. She landed on top of him, knocking the air out of both of them. When she was able to take a full breath again, she relaxed against his chest and giggled.

He sighed heavily and shook his head, but couldn't help but bury his hands in her soft hair. "So you decided to scale the side of my house? Are you out of your mind?"

She raised her head and looked at him, grinning. "Probably."

He smiled.

She hoisted herself up so that she was sitting and met his eyes. "I just had to see you before you left."

He sat up and faced her, suddenly feeling like going away to college was the worst decision he could have possibly made. "You know I wouldn't have gone without saying goodbye. I have my contact information for you." He grabbed a slip of paper off his desk, as well as a CD case. "This is the number for my dorm. Call me once you find an apartment and give me your number, okay?"

She took the paper and nodded.

"I won't have a computer right away, but once I have your new number, I'll call you and give you my email address when I get one."

She nodded again and looked down, playing with the paper absently. It was more than apparent that she was trying not to cry. Jake watched her and hated how sad and alone she looked. His heart couldn't take it. He needed to tell her how he felt... He would regret it forever if he didn't... He took a deep breath. "Kat?"

She glanced up at him with hope in her eyes. "Yeah?"

The deep breath he had taken wheezed right out of him, and he felt his courage deflate with his lungs. He couldn't. What if she rejected him? What if it changed their relationship forever and made it weird? He couldn't handle that. He would rather have her as a friend than not have her at all. He looked down at the CD case he was holding and sighed, extending it to her. "Here, this is for you."

She took it with a quizzical frown.

"It's the song I wrote for you. I recorded it at Lance's."

She smiled and pressed it to her chest, looking up into his eyes. "Thank you," she whispered. "I'm really going to miss you."

He smiled sadly and cradled her face in his palm. "I'm going to miss you too... But I'll visit. I'll come see you on breaks when I'm here with my family." He was trying to sound hopeful for her sake, but all he really felt was black depression and a desire to strangle himself for not having enough guts to tell her how he felt.

She nodded, but her smile seemed forced. "Promise you won't forget me?"

He sobered and he felt tears sting his eyes. "Forget you?" he whispered. He let his eyes roam over her beautiful, innocent face, and he traced his thumb along the line of her bottom lip. He remembered all too well how those perfect lips felt under his own. "I could never forget you. Not in a million lifetimes."

She wrapped her arms around him and squeezed hard, as if she didn't want to ever let him go again. When she managed to get a hold of herself, Kat pulled back and looked up at him with a tremulous smile. "Well, I should go," she said half-heartedly.

He nodded and ran his knuckles down her cheek. "Go out the front door. My parents won't wake up. I promise I'll call you. As soon as I get settled, I'll call you. Listen to that song... Think of me."

She smiled. "I will." She stopped at his door and looked back at him. "Goodbye, Jake."

Tell her! Tell her! Tell her how you feel, you moron! He let his breath out in a raspy, discouraged, and sad sigh. "Goodbye, Kat." He watched her go and felt his heart crumble. He shut the door and leaned his head against it, squeezing his eyes shut in pain and self-loathing. He whacked his forehead against the door a few times, cursing his own cowardice.

* * * *

Kat stood on the other side of his door for a moment, feeling kind of sick inside. She really didn't want to be away from him. The thought of not seeing him made her heart hurt. She swallowed hard; her chest felt tight. She hated how his room was all boxed up. It made her feel like he was leaving forever. She had this horrific feeling that she would never see him again, and it terrified her. Her heart felt like it was ripping in half, and she couldn't even begin to know why. She was so bad with her own emotions. She never had any clue what she was feeling or why she was feeling it, probably because most of the time she tried her hardest not to feel anything at all.

Right now, all she knew was that she had the worst, most foreboding feeling washing over her, and a voice in the back of her head was screaming for her to go back in there, throw her arms around him and beg him to take her with him.

She shook her head and forced herself to take the first few agonizing steps toward the stairs. *Get a grip, Kat*, she chided herself. He wasn't going away forever. He was going to college. It was what thousands of normal, American high school graduates did. It was what she was doing. There was nothing terrible about it.

But as she descended the stairs and made her way out of the Marsallis household, the feeling got stronger. She couldn't shake it no matter how much logic she tried to use on herself. Fat, hot tears rolled down her cheeks and didn't stop all the way to her house.

* * * *

Six years later

Kat tapped her fingers against her arm in irritation. She started to lean against the wall, but thought better of it. This was the sleaziest place she had ever been to. She sighed and knocked on the bathroom door. "Come on, Rochelle! How long does it take to pee anyway?"

"Hold on a sec! Geez!" Rochelle shouted back.

Kat rolled her eyes and glanced to the right. She had never seen such an obnoxious group of people in her life, and they were all still just hanging around, hoping to catch a glimpse of one of the band members.

She enjoyed going to concerts, but she usually liked to stand in the back where she had room to breathe and no one bothered her. Rochelle liked to be up in the front getting pummeled by moshers and attacked by crowd surfers. This group had been rowdier and more obnoxious than most, and they made Kat uncomfortable. She just wanted to go home and take a hot shower.

She jumped suddenly as she felt a hand on her shoulder, and she spun to see a burly man standing next to her. He had a long ponytail and was dressed all in leather like a biker. She took a step back as he leered at her.

"Hey, cutie, you lost?" he asked.

Kat didn't like the way he was looking at her. She knew that look, and she knew the feeling that flared to life inside of her as well. It was her inner warning mechanism. She'd had the same feeling every time her uncle had tried to molest her, and she'd had it the night Kyle had... She swallowed uncomfortably. And she'd had it when Jake had left. She knew what it meant now. It meant no good. "I'm not lost. I'm waiting for my friend," she stated matter-of-factly.

He let his gaze slide up and down her body. "Sure you are. I can be your friend too, you know." He placed his hand on her arm and tightened his grip.

Kat heard sirens go off in her head and she tried to yank her arm away. "Let go of me!" she cried, panic building inside of her.

The man shoved her back hard against the wall and was on her suddenly, forcing her legs apart with his knee and rubbing suggestively against her. She shrieked, and her vision blurred. *Not again! This can't happen to me again!* She tried to push him away, but he was too strong. She started to tremble and tears coursed down her cheeks.

Without warning, the pressure of the man's body against her was gone, and she blinked her eyes open just in time to see a strong arm shove her attacker backward. It pushed him into the far wall of the corridor and held him there.

Kat looked up and blinked. Van Marshall... His tall, lithe, well-muscled frame stood protectively by her while he held her attacker at bay. He was wearing what he had during the show, a simple black wife beater style tank and black pants, but he had donned a light leather jacket in preparation of the chilly night. His dark brown, almost black hair fell freely around his shoulders, and his handsome face was stern. "Get out of here," he said, his voice menacingly calm. "Now."

The man obeyed and Van turned to Kat. She looked up at him, astonished and bewildered.

Van gave her a gentle smile. "Did he hurt you?"

There was something in his face that made her ease, a sincerity that she hadn't seen in a long time. It was familiar somehow. She shook her head. "Thank you," she whispered.

"You're shivering." He pulled his jacket off and placed it around her shoulders. "There," he said with a smile, "see if anyone messes with you now."

All Kat could do was stare at him. Van Marshall had just saved her. The front man of the band that was climbing its way to the big time. His smile stirred memories she'd tried to block out, and tears of a different kind filled her eyes.

"Hey, Van!" one of his band mates called suddenly. "We gotta go, man!"

Van nodded and looked back at Kat just as Rochelle emerged from the bathroom.

"You keep the jacket, okay?" He winked at her and strode away, all poise and confidence.

Rochelle frowned. "Was that—" She looked at Kat and her eyes widened in alarm. "Kat, what happened?"

Kat scowled as she began to regain her composure. She smoothed her short hair and started to walk angrily down the hall toward the door. "No man will ever be able to overpower me again," she growled. "*No person* will ever lay their hands on me with cruel intent and keep their fingers intact."

Chapter One

Three years later

Rochelle winced as she entered the apartment and saw Kat deliver a particularly nasty kick to the punching bag in the living room. "Geez," she muttered, closing the door. "That one would have hurt."

Kat gave a short jab to the bag, followed by another. "Yep," she answered, "right in the crotch." She kicked at it again.

Rochelle smiled. "I got us some dinner at the deli on the corner. I got you a ham and cheese with only lettuce and tomato. I know you don't eat all the good stuff." She rolled her eyes.

Kat turned away from the bag. "Do you know how much crap you put on those?"

Rochelle frowned as she started to unwrap her sandwich. "Kat, you look like a tank. You're G.I. Jane. What is one sandwich going to hurt?"

Kat sat down next to Rochelle. "Mayonnaise is nasty, and I've spent too much time and effort to get into this shape. I'm not going to screw it up."

Rochelle shook her head. "You could beat up Jean Claude Van Damme."

Kat smiled and unwrapped her sandwich. "How was work?"

"We got a new assignment," Rochelle said, shooting her a glance.

Kat raised her eyebrows. "Figures. We get a new assignment on my day off. What's up?"

"We actually got a good assignment. They gave it to us

instead of Paul and Arnie."

"You mean no more documentaries about sea slugs or behind the scenes footage of obnoxious underground bands that only ever gets played on the cable public access channels?"

Rochelle turned her bright blue eyes to Kat and pushed her hands through her hair, turning to face her. "We're going on tour," she stated.

Kat blinked and looked up at her. "On tour? Like with a band?"

Rochelle nodded excitedly. "We are in charge of recording and editing an actual music DVD. The band wants footage from several live shows as well as backstage stuff and interviews with band members. We're supposed to tour with them for one month."

"Who are we covering?"

Rochelle grasped Kat's wrists, making her look up from where she had been peeling a rogue onion off her sandwich. "Bleeding Passion."

Kat felt herself pale. "You're not serious."

"I am!" she all but screamed. "You can talk to Van again!"

Kat frowned. "Yeah, right, like he'd ever remember me amongst all his adoring fans."

"I bet he didn't give any of them his jacket."

Kat rolled her eyes. "I bet none of them were getting assaulted either. Besides, we're going there to work, not schmooze with the band."

Rochelle stared at her. "Kat, of course we're going to schmooze with the band. How else are we going to get backstage footage? By magic? Using our telepathic abilities?"

Kat gave her a halfhearted scowl. "When do we leave?"

"In a week. Paul and Arnie were pissed. Paul loves Bleeding Passion."

"Who are they touring with?"

"A newer band called Thrill My Koi. Bleeding Passion is trying to give them some publicity."

Kat took the last bite of her sandwich. "Cool." She stood. "I'm going to go take a shower. I smell like a man." She headed into her bedroom and opened her closet to find some clean clothes. She sighed as her gaze fell on the leather jacket that had been placed around her shoulders two years ago, black with the Bleeding Passion logo on the back: an eye crying red rose petals instead of tears. That night had changed her life. She was a victim no longer. She had spent her entire childhood running from her lecherous uncle. Then, at nineteen, two years after her high school graduation, she had been date raped by a man she had only been seeing for about a month. The incident at the concert had decided her. Now, if anyone attempted to harm her, she could disable, incapacitate, or render unconscious. If that didn't work, she knew several ways to kill someone.

She grabbed a loose-fitting pair of pants and a clean shirt and headed for the shower. She cleared a space on the bathroom counter, moving aside Rochelle's many cosmetics. She shook her head. Rochelle's logic completely eluded her. Why would anyone want to spend forever just putting on makeup? All that did was attract attention.

Kat undressed and got in the shower, letting her mind return to the assignment they had just been given. She smiled. They had been seniors in college when she and Rochelle had stumbled into Bushman Productions, fresh meat for the apprenticeship program. They spent that whole year fetching coffee and doing menial chores for production teams just hoping that one day they would be hired onto the crew for real. They had been. Kat was put in charge of camera operations and editing. Rochelle had, by luck, been assigned to Kat as her assistant.

Bushman Productions specialized in making DVDs and videos of music groups, but they also had a small department devoted to low budget documentaries. That was where Kat and Rochelle had spent most of their time while the golden boys of the company, Paul Erickson and Arnie Fitzpatrick, got all the big stuff. The fact that Rochelle and she had been given the Bleeding Passion assignment was amazing.

Bleeding Passion had made quite a name for themselves since her short encounter with Van Marshall. This would give them the chance to finally prove that they weren't amateurs anymore.

Kat turned off the shower and squeezed the water out of the ends of her short, brown hair. It was cut just above her shoulders and the wet strands clung to her neck as she dried off. No one from her past recognized her with her short hair, but that was the way she liked it. She'd cut it right after the rape. She'd done it so that she wouldn't have to keep looking at that person in the mirror every day, the weak person, the victim. The event had changed her, and the long hair no longer suited her. She much preferred it short. It made her look older, tougher, and it took that innocent little girl look out of her face.

She sighed and glanced in the mirror as she wrapped the towel around herself. No one would know from looking at her that she was any different from anyone else. Her body had healed from its assaults, but her memory retained the scars. She shook her head to clear away the troublesome thoughts and put her clothes on. She headed back out into the living room where Rochelle was watching television. She picked up a book she had been reading and went out onto their small balcony, sitting down in a chair with a sigh.

She watched as the setting sun glistened off the windows of the buildings around her and she closed her eyes, letting the heat of the city wrap itself around her. She hated L.A. She really did. It had brought her nothing but heartache in her life. If she had her choice, she would live in a small coastal town where there weren't lots of people and she could go antique shopping or eat in a small café. Somewhere like San Luis Obispo or Cambria. A nice place where she could hear the ocean at night and watch the sun set on the beach. Peace and seclusion, complete tranquility. That's what she longed for.

Happiness.

She opened her eyes and sighed heavily as she could hear sirens and honking horns in the distance. She banished her silly fantasies and opened her book. Thinking about things that would never be was pointless.

* * * *

San Diego, CA

Van stared at his reflection in the bathroom mirror and ran his shaky fingers through his dark hair. He let out a deep breath and splashed some cold water on his face. He then eased himself onto the floor, putting his hand over his upset stomach. He heaved a sigh and leaned his head back up against the wall.

A knock sounded on the door of his hotel room and he

frowned. "Yeah?" he called. "Come in. The door's not closed all the way."

The door opened and Van's bass player and best friend, Lance, as well as their other singer, Nyah, entered the room.

Nyah's eyes widened as she saw Van sitting practically in the closet, and she rushed to him. "Van, are you all right?" she asked. "What happened?"

"You have another panic attack, man?" Lance questioned with a frown.

Van looked up at Lance and nodded.

"That's the second one this week," Lance pointed out.

"Must be stressed."

"Have you been taking your meds?"

He wrinkled his nose in distaste. Meds. It always made him sound like some kind of sociopath. He nodded. "Not that they ever do any good." He glanced down at Nyah, who was staring at him as if he were a frightened little boy. He frowned and looked back up at Lance, taking in his skaterish appearance. Baggy, tan cargo pants, Independent sweatshirt, blond waves poking out from under a gray beanie. He smiled. "You guys going out?"

Lance nodded. "We were going to get something to eat."

"What caused this?" Nyah asked, completely cutting off Lance.

Van looked at her. "Caused what? My panic attack? Nothing caused it."

She huffed. "Well something had to have caused it."

He clenched his jaw, his patience wearing thin. "Well, yes, actually. It was an over amount of adrenaline released into my body causing a fight or flight reaction that normally accompanies fear. I have a chemical imbalance. That's the cause." He stood to put some distance between the two of them.

She followed and took his arm. "My poor baby," she crooned. "Can I do anything? Would you like some tea?"

Van sighed again, irritated. "No, Nyah, tea has caffeine in it. Caffeine causes adrenaline. If adrenaline causes panic, then I don't think tea would be a good idea, do you?"

She said nothing.

"Anyway," Lance continued, "do you want to come with us?"

"No, I think I'm just going to stay here and chill."

"Baby, you should come with us," Nyah chided. "It's not good for you to be all alone when you feel this way."

Van looked down at her long black hair and sultry brown eyes, a woman used to always getting her way. "I've been alone feeling this way half of my life, thank you very much." He shook her off his arm. "If I needed my mother, I'd call her. I'm a grown man. I think I know what's best for me."

Nyah folded her arms and looked affronted. "Are you still pissed at me because of earlier? Geez, Van. I'm only trying to help you."

"If you ever listened to me when I spoke, maybe you would know what to do to help me."

She scowled, but said nothing.

Lance smirked. "You sure you don't want to come?"

Van waved his hand as if to dismiss his friend. "I'm just going to sit here and watch *Viva La Bam*. It's coming on in a half hour. It usually makes me laugh and takes my mind off of crap. Guilty pleasure and all."

Nyah snorted. "Bam Margera is such an idiot," she spat.

Lance looked at her like she had just said something absolutely sacrilegious. Van rolled his eyes. "Well, I like him, so I'm going to watch his show." He looked pointedly at Nyah. "I'll see *you* later."

She shook her head and started for the door. "Whatever."

Van sighed.

"Are you sure you're okay?" Lance asked.

Van looked up at his friend. "Yeah, I'll be fine."

"You going to be okay to perform tomorrow?"

Van forced a smile. "I always am."

Lance gave him an understanding smile and slapped him gently on the shoulder. "See you later."

Van closed the door as Lance left. He leaned against it with a heavy sigh. Panic attacks were no new thing to him. He'd been having them since he was fourteen. Lately, though, they'd been worse and he didn't know why. He wished they'd just stop. They left him feeling weak and powerless, like he had no control over his own body.He wandered over to the hotel bed and flopped down, closing his eyes. Nyah didn't help. She was clueless. If whatever was going on didn't include her as the focal point then she really wasn't interested. Sometimes, he didn't know what he'd seen in her at all. She was just a distraction, something to take his mind off of the emptiness he felt inside.

Only Lance really understood. He had been Van's best friend his entire life. They had crawled around in diapers together, learned guitar together, started Bleeding Passion together. The only thing they hadn't done was go to school together and that had been because Lance had been home schooled. Still, he had been in Van's first band and they had practiced almost every day. Lance was like a brother to him. He knew about the panic attacks and he knew about the emptiness.

Van sighed and sat up. He grabbed his acoustic guitar from where it was leaning against the wall and began to play absently. He loved his life. He was living his dream and his passion. He had what everyone wanted. He didn't understand the emptiness. He couldn't explain it. It was just there, gnawing at him. He had an idea of where it originated from, but he didn't like to think about it. It made him go back to his greatest regret in life and he didn't like to dwell on it.

He closed his eyes and let the music he was playing seep into his soul. He imagined the notes and chords flowing through his veins, calming him, numbing the aching emptiness and making him temporarily complete. He sighed as he felt himself relax and set his guitar aside. At peace for the moment, he turned on the television and started to watch the show that Nyah hated. It made him smile.

Chapter Two

Kat took a sip of her coffee, sitting placidly in the hotel lobby. She looked around for Rochelle, who had disappeared. She sighed and glanced down at her watch. They were supposed to meet Bleeding Passion and some of their crew ten minutes ago. They had yet to show up, and now Rochelle had vanished as well. This was a perfect way to begin their first real assignment. She shook her head and took another sip of coffee.

"Excuse me."

Kat looked up and saw a tall, slender woman with long, shining black hair.

"Are you the DVD person?"

Kat stood and smiled. "Yes, I'm Kat Vauss and—" She glanced around frantically and spotted Rochelle exiting a gift shop. She pointed to her. "—that is my partner, Rochelle Rollins."

The woman arched an eyebrow. "Oh...your *partner*?"

Kat frowned. "Yeah. My assistant. My co-worker."

The woman gave a fake-sounding laugh that made Kat cringe. "Oh, okay. That's wonderful. I'm glad. I don't care too much for lesbians, if you know what I mean. No offense."

Kat blinked. "Uh...none taken." She watched as the woman studied her nails, and Kat turned to Rochelle and flagged her down.

The woman sighed. "Rather unprofessional to have your *partner* just running around when you should be doing business, isn't it?"

Kat sighed, but it came out like a short growl. "Well, we were sitting here, waiting, but the people we were supposed to meet were late. Since *that* was very unprofessional, I figured Rochelle shopping in the gift shop would only be a minor inconvenience." She folded her arms. "Who are you anyway?"

The woman looked affronted. "I'm Nyah Densmoore," she stated. "The singer of Bleeding Passion."

"Oh, that's right," Kat said. "You *share* the lead vocalist position with Van Marshall. I didn't recognize you. You look different than when I saw you in concert."

Nyah giggled. "I lost ten pounds. I bet that's it."

Kat deliberately looked Nyah up and down and shrugged. "No, that's not it."

Nyah frowned.

"I think your hair was shorter," Kat decided.

"Oh, that too," she grumbled. She flipped her hair. "So, do you have any credentials? I mean, we only want to hire professionals. We don't want our video being shot by amateurs."

Rochelle, who had meanwhile returned, frowned. "We're not amateurs," she assured.

Nyah shrugged. "So you say, but we need proof. Anyone off the street could just say they know what they're doing."

Kat was starting to lose her patience with this woman.

"Nyah, quit harassing the camera crew," a resonant, silky voice commanded.

Kat tensed. She knew that voice. She may not keep up with everything having to do with pop culture, but she would remember that voice anywhere. She glanced behind Nyah to see Van Marshall striding toward them. She swallowed. He was so tall, and he walked with a graceful swagger that exuded pure sex appeal. His hair was tied back in a ponytail, revealing his handsomely sculpted features. He was striking. Striking in a way that made her heart hammer uncomfortably in her chest for a few minutes, as if it knew something her brain didn't.

He smiled and extended his hand. "I'm Van Marshall."

She took his hand. "Kat Vauss," she murmured. "This is my partner, Rochelle Rollins."

Van's smile faded, and for a brief second, he looked as if someone had slapped him very hard. He stared at Kat for a second, then his eyes moved to Rochelle, who was frowning thoughtfully at him. "Kat," he repeated, his voice strangely raspy. "Is that short for anything?"

Kat looked away nervously. "Uh...yeah. Katrina."

A slow smile blossomed across his face, and it made her insides squirm uncomfortably.

"Good name," he murmured.

She frowned. His subtle intensity made her uneasy. His eyes seemed to smile right along with his sensuous lips. Gray eyes... Soft... She eased unexpectedly. Something about his eyes....

"Van, shouldn't we get their resumes or something?" Nyah interrupted.

Van rolled his eyes. "Nyah, stop it. You're being ridiculous. Bushman Productions is very reputable. They did Fat Stinky's DVD and it was awesome. Besides." He met Kat's eyes again. "I have every confidence in these girls."

Nyah crossed her arms and huffed.

"Sorry I'm late," Van continued. "Our tour manager was giving me problems."

His eyes roamed over Kat. She had to fight not to turn around and head for the hills. Why was he staring at her? She clenched her jaw and touched her short, tapered and flipped hair self-consciously.

Van gave a quizzical frown and sighed. "We perform here in L.A. tonight," he said finally. "You don't have to start filming anything until after that. We thought you might like to see a show first so you can get an idea of how things go. It's going to be a little rigorous. We perform almost every night and we have a few signings and a video shoot in there also. We hit San Jose and San Francisco after this, then Phoenix. After that, we head to the east coast and work our way back. I know it doesn't make sense. That's what the tour manager was giving me problems about.

"You two will have your own hotel room and you'll go on the bus and planes with us. We want you to always be traveling with the band, not the roadies. It's kind of impossible to get footage of us if you're stuck on the roadie bus the entire time. Film whatever you think is interesting. I will leave that up to your judgment."

"Shouldn't we be meeting with your manager?" Kat asked. "Shouldn't he be going over these things with us?"

Van smiled. "You can meet him if you want, but I'm the one who called Bushman and asked for this DVD."

Kat raised an eyebrow. "Oh, in that case..."

"Come on, I'll introduce you to the rest of the band."

Kat and Rochelle followed behind him as he led them to the elevators.

"The guys are hanging out in our suite," he explained. They got in the elevator and Van glanced at Kat again. He shook his head. "Sorry, but you have really nice arms." He chuckled.

Kat looked up at him and offered a meager smile. "Thanks."

"Oh, I love to work out," Nyah gushed, "but I never lift anything more than five pounds. I like to stay fit, but I think muscles on a woman are disgusting." She laughed. "Unless, of course, you're a lesbian. Then it kind of fits."

Kat frowned. This woman was a nut ball.

"Well, I like muscles," Van said. "I think they're sexy." He smiled at Kat.

Her face grew stern and she gave him a sidelong look. "Don't think they're too sexy because I could kick your balls up into your throat before you even knew what was happening."

Rochelle's eyes bulged. "Kat!" she breathed in shock.

Van raised his eyebrows in surprise, but chuckled and grinned broadly. "That's awesome," he said. "There are far too few women who can kick a man in the crotch properly."

Kat looked at him. He smiled at her again and a pain shot through her heart. His smile, his eyes, were familiar. It reminded her of someone...someone she wanted to forget but knew she never would be able to. She glanced down as sorrow swamped her in the worst way.

"I do Tae Bo," Nyah remarked.

Rochelle glanced at her, then looked at Van. "Kat knows three different martial arts," she bragged.

"Really?" He smiled in a secretive way. "Impressive."

Kat sighed. She wished Rochelle wouldn't do that. She wasn't trying to flirt. She just wanted to do her job. Flirting was the furthest thing from her mind.

"Y'know, it's weird," Rochelle commented absently. "You look really familiar for some reason."

Van suddenly looked genuinely pleased. "Do I?"

She nodded. "I never thought you did when I saw you on TV, but in person..." She shook her head. "I can't figure it out."

He grinned broadly.

The elevator finally reached the desired floor and the four of them got out. Van led them to the hotel suite and opened the door. Three other men were lounging in the front room. One had wavy blond hair and was sitting at a table drinking coffee. One was dark like Nyah, and the other was tall with brown hair and a quiet demeanor.

"Guys," Van called. "Our camera crew is here. Come meet them."

All three of them glanced at the door and promptly stood up at seeing that they were two attractive women.

"May I introduce the rest of Bleeding Passion," Van said. "Lance Lawson, bassist."

The blond man grinned and shook their hands. "Good to meet you both. It'll be a pleasure having you."

Rochelle giggled. Kat rolled her eyes. Rochelle would flirt with anything halfway attractive.

"This is Jack Densmoore, drummer."

The dark one kissed both Kat's and Rochelle's hands. "I'm Nyah's brother," he said, "not that I like to admit it." He grinned devilishly at his sister.

Nyah scowled and stayed close to Van.

Jack fixed his green eyes on Rochelle and smiled again. Rochelle bit her bottom lip coyly. Kat sighed and turned to the tall one.

"And this is Erik Vandenburg, keyboardist."

Kat shook his hand as well. She then stood with her arms folded, waiting for their next instructions.

"So, tonight you guys will be able to watch the show from the front row," Van said. "I'm going to take you to meet the rest of our crew and our manager in a minute. He'll help you guys get situated. Do you have any questions so far?"

Kat and Rochelle shook their heads.

He smiled. "All right. I'll take you to meet the others. Our manager Hank will give you your laminates. Come with me."

Nyah continued to follow Van around like a lost puppy, which made Kat almost physically ill. She knew of the on-again, off-again relationship between Nyah and Van, but she thought it was disgusting that a woman would have such a lack of self respect that she would fawn all over a man.

Van led them to another room where he introduced them to an older but attractive gentleman who took Kat and Rochelle inside to get them acquainted with the rest of the crew while Van headed back to the hotel suite.

"I don't know about them, Van," Nyah commented flippantly. "They didn't seem professional to me."

"They're very professional, so shut it," he snapped. "You just don't like them because they're women." He shot her a look as he opened the door.

She huffed.

"Van," Lance said as soon as he entered the room, "did you know these chicks were going to be so hot when you hired them?"

Van smiled. "No, I didn't even know they were going to be women, but I agree... I honestly don't think two prettier girls exist." He was aware of Nyah's completely insulted look, but he ignored her.

Lance whistled. "That blonde was cute!" He went into the kitchen and looked in the refrigerator. "You okay to perform tonight, dude?"

Van nodded.

"No panic?"

"Not yet, but it depends on how much Nyah irritates me."

Lance chuckled.

As if on cue, Nyah sauntered up to Van and took his arm. "Quit being so mean, baby. Will you rehearse with me a little before the show? There's a note I've been having a some trouble with on *Epic Love*. I don't want to disappoint our fans by sounding awful." She gave a soft smile.

Van looked down at her and smiled, some of his annoyance dissipating. That was the one thing he would always love about Nyah. She may drive him insane, but she was an artist and a performer above all, just like he was. Her craft came before everything. He nodded. "Yeah, my voice could use a work out also."

She grinned. "Cool." She squeezed his hand and walked over to her brother.

Van sighed. "You know, she wouldn't be half so bad if she wasn't so neurotic."

Lance nodded and took a bite of the sandwich he had been making. "And narcissistic."

"That too."

Lance chuckled.

* * * *

Kat felt like she had been completely deafened after the show. She had been lodged right up next to a speaker and couldn't hear anything but obnoxious ringing in her left ear and muffled sound in her right. It gave her horrible vertigo. As she wobbled around backstage, she saw Rochelle run up to her.

"Wasn't the show awesome?" she cried.

"My eyes thought it was, but my ears didn't. How can you even hear?" She snorted. "Oh that's right, you *abandoned* me to go crowd surfing while I was smashed up against the speaker!"

Rochelle laughed. "It was fun."

"I can't hear," Kat reiterated.

"Didn't you think Van looked sexy?" Rochelle teased.

Kat thought of Van in his black leather pants and black sheer shirt. She tried not to remember his muscular arms and how the rest of his body had rippled beneath his shirt in intriguing secrecy and fluid grace. She tried not to remember how his dark hair fell in his face or how he completely captured the audience with his undeniable charisma. She also tried not to remember the veins in his neck, the tattoos on his body that she wished she could have seen better, or how she paid more attention to him than she really should have.

"Kat," Rochelle persisted.

Kat was jolted out of her reverie. She looked at Rochelle. "Huh?"

"I said, didn't Van look sexy?" She shouted it, thinking Kat's lack of response was due to her hearing.

"He looked like he always does," she replied. She left out that she had reluctantly thought he was sexy ever since he'd helped her that night at the club.

Rochelle rolled her eyes. "Whatever. The bassist winked at me during the last song."

Kat sighed. "Everyone winks at you."

"Hey, girls!" Van called suddenly, walking toward them. He ran his fingers through his hair and grinned. "How'd you like the show?"

"It was awesome!" Rochelle cried.

Kat smiled.

"Did you like it?" Van asked Kat directly, his eyes holding

that intimidating intensity again.

She shifted uncomfortably. "Yes, I was just in a bad spot. I can't hear."

He looked at her expectantly. "The music, though. You liked the music?"

She frowned, wondering why her opinion mattered so much. "Yeah," she said. She smiled a little. "You always write good songs."

He grinned. "Well, we're all going to head out soon. Just stick with us. Your equipment has already been loaded onto the bus. There's some food backstage if you guys are hungry. You don't have to hang out in the hall."

Kat nodded and gave him a tremulous smile.

He smiled warmly and started to walk away. Kat watched as his shoulders swayed slightly with his stride. She sighed. This was ridiculous. He was just a man and men were all the same, despite how beautiful some of them were. She nodded. Right. She just had to keep reminding herself of that.

Chapter Three

Kat tried to make herself as inconspicuous as possible on the tour bus by lodging into a corner on the sofa and losing herself in a book. They had several hours to travel before they reached San Jose and she wanted to do it as quietly as possible. She wasn't there to make friends. She was there to do a job. She pulled her knees up to her chest and sighed as she heard Rochelle's contagious laughter. She glanced up and saw her in the kitchen area, sitting in a booth. She was shuffling a deck of cards and talking with Lance, Jack, and the sound technician. She smirked. Leave it to Rochelle. She always made herself at home.

"Hey, Kat!" Rochelle called. "Wanna play cards with us?"

"Yeah we're gonna play strip poker!" Jack teased.

Kat was not amused.

Rochelle giggled. "Nah, we're just going to play silly games like Speed and Crazy 8's. Come play."

Kat smiled, but shook her head. "No thanks."

Rochelle sighed heavily and gave Kat a look that resembled pity. It irritated her, and she returned to her book. What reason would Rochelle have to pity her? She had her head screwed on straight. That was all. Just because she didn't go around flirting with everything male didn't mean she needed to be pitied. This was her job. It wasn't a vacation.

Over the course of an hour, Kat began to become less and less interested in her book and more and more aware of Rochelle's laughter. They had gone through Crazy 8's and Slapjack, which had been very entertaining to watch. Cards had flown every direction and everyone had been screaming. Kat was grateful they hadn't been playing Spoons. They were now playing Go Fish. Jack had stepped out earlier to remove his contacts and he was now wearing a pair of black-framed glasses. Rochelle was shuffling again, but this time she had a beer in front of her, and she kept flirting horribly with Lance. Kat couldn't help but smile.

"Go Fish," the sound technician muttered. "The first game everyone learns and the one I suck at the most."

Rochelle giggled. "Kat is the champion of Go Fish. She used to play me all the time and she never lost! Never! It was amazing!"

Kat stifled a grin.

"Yeah, well all champions have to retire," Jack said, shooting Kat a smug look. "She can move aside for the new master." He cracked his knuckles for effect.

Kat raised her eyes to meet his and gave him a mischievous smile. "You would be eating my dust if you played me," she stated.

"Bring it on," he challenged. "If you have the guts."

Kat's eyes narrowed. She stood, set her book down, and swaggered over to the table, her hands on her hips. "Let me in, Rochelle. I like to look my opponent in the eye."

Rochelle giggled and scooted out of the booth to let Kat sit across from Jack. She dealt the cards to just Jack and Kat, stating that she would rather watch the battle than participate.

Six games later, Jack threw his cards down and shook his head. "I don't get it." He laughed. "You're amazing. How do you do it? You're like the Gandhi of Go Fish."

Kat smirked and folded her arms placidly in front of her. "It's simple," she said, raising an eyebrow. "I've been looking at the reflection of your cards in your glasses."

The table went silent, and everyone stared at her for a minute.

Rochelle looked amazed. "Are you serious?"

Kat glanced at her. "Why do you think I stopped playing with you after you got contacts?"

Lance and Jack burst into laughter. "That is awesome!" Jack exclaimed. "You're brutal!"

Kat smiled, and Rochelle shook her head. "I can't believe it. All those years…."

Kat laughed. "Where's the bathroom?"

"Right at the back," Lance replied, still chuckling.

She made her way to the back of the bus, smiling to herself. She had to admit, that had been fun. She reached out to open the bathroom door when it flew open unexpectedly and smacked her full on in the face. She stumbled backwards, holding her nose.

"Oh!" Van exclaimed, going to her. "Geez! I'm so sorry!" He put his hand on her shoulder. "Are you okay?"

She blinked a few times and moved her nose around to lessen the sting. "That was refreshing," she muttered.

"I'm such a klutz. I'm so sorry."

She glanced up at him and didn't like the way her stomach lurched when she met his soft eyes. "It's okay."

"I didn't do any damage, did I?" he asked, feathering his fingers over her cheek briefly.

Little butterfly wings fluttered through Kat's stomach at his touch, and she somehow related his touch to his voice of velvet seduction. The combination was not good. It did something funny to her insides that she couldn't really explain. "I'm okay," she repeated in a lame voice.

"Sounds like you guys are all having fun over there."

She gave him a small, awkward smile. "I was kicking the crap out of Jack in Go Fish."

He grinned, and his gaze settled on her.

Kat swallowed and tried to maneuver past him to seek refuge in the bathroom. She shot him half a smile as she closed the door, letting out a monstrous sigh once she was safely inside. She touched her nose again and winced. She shook her head. He unnerved her terribly. She couldn't understand why. *I hate men. What makes him any different? Just because he rescued me once doesn't mean he isn't just as scummy as all the others.* She nodded. *Right. He is a rock star. He's probably even scummier. It doesn't matter that he wears sex appeal like a second skin, or that he has a singing voice that should be outlawed. He's still a man. Men are all the same.*

Feeling momentarily satisfied with this decision, she went back out. Maybe she would play another game with Rochelle and the others. She had other tricks up her sleeve.

"Hey, Kat!" his voice called.

She stopped in her tracks for a second, but no one would have noticed. She gathered herself and looked over at Van as she continued on her way to the table where Rochelle was. He was sitting where she had been earlier, holding up her book.

He smiled. "*The Complete Writings of Edgar Alan Poe.* Good choice."

Kat looked around as if hoping to find a way out, but she realized that was silly. She let out a heavy sigh, feeling ridiculous, and tried to smile back. "Yeah, he's one of my favorite authors."

He set her book down, but kept watching her.

Kat glanced from him to where Rochelle and the others were sitting. She saw Jack scowl, and everyone else laughed. He stood and pulled his shirt off. She grimaced. Great, now they really were playing strip poker. She was trapped. With no other choice, she headed toward Van. He smiled when he saw her coming and moved aside so she could sit down. He maintained his distance, which made her ease considerably.

"So, are you a big Poe fan?" she asked, somewhat sardonically.

"Of course," he stated. "I like anything that's dreary and depressing."

Kat's lips quirked in a small smile.

"So what made you decide to get into martial arts?" he asked, changing the subject.

She shrugged. "I just think a woman should know how to defend herself. You never know what could happen. Unfortunately, most chivalry is dead. The damsel in distress days are over. You'd better know how to take care of yourself because no one is going to do it for you." She thought of him helping her at the club. "Mainly," she added.

"Smart thinking. You got into media production then? Like you always wanted?"

She frowned at him. "How do you know I always wanted to be in media production?" Her heart did that bizarre thing again as she met his eyes. Like it was screaming something she was too stupid to pick up on.

He averted his eyes for a moment. "Well, I just assumed. Am I wrong?"

"No," she answered slowly. Okay, that was weird... "Rochelle and I got accepted into Bushman's apprenticeship program when we were seniors in college. We were hired onto the crew a year later and here we are. This is our first really big assignment. We've been given lame ones up until now. Don't tell your girl that, though. She seems to have it in her head that we don't know what we are doing." She frowned. "That and that I'm a lesbian."

Van chuckled. "She wishes you were a lesbian. She also wishes that she was my girl, but she's not. She tries to lay claim on me, but we're not together anymore. She drives me insane." He reached over to a bowl that was on the floor next to the couch and he offered it to her. "Chocolate?"

Kat looked at the chocolates and picked one out, smiling to herself. "I have very good memories of these," she murmured.

Van watched her with a soft smile on his sensual lips. "Want to share?"

She frowned. "My chocolate?"

"No. Your memory."

She looked away sadly and the deepest kind of sorrow welled up inside of her. Tears stung her eyes and she swallowed. "It was a long time ago," she whispered.

He gave her a look of concern, as if wondering why the memory should cause her such sadness. "Are you all right?"

She tried to mask her grief with a fake smile and nodded. "There's nothing better than chocolate," she said, trying to change the subject.

He regarded her with an expression that was solemn, but exuded warmth. It was one of those unnerving looks that made it seem like he was looking straight into her soul. It made her squirm and her pulse accelerate in a way that was extremely abnormal for her.

"Some things are," he said, his eyes holding hers.

Kat's heart lurched and she felt sick to her stomach. She looked away and pretended to be interested in a thread on the couch.

"Van!" Lance cried. "Dude! This girl's whipping us all! I'm gonna be naked soon!"

Kat and Van both looked over to see Lance sitting only in his boxers and one sock. Van laughed and Kat took the opportunity. She snapped her book open again and pretended to read, sticking her nose further into it than she needed to, trying to escape. She glanced at Van out of the corner of her eye. He looked at her and smiled knowingly, then stood and went over to Lance. She let out a relieved sigh and didn't move for the rest of the trip. She had never been so happy to see a hotel in all her life.

Hank helped Rochelle and Kat with their luggage and got them checked in. Kat listened to Rochelle go on and on *and on* about Lance's chest, Lance's torso, Lance's tattooed arms and rippling biceps, etc., etc., etc. as she put her pajamas on, glad to be in her own room and away from Van. Though she had refused to show any sign of life for the last leg of the journey, she noticed his continued quiet watching of her. He kept to himself, but she could feel his eyes burning into her. It had been the longest ride of her life.

"So I saw you talking to Van," Rochelle said.

Kat sighed as she set her suitcase inside the closet. "Yeah."

"What did you talk about? Did he hit on you?"

Kat rolled her eyes. "No, we talked about work and he gave me a chocolate. Big whoop. I'm gonna go find the ice machine." She left the room and wandered through the halls for awhile, trying to regain her usual composure. Van had rattled her much more than she would have liked. She was always in control, always cool and collected and reserved, but he had made her feel completely neurotic. The things he had said. The way he had looked at her. It was freaky. He made her remember things she had tried to forget a long time ago. Things that still hurt like they had happened yesterday.

She paced restlessly for awhile longer, until she felt like she had control over herself again, then meandered back to the room, never actually having located the ice machine. She stopped in the doorway and frowned when she saw a folded piece of paper on the floor. She picked it up and stared at it for a moment. Her name was written on the outside of it. She felt instant dread. This was something else that was going to freak her out. She could feel it. She opened it reluctantly.

"So as I lay here so restlessly,
Begging the silent night to comfort me,
My final thought, that peaceful place,
As I close my eyes, I still see your face
And my lips still linger of your taste…"

Kat stared at the paper and her heart started hammering to the point where she felt its pounding could be seen with the naked eye. She saw a figure move out of her peripheral vision and she glanced up to see Van standing in the doorway of his room next to hers. He leaned nonchalantly against the frame, his arms folded.

He smiled. "You don't recognize me, do you?"

She found it difficult to breathe. "Should I?" The words came out like a wheeze.

He stood straight and started toward her. She backed herself against the wall defensively, warning sirens going off in her head. She reached her arms out to push him away, but she stopped cold as he caressed her cheek with his knuckles. Her eyes fluttered closed and her chest felt so tight that it hurt. She started to tremble and her breaths came in short pants. She looked up at him in horror. "Jake?" she murmured. *Impossible...impossible...* The word repeated itself in her mind as a dozen horrifying memories barraged her.

He grinned. "Well, it's Van now."

Her trembling increased so that she had to slump against the wall to keep upright. "Impossible... I-I-" She shook her head, so bewildered that she thought she might be losing her mind. "I thought you were dead." Tears burned her eyes and she stole a glance up at him and forced a breath into her lungs. "You look so different." Was this really happening? Had her boyhood friend really morphed into this godlike man in front of her? Her heart tumbled and skipped over itself and she put her hand to her chest. Her heart...it had been acting weird ever since she'd seen him in the lobby. Is *that* what it had been trying to tell her? Had her heart recognized him even though her feeble mind had failed to?

Of course you didn't recognize him. Why would you be looking for him? That was nine years ago and you thought he was dead. Dead! What kind of a sick soap opera have I fallen into?

Her mind screamed at her while it tried to process everything that was happening. The result was her quiet trembling while she stared at him, yet through him, as terrible, painful memories whooshed to the surface.

He chuckled. "Well, you look different too, Kat." He frowned a little, as if wondering if he'd heard right.

She braved a full look up into his devastatingly handsome face and saw the subtle traces of her old friend, the angles of his face, the fullness of his perfect lips, his soft gray eyes that reflected such warmth. The tears hovering in her eyes overflowed, and she brought her hand to her mouth, horrified and elated and very confused. "I thought you were dead," she cried again. "All this time..." Tears coursed down her cheeks like rivers and she let out a mournful half-joyous, half-anguished sounding cry.

Van winced at the sound she made and placed his hand comfortingly on her shoulder. "Why would I be dead?" he asked, sounding thoroughly perplexed.

Kat shook so hard that she thought she might fall right out of her body. So many times she had wished for just one more look, one more touch. She had anguished for years over the supposed loss of him and she had been watching him on television and at concerts the entire time.

"Kat?" he prodded. "Why did you think I was dead?" His voice held a more serious note to it.

She tried desperately to get some kind of a hold on herself, feeling like a lunatic. "The summer after graduation you gave me the number to your dorms in college, remember?"

He nodded.

"Well, at the end of that year, I uh—" She swallowed painfully as more tears cascaded down her cheeks. She had never wanted to re-live this part of her life, ever. It had nearly destroyed her. "I tried to call you because you'd never called me to give me your email or anything. I wasn't really concerned because for awhile I couldn't even afford a phone, so, I mean, how were you supposed to get a hold of me? But, anyway, the woman who answered when I called your dorms said that no Jake Marsallis was registered there. So, I called your parents and your dad answered the phone. I don't think he really knew who I was or remembered me. Usually, when I was over at your house your mom was around, you know?"

He nodded slowly, as if trying to understand where she was going with this.

"I...really needed to talk to you...."

The look in his eyes showed mounting concern and he wiped her tears away with gentle fingers. "It's okay," he soothed. "Just take your time."

She shook her head. "So much bad stuff was happening. I needed you because I knew you'd listen. You always understood. Your dad answered the phone and when I asked for you, he—" Her bottom lip quivered, and she looked away. "He said that Jake Marsallis was dead. And then he laughed! He *laughed*!" She let out a little sob. "I thought it was so weird because your dad and you were always so close. I didn't understand why he was laughing, but I thought maybe it was hysterical grief or something, but then I couldn't understand why no one invited me to your funeral. Your mom knew I was still in L.A. I think she could have gotten a hold of me if she'd tried."

She shook her head. She was rambling. She never rambled. Then again, people she loved didn't usually come back from the dead either. He reached out to envelope her in a gentle hold, and she buried her face against his shoulder, relishing how he felt. So real, so alive. His skin was warm through his shirt and his body was firm, solid, real. "You can't even imagine how horrified I was. I asked your dad what had happened to you and he said..." She swallowed hard, having a difficult time getting the words past the horrendous lump in her throat. "He said that you had...killed yourself, or something like that after your first semester. He said it just like that. 'Killed yourself, or something like that.'"

"Oh my gosh!" he all but shouted. "Kat!"

She let out another sob. "You were so dark, so brooding, so reclusive. You weren't self assured or dynamic like you are now. It didn't seem very far-fetched."

"I was seventeen," he stated. "Nobody's right in the head at seventeen." He held her out in front of him so he could look at her. He smoothed her hair and wiped her tears again, shaking his head with a mortified expression. "Kat, my dad is an *idiot*," he stated. "Listen, I went to college for one semester and Lance and I started Bleeding Passion during that time. When we all decided we were serious about the band, we dropped out of school and made music our full-time career. I started to use Van Marshall as a stage name because Jake Marsallis represented an awkward boy I once was. Van Marshall was the man I wanted to be. We were signed at the end of the year, thanks to some connections Erik had from previous endeavors, and I got my name legally changed before we put the record out. All of my fans and friends knew me by it." He shook his head again and blew his cheeks out in an exhale. "No one had heard from you since I left for college. My father probably thought you were one of my friends playing a joke. I went home briefly right before we started recording and a bunch of my friends kept calling my house asking for Jake Marsallis, just to play around. They thought it was amusing. My parents weren't thrilled about the name change at first. They thought I was trying to do away with who I was. My dad probably thought you were one of my friends trying to get a rise out of him. He never would have said it otherwise." He winced. "'Killed myself, or something like that...'" He sighed. "Very funny, Dad. He's getting an earful, *immediately*."

Kat leaned against the wall, feeling weary. She had spent such a long time trying not to think about him, turning the station every time "It's Been Awhile" had come on the radio because it had reminded her of him. It had hurt her so badly to think that he was gone, and right after the rape... She had never been the same afterward. "I tried to contact your old friends to find out what had happened to you," she said quietly, "but I couldn't find anyone. I never really talked to Toby or Aaron so I had no clue where to find them, and I never even met Lance so I wouldn't have known that the Lance in your band was *your* Lance. I never would have made the connection. I thought about going to your house and trying to talk to your mom, but I couldn't bring myself to do it. It was a really bad time for me. Rochelle was worried that it might put me over the edge."

Van stared at her, and opened his mouth to speak, but it was obvious that he could think of nothing to say. Instead, he reached out and gave her cheek a slow caress, trying to convey as much warmth and care as he could with just one touch.

Kat closed her eyes and let out a shaky breath. "You've changed so much," she whispered.

His smile was gentle. "Not that much," he murmured. "Not really."

She looked up and met his eyes. Maybe not, but she had changed. So much so that she barely recognized herself. She wasn't the girl he had once known. "Jake—" She frowned. "Van—" That sounded weird too. She huffed. "*Mr. Marshall*, I need some time to think."

He smiled and nodded in understanding. "Kat, I'm so sorry for all of this. I didn't know."

She shook her head. "It's not your fault. It was just a really twisted misunderstanding. Really twisted." She wanted to say an atomic bomb sized misunderstanding, but she thought that would sound a little too dramatic. However, it didn't make it any less true. It had obliterated her. Jake had been the one man she had been able to trust, who hadn't hurt her. When she thought he had died, she'd killed a part of herself as well. The part that loved and trusted. Especially after what Kyle had done. She couldn't just wake that up again now that she knew he was alive. She wasn't the same anymore.

She forced herself to look up at him again. Her heart fluttered, and saw him for who he truly was. He was still there, just grown up. Van the confident man instead of Jake the insecure boy. What had once been a hunched, skinny kid was now a slender, tall, beautiful musician. What an amazing man he had grown into.

Van watched her for a moment and sighed. He wanted to know what had happened to her, why she had changed so much. She held such sorrow in her eyes. He wanted to hold her in his arms and soothe away her fears and troubles like he used to, but something told him that would be unwise right now. It had been so long...

He felt overwhelmed and pained at knowing that she had spent the last nine years thinking he had died. Again, he could think of absolutely nothing to say. There was nothing he *could* say. What words existed in the English language that could even come close to mending a wound of that size?

"I'll see you tomorrow?" he blurted in a pathetic attempt at verbalization.

A meager smile crossed her lips, and she nodded.

He smiled in his gentle way. "All right. Try to get some sleep."

"Jake." She sighed. "Van," she corrected. "Don't get me wrong...please. I'm really happy to see you."

He pulled her into his arms and allowed himself to hold her close for a moment. He didn't keep her there for long. She seemed so wary of closeness and he didn't want her to feel trapped. What had happened to his beautiful, affectionate Kat? "I'm so happy to see you too. Everything will be okay, I promise. I swear, I'll make up for it all."

She pulled away and gave him a strained smile as if to say, "Yeah right, buddy." He ran his knuckles down her cheek and she closed her eyes. He had missed that. He wondered if she had too.

"Goodnight, Van."

He leaned over to press a soft kiss on her forehead in a

non-threatening manner. "Goodnight, Kat."

She turned and sought refuge in her room.

Van sighed and walked slowly back into his room. Well, that hadn't gone exactly as he had planned. He was going to wring his father's neck when he spoke to him next. He felt horrible. While he had been becoming famous, Kat had thought he'd committed suicide. He couldn't stand the pain he had seen in her eyes. It was too much for him. She was never supposed to feel pain. He'd only ever wanted her to feel joy. This was his fault. He should have tried harder to contact her. He had been so immersed in music...what an ass he had been.

He frowned in a determined sort of way. He would take the sadness out of her eyes if it was the last thing he ever did. It was the least he could do after not being there for her through whatever had happened. He wouldn't abandon her again.

Chapter Four

Kat closed the door to her hotel room and leaned wearily against it. She eased herself onto the floor, staring forward. She felt like she had just been run over by a truck.

Rochelle popped her head out of the bathroom and her eyes widened upon seeing Kat. "Kat? Kat, are you all right? What happened?" She rushed to her and knelt down next to her. "You look like you've seen a ghost."

"I have," she rasped, her hands still shaking. She looked up at Rochelle. "Van Marshall is Jake Marsallis." Rochelle blinked and gave Kat the kind of look that she hadn't seen for awhile. The kind that made her think she feared for her sanity.

"Kat," Rochelle said slowly. "Jake is gone."

Kat rolled her eyes in irritation. "Look, I'm not insane Rochelle, okay? So quit it with the psychiatrist treatment. He's alive and staying right next door! Look!" She thrust the paper into Rochelle's hand, which was now crumpled from Kat holding onto it so tightly.

Rochelle read it and raised an eyebrow. "Are you serious about this?"

It didn't take a lot for Kat to get annoyed in the state she was in, and she felt it coming on like a wave. "No, I just thought it up in my head. Who else would know about that song? Who else would say that some things were better than chocolate while offering a chocolate to me?"

"He said that?"

"Yeah, plus there's the overwhelming evidence that he just told me himself outside! Go ask him if you don't believe me!"

Rochelle held up her hands in a gesture of surrender. "Okay, okay, calm down, Kat. What happened?"

"Well, he never died, obviously." She went on to relate

what Van had told her and soon Rochelle was sitting against the door next to her. "So, it was a really messed up misunderstanding," she finished, sounding exhausted from having to retell it.

Rochelle blinked and shook her head. "This is unreal... So you mean it was *Jake* who helped you at that club?"

Kat groaned and put her head in her hands. "Why is this happening?"

"You should be happy!" Rochelle cried.

"I am, but—" She held her arms out. "I don't know what to do, Rochelle! Don't you get it? The one beautiful man I ever cared for who never hurt me... I thought he was *dead!* How can I just pretend that never happened? I can't just smile and erase the past however-many years!" She started shaking again, unable to control the torrent of emotions she was feeling.

A loud knock sounded on the door. Rochelle scowled and made to get up, but Kat stood first. She yanked it open to see Nyah standing there.

Nyah frowned as she took in Kat's obviously haggard appearance. "Is now not a good time?"

Kat scowled. "For what?"

"Well, I was going to go over tomorrow's itinerary with you. See, I thought it would be easier for you to do your work if you had a clearly planned out schedule. I thought we could start out by interviewing me and then you could record me rehearsing later—"

"Nyah," Kat interrupted, her voice flat, "here's the deal; I run my own schedule. If Van wants to give me some kind of itinerary, he can. Hank can too for that matter. Otherwise, leave me alone. Contrary to what you may think, I am quite capable of doing my job and, if you bug me one more time, you won't be in the DVD at all. Got it?"

Nyah snorted and put up her hand. "Whatever. I was just trying to be *professional*."

"Better leave the hard work to the ones who *are* professional. You stick to holding a mic. That seems to be about as much as you can handle." She shut the door in her face.

Rochelle's eyes widened a little and she glanced at Kat, but said nothing. She knew better than to speak when Kat was in this kind of a mood.

Someone knocked on the door again and Kat let out a

growling noise. She yanked it open. "What now?" she spat.
Lance stepped back, looking surprised. "Sorry..." he said.
"I can come back tomorrow."
Kat sighed. "No, sorry. What is it?"
He glanced at Rochelle, then back at Kat. "I just wanted
to ask Rochelle something."
"Ask away," she grumbled. She pushed past him and
started down the hall.
"Kat!" Rochelle called. "Where are you going?"
"Somewhere I can think clearly," she hissed.
Rochelle sighed and glanced at Lance.
"Is she okay?" he asked.
"Lance, have you known Van all your life?"
He frowned. "Yeah, why?"
"He used to be called Jake Marsallis?"
His frown deepened. "Yeah."
"Do you ever remember him in high school talking about
a girl he knew named Kat?"
"Kat? Yeah, he talked about her all the time. He..." His
words trailed off as recognition dawned on him. He pointed
after Kat with a questioning look.
Rochelle nodded. "Come in. We need to talk."

* * * *

Kat stood staring at the Bleeding Passion jacket that was
hanging in her garment bag. She had no idea why she had
even brought it with her. She touched the logo tenderly and
let out a heavy sigh. She zipped the bag up and placed it with
the rest of her luggage. They were loading the bus that morning so that they were ready to go directly after the concert.
    "Hey, Kat," Rochelle called, lugging her bag over to the
door. "Where is the other band? Isn't there supposed to be
another band on this tour?"
    Kat frowned thoughtfully. "Yeah. I don't know where they
are. I'll check it out. I'm going to go get some breakfast. You
want anything?"
    Rochelle shook her head. "I'll be down in a minute. I'm
going to track down some roadies to load this stuff."
    Kat nodded and headed down to the lobby, grateful that
Rochelle had not tried to talk to her anymore about Van. She
had enough on her mind without Rochelle's hundred ques-

tions and her concerned looks. The elevator door opened and her stomach lurched as she saw Van standing at the continental breakfast table. *Why? Why does he have to be everywhere I go? Aren't rock stars supposed to hide out in their rooms and order room service? What in the world is he doing at the friggin' continental breakfast table?* She sighed and approached reluctantly.

Van saw her coming and he greeted her with a warm smile. "Good morning."

She gave him a small smile, but said nothing.

"Did you sleep all right?"

"Yeah, fine." That was, after she had lay in bed for about five hours staring at the ceiling and letting the past eight or so years of torment replay themselves in her mind. She grabbed a bagel and started hastily spreading cream cheese on it. "Are you doing anything before the show tonight?"

He smiled. "No, what did you have in mind?"

"I thought I could start interviewing everyone today. Then I was planning on getting some shots of the show tonight."

He nodded. "You have free reign of the stage. I already cleared it with security. Thrill My Koi starts opening for us tonight. I'll introduce you to them also."

"Good, I was wondering about that." She picked up her bagel, grabbed an orange juice, and turned to go. "I'll let you know when I'm ready for those interviews."

Van frowned as she started to walk away. "Kat!" he called.

She turned.

"That's all you're going to say to me?" He shook his head. "I haven't seen you in nine years!"

Her eyes narrowed. "And you never did anything to remedy that, did you?" she snarled.

He frowned. "What?"

"I called you, but I never heard anything from you. No phone calls, no letters, no nothing. Now you expect to come back from the dead and everything will be just like it was?" She started shaking again and hated herself for it. "I'm not the person you remember. You probably wouldn't even like me now. So, let's just pretend that you're a famous rock star and I'm the person hired to shoot your DVD and leave it at that, okay?" She spun and strode away before she could cry. She didn't like that being around Van made her feel weak. He had known her when she was weak and vulnerable, when she had been soft. She was different, different than he remembered, and he was different too. He was Van now. He wasn't Jake. Jake was dead, like his father had said. She nearly plowed over Rochelle as she was getting out of the elevator, but she didn't say anything. She pushed the button to close the doors as fast as she could and welcomed the empty silence of the elevator. She had work to do.

* * * *

Rochelle watched Kat blaze into the elevator in stunned silence. She glanced over at Van, who was at the breakfast table also watching the entire scene. "Hey," she greeted softly as she approached.

He smiled sadly. "Hey, Rochelle. How have you been anyway? You look really good."

She smiled knowingly at him. "You know we thought you were dead, right?"

He nodded. "She told me."

"It nearly devastated Kat. You were the one man she felt she could trust. It destroyed her when she thought you were gone."

Van sighed heavily. "Look, Rochelle, it's not like I knew. Do you think that if I'd known I would have just kept on letting her think I was dead? I would never have purposely caused Kat pain."

She must have sensed his defensiveness because she put her hand gently over his, stilling the stirring of his coffee, which was becoming faster the more agitated he got. "I know that, Van." He met her eyes and she sighed. "I've known Kat since freshman year of high school. I know all about her terrible parents and creepy uncle. I have seen Kat go through more pain than I can bear. The only time I have ever seen her completely free and happy was when she was with you."

Van's heart felt heavy in his chest. "I loved Kat," he murmured, looking back down at the table. "I've never loved another living soul like I loved Kat. All I ever wanted was for her to be happy."

"Well unfortunately, that didn't happen, Van," she said softly. "Some really bad stuff happened to Kat, and it changed her. She's not who you remember."

"So she said."

Rochelle rubbed his arm in a comforting gesture. "Don't give up on her. She's still in there, buried under the kung fu master borg who feels nothing. You touched that part of her last night, and it terrified her. I watched her assemble her fortress. It's impenetrable. The fact that you so easily strode right through it and touched her heart scared her really bad. Just give her time. She needs you."

He nodded. "I'm not gonna leave her alone again."

"I'm going to go find Kat." She turned. "Oh, Van?"

He looked up at her.

"Jake," she said with a wink. "You look really good too. *Really* good."

He blushed horribly and looked down.

She grinned. "Now I know why you look so familiar. I'm really glad you're not dead."

He chuckled. "Yeah, me too."

She continued on her way.

Van sighed and finished stirring the coffee he had been stirring for the past twenty minutes. Picking the cup up, he started back up to his hotel room, mulling over what Rochelle had said. He would never give up on Kat. It was because of her that he was who he was. He would never have made it this far without her. She had made him feel beautiful and talented. He owed everything to her.

The elevator reached his floor and he walked out slowly. He stopped when he saw Kat sitting on the floor at the end of the hall with her head in her hands. His heart twisted and he started to walk toward her.

"Van! There you are!" Nyah came tearing around a corner and took him possessively by the arm. "I've been looking everywhere for you." She started to guide him back toward the elevators.

Van glanced back at Kat over his shoulder, and he saw her look up at him. An angry and pained look flashed across her face, and she stood. She all but broke the door down getting back into her room, and the echo of it slamming reverberated all the way into the very depth of Van's soul. He went with Nyah numbly, feeling more empty than he had in his whole life.

Chapter Five

Kat couldn't remember when she had last been so tired. She washed her face and changed into some comfortable clothes, trying to escape the cigarette smoke stench that still clung to her. She sighed heavily, her ears ringing from the show. She hated that she had still watched Van with such rapt attention. She wanted to just forget about him, which didn't make sense. She had spent all these years wishing with all of her heart that she could see him just one more time. Now that she had him staying right down the hall from her and could see him every day, she wanted to forget about him? She was a seriously jacked up person.

She heard laughter from outside the bathroom and smiled. She left and grabbed her handheld video camera from the closet. Lance, Jack, Rochelle, and two members of Thrill My Koi were all in the room. Rochelle was good at making friends quickly, especially since she was blonde. That had always been a point in her favor.

Kat switched the camera on and turned the corner into the main part of the room. Rochelle was practically rolling on the ground while Lance tried to stuff a piece of cake in his mouth. Jack and Mark Henderson from Thrill My Koi were flashing twenty dollar bills at him in encouragement.

"Come on!" Jack cried. "Don't be a wuss! Eat it all!"

Lance gave him a pained expression. "Do you have any idea how much I just ate? That was an all-you-can eat sushi bar. I have a bunch of raw fish rotting in my gut right now. Along with a small tankard of sake."

"No one told you to eat so much. You ate half of Van's food too!"

"Dude, where did you even get this cake?" he asked,

making a face. "It tastes like cardboard."

Kat's smile broadened. They had all gone out to eat after the show. She hadn't. She'd stayed inside to unwind. Given her present state of mind, she figured going out while Van was in close proximity to her would be a bad thing. They were in San Francisco now and were staying there for two nights. They had a day off before they performed at The Fillmore.

Lance glanced up at Kat, and his eyes widened. "Oh, no way!" he cried, cake falling out of his mouth. "What are you doing to me? I'm a sex symbol!"

She giggled and zoomed in on his chocolate covered mouth.

"Just what all of America needs to see," he muttered.

Kat laughed and turned the camera off. She set it down and stood back, not knowing exactly what to do. She felt awkward and out of place. She wished she could be adaptable like Rochelle.

"I think you want some cake too," Lance decided. He stood and came after Kat with a handful of cake. Her eyes widened and she turned to try and escape. "Come on! Help me out!" he exclaimed. He grabbed her around the shoulders and tried to smash the cake in her face. "I'll split my winnings with you!"

She shrieked and pulled away with a laugh. "Get out of here," she said with a light shove. She pushed her hair back and giggled. "I'm going to go for a swim. Let me know if Lance ever gets it all down." Rochelle's laughter was the last thing she heard as she closed the door. She momentarily envied her ability to laugh so much.

She made her way down to the pool and let her mind replay the day's events. She had spent most of the morning in her hotel room trying not to lose her mind. She had done some Tai Chi and felt much better afterward. Thrill My Koi had shown up somewhere around noon and Hank had introduced her and Rochelle to them. They were a nice group of guys, but they had a tough-looking woman drummer with more metal in her face than Kat had in her car.

She had interviewed Erik and Lance, and Lance had refused to say anything to her until she smiled. He had been so annoying about it that she had finally resorted to laughter, and it had made her feel a little better as well. After the interviews, she had hidden out in her room until the show, being very careful to avoid Van. She didn't like how she felt when she was around him. He made her feel emotional and out of control, and that was a feeling she no longer tolerated. Kat had put her swimsuit on under her clothes, anticipating her swim, and she undressed quickly. She slipped into the pool, grateful that she was alone. She took a deep breath and started to swim laps, her mind still playing through her day.

After the show, everyone had boarded the tour bus and they had arrived in San Francisco in about an hour. Most of the band had gone to a restaurant to eat and Rochelle had claimed that they'd all had a blast, but Kat was glad she hadn't gone. She couldn't deal with Van, and she felt so out of place around everyone. They were all so lively and excitable. She just felt like a drag, like she was in the way. She preferred her solitude. Plus, she hated sushi.

After several laps, Kat got out and wrapped a towel around herself. She was putting her shoes on when she felt gentle hands on her bare shoulders. Her eyes narrowed and she acted without thinking. She pivoted and let her fist fly, not paying attention to who the person was before her fist made contact with his nose.

"Crap!" a familiar voice exclaimed.

Kat's stomach lurched. She turned and saw Van holding his nose. With a weary sigh, she put her hands on her hips.

"Geez!" he cried. "Holy crap!"

"Are you all right?" she asked flatly.

"I'm bleeding!" he shouted, wiping his nose and holding up his bloody fingers to show her. "You made me bleed, Kat!"

She huffed. "Well, you snuck up on me! You didn't even warn me first! That was a really stupid thing to do! Didn't the fact that Rochelle said I was heavily into martial arts clue you in?"

"I'd hate to cross you in a dark alley," he muttered.

"That's pretty much the point," she spat. "Anyone so much as looks at me funny, I kick their head off. That's how I live my life." She folded her arms. "Besides, if you recall, you brained me with the bathroom door on the bus last night so, as far as I'm concerned, you had it coming."

He glanced up at her and remembered her fire of fury from high school. It made him smile to know that not everything about Kat had changed. He tried not to think she was attractive. His intent hadn't been to ogle at her, but he couldn't help it. Her hair was clinging to her neck in wet strands and he could see all of the defined muscles in her arms. There was also something sexy about the way she was frowning at him. He had always thought her anger was a little bit of a turn-on. It showed the passion he knew she had so much of. "Kat, I did try to contact you," he blurted.

She frowned. "I beg your pardon?"

"When you said I hadn't done anything to change the fact that I haven't seen you in all these years, that wasn't true. I did try to contact you, but you moved out right after I went away to school and I couldn't find you. I called your house about ten times that semester I was in college, but your parents wouldn't give me your contact information."

She stared at him, and her hand went to her chest, as if it pained her. "They wouldn't?"

He shook his head. "They finally told me to give up because they wouldn't tell me where you were. They said that the last thing they needed was some gothic freak chasing after their daughter."

Kat paled, and her body language morphed from shock to rage. She clenched her fists. "But they'd let every other man chase after me and try to fondle me?" She turned and let out a shout, kicking at the wall. "What about what I needed?" she cried. "I needed you!" She kicked the wall multiple times, obviously unaware that it even hurt. Fresh tears coursed down her cheeks.

Van's eyes widened and he rushed over to her. She was seriously going to break her entire foot if she kept it up. "Whoa there, Pantera!" he chuckled. "Calm down. We don't need to destroy the hotel and get sued." He placed his hands gently on her shoulders again, just wanting her to know that he was there.

She stopped kicking and just stood there, shaking with fury. "They never did anything good for me," she murmured. "Ever."

He sighed and touched her wet hair. "Kat," he whispered.

She whirled, backing herself against the wall. "Don't even," she warned. "Just stop. Don't come near me. Why didn't you call Rochelle's parents? They would have given you my information?"

"I didn't know you guys had gone to the same college at

the time."

"You could have looked me up online. I'm sure I'm listed *somewhere.*"

"I—"

"Or why didn't you call my school? Or come to my school. You knew I was going to UCLA. I imagine I would have been easy enough to track down."

"Because I'm ass!" he exclaimed. His outburst caused her to fall silent and he shook his head in shame. "I got all caught up in my music career because everything happened so quickly and I freaking blew it, okay? I abandoned you because I'm a selfish ass."

She averted her gaze and focused on the tile. "Well, I appreciate your honesty."

"You don't even know how many times I've kicked myself," he continued. He ran his palms down her shoulders again.

She scowled and shrugged him off. "Just leave me alone, Van. Confession time is over."

He searched her face, and his heart twisted. *Does she really want to trust no one? To keep everyone at arm's length? Even me?* He sighed. "I'm not going to listen to you this time." He took a step closer. She brought her fists up, trying to warn him further. He gave her a half smile. "Beat me until I'm black and blue. It doesn't matter. I'm not leaving you again." He returned his hands to her shoulders.

Kat tensed and resisted his touch. His fingers seemed to burn into her skin with gentle urging. She clenched her fists so tight that they hurt. He was wreaking havoc on everything she had forced herself to become. His strong arms crept slowly around her and pulled her up against him, spreading his fiery trail all over her until she was enveloped in his warmth. She gave in and slumped against him, crying helplessly.

Without thinking, she wrapped her arms around his slender waist and dug her fingers into his lower back, feeling so completely undone. She wanted him to go away because he made her feel again, and feelings, emotions, were dangerous, but she also wanted him to never leave. She wanted to hold onto him with all her strength to make sure that he never disappeared from her life again.

"Why won't you just leave me alone?" she whimpered.

He stroked her hair softly and rested his cheek against

the top of her head. "I made that mistake once," he murmured. "I won't do it again."

"But you don't understand. I can't be who you once knew. I'm not that person anymore. If you had any inkling of what went through my head it would terrify you."

"I don't expect you to be the person I knew." He pulled away so he could look at her. "I would imagine we are both rather different. All I want is to get to know you for who you are now. I don't expect anything from you." As if he read the confusion she was feeling in her eyes, he smiled. He stood back and held his hand out to her. "I'm Van."

She frowned, but then cracked a small smile. She took his hand. "I'm Kat."

"It's very nice to meet you, Kat." He shook her hand slowly and closed his eyes for a moment, as if remembering her touch from all those years ago. She could only assume that's what he was doing, because she was doing it too. She remembered all too well the feeling of his hand against hers.

His voice was so soothingly soft that Kat felt her heart quiver.

Van smiled and let go of her slowly, letting his fingers linger for just a second. He watched her for a moment, his eyes full of concern and empathy. She could only imagine what she looked like. A trapped animal probably, confused and frightened.

"I think you're very beautiful," he murmured, brushing a wet strand of her hair back.

She looked up at him and blinked in bewilderment. His voice was so gentle and his words so matter-of-fact. She smiled just slightly.

"Can I walk you to your room?" he asked.

She shook her head. "I'm fine by myself."

He smiled. "I didn't ask if you were capable of walking to your room alone. I asked if you would horribly mind my company as you did so."

Kat sighed, her head aching. She couldn't even begin to comprehend what was going through her mind, and her heart felt like someone was squeezing it to death. She felt like her entire world was being demolished. She nodded wearily. "Okay, if you want."

He motioned for her to go first. He walked next to her, but not too close. He didn't want her to feel trapped, or like he was invading her space. He tried to pull his mind away from wanting to take her into his arms until she trusted him again. He knew that wouldn't do any good. Not yet anyway. "How did the interviews go today?" he asked, trying to sound casual.

"Fine. Erik's was pretty traditional, but Lance was a major pain in the butt. He wouldn't say anything because he said I was too serious and needed to lighten up. He wouldn't answer any of my questions until I smiled. He ended up being so stupid that I nearly laughed myself to death. It was very unprofessional."

Van grinned.

"And now I have a room full of musicians watching him try to stuff cake into his mouth and add to his already bursting gut. If I go in there and he's spewed all over everything, I'm coming to sleep in your room."

Van's heart skipped a beat. He didn't think she'd actually realized what she'd said, but the thought of having her sleep anywhere near him at all made his pulse beat just a little faster than usual. He cleared his throat. "Lance is a good guy. He's like my brother."

"How come I never met him?"

"He was home schooled and you never came to see my band practice." He looked down at her with a teasing frown.

She arched an eyebrow. "You never invited me."

He chuckled. "That's because we sucked."

"I have a hard time believing that you ever sucked at anything that had to do with music."

He couldn't help the boyish rush of heat to his cheeks.

"I think Rochelle is attracted to Lance," Kat said with a smile.

Van grinned. "Well, I think that Lance is extremely attracted to her. He practically drools when she walks into the room." Kat giggled, and he frowned thoughtfully. "By the way, what does Rochelle do exactly? She's supposed to be your assistant, but I haven't seen her do much assisting."

"She assists me in keeping all the guys away from me with her overabundant talent for flirting."

He laughed. "Well, she was always good at that." They reached the room and he turned to face her, offering her a warm smile.

Kat let out a shaky breath and let her eyes roam over his

beautiful face and long, shining hair. She sighed. He had blossomed into such a handsome man. No, handsome was too weak a word. Van was gorgeous, like art. Dark, gothic art. She looked down. "Van," she murmured, "I want you to know something, and I want you to remember this the next time I go on a psychotic rampage." She met his eyes. "If I could go back and know that I would one day see you again, I would stay the person you remember. It would be hard because of…what happened, but I would."

He gave her an understanding look that was full of warmth. "Kat, people change all the time for hundreds of different reasons. I've changed. I'm sure you can see that. We are molded and shaped by the things that happen in our lives. It would be silly and unfair of me to expect you to be the person I knew in high school. Just be you, Kat. That's all I want."

She studied him for a moment, then smiled. "Maybe I can interview you tomorrow."

"Sure."

She wrinkled her nose. "Don't tell Nyah, though. She'll try to sit on your lap or handcuff herself to you or something."

Van laughed. "Sounds like a plan. I'll see you tomorrow." He gave her a wink. "Have a good night, Kat."

She waved and watched him swagger off down the hall. She sighed, her tumultuous emotions somewhat quieted for the moment. He had always known how to treat her, always. Even now, he knew how to calm her, to reach out to her. She heard Rochelle's laughter through the door and smiled. She slid her key card through the slot and went in, almost afraid of what to expect.

Chapter Six

"You need to come with us, Kat," Rochelle insisted. "You can't possibly stay in the hotel room for the entire tour and Tai Chi yourself to death." She heaved an exasperated sigh as she followed Kat around the room. "It's just going to be Lance and me. Everyone else has other plans."

Kat frowned. "Just Lance and you. What would I do? Watch you make out?"

Rochelle blushed a little. "Gimme a break, it's not like we're dating. We just have fun together."

Kat rolled her eyes. "Third wheel, Rochelle. That's all I have to say."

"But you've never even been to San Francisco. Don't you want to see any of it? Aren't you even curious?"

"I have to interview Van today," she said. "We already made plans to do that."

"So?" Rochelle asked. "That will take, like what, twenty minutes at the most?" Her eyes lit up in the way they did only when she got an idea. "I know, we'll do the interview and then we can all go out together!"

"I don't want to go out, Rochelle. I have work to do," she grumbled.

Rochelle made a strangling gesture, obviously frustrated. "Look, you have a whole month to get the needed footage. You don't need to cram it all in during one week. If you run out of stuff to do too soon, you'll run out of excuses for not having a life."

Kat gave her a withered expression.

"Besides," she continued, putting her hands on her hips, "if you take the small camera out with us, you can get some great candid stuff."

Kat smiled in spite of herself. "I'm going to go do my interview now. Are you coming, or do I have to do everything by myself again?"

"Did you write down the interview questions?"

Kat handed Rochelle a few papers. "Already done."

"Excellent. Let's go." She opened the door and paused. "Kat," she called, "is there any particular reason why there's a hunk of chocolate outside the door?"

Kat frowned and went to the door. In the hallway, right in front of their room, was a king-sized chocolate kiss. She blushed. "Oh geez," she muttered.

Rochelle frowned. "Where did it come from?"

Kat scooped it up and started down the hall with her gear. "Are you coming?" she called.

Rochelle blinked, still obviously confused, then shook her head and followed after Kat to Van's room.

* * * *

Van sat reclining in the chair in his room, trying to will the awful tightening around his heart to go away. He rubbed at his chest in an attempt to soothe the ache. He couldn't have a panic attack right before his interview with Kat. That would be humiliating. He took deep breaths and closed his eyes, trying to calm his rapid pulse. The others had gone to Thrill My Koi's suite to give him some privacy for the interview. He relished the silence, hoping it would aid in relaxing him. He heard a knock on the door and he groaned inwardly. Now he had to pretend he was fine when he was anything but. He took a deep breath and forced himself out of the chair. He opened the door and gave Rochelle and Kat a prepared smile.

Kat looked up at Van and raised an eyebrow. She held up the chocolate. "Cute," she muttered.

He grinned and stepped aside to let them in.

"Where is everyone?" Rochelle questioned.

"In Thrill My Koi's suite," he answered. "Lance said to just call when you were finished so you guys can go out."

"Yeah, I was thinking it would be cool if we could all go," she suggested. "Me, Lance, you, and Kat!"

Van glanced over at Kat, who was setting up her camera and pretending not to hear.

"Kat's never been to San Francisco before," Rochelle continued.

He gave a half-smile, feeling anything but social. "We'll see. I don't want to push her."

Rochelle snorted and rolled her eyes. "The girl needs a shove!"

He chuckled and caught sight of his acoustic guitar. It was beckoning him to play it and calm his erratic heartbeat and frayed nerves. He almost launched at it, grasping for it like it was his only lifeline. "Here, I'll play for you guys while you set up." He sat down and let out a shaky breath. He closed his eyes and began to play a slow, melodic song he had written awhile back. Playing would make him feel momentarily better. At least then he could get through the interview.

Kat shivered in spite of herself as the soft notes filled the room. She stole a glance at Van and watched the expression on his face. He looked like he was in another place, like he was the music. His long fingers played expertly across the strings, and she smiled to herself, remembering the same look of rapture on his face all those years ago. "All right, I'm ready," she announced.

Van opened his eyes and smiled up at her. He set his guitar aside and went to sit in a chair across from Kat. She turned on her camera and focused it on Van while Rochelle read through the list of questions. She sat cross-legged on the floor, out of sight of the camera. She looked up at Kat. "Ready?"

Kat nodded. "Rolling."

"Hi, Van," Rochelle greeted with a grin.

He chuckled.

"Okay, tell me what it's like being a god among musicians," she started.

Kat coughed and scowled down at Rochelle. "That was *not* one of my questions," she protested.

Rochelle snorted. "My questions are better than yours. Yours are boring."

Kat stared at her. "Oh look who decides to have an opinion all of a sudden."

Van stifled a laugh.

Rochelle gave Kat a very haughty look. "I am your assistant," she stated. "I am assisting you in asking better questions."

Kat grumbled something under her breath and looked back through the camera.

"So what's it like?" Rochelle asked Van again. "Many people say you are the next rock legend."

Van shrugged self-consciously and smiled. "I never considered myself a rock legend. I'm just a man doing what he loves. If I make other people happy by playing my music, that is an extreme bonus. I play because I have to, not to become legendary. Music calls to me, it lives in me. I can't not play."

Rochelle smiled. "How did Bleeding Passion get started?"

"Well, Lance and I grew up together and we met Erik in college. We found Jack and Nyah when they answered an ad we posted for auditions. We weren't originally going for a six member band, but after we heard Nyah sing, we thought it would be interesting and unique to have both a male and female singer. We thought it would lend a different kind of sound, especially for gothic metal from America. A lot of the European metal bands have that kind of sound, but not many American bands do."

"You write all of the songs yourself, right?"

He nodded. "I write the songs and a lot of the music."

"I also know you are most of the brains behind Bleeding Passion. Is it difficult to be front man and lead guitarist as well as keep all of the business stuff in line?"

He shrugged. "Sometimes it seems a little overwhelming, but it's not like I'm by myself. The band decides everything unanimously, and our manager, Hank, takes care of most of the business."

"Where did the Bleeding Passion logo come from?"

"Lance and I came up with it when we started the band. We wanted a symbol that would show emotion, and we chose the crying eye because, in order to have tears, you have to be experiencing some kind of powerful emotion. Be it sorrow, joy, love, whatever. Also, it is commonly said that the eye is the window to the soul and the soul is where passion resides. The rose petals in place of tears signify romance and beauty."

Kat smiled. That was just like Van. He had always been so symbolic.

Rochelle nodded and glanced over Kat's questions again. "What made you decide to become a musician?"

Van's eyes sparkled for a second, like something had sparked to life inside of him. "There was no way I could have ever done anything else. It's in my blood; it's my calling. However..." He grinned. "I wasn't really set on being a performer until I had someone else's influence. I would have been content to just be a lyricist or something, always doing my work from behind the scenes."

"Who changed that?"

His lips quirked at the corners. "A girl I knew a long time ago." He looked directly at the camera. "She believed in me and made me feel beautiful and talented. I owe everything that I am today to her."

Kat almost stopped breathing. He was giving her way too much credit. He had been beautiful and talented long before she had entered his life. She swallowed and tried to focus on her job. Rochelle was asking a question about why he had chosen to play gothic rock and metal, but her words were muffled. For some reason, all Kat could do was stare through the lens at Van's gray eyes. They looked so soft and gentle, the same as she remembered. She'd always loved his gentle eyes.

"So tell me about you and Nyah," Rochelle said, cutting right to the chase.

Van stared at her for a second and chuckled when she raised her eyebrows at him playfully. "Nyah is an amazing musician and a good friend to all of us. That is all I'm saying on *that* matter." He gave her a pointed look.

Rochelle giggled. "Okay, what do you think about the whole sex, drugs and rock and roll philosophy?"

"It's moronic," he stated. "I am an artist. Getting drunk and stoned every night of my life and having sex with hundreds of faceless, nameless women is not an art form to me. I did not get into this business to be a mega star. I want to play music. So does my band. We have fun together. We go out, we drink, we pick up girls once in awhile, but we don't do drugs and we don't perform inebriated. It's just not something we do."

His response made Kat smile.

"Okay, one last question. What advice would you give your younger fans out there?"

He grinned. "If you have a dream, go for it and never quit. Even if the school bullies pull off your guitar strings, just buy new ones and play louder."

Kat couldn't help but grin. She focused for a minute on his face while he flashed his bright smile, figuring his fans would like that, then she turned off the camera. "Thanks, that was good." She started to put her equipment away.

"It was good because I didn't ask your lame questions," Rochelle teased.

Van smiled as Kat scowled playfully at Rochelle. He reached over for his guitar and started to play again.

Rochelle bounded across the room to call Lance, and Kat studied Van for a moment while she put her camera away. He seemed different, quiet, brooding, and all but attached to his musical instrument. "Are you okay?" she asked.

He glanced up at her and forced a smile. "I'm fine," he recited.

She frowned quizzically. "No you're not."

His fingers faltered for a minute and he had to look down at his strings. He cleared his throat and quickly recovered, but it was obvious that his composure was rattled by her keen observation.

"So are you guys gonna go?" Rochelle asked excitedly, coming back over to them. "Lance is on his way over."

Kat sighed. "Nah. I'm just going to stay here. I might work out downstairs."

Van wrinkled his nose. "I don't think I'm going to go either. I just want to play for awhile."

Kat noticed that he was hugging his guitar to his chest as if to use it as a barrier against the rest of the world.

Rochelle gaped at them. "You two are absolutely hopeless," she muttered. "Whatever. When neither one of you have any stories to tell when you're old, don't blame me." She shook her head and started toward the bathroom. "I have to pee."

Kat raised an eyebrow in amusement at Rochelle's frustration. "You would think that touring with a famous rock band would be a big enough story for her." She glanced back at Van and watched him play some more, intrigued by the way his fingers expertly sought the notes and chords. Her gaze traveled up to his face and he looked very much like Jake in that moment, hunched over, awkward, unsure of himself. It was a large contrast from the powerful man who dazzled crowds every night.

Apparently, some things didn't change. She walked slowly behind Van's chair, propelled by a memory she dredged up from the vaults of her mind. She reached out slightly trembling fingers and took a deep breath. She slid them lightly down the back of his neck.

Van froze, and his playing halted. He shivered and drew in a shaky breath. "What are you doing?" he asked, his voice hushed.

"I remember this used to help," she murmured. He craned his neck to look up at her with question in his eyes. "Your anxiety," she said.

He stared at her for a second, then smiled. "I forget you know me of old." He turned back around and let out a deep breath. His shoulders relaxed and some of the tension slipped out of his body.

Kat continued to caress her fingers up and down his neck, remembering how it had helped him during his terrible panic attack. After they'd become friends, she would do it in class. He'd had such horrible problems with his anxiety that it became second nature to her. She would listen to the teacher lecture, mindlessly trailing her fingers along the back of his neck all period. It would relax him and momentarily dispel his anxiety. He used to tell her that she had—

"Magic fingers," he whispered.

Kat smiled and studied his thick hair. She never would have thought he could have so much. He had always kept it relatively short in school. She wondered if it was as soft as it looked. Without even thinking at all, which was something she was not prone to doing, she reached out and pulled the tie from his hair. She ran her fingers through the silky mass and smiled. It *was* as soft as it looked.

Van sucked his breath in and made a noise in his throat. "That's even better than the neck thing."

Kat blushed, realizing just exactly what she was doing. Good lord, he must think she was a complete freak. One minute she was telling him to go away, the next she was threading her fingers through his hair. *What the heck is wrong with me? I'm a first-class nut job.* "This is not something I would normally do."

"You owe it to me after decking me in the nose last night," he teased.

She grinned, liking how he always set out to make her

feel comfortable, even when she was feeling anything but.

Rochelle came out of the bathroom then and stopped to stare at them in shock. "Did I interrupt?"

Kat glared at her and a knock sounded on the door. Rochelle went to open it, muttering something about her friend losing her mind.

"Do you feel better?" Kat questioned.

He nodded and looked up at her. "Thank you. That was very thoughtful of you." He smiled. "Took me back a few years... Made me remember why I thought so much of you."

She shrugged, feeling self-conscious.

He sighed. "Do you want to go out with Lance and Rochelle?"

His eyes reflected adoration, and her heart thudded against her chest. Her palms broke out in a sweat and she felt anxious and uneasy. "I don't think so."

"And what are you going to do instead?" Lance asked, coming into the room and striding over to them. He put his hands on his hips. "Sit in your room?"

She looked up at him and raised an eyebrow.

"You cannot pass through San Francisco and not see it." He snorted. "Quite frankly, Kat, I'm getting sick of your attitude."

She frowned. "My attitude? I've only been here for three days!"

He pointed at her. "You need to go out with us." He stabbed his finger at Van. "You too."

Van blinked at his friend. "Well gee, Lance, tell me how you really feel."

"I will!" he declared. "You're all acting old and boring. Come on!" He pointed at Kat again. "You do not want a piece of this, girl." He slapped his chest in a barbaric manner.

Kat couldn't help but chuckle.

"Come on, Kat. Please?" Rochelle begged.

She sighed and rolled her eyes. "Fine," she spat. "Just quit nagging at me."

Rochelle rolled her eyes heavenward. "Finally!"

Lance pointed his accusatory finger back at Van. "And you?"

Van held his hands up in an "unarmed" gesture. "I'll go," he said. "Anything's better than your wrath."

Lance nodded arrogantly.

Van chuckled and glanced up at Kat. "I guess we'll have to entertain each other."

She smiled, but still felt uneasy. She didn't like going out. She especially didn't like going out in strange places. It was outside of her safe zone and she didn't like that, but then again, everything that had recently happened was so far out of her safe zone that she couldn't even remember what "safe" meant. She took a deep breath, reassuring herself that if anyone tried anything funny, she could kick his or her head off.

Chapter Seven

Kat would never tell Rochelle this, but she had to admit that San Francisco was a beautiful place. It had been about two o'clock when they had headed out, and they'd taken a bus to Chinatown because Rochelle wanted to find an oriental dress for some reason. They had shopped around for about an hour and a half until Kat wasn't able to take the dead fish smell emanating from the markets anymore. They ate lunch at a small Chinese restaurant and then wandered up and down the sloping streets, talking and taking in all the sights.

Van had been to San Francisco several times, obviously, and he kept relating stories to Kat about his previous visits. She listened to him while she basked in the aura of the city, secretly delighted that she had decided to go along. She had tried to convince herself that all big cities were like L.A. so that she would not want to go anywhere, but San Francisco had a life of its own. Everyone seemed so colorful and full of energy, like each person had a different story to tell. She couldn't help but be caught up in the atmosphere. It made her feel somewhat less restricted, less stagnated.

Everywhere they went, people stopped Lance and Van, asking for autographs. One group of screaming Asian teenage girls had practically mauled them to death. Lance had brought his skateboard along, so he had made a quick getaway, but Van had been stuck in the middle of them with no escape. He was nothing but polite and friendly, speaking to each one of the girls like they were special and appreciated. She could understand why he had so many adoring fans. Not only was he gorgeous and amazingly talented, but he gave credit to the people who had made him so popular.

Popular.

It made Kat smile. That was one word she would never have thought to equate with Van. She could bet that everyone in high school who had once made fun of him was eating their words now.

They were now down on Pier 39 heading toward the aquarium and all the stores. Rochelle laughed about something while Lance skated along beside her. Kat had videotaped periodically throughout the day, feeling that she needed to do something productive, or maybe she was just making excuses so that she didn't have to admit that she was actually having a nice time. She no longer really knew. She was sick of her own brain. Her logic was anything but logical and it gave her a headache.

"Hey, what are these things anyway?" Rochelle asked, pointing to one of the many black bollards decorating the sidewalk.

"Those were used back in the day to tie the ropes around when a ship docked," Van supplied. "To keep it in the port."

She nodded. "It's cool to use them as decorations, especially down here on the pier."

Kat pulled out her camera and recorded some of their surroundings. They were apparently in a highly populated tourist area because there were so many people of all walks of life. It looked like a virtual melting pot. There were artists selling paintings and prints right out on the street, and one man was making paintings out of spray paint while listening to techno music.

"Excuse me," a soft voice came all of a sudden. "Are you Van Marshall?"

They all halted, and Kat continued to record as a young, maybe fifteen-year-old girl approached Van tentatively. She was dressed in a very earthy, hippie-styled skirt and shirt and she had brown braids sticking out from underneath a crocheted tan hat. She clutched a notepad to her chest.

Van turned to her and smiled. "I am."

Her eyes widened. "Oh my gosh," she breathed. "You have no idea—" She shook her head. "I was just drawing you." She indicated her notebook.

"Drawing me?"

She nodded. "I was listening to your CD and copying the cover." She opened her notebook and flipped to a page with a sketch on it. She held it out to him. "See?"

Kat zoomed in on the sketch. It was a good likeness.

"I drew all the other members of the band too," the girl added.

Van took the notebook from her and studied the drawing for a minute. He smiled broadly. "Do you have a name, sweetheart?"

She blinked in surprise. "Lola," she murmured.

"Lola," he repeated. "This is an excellent drawing. I think you made me look better on paper than I do in person."

She blushed a bright shade of crimson. "I don't think that's possible," she whispered.

He smiled. "Did you say you have one of Lance?"

She nodded. "I do, but it's not finished. I just have his head done. Do you—" She swallowed, obviously nervous. "Do you think I could trouble you to sign that?"

"Of course." He turned to the others. "Does anyone have a pen on them?"

"Oh, I do!" Lola announced. She rummaged through her small brown backpack and handed him one. "If Lance could sign his too, that would be great, even though it's not done yet."

Lance grinned. "Of course I will." He stopped doing whatever trick he had been trying to accomplish on his skateboard and went to stand next to Van.

"Are you going to the show tomorrow?" Van asked as he signed the sketch.

She nodded enthusiastically.

He grinned and handed the notebook to Lance as he finished signing it. "Well, I hope you enjoy it."

"Oh, I will!" she declared. "I love all your shows." She took the notebook back and clutched it to her chest. "Thank you so much."

"It was my pleasure. Take care."

She waved, still looking completely dazed.

Kat smiled and followed behind Lance as they all continued on their way. She loved how personable Van was with his fans. She focused her camera on Lance as he skated up the sidewalk, his wavy, golden hair blowing from the cool ocean breeze. He skated over to a curb near where a bunch of trees were planted and he ollied up to grind on it. He lost his footing and stumbled off his board, falling hard right into one of the bollards.

Kat's eyes widened and she turned off her camera.

"Lance!" Rochelle cried.

He seemed to melt down onto the sidewalk and rolled over onto his back. He pulled his knees up to his chest and groaned.

"You all right?" Van asked, standing over him.

"Man, I think I crushed my boys," he whimpered.

Van offered a hand and helped him up. "That's what you get for trying to show off," he teased. "I hate to break it to you, but you're no Tony Hawk."

Lance made a face at him and turned to Rochelle, who was more sympathetic.

Kat laughed. "I should change the name of this DVD to The Antics of Lance."

Van smiled. "The Humiliation of Lance is more like it." He glanced down at her as they fell into step with one another.

She was considerably more relaxed and actually found smiling to be less painful than it had been thus far. She enjoyed spending time with Rochelle, Lance cracked her up, and being with Van was much better now that the shock of his not being dead was wearing off.

"Hey look! It's a Hard Rock Café!" Rochelle exclaimed. "We should go in and see if you guys are on the wall!"

Van chuckled and turned to Kat. "Rochelle was always so excited about life. It's good to see that hasn't changed over time."

Kat nodded and glanced at her friend. "She loves everything about being alive."

He frowned thoughtfully. "Did she ever think I was a freak? I mean, she was always perfectly nice to my face, but behind closed doors, did she think you were nuts for hanging out with me?"

She shook her head. "Rochelle never thinks anyone is a freak. She liked you. Plus, she knew you made me happy, and she liked that." She looked down at the pavement as she said the last part of her statement, wondering what had prompted her to admit that.

Van stole a sidelong glance at her. He stopped at the entrance of The Hard Rock Café and sighed. "I think I'll just let Lance brave it in there. I'm finally feeling halfway decent and don't want to draw unnecessary attention to myself."

"Hasn't your anxiety gotten any better over the years?"

she asked. "Isn't there some sort of medication you can take?"

He shrugged. "I do take medication; it just doesn't do much. I've tried several different types, but nothing really seems to work. I've gotten considerably good at controlling it to where I don't flip out in public anymore, but it never really goes away."

He glanced down at his watch. "Look, I made plans to have dinner with a friend of mine tonight, and it's already almost six o'clock. I have to go all the way across town on a bus so I have to get going." He met her eyes, seemed to debate with himself for a minute, and then asked, "Would you like to come with me?"

Kat felt everything inside of her tense up. She shook her head instinctively. "No, that's all right. I'll just go home with Lance and Rochelle." He arched one dark eyebrow and she frowned. Right, so she could tag along and feel left out because she wasn't a party animal. They would probably want to go to a club and drink or something while she sat in the corner dodging all of the sleazy drunk guys.

She shook her head. "Never mind. I'll just catch a cab back to the hotel." Why was he riding a bus anyway? Shouldn't he have a limo or something? Van was the most down to earth rock star she had ever met, but that didn't really surprise her. He wasn't in the business for the luxuries. He just loved to play music.

Van forced his breath out in a rush. "Kat," he said, his voice carrying a slight bite of frustration, "did you have fun today?"

She blinked at him, a little taken aback. "Yeah," she answered slowly.

"Have I made you feel uncomfortable at all?"

She shook her head, not adding the fact that he being so devastatingly good-looking always made her feel a little uncomfortable.

"Then why do you insist on isolating yourself? I get up on stage in front of hundreds of people every night and I have panic disorder. Years ago, I met this gorgeous, pushy girl who insisted on going to the music store to buy me guitar strings and then invited herself over to my house. I thought my life was over, but I dealt with it. Now imagine if I hadn't taken that opportunity and gone with it. Imagine if I'd told her to just go home because having her near me made me uncomfortable. I might not be where I am today, and my life would have been a whole lot less beautiful."

She stared up at him, then cracked a small smile and averted her eyes shyly. How had she ever been that bold? It seemed like a lifetime ago.

"All I'm asking is for you to come and have one measly meal with me. I don't want to leave you here with Lance and Rochelle so you can watch them google-eye each other all night, and I don't want to send you back to the hotel all alone when I know there is still so much beauty I can show you. Besides, you've made it quite clear that you could kick the crap out of anyone that comes within speaking distance, so what's the problem?"

She wanted to smile, but at the same time, wanted to be angry with him for making her sound foolish. She decided on a frustrated-sounding huff and folded her arms. "Who is this friend of yours anyway?"

"Do you know the band Fat Stinky?"

She nodded.

"We toured with them awhile back, and the bass player ended up bringing some friends along for a couple shows. I hit it off with them and we keep in touch. One of them lives here in San Francisco, and when he found out we were going to be here, he asked if we could get together. We're eating dinner at the Cliff House. He's harmless, Kat. Really. Besides," he touched her chin with his finger and smiled, "you know you can trust me."

She studied his eyes for a minute and sighed. She felt like a friggin' yo-yo. He was wreaking havoc on her carefully constructed way of life. "All right," she found herself saying, unable to think of any good reason not to go.

Van was unable to hide his surprise. "Really?"

She nodded and looked down again, feeling awkward. She felt a lump rise in her throat and tears stung her eyes. She hadn't realized how much time she spent by herself. She worked, worked out, and went home. She didn't go out, she didn't socialize. Now, when she tried, it felt foreign and uncomfortable. She missed feeling sure of herself.

Deep inside, she wanted to laugh like Rochelle again. She just didn't know how. She felt broken and she hated it. She hadn't felt that way before Van. Or, at least, she hadn't realized she'd felt that way. He made her feel things she'd tried to make herself forget. He was a piece of past that belonged to the old Kat. Now that he was back in her life, the new Kat didn't know what to do to bridge the gap between her old life and the one she lived now.

"You aren't in there," Rochelle declared, coming out of the Hard Rock Café. "I looked everywhere. Lance got attacked by fans, though, so he's stuck in there."

Van smiled. "Don't let him fool you. He loves the attention. Hey, Rochelle, I made dinner plans with a friend of mine and I have to get going. Kat's going to come with me, so you guys have fun, okay?"

Rochelle glanced at Kat and raised an eyebrow in surprise. Kat made a face at her to cover over the fact that she felt self-conscious. Rochelle probably thought she had lost her mind. Maybe she had. She didn't know anymore.

"Tell Lance I'll see him later," Van said. "Come on, Kat, we've gotta move."

She nodded and followed after him. They walked several blocks, passing some men with dreadlocks playing on steel drums and some men that were painted completely silver acting like robots. She was going to ask Van about them, thinking it was rather odd, but they were running to the bus stop before she could even formulate a thought, and soon they were heading through the city.

Kat studied the Victorian style homes lining the streets as they drove by and thought that it looked like she'd stepped back in time.

"I wish we were spending more time here," Van said. "San Francisco is one of my favorite cities. I like to ride the cable cars and shop down on Fisherman's Wharf. You see so many interesting people." His lips turned up at the corners. "I remember the first time we came to San Francisco for a gig. It was something Erik had managed to set up and we were all scared to death. It was the biggest one we had played up until that point. I was awestruck the entire time. That was the turning point. I remember sitting in my hotel room, looking out the window at all the rooftops around me knowing that I was in a beautiful city to play music, that I was getting paid to entertain people with *my music*." He shook his head. "That was it for me, the defining moment. I knew then that this was what I wanted more than anything."

She looked up at him and couldn't help but grin.

He smiled. "We have a signing tomorrow from noon to four if you want to come along and record some of it."

She nodded.

Van's friend called right as they reached the restaurant, telling them that he was running about an hour late because of having to work overtime. He looked around as they tried to think of something they could do for an hour and he pointed down toward the beach. "Do you want to take a walk while we wait?" he asked. "There are these old ruins right down the road that used to be a public bath house in the eighteeen hundreds. They're interesting. Want to check them out?"

She nodded and followed him down the road until they came to a sandy cliff that overlooked a bunch of concrete slabs that were worn and overgrown. They looked like they had once formed grand pools, but were now only filled with sea water and algae.

They descended winding steps that led down the cliff and headed along a path around the ruins. The sun had started to sink and tendrils of fog rolled in on the waves. Kat admired them as she walked with Van. The fog called to her for some reason, and she found it strange. Fog was mysterious and almost seemed dangerous. She usually shied away from things that were dangerous, but she found the fog intriguing.

She fell into silence, and knew Van noticed. While she stared off toward the ocean, she felt his astute eyes trace over her.

"Are you okay?" he asked.

She looked up at him. "Yeah, why?"

He shrugged. "You just seemed lost somewhere."

She shook her head. "It's dumb. I was just wondering why I find fog so intriguing when it's so ominous."

"Fog encompasses everything. You can lose yourself in fog, become someone else if you want."

"You think so?"

"Sure."

She glanced over at a cave that she spotted in a cliff nearby and pointed to it. "Let's go over there."

Van followed her. It was dark in the cave and the sound of the waves against the cliff was thunderous. Kat closed her eyes and allowed herself to relish in the cacophony. She loved the sound of the sea. She always had. It was so powerful, so strong.

She loved the ocean, but couldn't appreciate it in L.A. The beaches were always too full of people. It took away the natural peace and beauty to have a ton of butts in thong bikinis being paraded in front of you. Besides, L.A. had tainted everything for Kat. She hated L.A. But this... This was beautiful. The fog wrapped around her and she closed her eyes, soaking up the peaceful sound of the crashing waves. It sounded and felt like freedom.

Van continued to walk through the cave to the other side, which opened up to a bunch of rocks and jagged cliff edges. The ocean pounded itself against them, sending salty spray up into the air as the fog started to blanket everything. "Kat, come look!" he called.

She followed, and gasped when she reached him. "This is so beautiful," she murmured. She started to climb down the rocks and out toward the crashing waves.

"Be careful," Van warned. She shot him a look that made him chuckle as he moved in her direction. She sat down on a rock that was the closest she could get without being drowned. He sat next to her.

"How is it that something can be so angry, yet give off such a feeling of peace and beauty?" Kat murmured.

He glanced over at her and studied the stern set of her features. She had never looked stern before. She gazed out at the ocean in a mesmerized silence, her hair blowing playfully around her face. He sighed. It appeared to him that her lovely eyes had seen far too much. "It seems angry," he said, his voice soft, "but it's not really. It's just trying to get your attention. It draws you toward it with its fury so you can stop and admire its serenity."

She slowly turned her gaze to meet his and his heart turned over at the dull sadness reflected in her blue-gray depths. "You're a lot like the ocean, Kat," he murmured.

She frowned. "How so?"

He let his eyes roam over her face for a moment. "You're so tumultuous, yet so very beautiful. I thought it once, a long time ago, and I still believe that you are, by far, the most beautiful woman I have ever seen."

Color crept into Kat's cheeks and she looked away. She worried her bottom lip with her teeth. "Beauty is a curse," she muttered. "I don't want to be beautiful."

"You can't help but be. You were made magnificent."

She shook her head as if fighting tears. "But I don't want to be anything other than boring and dull. I try. I try to be as plain as possible. I don't wear much makeup. I don't wear revealing clothing. I don't do anything Rochelle does. I don't attract attention to myself, and yet..." She drew in a shuddering breath, and shook her head again.

Van leaned a little closer to her in concern. She looked like she was trying to dispel some sort of troublesome memory, and he felt like she was on the verge of telling him something very important. "What?" he urged gently. "What is it?"

"I was raped, Van," she admitted, her voice so soft and small he could barely hear it.

He stared at her in shock, unable to think of anything to say. How could anyone even think of touching Kat in a harmful manner? Who in their right mind would want to hurt her? "Kat," he stammered. "Kat, I—" He shook his head in disbelief. "When?"

"In college. I started dating this guy and he date raped me. After having to dodge my uncle my whole life, it kind of just broke me, you know? I called you because, for some reason, I always felt safest with you. Safer even than when I was with Rochelle." She stared down at the rock she was sitting on and picked at some dried moss. "After I thought you were dead, I just shut myself down. I became all about work and duty. I only went out when Rochelle begged me to. After another incident I had with a man, I vowed I would never let anyone touch me again. I figured there had to be something about me that attracted people like that, so I became a martial artist, never went anywhere unless I had to, and became cold and distant. It was the only way I could cope, the only way I knew how." A tear slipped down her cheek. "The only person I didn't shut out was Rochelle, but I even kept her at a distance. I didn't like feeling weak, and I knew that she was worried about me, especially after I thought you had died. I couldn't take the concern in her eyes. I didn't want anyone to pity me or think of me as anything but strong. People take advantage of weak people. No one messes with someone who is strong."

Van reached out to her and pulled her into his arms,

holding her tight, wanting to protect her from everything and take away all of her pain. His heart was breaking for her. It was bleeding at the thought of her going through all of that on her own. "I am so sorry," he whispered.

She shrugged. "It's not your fault, Van."

"And it's not yours either." He held her out so he could look at her. A wave crashed behind her, and he touched her wayward hair, letting his fingers trail down the line of her jaw. "You did not attract any of that. Anyone who would hurt you deserves to be killed," he spat. "I would have killed him…" He squeezed his eyes shut for a moment and tried to get a handle on his emotions. The last thing she needed was to hear him go off about murdering someone. He was sure that wouldn't make her feel at ease. "If I could take it all away, I would. I'm sorry I wasn't there, Kat. I'm sorry for the horrid misunderstanding. I should have tried harder to find you." He shook his head, feeling guilty and terrible. He could have prevented this.

Kat smiled in understanding. "Things happen, Van. You couldn't have stopped it."

"I could have stopped it if—" He shook his head again.

She frowned. "What?"

He heaved a sigh. "Nothing. Never mind." He'd almost told her what he'd wished for ever since he'd said goodbye to her. He'd almost said that he could have stopped those things from happening if he'd stayed with her, if he'd asked her to be with him like he'd wanted to. He could have pro-tected her. She had been hurt because of his cowardice.

"We should probably go meet your friend," Kat said sud-denly.

He glanced down at his watch and nodded dismally. He stood, helped Kat back across the rocks, and led them back to the Cliff House, kicking himself for his stupid mistakes the entire way.

Chapter Eight

Kat was unable to speak for the entire first part of dinner. Van's friend, Torrey, was the most beautiful man she had ever seen in her life next to Van. He was tall and slender, like Van was, with intense eyes and jet black hair that glistened down half of his back. He was one of those people that held eye contact with someone the entire time he was talking and it made her want to run away. She had stared at her plate all through appetizers to avoid staring at him. She was sure his wife Taegen wouldn't appreciate that very much. She knew that ogling at him was stupid, but she wasn't dead. She was still human, despite all of her carefully constructed barriers against everything male, and there was no denying that Torrey was a very good-looking man.

"So, Kat, how do you know Van?" Torrey asked her.

Kat suppressed a groan. *Crap, I didn't succeed in making myself invisible. I'll have to try harder next time.* She braved a glance up at him, and he smiled easily at her. "I actually went to school with him," she replied quickly, averting her eyes again. Good lord. Men like Torrey and Van should not be allowed in public. It wasn't fair to all the ordinary men out there, and it certainly wasn't fair to all of the woman who were with those ordinary men.

She cleared her throat and tried to get a grip. "We lost contact for several years," she continued. "I work for a production company, and my partner and I were hired to record footage for a DVD on Bleeding Passion. I didn't know Van was Van when I met him. He went by another name in high school, and I didn't recognize him."

"It was an amazing coincidence," Van said.

Taegen rolled her eyes. "You want to talk about amazing

coincidences? I first saw Torrey on a train during, like, the worst day of my life. I didn't talk to him or anything because I was on this whole hating life kick." She made a face as if she thought the idea had been a stupid one. "Not an hour later, I saw him in Golden Gate Park and he talked to me. We had a really nice time together, but I was a complete lunatic at the time."

Torrey chuckled and reached over to play with her flaxen hair while she talked.

"I wouldn't even tell him my name because I was so terrified of commitment. We kept calling each other 'beautiful stranger' and 'pretty lady.'" She rolled her eyes again.

Torrey grinned. "Hey, I liked it when you called me that."

"It was so lame!" she cried. "Like I couldn't think of something better than that? It was so cliché!"

Kat giggled.

"Anyway, he took me home, and I was so sure he'd disappeared from my life forever. I spent several days kicking myself for being such an idiot, and then I was in this record store in Berkeley and this guy tried to pick me up. He wound up being a friend of Torrey's, and Torrey was right outside in the car!"

"Not to mention I painted this portrait of some woman I dreamed up late at night," Torrey went on. "And it ended up looking just like Taegen. And this was before I'd even met her."

"It was bizarre," Taegen said. "I say, don't ignore the coincidences. When there are too many, you need to pay attention."

Van smiled and glanced down at Kat.

Kat smiled at the lively couple. "How long before you got married?"

Torrey frowned thoughtfully. "What was it, a week, I think?"

Kat choked on her bite of food and stared at them in shock. "A week?"

Van chuckled. "Yeah, they got married on my tour. We all went dancing one night in Las Vegas and Taegen spent the whole time drinking O'Doul's non-alcoholic beer. She didn't know it was non-alcoholic and convinced herself she was drunk."

Taegen groaned and put her face in her hand.

Van laughed. "They got married on a whim in some chapel and she almost had a heart attack the next day when she realized she'd been completely sober the entire time."

Taegen gave Van a pained expression. "Do you have to tell that story? That was humiliating. Maxim yelled at me because of that."

Torrey laughed. "Speaking of Maxim..." He checked his watch and pulled his cell phone out of his pocket. "He was supposed to propose to Alyx tonight."

Van raised his eyebrows. "Really?"

Torrey grinned. "Yeah. I'm going to call Javan and see if he really did it."

Kat frowned. "Who are we talking about?" she asked Van.

"Torrey and Taegen's friends Maxim, Alyx, and Javan. They were with Torrey and Taegen when I met them. Maxim and I bonded because we were both shy and creative. I email him once in awhile. Alyx is his girlfriend."

"So were you guys friends in school?" Taegen asked while Torrey talked on the phone.

Kat smiled. "Yes, we were good friends."

"Kat saved me from going insane my senior year," Van teased. "About four months before graduation, we got very close. She helped me realize that being a musician was my purpose. I owe my success to her."

Kat shook her head adamantly. "That's not true. You were brilliant before I ever stumbled into your life."

Van looked down and met her eyes. His gaze reflected so much warmth that she swore she could actually feel it.

Torrey flashed a perfect grin. "Taegen and I have tickets for your show tomorrow. We're looking forward to it."

Taegen frowned thoughtfully at him. "What's going on?"

"I'm on hold," he replied.

Van smiled. "I love playing The Fillmore. We play in Phoenix next. That should be interesting. Strange things always happen when we play in Phoenix. The last time we were there, the power went out. We wound up only having back-up lights and had to play an entire acoustic show. It was ridiculous. None of us were prepared to have to play acoustic. Lance kept messing up on chords and Nyah and I nearly lost our voices trying to get everyone to hear us. The time before that, I got food poisoning." He snorted. "Yeah, try to put on a good show when you're puking in a can between songs and have to keep giving the other band members unexpected solos because you've got an extreme case of the runs."

Kat made a face, and Torrey laughed in a way that made her stare at him in wonderment. Even his laugh was beautiful, carefree and melodic. She envied his laugh even more than Rochelle's. He had such a laid back attitude. She sighed, wondering if everyone else on the planet enjoyed life but her. She looked down and twisted her fingers in her lap, feeling very isolated all of a sudden. It wasn't isolation like she was used to, not the kind she chose for herself so she wouldn't get hurt. This was different.

This was lonely.

She felt warm fingers encompass hers and she looked up at Van. He smiled at her and squeezed her hand lightly. The lonely feeling subsided a little and she remembered how comforted and safe she used to feel in his presence. The memories of him she had tried to banish were coming back stronger and faster than she had anticipated. She glanced down at his hand and studied his fingers. Musician's fingers.

He was really very different from how she remembered him. His features, which had always been attractive in her opinion, had morphed into such masculine beauty, and he carried so much more self-assurance than he had before. She would never believe he was the same brooding, awkward boy she had known if he didn't have the same soft eyes, gentle mannerisms, and elegant hands. Hands that produced sonorous perfection.

She slowly pulled one of her hands out from underneath his and placed it on top, caressing the back of his hand for a moment. She smiled as she felt his fingers tighten around the hand that was still beneath his.

"Hey, Max, congrats man!" Torrey exclaimed suddenly with a loud laugh.

Van met Taegen's eyes and smirked. "I take it things went well."

She smirked.

"Yeah, guess what?" Torrey continued. "Van's here! Talk to him!"

Van blinked as Torrey thrust the phone at him. He took it in his free hand, still keeping his other one on Kat's. "Hey, Maxim."

"So how do you like life on the road so far?" Torrey asked Kat, snapping her attention back to the conversation.

She looked up at him. "Well, I haven't been touring with them for more than a few days, but it seems very hectic."

"Do you get along with the other band members?" Taegen asked.

"For the most part," she replied with a polite smile.

Van chuckled. "Nyah drives her crazy," he supplied as he said goodbye to his friend and passed the phone on to Taegen. "She's insistent on thinking Kat is a lesbian and tries to undermine her work all the time." He rolled his eyes. "That's Nyah, though."

"Are you still seeing her?" Torrey asked.

Van shook his head. "We haven't been seeing one another for awhile, not that she'll admit it. She may be a very talented woman, but she's so self-absorbed and shallow that it's not even worth it. Half the time, she never listens to a word I say. I need something much more than Nyah could ever offer." He stole a sidelong glance at Kat. "She could never understand me."

Kat made a face. "That's because Nyah has about as much depth as a cow," she grumbled.

Torrey had been taking a sip of his drink when Kat spoke and he spurted some out of his mouth. Van erupted into laughter.

Kat smiled. "Sorry," she chuckled, "but it's true."

"It is," Van agreed. "I once wrote an abstract song about the complicated relationship between a man and a woman, and she thought it was about reincarnation."

"Now that could either mean that Nyah has no artistic depth," Torrey said with a teasing grin, "or it could mean that you make absolutely no sense."

Van gave him a flat look, and Kat giggled. "Well, I think I make perfect sense, and that's all that matters," he said. "Anyway, she's a great performer, but she's no poet, and she can't think past her lipstick and her weight." He laughed. "You should have seen how threatened she was by Kat. Kat knows three different types of martial arts, and she gets into the elevator all svelte and toned. She made Nyah look like a pudgy little girl."

Kat felt herself flush. It was strange to hear such compliments directed at her.

She looked down at Van's hand again. She lifted it enough to slip hers under it and twine her fingers with his. He faltered with what he was saying for a minute and looked down at her in surprise. She gave him a reassuring smile. She was just holding his hand. He deserved at least that after what she had put him through the last few days. Besides, she felt better knowing he knew about the rape. He could better understand where she was coming from and why she was the way she was. That helped tremendously in her not feeling like a complete freak.

Van kept his fingers linked with Kat's for the remainder of the evening, and she found herself slowly relaxing as she talked with Taegen and Torrey. They were both vibrant and easy to be around, even if she found Torrey's extreme good looks to be unnerving. He told amusing stories about his friends and co-workers, and Kat barely noticed that soon she was actually laughing instead of just smiling politely, feeling comfortable in the presence of strangers for the first time in years.

It was cold outside when they finally left the restaurant. The tide had come in and covered over the old stone ruins. The waves crashed against the cliffs with a vengeance, and the fog was thick and milky against the dark of night. Van and Kat waited for Torrey and Taegen, who were paying their bill inside.

Kat sighed, and Van glanced down at her. She looked pensive. "Are you okay? What are you thinking?"

She glanced up at him. "I'm thinking your friends are too good-looking," she replied, grinning mischievously.

Van's heart almost stopped at seeing her smile. She looked like he remembered her, playful and teasing. Without thinking, he reached out and cupped her cheek in his palm. "I'm glad you came with me tonight," he murmured.

She smiled and closed her eyes at his touch. "So am I. Your friends are nice."

"They're a lot of fun." He reluctantly pulled his hand away from her soft skin.

"I can't believe they got married after only a week and are still together! That's crazy!"

He smiled. "They loved one another the moment they saw each other." He shrugged. "I guess sometimes, you just know." He met her eyes with a hidden message in his own.

Kat swallowed hard and looked away.

"Ready to go?" Torrey asked, coming out the door with Taegen. "Or did you guys want to go somewhere else?"

"We should probably just go back to the hotel. I have a signing and a show tomorrow and I need to get a good night's sleep or I'll be feeling like crap in the morning," Van said.

Torrey nodded. "Understood." He ran his hand down the length of Taegen's hair and kissed her on the head as they walked back to the car. Kat and Van's hands brushed against each other as they followed and, without much thought from either one of them, they linked fingers again.

* * * *

The roar of the crowd was deafening as Bleeding Passion ran backstage after their show. Kat was putting her equipment away and smiled at the way their fans screamed for an encore.

"We have a good crowd tonight," Lance commented.

"That's because I think everyone at the signing today is out there in the audience and is jazzed they got to meet us," Erik said.

"Some guy in the front keeps screaming my name," Nyah said, glancing at Van to see his reaction. "Maybe I should find him after the show and invite him backstage."

Van ignored Nyah and looked at Kat over his shoulder. He met her gaze and grinned.

Kat smiled, her heart doing something of a somersault at the warmth she saw in his eyes. She looked down and concentrated on what she was doing, wondering how something as simple as a smile or a look could wreak havoc on her insides. It drove her crazy. She had conditioned her mind to view any kind of attraction as off-limits. Why couldn't her body do the same? She glanced at Van again as he prepared himself to go back out on stage. He guzzled water from a bottle and poured some of it over his head. He exchanged a look with his band mates and they all trooped back out onto the stage.

Kat could see him from where she was in the wings and he raised his arms up, drawing further noise from the crowd. He pulled his guitar over his head and nestled it against his hips. It seemed to meld with him as he walked over to the microphone and addressed the crowd.

"Thank you, everyone, you've been fantastic," he said.

The crowd cheered.

"It's all of you who make Bleeding Passion what it is, so we thank you from the bottom of our hearts for making our dreams real." He blew a kiss out to the audience, then broke into the intro of one of their chart toppers. It was dark and slow and it always made Kat have chills. She watched as he played, his long legs spread in a power stance, water droplets cascading down his hair and shoulders like sparkling jewels. His lithe body moved in unison to the notes and chords his fingers produced with fluid grace, and she could do nothing but stare in awe.

She was watching the fusion of man and music, and she didn't think she had ever seen anything more intoxicating. Her eyes were drawn, once again, to the tattoos she could barely see through his black fishnet shirt. She could not quell her curiosity about them. She wanted to see what things Van had thought so important to him, or so beautiful, that he would permanently draw them onto his body.

"I don't think I could ever get tired of watching them perform," Rochelle said, coming up behind her suddenly.

Kat turned to look at her over her shoulder, then looked back at Van. "He's always been so brilliant," she murmured. She wasn't sure if Rochelle had actually managed to hear her, but she couldn't miss the way her friend smiled, as if she knew something that Kat didn't.

Chapter Nine

"I've always loved playing in Phoenix," Nyah said to anyone who would listen to her as she stared out the bus window. "The fans are great there."

Kat was reading her book on the couch across from her and she glanced up. That must mean that the fans loved *her*. Nyah only gushed about something when it had to do with her.

"Phoenix has such a great metal scene," she continued. "When Van and I were dating, we played a lot of shows there. We got good turnout. Everyone said our chemistry on stage was phenomenal." She gave Kat a smug look.

Kat placidly turned a page. "Yeah, too bad your chemistry off stage wasn't as great, or you might still be together, huh?" she said without looking up.

Nyah scowled at her and shut up for about half a second. She tapped her fingers restlessly on the back of the couch, then got up and went to sit next to Kat. "Ugh, how can you and Van read such dreary stuff?" she muttered. "I could never understand that. Van is a man who needs light in his life. He's too brooding as it is."

"He's the lead guitarist, composer, lyricist, and singer of a gothic metal band. I would think that his being brooding is what's making your bank account fat." She looked around, hoping to find some way of escape. She imagined she could always hide in the bathroom, but the light was bad in there. It would be hard to read sitting on the toilet.

"We used to always go to this place in Phoenix when we were dating," Nyah continued. "It was our special place."

Kat heaved a weary sigh. "And where was that?"

"Oh, Hooters," she replied.

Kat blinked several times and frowned. Hooters was their special place? Yeah, now there was a relationship based on depth and beauty.

"I wouldn't be surprised if we went there again," Nyah said dreamily, twirling her fingers through her midnight hair.

Kat shrugged. "Me either. I hear they have really good wings." She stole a sidelong glance at her and smirked. "Plus, the scenery is supposed to be really nice."

Nyah shot her a scowl. "Van never looked at the scenery," she spat. "He only looked at me." She smiled and sighed.

Kat put her book down in irritation. "Are you certain he was only looking at you?"

Nyah frowned. "What is that supposed to mean?"

"Well, people don't readily share their private lives with strangers unless they're trying to invoke jealousy or convince themselves of something."

Nyah snorted. "Don't pretend to know anything about Van. Other than Lance, no one knows him better than me." She flipped her hair over her shoulder.

"What was his name before he changed it to Van Marshall?" Kat questioned. She knew this was amazingly childish, but she couldn't help herself. This woman needed to be put in her place.

Nyah rolled her eyes. "Oh you want to play, do you? Fine, it was Jake Marsallis. Everyone in the band knows that. Anyone who can use a computer knows that. Here's one for you. Why did he pick Van Marshall as his name?"

Kat frowned and looked away.

Nyah smirked triumphantly. "Not as smart as you thought? Van after Van Halen. Van Halen is a guitarist, by the way."

Kat scowled and felt her temper rise. "I know who Eddie Van Halen is," she snarled.

"Well, anyway, Van after Van Halen and Marshall after the guitar amp."

If she hadn't been so perturbed, Kat would have smiled. It was so fitting that he would choose a name that made music part of himself.

"Do you give in now?" Nyah simpered.

Kat turned and gave her a measured stare. "Who was his first kiss?"

"Some girl in high school," she replied flippantly.

"What was her name?" Kat prodded.

Nyah rolled her eyes. "Stop grasping. I don't know and neither do you."

"I do know," Kat countered, "because it was me."

Nyah stared at her, and her smile faded. "Yeah, right," she said, but her voice had lost some of its gloating power.

"Van was in my graduating class," Kat continued.

Nyah swallowed hard. "Oh, yeah? Well if that was the case, what did he always have you do when he was having anxiety problems?"

"Caress the back of his neck. It relaxed him."

Nyah's face twitched as if that had been a blow. "Well, what did he sing to you at that show he did?"

She frowned. "The Senior Show? He played a song he'd written entitled *Restless*." She smiled whimsically as she thought of the CD case he'd given her before he'd gone away to college. She'd locked that in her memory box at home in her closet and hadn't been able to look at it since she'd thought he'd died.

Nyah looked away and drew in a shaky breath. "Fine, if you're so smart, what did he say you tasted like after he kissed you?"

Kat frowned as she saw Nyah's eyes get glassy. How would she even know that? Van had discussed the details of their kiss with Nyah? That was a little messed up on more than one level.

"Come on, tell me!" Nyah demanded.

Kat hesitated, feeling like this had ventured into bizarre territory. "He said I tasted better than chocolate."

Nyah bit her bottom lip and looked down. "You," she whispered. She shook her head. "You win... You've always won." She squeezed her eyes shut and jumped up, practically running to the back of the bus.

Kat frowned. She always won? What did that mean?

"Tell me one thing!"

Kat jumped as Nyah came barreling back out, her eyes flashing fire.

"Did you come here on purpose?"

"Pardon me?"

Nyah wiped hastily at the tears that were streaming down her cheeks. "Did you come here to find him?"

"What? I didn't even know who he was, Nyah! I thought he'd committed suicide! I lost contact with him after high school. I had no idea he was Van Marshall. Besides, what does it matter anyway? And why would he talk to you about our kiss?"

Erik and Jack had been sitting at the booth in the kitchen and they glanced at Kat and Nyah.

Nyah shook her head and stabbed her finger in Kat's direction. "What *didn't* he tell me about you? I probably know more about you that you do! Well, for all of your knowledge, there are some things you *don't* know." Suddenly, the bus came to a stop and Nyah scowled. "What are you doing?" she shouted at the bus driver. She looked out the window. "We're in the middle of nowhere!"

"I'm overheating," the bus driver replied. "I think I blew the radiator hose."

Kat turned to look out the window. There was nothing but brush and dirt and a few saguaro cacti. "Where are we?"

"I don't know," the bus driver replied.

"You don't know?" Nyah exploded. "How can you not know?"

"I took a wrong turn somewhere."

"What's going on?" Van asked as the rest of the band came out from where they had been watching a movie in the back.

"This idiot got us lost!" Nyah shouted. "And we're broken down!"

Van gave Nyah a somewhat surprised look, as if he wasn't completely sure of why she was so upset. "Lost?" he questioned. He went up to the bus driver. "Where are we lost at?"

He shrugged.

Van stared at him in disbelief. "You're kidding me? You haven't the slightest clue?"

"I just passed a little town. I'm going to try and make it back there. We can fix this thing and ask directions."

Van stared at him for a second longer, then turned to Lance with a bewildered look. "Shouldn't he have, like, told us or something? Shouldn't he have a map?"

Lance shrugged. "I don't know, man. This guy's new. Our old driver retired after our last tour."

Nyah let out a frustrated sigh. "This is so stupid!" She

stormed to the back of the bus, followed by Jack, who un-
doubtedly wanted to make sure she was all right.

Lance blinked. "Dude, what is her problem?"

Van rolled his eyes and shrugged. "This is really incon-
venient. We perform tomorrow. This is going to throw us off
schedule really bad."

The bus driver loped back to the town he had seen and
made it to a gas station just as the bus started to smoke.
Rochelle, Van, Lance, and Kat all headed to what looked like
a convenience store next to the gas station while the bus
driver went to ask for help.

"What happened to the roadie bus anyway?" Lance
grumbled. "And Thrill My Koi's bus? How are we out here all
by ourselves? This is ridiculous."

A small bell rang on the door as they entered the store
and honky tonk music played in the background. Everything
looked dilapidated and run down and seemed to be covered
in a fine layer of dust. Flies buzzed absently from window to
window, and the things that were for sale looked practically
ancient.

Rochelle grasped Kat's arm as she looked around. "Okay,
did anyone see *Texas Chainsaw Massacre?*"

"Dude," Lance said seriously. "That's not even funny."

"Where are we?" Van asked. "This is insane. Why did he
get lost and just keep going?"

"Maybe it was part of his plan," Lance said. "Get us
stranded out here so they can have us." He looked at Van.
"He is a weird guy, Van. Did you notice that his eye twitch-
es?" He did an imitation. "It's creepy."

"Okay, Lance, you're not helping," Rochelle said, taking
another nervous glance around. "Where is everyone?"

"They've already been taken," Lance said. "They're all cut
up and hanging from meat hooks in the back."

Rochelle made a squeaking noise and pressed closer to
Kat.

"Gimme a break," Kat muttered, rolling her eyes. "Why
would a bunch of hillbilly cannibals go through an elaborate
plot to get a busload of rock stars when they can have anybody who just wanders through?"

Lance snorted. "Because Van is a sexy hunk of man flesh,
that's why!"

Van frowned. "Thanks...I think."

"I mean, what kind of a trophy would that be?" Lance continued.

"That's it, I'm getting back on the bus," Rochelle declared. "Two guys and two girls. It's too cliché." She turned to go and almost ran right into an old man who had come up noiselessly to stand behind her. She let out a blood-curdling scream and Lance shoved Kat out in front of them, hiding behind her.

"Stay back!" he shouted. "This girl's a kung fu master!"

The old man blinked, and his eyes looked magnified by his enormously thick glasses. "You're not from these parts, are you?"

"No, our bus broke down," Van explained. "We're on our way to Phoenix and we got lost."

"City folk," the old man wheezed. "You're a long way off."

"You can't have Van," Lance announced. "We'll let you have Jack, but you can't have Van."

Kat rolled her eyes.

"Hey, Grandpa, do you—" A young man blew into the store dressed in all black. He had wide leg pants on with bondage straps on the back and his hair was black and purple. He had black eyeliner and black nail polish on. His eyes widened as he stared at Van and the others.

Kat stared down at the boy with the same shocked expression. She could have sworn she was staring at the ghost of Van's youth.

"Van Marshall," the boy whispered in awe, "and Lance Lawson. Holy crap!"

"You know these whippersnappers?" the old man asked.

The boy's eyes bulged. "Know them? It's Bleeding Passion, Grandpa! They're the best metal band on the planet! Everyone in America knows who they are!"

Van smiled.

"What are you guys doing in Turnbeck?" the boy asked.

"Turn *back*?" Lance questioned in horror. "Your town's name is Turn *back*? That's it. I'm getting out of here."

"Turn*beck*," the boy corrected.

"Is that even on the map?" Van asked.

He laughed. "Probably not. It's really small."

"Our driver got lost," Van explained, "and then we broke down. He's trying to get the bus fixed now."

The boy shook his head. "Our mechanic is on vacation.

He doesn't get back until tomorrow."

"Tomorrow?" Lance cried. "You mean we have to stay here overnight?"

"Is there anyone else who lives here that can fix a radiator hose?" Van asked.

"The mechanic's shop is the only place to get spare parts," the boy replied.

"I don't like this," Lance whispered to Van. "I don't like this at all."

"Lance, stop being such a wuss," Van spat. "Good lord."

Kat smiled.

Van sighed and turned back to the boy. "I don't suppose you have a hotel around here or anything?"

He shook his head. "We're mostly just a bunch of white supremacist Nazis who run meth labs and eat people."

Lance paled.

The boy laughed. "I'm kidding! Actually, this town is just boring. I don't even know why it's here. Some old man spit one day and here it is. I'm getting out of here as soon as I can."

Van indicated the boy's clothing. "There a lot of goths in Turnbeck?"

He shook his head. "Just me. Mostly this is a place of old-fashioned people who like seclusion. I just live here. You can't pick your family."

Van smiled. "What's your name?'

"Ozzy," he replied. "Ozzy Osbaum."

Lance blinked. "Are you serious?"

He laughed. "Yeah, my parents are insane stoners. My mom was listening to Ozzy when she had me and that was the first name that popped into her head."

"Your mom was listening to Ozzy Osbourne in the delivery room?" Rochelle questioned.

He nodded. "Ozzy's her favorite."

Lance shook his head. "Man, this is getting weirder and weirder."

Nyah burst in the doorway with a dramatic wave of her arms. "We're stuck here! We can't leave until tomorrow! There's no hotel or anything!"

"Yeah," Van said, raking his fingers through his hair. "Did anyone try calling Bob, the mechanic on the roadie bus? We could tell him where we are, and maybe someone could come and help us out."

"We're in a complete dead zone," Nyah grumbled. "Everybody's phone is in search mode."

"Nyah Densmoore," Ozzy breathed, staring up at her in awe. "Man, you're hotter in person than you are on TV."

Nyah glanced down at him and her face lit up.

Ozzy's eyes took on a dreamy quality. "I want to lick honey off of your naked, beautiful body."

Rochelle stifled a laugh, and Nyah raised an eyebrow.

"Dude, how old are you?" Lance asked.

"Eighteen next month."

Van shook his head and chuckled. "Ozzy, is there somewhere we could go to get something to eat?"

Ozzy nodded and grinned. "I'll show you. I can be your guide."

"Guide?" Lance muttered. "You can see the entire town in one glance."

Van smiled at the teen. "Thanks, Ozzy. Lance, once we get somewhere with a pay phone, call the others. We have to at least let them know where we are."

They followed Ozzy back outside, Lance sticking close to Kat the entire time.

Chapter Ten

Lance and Kat had been sitting on the stairs of the tour bus for the past hour. They had seen the entire town of Turnbeck in about fifteen minutes and came to the realization that they were basically stuck overnight in a town that looked like a throwback to the 1800s. Ozzy had kidnapped Van, Nyah and Rochelle, and they were all back at his house talking about music and playing guitar. Kat had declined the invitation, wanting to be as far away from Nyah as possible. She had no idea what her outburst had been about on the bus and didn't desire another confrontation.

Lance refused to leave Kat's side, so he had gone with her back to the bus. She'd sat down on the stairs with her book, and he'd sat behind her. They hadn't moved since.

Lance squinted his eyes and frowned as he watched a man sitting outside the scary convenience store. "Check it out," he said. "This is like the hick capital of the nation." He pointed over to the man. "This guy has been spitting tobacco for the past hour and doing nothing else."

Kat glanced up at the man. He was leaning against the wall and she made a face as he turned his head and spit a wad of brown liquid onto the ground. She sighed and turned back to her book. "The sad thing is, Lance," she said, "that you have been sitting here watching him spit tobacco for the past hour and doing nothing else." She glanced up at him over her shoulder. "What does that say about you?"

"Hey, it's not my fault you decided to do something that didn't include me," he said defensively.

She frowned. "Can't you entertain yourself? I'm sure you're safe from the evil, psycho zombies if you're inside the bus."

"Hey, have you noticed that Van and the others aren't back yet? They're probably being digested right now. I'm sticking close to you in case they come after us next."

"And what exactly am I supposed to do about a bunch of deranged cannibals?" she asked in exasperation.

"You're a martial arts expert! So you can go all Matrix-style and karaticize!" He moved his hands in chopping motions like he was doing karate.

Kat rolled her eyes and couldn't help but smile. "Bruce Lee is rolling in his grave right now," she muttered.

"It's so freakin' hot out here!" he wailed.

"It's Arizona, what do you expect?"

He groaned and put his chin on his hand, tapping his fingers against his jaw. "I'm bored, Kat," he whined.

"Then do something! Play your guitar or something. Go and entertain the tobacco guy so you can both have something better to do than what you're presently doing."

Lance frowned at her, but his eyes lit up a second later. "Hey, that's an awesome idea! What do you think a town like this would do if we put on a free show? Do you think they even know what metal music is?"

Kat absently turned a page. "Well, Ozzy Osbaum's parents do."

"When Van gets back, I'm going to tell him we should put on a show. That would be totally fun." He grinned at his own idea.

"One problem. All your roadies and equipment are on the bus that didn't get lost."

Lance flung his hands up in the air in exasperation. "How did the bus driver manage to completely isolate us? It was practically impossible!"

Kat shrugged.

"Well, we still have some equipment," he continued. "It's enough to put on a makeshift show for a tiny little town. It's not like we'll need a whole lot of speaker power for the ten people who live here." He stood. "I'm going to go find Van." He stepped over her and down the stairs.

"Suddenly the cannibals don't bother you?" she asked with a smirk.

He stopped and turned back to her. He grabbed hold of her wrist and pulled her up, toting her along beside him. Kat sighed and rolled her eyes, but said nothing.

Soon, Lance's project was underway and Van and Jack had figured out how to create a makeshift stage in the middle of one of the many barren places around the town, using the bed of a semi truck as a platform. It took them about two hours to get everything set up, and Kat had recorded it all. She had plans to speed it up when she took it to the studio for editing and show how the stage had come into creation at double the speed.

Ozzy was almost spontaneously combusting he was so excited, and he was blasting music on their pathetic, half-cracked PA system from a band called *Bella Morte* while the members of Bleeding Passion were getting ready in his family's doublewide trailer.

He had alerted the entire town, all 100 or so of them, about the concert, and they were all either standing around, waiting for the show to start, or lingering in the distance out of sheer curiosity. Ozzy's girlfriend and her father were barbequing hamburgers for everyone, and Kat was sitting in a fold up chair by the stage, listening to Ozzy's music, smelling the heavenly aroma of grilled meat, and watching the sun sink behind the distant mountains. She smiled to herself, thinking that the way the setting sun made the mountains look purple was very beautiful.

She felt at peace and content, enjoying the serenity of the desert and the simple camaraderie all of the townspeople seemed to share. Everyone had turned out. Even the people who had no clue what was happening had at least come for the barbeque. She sighed, thinking it was somewhat odd that she was where she was. She had forever seen herself shooting boring documentaries and going home to frozen dinners and Rochelle. Not that she minded Rochelle, but the routine sucked. Touring with a famous rock band whose front man just happened to be someone she had once cared a great deal for was anything but routine. So was this silly concert, but she couldn't deny that she was having a good time.

* * * *

Van stepped out of the trailer, preparing himself mentally for this unconventional show. He looked up and his breath practically stopped. The sunset made everything seem amber-golden and hazy. Kat was sitting placidly in a chair by the stage, and the sun's rays reached out and touched her, streaking her hair with red and gold. She had a slight smile on her lips that made her look peaceful and so beautiful that it hurt. He placed his hand over his heart, wondering if he could ever get it to beat normally again when she was around. He doubted it. He had never seen anything more beautiful, never in his whole life.

The lyrics of the current song suddenly seemed painfully clear. The band was unknown to him, but the words assaulted his ears with their truth. *"Hold me until this world dies, and say you'll stay here through the night. Sing to me the song I once knew, of the passion and fire living in you. And I shall dream of our souls intertwined as another sun rises and sets in my eyes. Without you, I dream. I live and die all night long. Only to be reborn at dawn."* He let out a shaky breath and started toward Kat, unable to stop himself. How many nights had he slept the sleep of a restless, tormented man, dreaming of her and her decadent kisses? Her kindness? Her warmth? She had absolutely no idea what kind of effect she had over him, what effect she had always had. She had always held him right in the palm of her hand.

Kat glanced up as a tall shadow fell over her. Her heart leapt uncomfortably in her throat as Van stood there, his dark hair flowing freely around his shoulders. That always caught her off guard. When he wasn't performing, he usually wore his hair tied back, and every time she saw him with his hair down, she was struck dumb by how completely stunning he was. His hair set off his features perfectly, the way the right frame might complement a piece of art. She let her gaze take in all of him for a minute.

He was wearing a simple black shirt that showed off his beautifully sculpted arms and a pair of baggy pants that were black and dark gray camouflage. He smiled softly at her and held his hand out as if to help her up. She frowned in curiosity and placed her hand in his.

Van pulled Kat gently out of the chair and turned her so that the sun was setting behind her. Kat would normally have felt uncomfortable by the intensity in his gaze, but his smile softened his features and she couldn't look away from him. She could see the sun setting in his eyes, and she briefly thought that she'd heard something like that in the song she'd been listening to a moment ago. It was fantastic, and strangely intimate to watch.

Van took his hands and ran his fingers through her soft hair. "I am reborn," he whispered, quoting the last portion of the lyrics they had heard. Her heart started to beat ridiculously fast. He pulled one of her hands up to his mouth and pressed a kiss to her palm, closing his eyes as he did so. She couldn't breathe. It was such a simple gesture, but the way his lips lingered on her skin and passionate way he looked at her, it made it seem so erotic.

Van opened his eyes and met Kat's again. He smiled enigmatically and looked like he was hiding a very important secret. Kat didn't want to look away from him, ever. Somewhere in the back of her mind, she thought it was a strange desire to just want to stare at another person for all time, but she didn't care. She reached her hand out to lightly touch his cheek. She didn't know why. Maybe to assure herself that he was real, or maybe just to touch him. All she was sure of was that she couldn't have stopped herself if she'd wanted to.

He closed his eyes and leaned in to her touch, trapping her fingers against his face by placing his hand over hers. Kat was heaven to him. She had always been heaven. He felt her touch all the way through his blood and into his heart. If she only knew. If she only knew what she did to him, how he had longed for her for so many years.

He was reborn, just like the song said. She had brought him back to life just by stepping back into his world. Just by gracing him with her presence. Even though she was so different, she still filled his world with color and light like she always had.

His heart had been so empty, so lonely. Even with his music, even with all his dreams being fulfilled. He hadn't realized just how much he'd needed Kat. She'd always been the missing piece. The whole time, it had been her.

Out of the corner of his eye, Van saw Nyah stride out of the trailer, flipping her ebony hair over her shoulder. She stopped short at seeing him with Kat and she stared at them for a moment before whirling in retreat, barreling over Rochelle who had been following behind her.

Van turned to glance at Rochelle as she was knocked backwards onto the ground. She landed on her butt in surprise and stared after Nyah, who didn't give her so much as a backward glance as she strode off. Rochelle scowled. "Why do I spend so much of my time getting mowed over?" she growled as she pushed herself up.

Her intrusion successfully broke Van and Kat's personal moment and he slowly slid Kat's hand off his cheek. He kept a hold of it for just a moment, however, reluctant to break the connection.

"That woman is really annoying," Rochelle continued. "Did you see that? She ran me right over without a care in the world! What did I ever do to her?"

"We exist," Kat grumbled. "For some reason, that bothers her."

Rochelle shook her head, but let it go and turned her attention to Van. She grinned. "Lookin' sexy!"

Van smiled shyly.

Kat smirked. "Yeah, you sexy hunk of man flesh."

He reddened a little. "Lance has problems."

Rochelle giggled. "Are you looking forward to the show?"

He nodded. "It's cool to deviate from the norm. This will be a fun detour. Where's Ozzy?"

Rochelle rolled her eyes. "Accosting the rest of the band with his camera."

"At least Lance finally got distracted and left me alone. The guy was practically attached to me all day," Kat said.

The other members of the band filed out of the trailer, followed by Ozzy who shouted like he was running everything. "All right, everybody! Let's get this show on the road! Everybody prepare to be blown away! Dad! Put out the joint, man! Grandpa! Sit down!"

Kat grinned, and Van chuckled. The befuddled onlookers all started to meander toward the stage. Van looked down at Kat and his heart made a small sigh. He ran his knuckles down her cheek in his trademark gesture and flashed her his secretive grin before joining his band mates.

Rochelle glanced at Kat and frowned. "What was *that*?"

Kat frowned. "What?"

"That look!"

She swallowed and tried to look innocent. "What look?"

"Gimme a break, Kat! That look Van just gave you! He had desire written all over his face."

Kat flushed and looked down. "I don't know what you're talking about." She played with the ends of her hair self-consciously.

Rochelle folded her arms and gave her a knowing stare. "Kat, you aren't that dense. I know you aren't."

Kat gave her a sidelong glance.

"I totally saw you while I was getting run down by Nyah! What's up? Something's different! You let him touch you, and you don't freak out whenever he's around. I want details, and I want them now."

Kat smiled softly. "I told him about the rape."

Rochelle couldn't mask her surprise.

She shrugged. "We were talking, and it just seemed right. I figured he had a right to know why I was so weird. I felt better afterward. Telling him made me feel like he understood where I was coming from."

Rochelle smiled. "Van's always cared so much for you. Of course he'd understand."

Ozzy's voice cut through the murmuring of the crowd as he jumped up on stage. "Are you all ready to rock?" he bellowed.

The small group exchanged confused glances while Ozzy's mom whistled shrilly and started jumping up and down. Her frizzy, red hair took on a life of its own, as did her massive breasts.

Rochelle stared in horror. "Oh gosh."

Kat laughed.

"I said, are you ready to rock?" Ozzy screeched again.

A few of the younger people muttered some incoherent half-cheers while Ozzy's mom continued to jump even higher.

"That is so wrong on so many levels," Rochelle said as she stared in morbid fascination at the big-busted woman.

"Ladies and gentlemen, prepare to have your ears assaulted by the best metal band on the planet, Bleeding Passion!"

Rochelle and Kat cheered to help the crowd out as the musicians filed out onto the stage. Van raised his hand to the crowd in greeting, but all that could be heard were crickets, cicadas, and Ozzy's mom, howling away.

Van chuckled and adopted a relaxed pose. "Good evening, Turnbeck," he greeted softly. "Before you all run out of here in fright, let me first tell you how much we all appreciate your hospitality. You have all been very kind to my band mates and me, and that is the reason for this performance.

It is our thanks to you kind people for taking in strangers and treating them as your own."

Kat smiled, and the crowd did too.

"I hope you enjoy the show."

Jack counted off with his drumsticks, and they started into a powerful melody, saturated with their trademark haunting sound.

The show went well, and Van had everyone up and moving three songs in. He had so much stage presence that it was impossible to ignore his urgings to join in. Even Ozzy's grandpa bobbed his head to the beat. Nyah seemed somewhat less passionate than usual, but Ozzy didn't care or notice. He screamed the loudest when she was singing.

Kat recorded the entire performance, getting a lot of footage of the town and speaking to a few people to get their thoughts on the free show. She figured that this little "detour," as Van had called it, would be very interesting to Bleeding Passion's fans.

Everyone cheered when the band finished, even encoring them back on for two more songs. Kat put her camera away toward the end with a smile on her face. She seriously thought that, even though getting lost sucked, this experience might have been the best moment on the tour thus far. It seemed that Bleeding Passion could add several more people to their fan list after this.

She walked to the bus to put her equipment away and stopped when she saw a man standing by the door upon her exit.

He smiled. "Hello."

Kat glanced both directions to see if anyone else was around, and her stomach lurched with the realization that she was all by herself. She raised herself taller. He was young and clean cut, which made him stand out amongst his neighbors who mostly had straggly beards and missing teeth. He didn't look threatening...yet.

"Are you a part of the band's crew?" he asked with a smile.

"I'm the videographer," she replied.

"I think you're the most beautiful woman I've ever seen," he said with a self-conscious chuckle. "I was watching you during the show. We don't have many beautiful women around here."

Kat maintained her distance and nodded. "Well, thank you."

"My name is Billy. Do you want to come back to my place and hang out? I know you guys are here for the night."

She shook her head. "No, thank you."

He pouted in a playful manner. "Are you sure? I could make you a drink."

She shook her head adamantly. "Thank you for the invitation, but no."

"Is there a problem?" Van came out of nowhere, stepping casually between Kat and Billy.

Billy grinned up at Van. "Oh man, that was an awesome show."

Van gave a polite smile. "Thank you."

Billy looked back at Kat. "Last chance?"

She smiled a tiny bit and shook her head. "No." She felt Van's fingers begin to play casually with her hair.

Billy's eyes widened. "Oh," he said as if coming to a sudden realization. "I get it. Sorry to bother you guys. Have a good night."

Van turned to Kat as Billy walked away. "Was he bothering you?"

"No, not really. He was just a young, deprived guy. He was actually quite polite. You didn't have to step in, Van. I can take care of myself."

"I know," he stated simply. He turned his gaze up to the sky and released a serene sigh as he looked at the sparkling expanse. "Look at the stars," he breathed. "You forget how many there are until you're some place with no city lights."

Kat joined him in looking up at them. "It makes you feel small, doesn't it? Knowing that we're just a speck in such a vastly infinite thing."

He glanced down at her. "I always thought you were prettiest in the moonlight," he murmured.

She frowned and looked at him. "You've never seen me in the moonlight."

He smiled. "Yes, I have. Do you remember when you asked me to go to prom with you and I said no?" She nodded, and he shook his head. "I wanted to go so bad. The thought of being at the biggest high school event with the most beautiful girl in the world was such a wonderful thought to me. I wanted to dance all night with you, but I felt awkward and embarrassed and my anxiety was so bad back then."

"I know, Van. I understood."

He looked at her. "But I went, Kat."

"You went?" Her voice went up in surprise.

He nodded. "I rented a black tux and my mom made me this black cloak because you know I could never just do something normal."

Kat grinned. "It was what I loved about you."

"So there I was in my black eye makeup, looking like some kind of gothic Phantom of the Opera, and I made it as far as the courtyard and had to sit down to collect myself. Right when I had gathered most of my courage, you suddenly came out to get some fresh air or something. You were wearing a silver dress and the moon was full..." He closed his eyes and smiled blissfully at the memory. "You were *so beautiful*. I wanted to go to you so badly, but I just couldn't. You made me lose my ability to move, or speak, or even breathe. I just...stared at you. You left with Rochelle shortly afterward." He met her eyes. "So I never got to talk or dance with you that night, but I saw you. I saw you and always remembered how you looked in the moonlight." He ran his forefinger down her cheek. "How you look right now."

She stared at him, speechless. He was so open with his feelings and emotions. It amazed her because she was so guarded with her own. Little tremors that felt like electricity ran up and down her spine. Had his touch always been so gentle? Had his presence always been so warm? She leaned closer to him instinctively. He had his hands resting on her arms, and he was close enough to her that she could feel his breath. It was sensual, not lusting. It didn't frighten her like it should have.

"No one ever tasted like you," he whispered.

She looked up at him. "I've never known a real man's kiss," she murmured. "I've known a cruel sadist's and yours, although the sweetest of all, was a boy's kiss. We were children. What would a real kiss feel like, I wonder?"

Van reached up to gently cup her face in his hands. He feathered his thumbs across her cheeks and gazed at her as if she was the most exquisite treasure he had ever seen.

"That was awesome, Van!" Ozzy's voice came tearing its way through the night, blinding Kat and Van with reality.

"That was the best show ever!"

Kat looked down and took a step backward. *What in the heck am I saying? Real man's kiss?* She shook her head. *What, am I possessed?*

Van turned to Ozzy with a prepared smile and started talking to the excited youth. Kat stared at him for a long moment, then shook her head again, trying to regain her senses, and got back onto the bus.

Chapter Eleven

The town of Turnbeck was only a distant memory to everyone by four P.M. the next day. That morning they had eaten breakfast with Ozzy's parents while the bus driver had tracked down the mechanic. He'd managed to figure out approximately where they were on the map and, by the time they left, had a good idea of how to get back on the road to Phoenix.

Ozzy had begged Van to hire him on as a roadie, but Van had to turn him down seeing as how he was not yet of legal age and his parents weren't too thrilled about losing their only son so soon. The band had autographed one of Van's many guitars, however, and gave it to him as a gift. Van had also given him his email address so he could keep in touch with him if he wanted to. Ozzy had been absolutely thrilled.

Kat remained relatively quiet all morning because, whenever she looked at Van, she tended to stare longer than she liked. Why was she all of a sudden noticing how his eyes crinkled when he laughed, or how he smelled like patchouli? Had he always smelled like patchouli? She couldn't remember.

And why did she play back in her mind over and over again, like a CD that kept skipping, how his touch felt? She didn't understand. She hated men, feared them, and generally avoided people of all kinds. Why did all of that seem to fly out the window when she was with Van? Why did she sit close to him when she got the chance? And why was she fixated on the way his shoulders swayed when he walked? They were his shoulders. What was so spectacular about a pair of swaying shoulders? She noticed weird things. Things she would normally never notice. She had practically asked him to kiss her the other night. What had that been about? Physical contact was forbidden. Why did she not hate Van's?

Kat felt a bit frazzled by the time they got to Phoenix. Thrill My Koi and the roadie crew were relieved to see everyone all right, considering they had been almost unreachable for the past 24 hours. The venue they were playing at was an outdoor arena, and all sorts of people had turned out.

Kat watched the crowd file in from the wings as the roadies checked the sound systems, and she smiled as she took in the eclectic group. There were goths and teenage girls, punks and middle-aged moms and dads. There was one boy who looked like Dr. Frankenfurter from *The Rocky Horror Picture Show* standing next to a woman who was dressed all in pink with a belly button ring, bleach blonde hair and rosy-colored sunglasses. Everyone loved Bleeding Passion. Even though they were labeled in the Gothic Rock category, their music defied stereotype.

She turned and headed backstage to get her camera, preparing for another night of taping. She technically didn't have to get footage of every show, but she thought it was better to get many shots from different places so, when she was editing, she would have a lot to choose from. She walked past Van's dressing room and stopped as she heard soft strains of music coming from inside. The door was open a crack and she moved closer, unable to quell her curiosity. The lyrics immediately caught her attention, speaking of an unending path of black and traveling on an arduous journey.

She tried to peer through the crack in the door. She could see Van sitting in front of a mirror, putting black eye makeup on, singing quietly along with the song. She marveled over the beautiful lyrics, wondering if he applied them to his own life. It saddened her to think that he sometimes felt like he was walking a dark path in solitude, but the rest of the song, it was about seeing through the darkness a way back home and finding where you belonged in a stranger's eyes... She wondered what exactly that meant to him. She knew it had to have some kind of significance. Everything had significance to Van.

She continued to ponder over the lyrics as she wandered blindly up the corridor. Several lines in particular stuck in her head. They spoke of knowing yourself less and less with every step you took and how every vow was broken as you made your way toward someone's heart. She frowned. Actually, a lot of the song hit frighteningly close to home. How often did she feel all alone, lost in the dark? Too often. Was it possible for her to find her way back home as well, to see dawn again? She sighed. Maybe she just thought too much. She was beginning to think that this was the case.

She sighed and realized she was heading the wrong direction. She rolled her eyes and tried to remember what she had been doing before she'd tried to spy on Van. She made a swift turn to go back the other way and plowed right into Erik, who had been eating something. Whatever it had been was now decorating the front of his shirt. Kat let out a shout of surprise and stepped back.

Erik looked down at his shirt and sighed. "Well, I guess that means I'll be wearing something different tonight."

"I'm so sorry!" Kat exclaimed.

He smiled. "It's all right. I don't really like this shirt anyway, and that burger was actually pretty awful so you probably saved my life."

"What's going on? Is everyone all right?" Van poked his head out of the door, squinting one eye shut.

"Yeah, I'm just half past stupid or something," Kat muttered. "I just ran Erik over."

"Why are you squinting?" Erik asked.

"When Kat shrieked, it startled me and I jabbed my eyeliner pencil in my eye."

Kat's eyes widened, and Erik chuckled. "I'm going to change my shirt," he declared. "You fix your eye. The pirate look doesn't suit you." He meandered past Kat and continued on his way.

"Are you all right?" Kat asked Van, going over to him.

He laughed. "I'm fine. What are you doing back here? You're usually out in the wings setting up."

She cleared her throat. "Yeah, well, I was just passing by. What were you listening to? The music was nice."

He motioned for her to follow him back into his dressing room. "I have to finish. Come in. I can talk while I'm getting ready."

She obeyed and stood behind his chair as he sat down and tried to open his watering eye.

"I was listening to HIM," he replied. "Remember them?"

"I remember your poster, but I never did listen to any of their music." He scowled at her playfully and she looked down. "I kind of didn't want to listen to anything that reminded me of you."

His smile was soft. "Well, their music is still as good now as it was then. You should listen to it."

She smiled, but omitted that she technically had listened to it while she was spying on him out in the hall. "You usually don't wear a lot of eye makeup," she observed.

He shrugged. "Sometimes I just feel darker than usual, I guess."

She frowned in concern. "Are you okay?"

He nodded. "It's just hard to give one hundred and ten percent to your fans when you can barely bring yourself to get out of your chair."

"Is your anxiety bothering you that badly?"

"It's always with me, like an extra shadow, but it doesn't run my life. I have never canceled a show because of it, and I never will."

Kat smiled, admiring his strength. "You'll be all right when you get on stage."

He nodded. "My music lets me fly above my limitations."

"Then your fans will never be disappointed."

He grinned.

She stood closer to the back of his chair. "Want me to help you a little?" she queried.

He met her eyes in the mirror and smiled. "Do you have to ask?" He closed his eyes in obvious ecstasy as her fingers slid through his hair. He eased almost instantly, and she let her hands travel down the back of his neck on their journey. He made a small noise of pleasure in his throat. Kat smiled, enjoying the softness of his silky strands as they slipped through her fingers. "Is that better?" He nodded and she leaned forward and wrapped her arms around his neck in an embrace. "You are always brilliant and always beautiful. No one would ever know your weakness."

He put his hands over hers, meeting her eyes in the mirror again. "You cure my weakness well enough, Kat."

She felt her face turn hot at his words and her stomach somersaulted. She pulled away gently, but left her hands on his shoulders.

He turned to look up at her and smiled.

"Have a good show, okay?" she said.

He nodded.

"I...uh...have to go find Rochelle, or...something." Her brain, it liked to stop functioning when she was around Van.

"Hey, Van, these were on our bus. I don't recognize them. Are they yours?" A roadie burst in carrying a garment bag.

Van frowned and stood. "Hang it up. I'll check."

The roadie obeyed and left.

Van unzipped the bag and blinked in bewilderment. "Holy cow," he muttered. "Where did this come from?"

Kat looked up from the spot on the floor she'd been staring at while she tried, once again, to rein in her erratic emotions. Her eyes widened. "Hey!" she cried. "What the heck? Those are mine! How did they get on the roadie bus?"

Van turned to stare at her. "These are *yours*?" She nodded and he opened the bag wider so Kat could see inside. "Where in the world did you get this?" He pointed to the black Bleeding Passion jacket.

Kat swallowed and stared at it, feeling humiliated.

"This was custom made," Van continued. "I had this done myself. It's one of a kind. Where on earth did you get it?"

She heaved a sigh. There was no way out of this one. "You gave it to me," she surrendered.

He stared at her for a moment. "Are you serious?" he murmured. "You mean *you* were the girl at the club in L.A?"

"Unfortunately," she muttered. "Remember that other experience I said I'd had? The one that made me turn into the *Karate Kid*? Well, that was it."

Van couldn't believe it. He had been face to face with her and hadn't even recognized her? Was he insane? He had touched her, helped her, and he hadn't even thought she looked remotely familiar? He'd spent the last two years wondering what had compelled him to give the stranger his jacket. He'd loved that jacket. "Why didn't you tell me?"

Kat rolled her eyes. "It's embarrassing, Van! I mean, come on! 'Hey, I haven't seen you in nine years, thought you were dead, but now that I know you're not, do you remember pulling a sweaty biker off of me at a dingy club three years ago?'"

He smiled. "You kept the jacket even though you didn't know it was me?"

She snorted. "Well, yeah, it's not every day a famous rock star gives you his jacket."

"But I wasn't completely famous then."

She shrugged. "I knew you would be."

"Did you?"

"Of course. I didn't know you were you, but that doesn't mean I thought you were any less talented."

He grinned. "Were you ever going to tell me?"

"I hadn't planned on it. I don't even know why I brought the jacket. I'm a spaz. Half the time I don't have any clue why I do what I do."

He chuckled and touched the sleeve. "I loved this jacket."

She smiled. "You should wear it."

"But I gave it to you. If I wear it on stage, it'll get all sweaty and nasty. It's a hundred and ten degrees outside! It'll smell like butt by the end of the concert, and then you'd never want to wear it again."

She laughed.

He smiled and pulled it out of the bag. He placed it around Kat's shoulders in much the same way he had all those years ago. "You wear it. It deserves to be worn by someone beautiful. Besides, you are part of Bleeding Passion now." He gave her a somewhat bashful smile reminiscent of his youth. "Actually, you always have been."

She swallowed hard and forced out a nervous laugh. "You want me to wear it? So *I* can make it smell like butt? I don't think so." She took it off. "Let's just put it back in the bag where it's safe."

He chuckled.

She sighed and pushed her hand through her hair. "So, we're going to New York after this, right?"

He nodded. "We're there for about a week. We perform twice and then have a video shoot for three days."

"Isn't making a video a lot more than just three days of work?"

"Yeah, but they only need us for three days. Most of the work is the preparation and the post-production." He glanced at her and smirked. "But I imagine you would already know that."

She grinned, dismissing it. "Will I be allowed on the set to film while you're doing the shoot?"

"Of course. You are allowed everywhere I go." He smiled

coyly at her.

Kat let out another nervous laugh. "You know what, Van Marshall? I think I need to get out of here while the getting is good."

He grinned devilishly and approached her at a slow, leisurely pace. "Why's that?"

"You are flirting way too much for me to handle." She giggled and skirted him. "Well, uh, I'd better go find Rochelle. She's going to wonder what happened to me."

He smiled and turned to the portable CD player he had sitting next to him. He popped the CD he had been listening to out and put it in its case. He stood and handed it to her. "Listen to that," he demanded.

She rolled her eyes. "Yes, sir," she said in playful sarcasm.

Van had to fight hard to resist the urge to touch her face. He wanted to touch her all the time. She was like an addiction to him. He waved as she bade him goodbye and left the room. He shook his head and sighed.

He couldn't believe she was the girl he had given his jacket to. He remembered that night. The girl being attacked by that letch. He had seen it happening as he and his band mates started to head out of the club. It had angered him beyond anything imaginable. He hadn't even thought about it, he'd just gone and intercepted. There had been something about her. He hadn't even thought about giving her his jacket. It had come naturally, like she was supposed to have it.

And it had been Kat. His Kat. Different hair style, thinner face, but still Kat. He couldn't believe how stupid he had been for not recognizing her.

He sat back down in front of the mirror to apply some finishing touches to his eye makeup when the door opened again.

"Baby?" Nyah's voice called. "You in here?"

He suppressed a groan and released a sigh instead. He wished she'd stop calling him that. They hadn't been together for a whole year now. "Yeah, I'm here," he replied.

She walked in slowly and smiled at him. "I always like it when you wear the black eye makeup."

He smiled a little.

She sauntered over to him and put her hands on his shoulders. "Remember when we first started? We'd always play in Phoenix because our fans were so loyal here. I love coming back here."

He nodded. "Phoenix has fabulous crowds."

"Do you remember our special place?" she asked with a grin, giving his shoulders a little squeeze.

He chuckled. "Hooters? How could I forget?"

"Maybe we could go there before we leave," she suggested in her silky voice. "Just you and me."

He wondered why she could never just have a normal conversation with him. "Nyah, you do realize we're not together anymore, right?"

She straightened and pulled away. "Of course. I'm not stupid," she spat. "I just thought it would be a nice memory, that's all." She glanced over at the jacket in the garment bag and frowned. "Where did that come from? I thought you lost it."

"No, I gave it to someone," he muttered.

"How did it end up back here?"

He really did not want to tell her this. "Turns out the person I gave it to was Kat," he grumbled. "I just didn't recognize her."

"Kat?" Nyah hissed. She whirled to stare at him. "How is that even possible?"

He shrugged, thinking of Torrey and Taegen. "Life is full of strange coincidences. I just think it was a sign that one day she would be in my life again." He smiled whimsically.

Nyah looked down. "I don't know how you ever got along with her. She's rude and antisocial."

Van turned in his chair to fix her with a stare. "I would be rude and antisocial too if someone treated me the way you treat her. You've had a massive attitude problem ever since you met her."

Nyah snorted and put her hands on her hips. "You're so blind, Van. She's not your high school sweetheart anymore. She doesn't have what you need. Don't be deluded by some teenage fantasy. She doesn't know anything at all."

He frowned, a protective kind of anger flaring to life inside of him. "Kat knows more about me than almost anyone. She still knows what I need."

"Oh, come on!" Nyah exclaimed. "You haven't seen her in years! She can't possibly know you like I do."

"She knows me better than you, Nyah! Much better! She

actually listens to me, which is more than you ever did. You always knew how to alleviate my anxiety, to help me relax, but you never did because you're selfish! Kat helps me; she makes me feel better; she makes *me* better. She is more beautiful than half the people I know and you need to get over whatever issue it is you have with her!"

Nyah shrugged flippantly in the way she did when she wanted to put across that something didn't matter to her. "Whatever. She'll be gone soon anyway and good riddance to her."

Van let out something that resembled a snarl and it got Nyah's attention. He met her eyes very calmly, but he knew his gaze was icy. "If I have anything to do with it, Kat will never leave my side again. Watch it, Nyah. You should tread carefully. If you start causing tension in this band because of your problems, it's over. You're not as indispensable as you think you are."

Nyah stared at him for a second, shock and hurt washing over her features. She whirled and fled from the room.

Van sighed and leaned back wearily in his chair. He rubbed his temples and wished he hadn't given Kat his CD. He could really use it. It was his relaxation music. He shouted an angry, frustrated cry to the ceiling before turning back to the mirror to make the black lines around his eyes thicker and darker.

Chapter Twelve

Kat was exhausted as she got off the bus and headed in-to the airport. She hadn't slept well at all the night before for reasons that were unknown to her, and she just wanted to get on the plane and go to sleep. She wasn't sure if it had been the hotel mattress or what, but she had tossed and turned all night.

"I've never been on a private jet before," Rochelle said. "This is going to be so exciting."

Kat smiled. "It doesn't even matter to me what it is. It could be a spaceship for all I care. I just want somewhere I can close my eyes."

They were mobbed by fans in the airport, but they fought their way through and made it to the gate in one piece. Kat slumped against the wall while Hank took care of the neces-sary arrangements. She glanced over at Van, who was laughing with Lance. She watched how his face lit up when he smiled and how he stood with a casual strength and ele-gance. It was such a change from Jake, who had been tall and lanky, awkward like all teenagers. He had turned into such an amazingly sexy man.

"Um, bad news guys," Hank said, snapping Kat's atten-tion back to the business at hand and away from Van's frame. "It seems our plane is experiencing some mechanical problems and is unable to fly."

Lance raised his eyebrows. "Yeah, that's not good."

"Luckily, the crew's plane is still in working order, but we sent them ahead an hour ago. So, as it stands, we have no plane. What we're going to have to do is see if there are any regular commercial flights going to New York that still have open seats. We'll probably have to fly separately."

"You mean fly coach?" Nyah protested.

Hank rolled his eyes. "If you want to be there to perform tomorrow night, possibly. Thrill My Koi's plane left earlier also. It's our only option."

She folded her arms and snorted in disgust.

"I'm going to go see what openings are available," he said. "I'll be back shortly."

Kat groaned and sank down so that she was sitting on the floor.

"This is ridiculous," Nyah spat.

Rochelle sat down next to Kat and sighed. "So much for the private jet." She shrugged. "Oh well. Better than exploding into little bits, I suppose."

Kat raised an eyebrow and let her head loll over to one side to look at her. "You think?"

Hank came back about twenty minutes later carrying some papers and wearing an annoyed frown. "Okay, here's the deal. I was able to fit most of you on United flight one-one-seven that leaves in about two hours, but two of you will have to go on America West twenty-eight-sixty-four, which doesn't leave until about five."

"So we get to duke it out to see who flies later?" Jack asked.

Hank nodded. "Pretty much."

"One of us should go on the later flight," Kat proposed to Rochelle. "That way we can both tape whatever goes on."

Rochelle nodded in agreement. "Rock, paper, scissors."

They did a quick game, and Kat groaned aloud when she lost. She just wanted to sleep! "I'll stay for the later flight," she grumbled.

Hank nodded. "Okay, Kat and...?"

"Me," Van volunteered.

Kat blinked in surprise and looked over at him.

He gave her a soft smile.

"All right," Hank continued. "Your flight leaves at five o'clock tonight and has a plane change in St. Louis. I have the flight reserved, you just have to go and show them your IDs. I didn't know whose names to put on the tickets, so..." He handed Van a paper. "Here's all the information you need. Just go to the check in station and they'll direct you from there. Everyone else, come with me. We're in the wrong terminal."

Rochelle stood and gave Kat a wicked grin.

Kat rolled her eyes. "See you in New York," she muttered.

Nyah tugged on Van's arm, trying to say something to him as Kat hauled herself up off the floor and approached him. He ignored her and yanked his arm away with a scowl. She turned and followed the other band members reluctantly.

Kat sighed. "Okay so why did you volunteer so readily once I said I was staying?" she half-teased.

"Someone has to protect you." He grinned and winked at her.

She raised an eyebrow, too exhausted to do much of anything else. "Let's just get checked in and get to our gate. I'm so tired I can barely stand."

* * * *

Kat's eyes fluttered open and it took her a minute to realize that she was in the airport terminal, slumped down in a rather uncomfortable chair, and propped up against Van's shoulder. She groaned and rubbed at a sore spot in her neck from sleeping so contorted. She hadn't meant to fall asleep, but after eating lunch and dealing with the steady stream of fans that had constantly barraged Van, she'd been even more tired than when she started. She blinked the remnants of sleep from her eyes and glanced at her watch. Their plane should be arriving any minute.

"Welcome back," Van said, smiling down at her. "You were asleep forever."

She yawned and sat up straight. "Sorry I was leaning on you," she said with a stretch. "Did I drool on you?"

He grinned. "I don't think so." He flipped absently through a *Metal Edge* magazine. "Some airport employee just went tearing through here screaming for security," he said. "Don't know what that was all about."

Kat slumped back in the chair, still trying to wake up her sluggish brain. "What was Nyah bothering you about before we left anyway?"

He rolled his eyes. "She was trying to convince me to let Lance go instead. She's so jealous of you."

"What in the world for?" Even as she said it, her bizarre conversation with Nyah outside of Turnbeck filtered through her mind.

He glanced down and met her eyes. "Because she'll never be half the woman you are, and she knows it."

Kat's heart did that flip thing again, and she averted her eyes.

"Look, our plane is here," Van announced, putting his magazine away.

Kat glanced up to see the plane pulling into the gate. She was grateful she had slept through most of the boredom of waiting. Maybe she could sleep some more once they were on the plane.

"Attention passengers of Flight twenty-eight-sixty-four for St. Louis. We are currently not letting passengers deplane at this time. Please stand by for further information."

Kat frowned and looked up at Van. "What does that mean?"

"I don't know, but I hope they get on with it. This is really boring."

She sighed and held her hand out to Van. "I'll thumb war you."

He laughed and took her hand in agreement. They played several rounds, which Van won every time.

"This sucks!" Kat cried as she found her thumb pinned under his again. "You're cheating!"

"It's a thumb war! How could I possibly cheat at a thumb war?"

She giggled. "Your fingers are too long."

"And this is my fault?"

"Attention all passengers, there has been a security breach. All of those in Terminal Four need to return to the security check point. I repeat, all passengers must return to the security check point."

They both frowned. "You have got to be kidding me," Van grumbled.

Kat heaved a sigh and stood. "This would happen to us."

They followed the rest of the hordes down the length of the terminal and stopped in horror upon seeing the security check line. No one was being let back through yet, and there was no telling where the line actually ended. People swarmed everywhere in confusion and bewilderment. A lot of people were just sitting on the floor in boredom.

"Good lord," Van breathed. "Where are we supposed to

go?"

Kat scowled and started pushing her way through the crowd, trying to locate the end of the line. Everyone was talking at once and all asking the same questions to people who didn't know anymore than the next guy. Separate lines snaked and branched off of one another, all converging into a massive cluster, which Kat supposed had once been the main line. She took a place in one of the shorter lines and glanced at Van in disdain. "This is ridiculous."

He heaved a sigh and shoved his hands into his pockets. "Great," he muttered. "Stick the guy with anxiety in a crowded friggin' room."

Kat gave him a sympathetic look and reached over to touch his arm briefly.

Time dragged on, and people started to get more and more frenzied. The terminal pulsated with the heat of so many bodies so close together and one of the airport vendors tossed bottles of water into the crowd. Kat dodged the elbow of a guy next to her, who had been flailing his limbs in boredom for the past hour, and she stood on her toes to try and see if anything was actually going on. It was like being stuck at a bad concert, and the band was *really* late. "Can you see anything at all?" she asked Van.

He shook his head miserably. "Just endless amounts of people."

A man standing next to Van jumped up on a planter nearby and scanned the crowd.

"Can you see anything?" a woman asked him.

"They still aren't letting anyone through," he reported. He leaned forward a little, as if doing so would help him see farther, but he stumbled and fell into the crowd. Shouts of irritation came from the people he had bumped into on his way down.

"Good lord, these people are like animals," Kat breathed. Everyone was beginning to look more trapped and crazed. "Put people in a strange situation, and watch it go sideways in no time."

"Oh my gosh! It's Van Marshall!"

A shrill shriek followed the exclamation, and Kat grimaced.

A blonde girl who looked seventeen or so charged through everyone, knocking people aside to get to Van. He raised an eyebrow and looked genuinely horrified right as the girl launched herself at him. He held his hands up to fend her off, but she was all over him, clawing at his clothing in hysterics.

"Oh my gosh! Oh my gosh! I love you!" she cried. "You're the man of my dreams! It's fate! We were meant to meet here and spend eternity together! I want to be the mother of your children!"

He tried to back away, blindly running into people as the girl continued to maul him. Kat noticed the panic-stricken look on his face, and he started to take breaths that were much too deep and much too fast.

She grabbed the girl by the back of the shirt and yanked her off Van, delivering a harsh slap across her face. It stunned her enough so that Kat could grab Van's hand and lead him away from the claustrophobic crowd.

"Kat!" he cried. "Kat, I can't breathe! There are too many people! Get me outta here!" His voice was frantic and he looked wild. He clutched at his chest, taking deep, gasping breaths. "I can't breathe!"

She looked around for any free area of space and spotted an unoccupied area by the bathrooms. She pulled him behind her over to the empty space and made him sit down. He sat against the wall, shaking horribly and looking so frantic that she had to force herself to remain calm.

She knew he was having a panic attack, but it was unnerving regardless. He squeezed his eyes shut, as if he was desperately trying to get a hold of himself. Beads of sweat formed on his forehead and he turned a deathly shade of white. She reached over and started to rub the back of his neck in a soothing motion. "It's okay," she murmured. "Van, it's okay. Just breathe. Slow and easy."

He shook his head frantically. "No air...too many people..." Tears trickled out of his eyes and down his cheeks.

"Come here," Kat commanded. "Lie down. Face yourself toward me." She guided his head down onto her lap. "Keep your eyes closed. There's no one here but you and me, okay? Just concentrate on me." She raked her fingers through his soft hair, hoping that the gesture would help some.

Having him shake so violently and clutch at his chest like he was having a heart attack was not something she had seen in a very long time. Only once, and that had been before she'd really known him. She noticed that her hands trembled, and she took a deep, calming breath. It was disturbing to see him this way. It had been disturbing back then, but it seemed ten times worse now. Probably because, back then, he had been an awkward teenage boy. Now he was a poised celebrity, elegant and beautiful. The incapacitating panic seemed so much worse as it tore through his strong, graceful body.

Van faced Kat's torso, his head pillowed in her lap, and he curled his body around her as much as he could. She continued to stroke his hair, caressing her fingers across his forehead and down his jaw. It made her want to weep to see such a powerful man curled in a ball like a child.

She studied his beautiful features as she traced her fingertips along the angles of his face. She thought of the Jake of her past. Had he always had such defined features hiding underneath his dark, boyish face? She remembered his spiky black and crimson hair and smiled as she ran her fingers through his long, thick locks. Dark brown...like dark chocolate. She grinned. Chocolate....

She ran a finger across his lips, remembering his innocent kiss. He smiled just slightly and kissed her fingertip. Kat smiled and caressed his face again. "Are you doing any better?"

"A little," he rasped, "but I can't stay here much longer, Kat. I'm going to lose it. I felt like I was suffocating back there, and it seemed like the room was spinning while it slowly trapped me. I haven't had an attack like that in a really long time."

She looked at her watch. They had already been standing around for three hours. She glanced at the swarm. It didn't look like anyone was going anywhere anytime soon. "What time do you perform tomorrow?"

"Six o'clock."

"Let's see if we can transfer our flight. Can you stand?"

He sat up slowly and nodded. "I'll be okay."

She did not like how pale he looked. She touched his cheek. "Are you sure?"

He met her concerned eyes and took her hand in both of his. He pressed a kiss to her fingers and forced a small smile. "I've been dealing with this forever, Kat. I'm okay."

She stood and reached her hand out to him. She helped him up, then threaded her fingers through his, guiding him back through the throng and to the escalators. It was much calmer downstairs, and they headed to one of the check-in stations.

"What's going on up there?" Kat asked the person at the desk.

The woman shrugged. "We're not entirely sure. Someone snuck past security with a weapon or something. We have to make sure the terminal is secure before we can let anyone back through. What can I do for you?"

"Do you have any flights going out tomorrow to New York City?"

She looked through her computer and nodded. "We have one at seven o' five a.m. It stops once in Denver, and then you have a plane change in Chicago."

"Chicago?" Kat grumbled. She heaved a song-suffering sigh. "Fine. Can you transfer us to that flight?"

She nodded. "Can I have your names, please, and see your tickets?"

Kat handed their tickets to her. "Katrina Vauss and Van Marshall."

The woman paused and glanced up at Van. "Are you...*the* Van Marshall?"

He smiled wearily.

She blinked in obvious surprise. "Don't worry, I will take care of this for you, Mr. Marshall. I am very sorry for the inconvenience. If you give me a moment, I will make reservations for you at the nearest hotel and get you a rental car. I'm aware of the predicament you're in because of your private plane."

Van glanced down at Kat and gave a small shrug. "Being famous has its perks."

She smiled up at him, keeping her hand in his. She knew he was still feeling very uneasy and she caressed the back of his hand with her thumb in a comforting motion.

The woman took less time getting everything set up than Kat thought she would and soon they headed outside to pick up their car. They were immediately blasted by pouring rain and Kat let out a startled cry. "What in the world?" she exclaimed. "I thought this was supposed to be a desert!"

"Monsoon," Van stated. "It figures."

They ran to where their car waited and jumped in, sodden and dripping. Kat let out a slow, frustrated breath that sounded more like a hiss. "That was invigorating."

Van smirked. "We're only checked into a Best Western," he remarked. "The airport went all out."

"Maybe they don't like metal music," Kat muttered. She turned on the car and headed for the hotel via the directions the woman had given them. They arrived in a matter of minutes and Kat checked them in while Van was still in the car so he wouldn't have to deal with anymore people recognizing him. He didn't need the stress.

Van heaved a huge sigh once they were safely inside the hotel room. He looked exhausted, and he sat down on one of the beds, letting his shoulders slump. "I always feel like I've been run over after I have a panic attack." He said it absently, his voice laden with dismal fatigue. He rubbed at his chest as if it ached.

Kat glanced at him as she set her things aside. He looked about five years older. His broad shoulders drooped and she could see that his hands were still shaking slightly. Without saying anything, she went into the bathroom and drew a steaming hot bath. She knew hot baths always relaxed her. When she emerged, she walked quietly over and knelt in front of him, taking both of his hands in hers. She gave him a gentle smile. "How are you doing?"

He shrugged. "I haven't felt panic like that in a long time. It was hard being in that crowd anyway, but as soon as that girl hit me..." He shook his head. "I just couldn't deal with it."

"You don't need to explain yourself to me, Van. I remember before you really knew how to control your anxiety."

He nodded. "Yeah... You remember that time I flipped out in class?"

"I remember. Of course I remember. You scared everyone to death."

He rolled his eyes. "Thus sealing my high school fate as a complete freak."

She stood up and touched his face. "You're not a freak, Van. You were just a boy. You didn't even know what was wrong. I felt so bad for you that day. I didn't even know you then."

He looked up and met her eyes. "And what made you befriend me when everyone else fled in terror? You were there for that panic attack. You saw me acting like a complete lunatic, and yet, you still befriended me. You came up to me, touched me, soothed me even though Mr. Reynolds yelled at you not to. Then later, you sought to offer me your friendship. Why?"

"I don't scare easily." She raised her eyebrow in an attempt at playfulness.

He gave her a pained, forced smile.

"Come on," she urged. "I made a bath for you. So you can relax."

He stared at her for a moment, his eyes reflecting surprise. He shook his head. "How do you always understand?" he asked in awe.

She frowned. "What do you mean?"

"You have always known how to treat me. Even when you didn't know me. How do you always know what I need? You're amazing." He stood and wrapped his arms around her in reverence. "Thank you, Kat," he whispered.

Kat felt a tremor go through her at the emotion she heard in his soft voice. She closed her eyes and leaned into him without realizing it. He pulled away gently and smiled down at her.

"I'll call Rochelle and tell her what happened," Kat said. "She'll pass on the word."

He nodded and ran his knuckles down her cheek before heading into the bathroom. Kat sighed and went to her purse to find her phone. She tried to ignore the way her heart was beating fast from Van's nearness, but she realized she didn't really want to ignore it. That realization both invigorated and terrified her.

Chapter Thirteen

Kat had changed into some warm, dry clothing and was lying on her bed watching TV when Van finally emerged from the bathroom. "I thought you were never coming out," she remarked with a smile. She glanced over at him and her eyes widened. He'd left his shirt off, and what Kat had been trying in vain to see through his sheer shirts at his shows was now in plain sight. Her breath caught at the sight of him. He was so incredibly beautiful.

"It felt good," Van said. "I wanted to stay in there forever." He shot a glance toward the TV and his face lit up. "Hey! You're watching *Viva La Bam*!"

She tore her gaze away from the exquisite radiance that was Van's perfect body, and she looked back to the TV. She nodded. "He's hilarious."

"I love him," he said. "Nyah hates this show." He sat down on the end of his bed and started to watch.

"I remember the poster you had of him in your room," Kat said with a smile.

He grinned. "That's right. Bam's a cool guy."

She let her eyes wander over him again. He was sitting cross-legged with his back toward the wall. She could see one tattoo on his left shoulder and one around his right bicep, but she couldn't make out what they were. She did see that he had two music notes tattooed across his chest, right where his heart would be. She smiled. The music in his soul. The song in his heart.

Van must have felt eyes on him because he turned his attention to her.

Kat felt her cheeks turn pink at being caught. She shrugged sheepishly. "I was trying to see your tattoos," she admitted.

He smiled. "Well, come look then."

Her heart started pounding again, but she went over to him anyway. She had been dying to see what they were. She wasn't going to give up her chance now. The tattoo around his bicep was a simple tribal arm band, and the one on his left shoulder was the band's symbol. Somehow, she felt like she should have known that.

"I have one on my back too," he said. "It's my favorite." He turned so that she could see it.

Kat drew in her breath and marveled at it. It was an electric guitar going all the way down his spine, and it had wings sprouting out of the neck that expanded across his shoulders. The guitar was red, like the one he had played in high school. "Oh my gosh," she breathed. "It's beautiful." She stood and went to him. She reached out without thinking and touched it, running her fingers down the length of the guitar.

"Your music gives you wings to fly above your limitations," she murmured.

He smiled over his shoulder. "You always understood my symbolism."

She grinned as she turned her attention to tracing the outline of the wings. "I used to stare at your drawings when we displayed our art in class. I was always amazed at how you could say so much in so little."

"You saw the meaning in what everyone else only thought was twisted," he said.

"I always saw who you really were."

He turned so he could look at her. "You always saw straight into me."

Kat glanced up and met his eyes. Her heart shivered.

Van reached over to cup her cheek in his palm. "I have tasted you in my mouth every day of my life since that time in my room," he whispered. "You've haunted me all these years."

Her eyes drifted closed for a moment as she relished the feeling of his touch. Touch... She hated it from everyone but him.

"So as I lay here so restlessly, begging the silent night to comfort me, my final thought, that peaceful place, as I close my eyes I still see your face," he sang softly. "And my lips still linger of...your...taste..." He whispered the last part over her lips and lowered his softly to hers. The breath left his body at the silken softness of them. He had dreamed of her kiss for so long, ached for it. He cradled her face in both of his hands and kissed her with deliberate slowness so that he could savor her.

He was not prepared for the sweetness of her mouth. It was something he had yearned to have for years, but his memory of her was nothing compared to the reality. It was just a kiss, something so simple and so common. Yet, at that moment, it was something sacred and sinful at the same time. Something men would die trying to find. It was perfection and divine bliss. He tangled his fingers in her hair, wanting all of her forever. She was intoxication. She was everything. He only saw in black and gray when he was not with her.

Kat's head spun and her chest felt painfully tight as her heart hammered against it. She was lost in the complete gentleness of him. His lips felt so much better than she remembered, soft and tender and full of emotion. Not lust, not control. Just pure, raw emotion. It was all-consuming and overwhelming. She felt as if he was climbing straight into her. She opened her mouth for him and let his velvet tongue slip over hers, wanting what she had sampled so long ago.

She trembled when she pulled away, but it was out of something very far from fear or worry. She met Van's eyes and let out a shaky breath. "Wow," she breathed, "so that's what a real man's kiss feels like." She felt stupid for her lame response, but it was true all the same.

He smiled and caressed her face with both of his hands, as if to memorize her features. "You were always alive in me," he murmured. "Even when I thought I'd never see you again, I carried you in my heart. You never left me, Kat. Not for a second."

She looked away. "You never really left me either, Van. Something inside of me broke when I thought you had died."

He lifted her chin with his finger. "I'm alive," he stated, "and I'm here."

His eyes seemed to say more than his words, and the message frightened her. She trusted Van, but she did not trust what she didn't understand. She didn't understand what she felt when he looked at her like he did, or touched her, or kissed her. She wanted to sleep in his arms with no care or worry, but her defenses were still so strong.

Van did not press her further. He merely smiled and let his heated gaze rake adoringly over her for a moment. "Thank you for taking care of me tonight," he said, smoothing her hair.

She smiled, feeling a little self-conscious, and shrugged. "I don't even know if I did anything right."

"You did everything right," he assured her.

Her small smile grew.

He moved away from her and lay down. He kept his hand over hers, but that was all. He idly caressed his fingers over hers, and he turned back to the show.

Kat swallowed and sat there for a moment, staring blankly at the TV. She felt bereft. She glanced back at him and sighed. "Van?"

He met her eyes.

"Would you mind if I laid next to you?"

He smiled and picked up her hand, tugging her over to him. "Of course not. I just wanted to give you some space. I didn't want you to feel like I was crowding you."

She grinned and lay beside him, resting her head against his shoulder. She loved how attentive he was. He was always thinking of her, always taking her feelings into consideration. "I don't feel crowded when I'm with you, Van," she admitted, her voice small and faint. "I never have. I just have issues."

He pressed a tender kiss to the top of her head. "I know that, sweetheart. We all have issues. You don't need to explain that to me any more than I need to explain my panic to you. Let's just watch the show." A deep, throaty chuckle rumbled through his chest. "Maybe if I can focus on whatever it is Bam is doing to his poor family this week I can ignore my desire to kiss you completely breathless." He laughed again. "I'm sure that wouldn't be conducive to making you feel like you can trust me, would it?"

Her face flamed and she buried it against his shoulder in embarrassment, but she was grateful for his good humor. It took some of her apprehension away. Not to mention, it was nice to know that he felt such strong desire for her, but was more than willing to keep it in check to make her feel comfortable. That meant more to her than anything.

They watched the show together, and Kat noticed toward the end that his breathing grew deep and rhythmic. She finished watching the episode and turned off the TV, then watched him for a minute as he slept. She ran her fingers through his hair and braved placing a small kiss to his lips, wanting to feel their warmth again just for a second. She decided against waking him. He had been through too much. She also seemed to be having a moment of lucidity, so she decided she may as well enjoy it.

She smiled, curled next to him, and closed her eyes.

* * * *

Kat gazed out the window of the plane, watching the clouds float by. She let her mind replay the morning, recalling how she had awakened feeling safe for the first time in her life. She didn't feel like she had to be on her guard all the time when she was with Van. She didn't need to always be looking over her shoulder. She closed her eyes as his fingers absently started to toy with her hair. She glanced over at him and he smiled, then went back to the magazine he had been reading, still keeping his fingers in her hair.

She sighed and let her mind return to the happy memories she held of Van. She had shied away from them for so long. First, because they had caused her pain, and then again out of fear. Now she embraced them. He had only been a part of her life for a short while, but he had affected her so much. The happiest moments of her life had been those last few months of high school.

She turned to look at him and studied his profile. He seemed to have transformed from the night before, morphing back into the smooth, confident person all of America was in love with. No one would ever know his weakness. No one but her, because he trusted her enough to show it. Her eyes lingered on his lips for a minute and her heart flipped uncomfortably at the recollection of his sensual kiss.

Van glanced at Kat out of the corner of his eye and smiled to himself. He met her eyes briefly and she looked away. It was more than obvious that he fought the urge to chuckle, and she frowned. Dang it. She'd been caught again. He ran one finger slowly down her cheek and she closed her eyes. He leaned over and pressed a soft kiss to her cheek, then lifted up one of the earphones she was wearing. "What are you listening to?" he asked, trying to hear for himself.

She swatted him away playfully. "The CD you demanded I listen to," she stated.

He grinned. "Do you like it?"

She nodded.

"I knew you would." He paused, then lifted her earphone up again. "You look beautiful today," he whispered.

She blushed and smiled shyly.

"We have one whole day off in New York. Will you let me show you around once we get there?"

She swallowed. New York City. Of all places for her to feel unsafe, that had to be the worst, but she would be with Van. He would never let anything happen to her. She blinked with the sudden realization that, for the first time ever, the first thought in her mind had been that someone else would take care of her instead of reminding herself that she could beat up anyone who looked at her funny. She wasn't sure how to react to that.

"Kat?" Van prodded. "Please? New York is too amazing to miss out on."

She raised an eyebrow and met his eyes, putting the CD on pause. "Are you asking me out on a date, Van?" she asked with a playful smile.

His eyes softened and he brushed a piece of her hair back. "Yes," he said in all seriousness, "I am."

She looked down, her smile fading out of feeling awkward. "I haven't been on a date in a long time," she murmured.

He smiled. "Kat, it's just me."

She sighed. He didn't understand. He made it sound so trivial, like she was going out on the town with her brother. What he didn't realize was that she'd never looked at him as "just Jake," or "just Van." He had always been special, and he didn't know how her heart twinged at his nearness.

"Kat?" he asked again, frowning in concern.

She looked up at him and smiled at his obvious distress. She nodded slowly, knowing she could never refuse him. "Okay."

He grinned. "You won't regret it, I promise. Just leave the entire day open."

She continued to smile, but her stomach was doing somersaults. She hated how out of control she felt around him. It was so not like her. She sighed and pressed play on her CD player again, hoping to lose herself in the beautiful music and not have to think about her problems.

She tensed slightly when she felt Van's fingers brush against her own. He took her hand and twined his fingers with hers, bringing her hand to his lips and pressing a kiss to her knuckles. He did it all absently while flipping through his magazine, as if he did it all the time. It was almost subconscious, like he couldn't help but touch her. It was strange to her and so foreign, but not unwelcome. His touch was divine, just confusing. She leaned her head against the window, wondering if she would ever feel sane again.

Chapter Fourteen

Nyah was watching Van in the dressing room as he put his hair back in a ponytail after the show. He and Kat had not arrived until late in the afternoon and had barely been given any time to think before being rushed to the auditorium to prepare for the show. He knew she had been banking on him being exhausted and riddled with anxiety, but he actually looked and felt better than he had in quite awhile. He knew it irritated her.

She frowned and picked at her fingernails. "So," she said, "what did you and Kat do while you were stranded in Phoenix?"

He shot her a piercing scowl.

She gave him a helpless look. "What? I was just curious."

"We were stuck in the airport for the entire day and then got caught in a monsoon after not being allowed on our plane. Not to mention I had a monstrous panic attack. What do you think we did? We went to sleep."

"You performed really well tonight," she said softly. "I mean, you always do, but you looked and sounded so alive tonight."

"We had a good crowd." He wasn't about to tell her that the reason he seemed so alive was because he had sampled heaven and was still floating on the clouds. He heard Nyah sigh and glanced at her. "They loved you tonight. Did you see that one kid in the front row? He was practically drooling." He chuckled.

She smiled. "Lance almost tripped me with his cord once. During the bridge on *Battleworn,* he zipped past me and it caught on the heel of my boot. I thought I was going to bite it."

He grinned. "Do you remember when you and Jack first joined the band and we played at that tiny little club in Petaluma?"

"When Jack's drumstick broke?" she asked.

Van laughed. "And pelted Erik in the back of the head. Jack looked so confused and was so flustered that we had to stop the show."

Nyah giggled. "He was such a dork back then. We were all so naïve."

"They were good times, though."

She looked up at him. "They were," she murmured.

He glanced away.

"Hey," she began, "I was thinking, we have the whole day open day after tomorrow. Maybe you and I could—"

He sighed and met her eyes, finding it almost painful to do so. "I already told Kat I would take her out." To his surprise, she didn't yell, scream, or become irate. She merely dropped her gaze to her lap and said nothing. He thought that reaction was much worse. Nyah was a volatile person. All of her emotions were extreme. To see her react quiet and demure over something that should have caused her to get hostile was just downright disturbing. "But how about we all go out tonight?" he suggested. "The whole band together. We could get some drinks and just hang out." He offered an encouraging smile.

She shook her head. "No, that's okay. I think I'm just going to call it a night. I'm kind of tired." She stood and headed toward the door. She stopped for a second, looking hesitant, then spun. "Van," she said. "I blew it, didn't I?"

He frowned.

"I blew any shot of ever being with you."

He swallowed uncomfortably.

She sighed. "I know sometimes I'm an awful shrew and I may not have treated you very well, but I couldn't deal with knowing that, no matter what I did, I would always be second. I could never be Kat, no matter how hard I tried."

His frown deepened. "Nyah, we weren't even together when Kat joined our crew."

She shook her head. "She didn't have a name then, but she was always there just the same." She smiled sadly. "You never realized it and that's where I went wrong. I should have told you. I should have told you that when you looked at me, I saw the memory of someone else behind your eyes. I wanted to be your one and only, and I knew I never could be, so I took it out on you. I wanted to take you by the shoulders and shake you until you understood, but I should have just told you. Maybe it would have saved us both a lot of pain." She sighed. "For what it's worth, I did love you, and I'm sorry." She turned and strode from the room, leaving Van stunned.

He sighed and brought his hand to his forehead, an instant headache forming. He left the dressing room and went to go find Lance, but he stopped as he walked through the wings behind the stage and saw Kat filming the roadies tearing down the set. One of them chased another around, laughing like a psychopath and trying to beat him in the head with a pair of drumsticks. Van chuckled and folded his arms, watching.

The one being chased headed straight for Kat, a fake terrified look on his face, and he made like he ran head on into Kat's camera. She laughed.

"That's one high quality, professional roadie crew right there," Rochelle remarked, coming up to stand next to Van.

Van watched the same pair, only this time, the one that was being chased earlier pretended to strangle the other with a power cable. Van laughed. "I'm almost afraid to see what's going to be on this DVD."

Rochelle shared in his laughter. "Thrill My Koi had a drunken party last night. Lance and Jack were pretty wasted. That was really great footage."

"Great," he muttered with a wince.

She laughed. "Do you ever drink?"

He shrugged. "Not often. It messes with my anxiety medication."

She nodded. "Kat never drinks, ever. She never does anything that could potentially impair her judgment or her ability to properly break someone's neck if she had to."

"I can't believe she's so into martial arts." He shook his head, his memory filling with images of the sweet, gentle girl he had known in high school.

Rochelle met his eyes. "She's lethal, like a *Kill Bill* assassin. It's insane. Even her sensei couldn't believe how fast she took to the arts."

He raised his eyebrows. "I never would have pictured

that."

"I'm pretty sure she wouldn't have either," she said, "but I also don't imagine she pictured the rape or the other attempts at an attack."

"I want to protect her forever," he admitted, his voice soft.

Rochelle glanced up at him. "She's warmed up to you."

He gave her a sly look and nodded.

She raised an eyebrow.

"She agreed to go on a date with me on our free day," he said.

"She did?"

He nodded again and bit his bottom lip coyly. "And she is still the most magnificent kisser."

Rochelle's eyes bulged. "She let you kiss her?" She grinned. "Oh my gosh, it's a miracle!"

He gave a shy laugh and looked away.

"So, where are you going to take her on your date?" Rochelle prodded.

"I haven't completely decided yet. I just want to show her something beautiful. I want to fill her life with beautiful things."

Rochelle smiled and took his arm affectionately. "I never would have pegged you for such a romantic, Jake Marsallis." She leaned her head on his shoulder.

He chuckled softly and placed his arm around her in a half-hug. Kat turned the camera on them and he raised his eyebrows. Rochelle grinned and waved.

Kat smiled and turned the camera off. She left the stage and made her way down to them. "What are you guys doing?"

"Bonding," Rochelle teased.

She smiled. "So, what have you recorded so far?"

"I got a bunch of good footage last night and I've been recording the shows from different angles."

Kat nodded. "Good. I keep getting some random stuff that ought to be amusing to the viewers." She groaned. "It's going to be a pain to sift through all of it in editing. Do you realize how much footage we're going to have at the end of the month?"

"I don't even want to think about it," Rochelle said, rolling her eyes.

Kat frowned in thought. "You know, I had this idea to maybe tape an entire live show. Don't you think that would be cool?"

Rochelle nodded in agreement. "Let's do it tomorrow."

"It'll be tiring with just the two of us trying to get all the angle shots, but I have some good ideas we can work with."

Van smiled to himself as he listened to Kat talk. She was so focused and professional with her job. She had always taken everything she had done very seriously.

"Rochelle!" Lance called, coming over to them. "Jack, Erik, and I were thinking of going to the Empire State Building." He smiled. "I think Erik has a thing for Alana in Thrill My Koi. She's never been there before, and I think he wants us as cover."

Rochelle grinned. "The Empire State Building!" she exclaimed. "That sounds like so much fun!"

Van smiled. "It does sound cool. I haven't been in ages. Kat, do you want to go?"

She gave Lance a small smile. "Sure."

Lance raised a surprised eyebrow. "You actually agreed without a fight. You're learning." Kat rolled her eyes, and he grinned. "Well we'd better head out soon then. Let's meet at the back door."

Van nodded. "See you in a few."

Lance turned and headed back toward the dressing rooms, motioning for Rochelle to follow.

Rochelle giggled and winked at Kat. "See you soon."

Van smirked. "Some things never change."

"What, Rochelle?" Kat laughed. "No, Rochelle has stayed pretty much the same."

He leaned against the wall he was standing next to and toyed with a piece of her hair. "Not like you."

She looked down with a sigh. "Yes, I am very different."

He lifted her chin with his forefinger so he could look into her eyes. "Not that different," he murmured. "Not inside." He cupped her cheek with his palm. "You have an inner beauty that's impossible to extinguish. It radiates from you."

Color touched her cheeks and she smiled. "You're sweet, Van."

He shook his head. "Not sweet. Truthful." He grinned and leaned in to press a kiss to her jaw. "And you're still an amazing kisser," he whispered, nuzzling his nose against her ear.

Her cheeks flamed and she giggled. "Never mind. You're not sweet, you're terrible."

Van chuckled and caught movement out of the corner of his eye. He straightened just in time to see Nyah retreating. He kicked himself mentally. "Nyah!" he called.

She turned and looked at him forlornly.

"We're all going to the Empire State Building." He gave her a warm smile. "Come with us."

She shook her head. "I'm tired. I think I'm just going to sleep."

"But it's New York," he urged. "You love New York."

A very faint smile touched her lips. "It's okay, Van, don't worry about me. I'm fine." She met Kat's eyes briefly and it looked like she tried to smile, but didn't succeed very well.

Van felt his heart twist painfully. Even during her worst, he had never wanted to hurt Nyah. Seeing pain in her eyes stabbed at him. To know that the whole time they'd been together she had felt second best and less than Kat made him feel sick. He would never have intentionally made her feel that way. His feelings for her had been genuine at the time. Going into the relationship, he hadn't realized that his undying love for Kat was still so strong. "But it wouldn't be right if you didn't go," he insisted, feeling horribly guilty. "The rest of the band is going. You're a part of the band, Nyah."

She swallowed and looked away. "I've been to the Empire State Building before. It's not that exciting. I'm just going back to the hotel." She pivoted on her heel and continued on down the corridor.

Van let out a long breath.

Kat frowned and placed her hand on his chest in a comforting gesture. "What's wrong?"

He shook his head. "Nothing." He forced a smile and met her eyes. He took her hand from his chest and placed a kiss to her palm. "Come on, the others will be waiting for us."

She nodded, and they headed toward the back door.

* * * *

Kat had never seen anything quite as beautiful as New York City from the top of one of the tallest buildings in America. The lights sparkled like glitter as far as she could see, and the warm night breeze touched her face softly. She sighed and looked over at Rochelle. She was laughing again, as always. Jack and Lance teased her about something and she tried to video tape them. Erik stood a little ways off talking to Alana, inching closer to her.

She felt hands on her shoulders and looked up to see Van smiling down at her.

"Beautiful, isn't it?" he asked.

She nodded and turned back around to gaze at the breathtaking city below. Van ran his hands down her arms and wrapped them around her, pulling her close up against his solid frame. She closed her eyes and tried to keep herself from falling over. He had no idea how being so close to him affected her.

"I always wanted to stand up here with someone in my arms," he breathed. "It always seemed so romantic to me."

She smiled and her heart started to hammer at the way his breath tickled her neck. Images of his kiss the night before barraged her mind, and all she wanted to do was stare at his back again. *What is with that? It's just a man's back. What is the obsession with his back?* She sighed and thought of his beautiful tattoo. She wanted to trace it again. She wanted to memorize every perfect line of him. She frowned. This was so weird. She'd never had a thought like that in her life. What was it about Van? What had it always been? It drove her nuts.

Van pressed a kiss to the top of Kat's head as he thought about their date. He would show her magic and beauty and make her see that life with him could always be beautiful. It was what she deserved and what he would always give her.

Chapter Fifteen

"Get up!" Rochelle's shrill voice pierced Kat's slumber and she groaned as Rochelle leapt up onto Kat's bed and started bouncing on it. "Today's your date with Van! Get up!"

Kat opened one eye. "What is your problem?" she grumbled.

Rochelle flopped down on top of Kat, making all of her air go out with a *hmmph* noise. "It's your date!"

"Yeah, so?" She tried to rub the sleep from her eyes with one hand and push Rochelle off of her with the other.

"So get up! You need to look your best! I'll help you pick out something to wear. Heaven knows what'll happen if I leave it up to you."

"What's wrong with the way I dress?" she hissed. She pushed at her again. "Get *off* me!" she cried. "I recorded an entire two hour show last night. My shoulders are killing me. The last thing I need is your unbudgeable body squashing me!"

Rochelle rolled over with a giggle.

Kat groaned again and yawned. "Now, again, I ask you, what is wrong with the way I dress?"

Rochelle flashed Kat a mischievous smile. "Nothing, if you're trying to attract an Amish dude. Come on, Kat. You know Van would never do anything to hurt you, so there's nothing wrong with showing off a little bit." She yanked the covers off her. "Come on, get in the shower. I'll pick out something for you to wear."

Kat muttered something under her breath and sat up. There was a sudden knock on the door and Rochelle ran to open it. Kat combed her fingers through her hair and yawned again, then glanced up at Rochelle, who was approaching with a bewildered expression. She handed Kat another king-sized chocolate kiss and a note.

Kat rolled her eyes and smiled a little. She reached out and took them from Rochelle, then shook her head and opened the note. *"Good morning, beautiful. I hope you had a wonderful night. I can't wait to see you today, but first you have to go with Lance and Rochelle. They are going to take you to South Street Seaport. Find an evening gown you like. Lance has the money to buy it. When you're finished, meet me at the Metropolitan Museum of Art. I will wait for you there."* Kat frowned and looked up at Rochelle. "You in on this?"

Rochelle shrugged. "I guess so. Lance just kind of informed me that I was. I guess he volunteered me. Isn't that nice of him?" She rolled her eyes.

Kat sighed. "This is silly." She folded the note back up. "Why do I have to find an evening gown?"

Rochelle heaved an exasperated sigh. "Maybe he's going to take you somewhere nice, Kat. Geez, sometimes I wonder if you're a woman at all. Get in the shower. I'm not going to wait for you half the day just because you're a coward and don't want to go on a date."

Kat frowned and opened her mouth to protest.

"Get in the shower!" Rochelle commanded.

Kat raised her eyebrows. "Yes, dictator. Geez. Should I salute when I address you?" She stood and made her way into the bathroom while Rochelle smiled and headed for Kat's suitcase, intent on finding something she assumed was suitable.

* * * *

Lance looked uneasily up at the sky as dark clouds began to roll in. "I don't know about this weather, guys," he cautioned.

"No kidding," Rochelle complained, tugging at her shirt collar to try and cool herself off. "It's, like, a million degrees out here. My makeup is going to melt off."

Kat sighed in frustration and looked over the dresses in the window of a store. There were so many different kinds of stores in the shopping area on the pier at South Street Seaport, but she couldn't seem to find anything that jumped out at her. She needed to find something perfect, and she was beginning to think that was impossible. "Here's the problem," she said. "I don't *like* any of these dresses."

Rochelle flung her hands up in the air in frustration. "It's a dress, Kat. It's not disarming a bomb. The decision is not that crucial."

"Yes, it is," Kat muttered under her breath. Rochelle didn't understand. This was the first date she'd been on in years, and it wasn't just with some random guy. It was with *Van*.

"We've been looking for two hours," Lance pointed out. "I think Van might start to worry after awhile." He glanced up at the ominous sky again just as a roll of thunder sounded. "We need to get inside, like pronto."

A cool breeze drifted over them and Rochelle closed her eyes, basking in it. "No way, it's just starting to feel nice out here."

"You don't understand," he said. "With humidity like to-day—" Without warning, rain began to pour down on them in driving sheets, soaking all three of them instantly.

Rochelle shrieked and jerked the door of the dress shop open. They all ran inside and stood there, sopping and stunned.

"I told you," Lance said, shaking off his arms. "I've been to New York in the summer before. On one of these humid days, if you hear thunder and all the people around you disappear, take cover."

"Look at my hair!" Kat cried suddenly. "It's ruined!" She let out a frustrated growling noise. "I am sick of being wet! What is it with these states and the sudden intense rain? You only tour in states that drench you? My shirt is completely soaked through! I look like a drowned rat! Why don't you just send me down to the sewer!"

Lance and Rochelle exchanged a knowing glance. For someone who always acted so collected and indifferent about everything, Kat's actions and words betrayed her emotions about her date. She knew it. She knew they knew it, but she didn't care. She had bigger problems at the moment.

"It's okay," Rochelle assured her. "Your shirt will dry by the time you get to the museum, and your hair doesn't look bad straight."

She glowered at Rochelle. "It's flat and lifeless."

"We'll find you a cute hat, okay? While we're stuck in here, you may as well look at some dresses."

"But I don't like any of them!" she huffed.

Rochelle smiled and linked her arm with Kat's, guiding her over to the eveningwear section. "Kat, you need to calm down. I have never seen you so flabbergasted."

Kat sighed in agitation. "You don't understand, Rochelle. This is the first date I've been on in ages."

"But it's just Van."

She shook her head. "You all keep saying that, but he's not 'just Van.' He's Van, pure and simple. He's never been 'just' anybody. Everyone always saw him as 'just' whoever he was, but he's always been so much more to me than that. I feel like I'm going to puke."

Rochelle grinned. "Just find a dress you like. He'll think you're beautiful no matter what you wear. He adores you."

Kat sighed and started to look through the dresses.

Rochelle tried to suppress a grin, but failed

* * * *

Kat sat on the bed in her hotel room, absolutely petrified. She stared ahead blankly and her hands trembled. She felt ridiculous. For someone who prided herself on always being calm and collected, she felt like her life was over. She realized that was a bit dramatic, but she couldn't help it. If she was going to have lunch, or going for coffee, this wouldn't be a big deal, but this was a "date." That word alone terrified her.

The last time she had been on a date, the unthinkable had happened and, while she trusted Van, the memory association was not happy. Besides, "date" always had a looming sort of sound to it. It was like relationship purgatory. You were interested enough in one another to chance going out on a "date," but you weren't certain yet if you were compatible enough to involve yourself in a long-term relationship. It was just, all in all, a terrifying word, especially when you were going out on a date with Van Marshall, who just happened to be the sexiest man on the planet.

The fact that Kat had technically known him for years didn't seem to matter. She seriously felt like her life was over.

"Kat, you need to breathe," Rochelle coached as she looked at her. "What are you thinking anyway?"

Kat stared up at her. "You don't even want to know," she replied truthfully. "It would frighten you."

Rochelle grinned. "You look beautiful. Didn't Van make you feel less nervous at the museum?"

Kat sighed and stared down at her hands in her lap. Van had been very sweet to her. They had gone through the entire museum, staring at paintings of all sorts and sharing ideas on what they thought the artist was trying to convey. It made her feel like they were back in art class, which she imagined might have been his intent. He had casually held her hand for most of the day, but Kat was quickly coming to realize that Van's most casual gestures were usually the most intimate to her.

They had eaten a simple lunch at a hotdog stand and then he had instructed Kat to go back to the hotel room and change into her gown. He told her he would pick her up in an hour, which meant he should be knocking on the door any second.

"It's not that he makes me feel nervous," she murmured. "He just makes me feel like..." She sighed. "I don't even know how to describe it. All I know is that he's so beautiful and I'm so...." She shook her head.

Rochelle frowned. "What?" She sat down next to her. "Kat, it's okay to feel beautiful and sexy once in awhile, especially with someone you trust."

Kat shook her head. "It's not that, it's just..." She sighed. "Earlier didn't really feel like a date because we were just going to a museum, looking at art, you know? This feels like a date. Waiting for the guy to pick you up, butterflies in your stomach, wondering if you're pretty enough, if he'll think you're pretty." She shook her head. "Rochelle, the last time I went on a date was bad. We know this."

"But Van would never—"

"It's not that. It's not Van I have the problem with. It's just, I have all these horrid memories and I feel..." She sighed again. "Tainted, Rochelle." She met her friend's eyes. "I'm used."

Rochelle's eyes widened. "You are *not* tainted!" she exclaimed. She clasped Kat's hands in hers. "You listen to me; that was not your fault. Your uncle, the rape, that guy in the club, none of those instances were your fault. You are not used. You are perfect. You're talented and focused and insanely strong. You're a wonderful friend. Jake thought you were perfect long ago and he still does. When are you going to believe it?"

Kat sighed. "I know I don't make sense, and I probably sound like a complete moron, but I just don't feel worthy of him. Not now, not after all that's happened. He's so talented, and he shines so brightly. What am I? I can't even stand the thought of going on a date because of the memories the word invokes. I'm messed up. I have problems. What in the world could I possibly offer him?"

"You saw him, Kat. All those years ago, you saw past his crazy-colored hair, black eye makeup, and anxiety disorder. I imagine that meant more to him than anything."

"But I was stable back then. Now I'm a complete spaz. We're not in high school anymore. This is real life. What if— what if something happens?"

Rochelle frowned. "Like...?"

Kat huffed in exasperation at Rochelle not being able to read her mind. "Like what if we fall in love or something? How is that supposed to work? He's on tour all the time. Women are always throwing themselves at him. I just think this is a really bad idea. Somebody could get hurt."

Rochelle took Kat by the shoulders. "You're right," she stated forcefully. "Kat, you're right. Someone could get hurt. He could hurt you or you could hurt him, but let's imagine just for a second that you don't have the Great Wall of China as a defense around yourself. Let's pretend that you just stop trying to rationalize why you shouldn't do something that you might not be able to control. I know that your logic is the only way you were able to get through all the stuff that happened. I understand that. But, sometimes, when we, as humans, think too much, it's just an excuse for trying to cover over emotions that might frighten us. You like Van. It doesn't matter whether or not you used to know him. The fact remains that you like him and he likes you. Go on this date and have a good time. If you fall in love, so be it. Let it happen. Don't worry about the what ifs and the maybes. If it doesn't end up working out, at least you'll know what it felt like to let another person inside. You won't have to wonder the rest of your life what it might be like to have someone share your heart."

Kat blinked at Rochelle in stunned silence. She let out a slow, calming breath just as they heard a knock on the door. Rochelle stood and announced that she would get it. Kat nodded and closed her eyes for a minute, letting Rochelle's words sink in. How did her flirty, carefree friend manage to have such an amazing amount of wisdom? "Just take the chance," she murmured to herself. "Come on, Kat. Just do it. Let yourself go for once in your miserable life." She stood and headed to the bathroom for a quick last minute check, but she stopped just long enough to peek her head around the corner and steal a look at Van. She needed to prepare herself.

Rochelle opened the door and there he was, in a magnificent tux with tails. His dark hair was hanging loosely around his shoulders and he was holding a long-stemmed rose.

"Nice," Rochelle commented in her usual, flirtatious manner.

Van bit his bottom lip shyly, an action very much Jake Marsallis. "Is Kat ready?" he asked.

Kat darted back into the hall, definitely deciding she needed to primp a little bit more.

Rochelle's voice came, "Just give her a sec. She's really nervous."

* * * *

Van closed his eyes for a minute, trying to will his heart to beat normally. Anxiety. Something he was so familiar with, but this kind was so much sweeter. This had a reason. This was anticipation. He glanced toward the bedroom as Kat finally appeared, and he stared in wonderment at her. He put his hand to his chest. She wore a white dress with small, golden flowers trailing up the bodice and down one side of the skirt. They sparkled. Her short hair was flipped up like always, but she had soft makeup on, which made her lovely features stand out more than usual. Her beauty was so intense he wanted to cry.

Kat looked down in a shy gesture.

Van smiled and approached her. He lifted her chin and gazed into her eyes. "You are so exquisite it hurts," he whispered.

She swallowed hard. "Where are we going?" she managed to ask.

"To heaven," he replied.

Rochelle raised her eyebrows and apparently decided it would be a good time to remove herself.

Van handed Kat the rose and offered his arm as they left the hotel.

* * * *

Kat was quiet the entire time they were in the cab, feeling completely awkward and out of place. She watched the buildings go past her window, hoping that staring at the city might aid in calming her nerves. It didn't seem to work. They ended up at The Plaza hotel where Van escorted her to a restaurant inside.

"We'll get dinner here," he said. "Then we're going to Times Square."

"What for?"

"A play."

She smiled up at him. "We're seeing a play?"

He nodded as he pulled her chair out for her to sit. "*Beauty and the Beast.* I hope you like it."

"I've always wanted to see that play. It's my favorite Disney movie."

He grinned. "I'm glad I picked it then." He scooted her chair in as she sat and he pressed a soft kiss to the base of her neck.

Kat's heart stopped for second. She was positive it had. She let out a shaky breath as the place where he had kissed seemed to burn even after he was gone.

Van sat and reached across the table to take her hand. "What's wrong?" he asked. "You seem nervous."

She looked up at him. "Van, do you remember how you felt the day I bought your guitar strings for you and then invited myself over to your house?"

"Of course I do." He chuckled. "I felt like I was going to die. You were so popular and beautiful and I felt like such a loser. I didn't know what in the world I was going to do."

She nodded. "Yeah, I think we switched places."

His eyes softened and he gave her a warm smile. "Kat, you could never disappoint me."

She looked up at him, and his eyes caught hers. She felt warmth steal through her entire body and somewhere, something just decided to give. A slow smile blossomed across her face and she sighed, running her thumb back and forth across his hand.

The waitress came then, and Kat was distracted by starvation for a little while. They shared pleasant conversation through dinner, mostly talking about music, life on the road, independent films, and Bam Margera. Slowly, Kat began to feel her nervousness subside. Van told her stories that made her laugh, and she began to feel less and less self-conscious.

Dinner was finished and they made their way to the theatre, Kat taking in all the sights as she did so. New York was a bustling, insane place. While San Francisco had been very busy as well, New York seemed to run at a frantic pace. There was so much to look at that it was overwhelming.

Van had gotten them seats in the front row and Kat watched the show in amazement. The only live plays she had ever been to were the ones in high school. She was enthralled at the way the actors could fill the entire theatre with their voices and presence. Van kept his casual hold on her hand all through the show, and Kat began to realize that she loved the feeling of his hand on hers. His touch was always gentle and warm.

Kat was disappointed when the play came to an end. It was such a fascinating experience that she had wanted it to last forever. She joined the other audience members in a standing ovation then sat back in her chair with a sigh. "That was breathtaking," she said. "The whole thing was so amazing! I can't believe how they did the end when he transforms! It looked so real!" She met Van's eyes and smiled. "Thank you."

He grinned and pressed a kiss to her forehead. "Wait here," he commanded. "Don't move."

She frowned, but obeyed. She studied the way the theatre looked with all of its ornate finery and read her program about three times, but started to feel uneasy when she realized there was no one left in the theatre. Where had Van gone anyway? Getting more and more irritated, she contemplated going and calling a cab, but before she could move, the curtain on the stage lifted to reveal about a hundred lit candles. They bathed the enormous stage in an ethereal amber glow.

Van came striding up onto the stage and she raised her eyebrows. He carried his acoustic guitar and grinned. He dragged a stool out from the wings and sat down on it. "Good evening, everybody," he said, acting like there was a full audience. "As you may know, I'm Van Marshall, singer and guitarist of a band called Bleeding Passion. Some freaks out there say I'm the next rock legend, but I think that's ridiculous." He looked at Kat. "You see, my music career started out really poorly. It wasn't much different than this, actually. Me, all alone on a stage with my guitar. I started to play and some arrogant idiot ripped off my strings."

Kat giggled.

He shrugged. "I pretty much thought that was it at that point, but then a miracle happened. An angel stepped into my life and graced me with her beauty. She has no idea how much she affected my life. I lost contact with her for years, but her memory haunted me every day. I couldn't even last in a relationship because of the memory of her. I had so many regrets. I thought I'd let my chance slip by out of fear, and that made me sick inside. But then, I was given another chance, a chance to be the man I'd wanted to be when I first saw her but didn't know how to be. The only problem was, she had changed and her views were something like this—" He started to play Queensryche's "I Don't Believe In Love," and he sang out the chorus.

Kat couldn't help but grin.

Van continued. "It was discouraging, of course, but she had her reasons. She had been hurt beyond repair, and it killed me to know that I had not been there for her. Unfortunately, I can't take back my past mistakes. I can't go back to a time when I could have protected her and change the course of her future. All I can do is try to heal the scars that the past has left behind and show her how much I am devoted to being beside her for whatever life might throw her direction." He met her eyes. "I never really got a chance to tell her how much she means to me." Without taking his eyes off her, he broke into HIM's "In Joy and Sorrow.'

Kat felt tears sting her eyes as she listened to his gorgeous voice. He always put so much emotion into his singing. She didn't just hear him singing, she felt it. Even when he was singing someone else's song. The lyrics spoke of finding your home in someone's arms through joy and sorrow, thick and thin, no matter what. That was not a light statement.

Van finished the song and let his guitar rest across his lap. He sighed and ran his hand through his hair. "Basically, I just want her to know that I'm here for the good times and the bad, that I'll never leave her alone again unless..." He averted his eyes for a moment. "Unless she wants me to, which I really hope isn't the case. She has made me what I am today. I'd like her to take this chance and trust me." He met her eyes again and held his hand out. "Come and dance with me if you're willing."

Her heart flipped dramatically in her chest, but she stood quickly, even though her legs were wobbly. She made her way up onto the stage and placed her shaking hand in his. She couldn't wrap her mind around what he had just voiced. It was overwhelming.

Van set his guitar aside, then met her as she climbed the stairs onto the stage. He kissed her fingers and smiled as he placed his other arm around her waist. "You won't regret this," he promised. "I will never hurt you. You will never know pain or betrayal with me. You will always feel empowered, and confident, and loved."

Tears stung her eyes, and a beautiful melody started to play out of nowhere.

Van smiled down at her and gently guided her closer to him. She placed her free arm on his shoulder and could not help but feel a jolt when her body pressed against his. She marveled over the fact that she seemed to match perfectly with him, like their bodies were meant to fit together. Even with him being so much taller than her, they fit. Like two parts of one whole. She braved a look up at him as they began to sway to the music.

"How did you pull all of this off?" she breathed.

He grinned. "Like I said, being famous has its perks."

She stared up into his soft eyes as the haunting lyrics began. Fog started to roll in from the wings of the stage, covering the floor and making Kat gasp.

"I told you we were going to heaven," he whispered against her ear.

She closed her eyes and rested her head against his shoulder, loving how it felt to be so close to him. He held her hand over his chest and she could feel his strong heartbeat.

She'd never thought she was capable of feeling this way, not after what had happened. She thought Kyle had broken the part of her that felt desire. Van made her forget all of that. She had no fear when she was with him, no recollection of old pain. All she felt was warm and protected.

Van held her, amazed at having her in his arms. Even though he was a lot more sure of himself than he had been in high school, deep down he still had moments when he felt awkward and gawky. He had been terrified that she would reject him. The fact that she hadn't made him want to scream at the top of his lungs in exuberance. He had dreamed of being close to her for so long. She completed his soul, made him a whole person. He couldn't comprehend how he had been living without her all these years.

He ran his hand down her bare back, feeling the lithe muscle. He smiled. Maybe, over time, some of that would disappear. She no longer had to worry about protecting herself. He would never let anyone harm her. He blinked in surprise as she seemed to unconsciously slip both of her arms underneath his tuxedo coat and wrap them around his waist. He closed his eyes as her soft body pressed against his, and he shivered when her lips placed a kiss to his neck. He stopped dancing and slowly wrapped his arms around her, relishing in the splendor that was all her. "I've loved you my whole life," he admitted in a hushed voice full of raw emotion that he couldn't have kept from her if he'd tried.

Kat absently ran her fingers back and forth over his lower back. "Van," she murmured, her voice raspy with emotion. She shook her head as if trying to collect her thoughts. "I spent my entire life in fear up until the point I decided to take matters into my own hands. I was always running from someone, always looking over my shoulder. The only person I ever felt safe with was you. Even when you were so shy and reclusive..." She chewed on her bottom lip. "I just never felt like you would let anything happen to me."

She pulled away from him enough to be able to look into his eyes. He gave her a soft smile. He would protect her with his life. He would sacrifice anything to keep her safe.

She reached up to take his face in both of her hands. She ran her fingers across his cheeks, as if savoring the texture of his skin. She smiled again and brought his face down closer to hers. She raised her lips to his and nibbled on his bottom lip in a naughty taunt before kissing him fully.

Van held her tight and kissed her with all of his desire. *She* was his desire. His desire, his light, and the fire in his soul. She always had been. Until the day he died, he would thank her every day for making him what he was. He poured as much of his heart and love into the kiss as he could, hoping she could feel what he was feeling even on the smallest level.

Kat pulled away first, breathing heavily. She looked down and ran her hands across his chest, tugging ever so slightly on the lapels of his tux. He wondered what she was thinking. Half the time she looked like she was waging war inside her own brain. She moved her gaze back up to his eyes and her arms circled his neck.

"Van," she whispered.

He tucked a strand of hair behind her ear. "Hmm?"

"I feel music in your kiss." She played with the hair at the nape of his neck. "You taste like passion."

He stared at her, dumbfounded and awestruck. He felt the sudden sting of tears and had to fight not to weep. He wrapped his arms around her and all but crushed her to him. He couldn't help it. He wanted to be gentle and suave, but he couldn't after hearing her say a thing like that. He trembled a little with the intensity of his emotion and buried his face in the crook of her neck.

Kat smiled and just let him hold on, relishing in having his arms around her, loving how his breath felt against her skin. "Today has been beautiful," she murmured. "Thank you for everything."

He managed to detach himself enough to look down at her. "All I ever want to show you is beauty."

She trailed her fingers down his cheek to his jaw, then across his full lips. He closed his eyes and kissed her fingertips. She smiled. "I don't want the night to end."

He pressed a gentle kiss to her forehead. "It doesn't have to."

She arched an eyebrow.

He pulled away from her somewhat reluctantly and offered his arm.

She smiled and took it. "What about the candles and all the stuff?"

"My accomplice will take care of it."

She let him lead her off the stage and out of the theatre. She didn't know where he was taking her, and frankly, didn't care. For the first time in ages she didn't feel like she needed to be in control. It was liberating, and she planned on enjoying it.

Chapter Sixteen

Kat couldn't properly express how it felt to stroll through Central Park with the wonderful warmth of Van's hand on hers. It felt like she had waited her entire life to reach this point. Something extraordinary had happened. She felt no fear, no apprehension. She wandered through one of the most traveled parks in the U.S. and wasn't the least bit concerned about what might be hiding in the shadows or lurking in dark corners. All she felt was Van.

Until this point, she thought it impossible for anything to feel better than Jake's soft kiss, but kissing him now made the memory seem small and silly. She had turned herself into a machine, someone who didn't feel, and he made her heart melt. He made her feel so much more than she ever thought was possible. It was intimidating and a little frightening, but too wonderful to run from. She was tired of running.

Van glanced down at her as they walked, and he gave her a smile that reflected complete elation and blinding joy, like he was so happy to be there with her that he couldn't possibly keep it all inside. "I wish I could show you more of New York," he said. "I've barely even scratched the surface."

She smiled. "What you've shown me is very nice." She shrugged. "I'm not a big city person anyway."

"No?"

She shook her head. "If I had my way, I would live in one of those small coastal towns in California. You know, like Cambria or San Luis Obispo. They're so peaceful. I want to just be able to eat dinner on the beach anytime I want, or go down to the farmer's market and watch the local people perform their talents on the streets." She smiled, feeling silly. "I guess I'm really just a simple person at heart."

"There's nothing wrong with that."

She looked away for a second. "Not like the life you're used to," she murmured.

"My career complicates my life, but it also gives me the ability to live any life I choose. I think I could be very happy living in a small coastal town." He stole a sidelong glance at her to observe her reaction to his words.

Kat bit her bottom lip and smiled, her cheeks turning hot. For a moment, she allowed herself to picture living in a house by the ocean with Van. The thought took on a life of its own, and she envisioned herself waking up next to him. She pictured laughing with him over breakfast and walking hand in hand with him down the beach. She pictured them in front of a fireplace, her nestled in his arms, kissing him. Her imagination continued to play out the fantasy until she was visualizing things she had never even allowed herself to think before. No, that wasn't it. She'd just never had anyone that she'd wanted to think that way about. The thought of intimacy with anyone had been nauseating after the rape, but the thought of intimacy with Van... She shook her head.

Van frowned thoughtfully. "What were you thinking about?"

"Nothing." She felt her face flush once more.

He chuckled. "Whatever it was, it must have been good because you're blushing."

She scowled half-heartedly at him.

He grinned and pulled her into his arms, closing his eyes as he held her tight. He nuzzled his lips against her neck and nibbled lightly. She shivered.

"I never want another day without you," he whispered. "I ache without you."

There was a strange tightening in Kat's chest and the tears burned behind her eyes again. Flashes of memory barraged her without warning and she clutched him close to her, holding on. Every once in awhile, it still blew her mind that he was really alive and with her. At times, simple things like the solidity of his body, the reality of his touch and sound of his voice were so overwhelmingly beautiful.

Van pulled away enough to look down at her. He touched a falling tear and wiped it tenderly. "What is it?" he asked. "What's wrong?"

She looked up at him and gave him a meager smile. "I

was just thinking about us. I was remembering you."

"And that made you cry?"

She giggled. "No. I was thinking about how wonderful it is that you're alive. Wonderful doesn't even describe it." She shook her head. "I can't even begin to tell you how devastated I was. I've never felt pain like that. The thought of never seeing your smile, or your soft gray eyes..." She sighed. "Even though you went away to college and I stayed in L.A, I always thought we would find one another again, that we would always be in each other's lives somehow. I didn't realize how much I craved your companionship. I've never felt so alone."

He took her face in his hands and stroked her cheeks with his thumbs. "I would take it all away if I could, Kat. If I had known..."

"How could you have known? It wasn't your fault. Besides, we ended up finding one another again anyway."

He grinned and slipped his arms around her waist. "What do you think would have happened if I had never gone away to school and we had never been separated?"

She sighed and met his eyes, realizing that she felt happy. Really happy. It had been so long that she had forgotten what happiness felt like. Warmth wrapped itself around her heart and she ran her fingers through Van's hair. "I don't know," she murmured, "but I'd really like to find out."

He lowered his lips to hers with soft tenderness, as if savoring the feel of her.

She nestled herself in his arms and closed her eyes, resting her head against his chest in contentment. "I've never been close to anyone but you," she murmured. "The guy that raped me...we dated a little, but we weren't close like this."

His arms tightened around her. "No one will ever hurt you again, Kat," he whispered. "I promise."

She smiled. "And since I just so happen to know several ways to kill someone, no one will ever hurt you either."

He chuckled and tangled his fingers in her hair. "It's so good to see you laugh and tease like you used to. I knew the Kat I remembered was still in there somewhere."

She nestled into his arms again, enjoying the feeling of being free of her oppressive discipline and allowing herself to feel feminine for the first time in far too long.

* * * *

Nyah slapped down her washcloth in annoyance as she finished cleaning her face. She heaved a sigh and went to flop down on her bed. She grabbed the bottle of wine she had been attacking and took a long drink, giving a blank stare to the wall. She had gone over to Van's room earlier, hoping maybe they could go out to eat or something. She didn't want much, just a little time with him, like the way things used to be before they got all weird. Lance had reminded her that he was still out with Kat. She scowled at the thought and took another drink.

Memories came unbidden to her, memories of Van. She remembered what she'd thought when she'd first met him years ago. She and Jack had been so nervous. They had auditioned for bands before, but had never had any luck with their music. Jack had been given offers, but not a lot of bands wanted a female vocalist, and they came as a pair. She could play guitar as well, but no one ever took her seriously. Rock was such a male dominated world. It was difficult for someone like her to be seen as a true musician.

Van had been the most beautiful man she'd ever seen. As soon as she'd walked in the room and he'd turned to greet them, her heart had stopped. His hair was short back then, dyed black with crazy streaks of blue and purple, and he'd been more lanky than masculine, but his eyes... For the rest of her life she knew she would never look into another pair of eyes like Van's. They were so gentle, so soothing. He'd made her feel instantly at ease.

Van had been the first person to ever take her seriously as a musician. He respected her for her talent and gave her a say in everything. He treated her as an equal band member and not just eye candy used as promotion. She had never thought he would be interested in her romantically. The day he'd asked her out had been bliss for her, and when he'd first kissed her, she knew she would be lost forever.

There was no one in all the world like Van. But she'd never been enough for him. There'd always been a shadow lurking behind his eyes. She would have given him everything, but he'd always held her at a distance. He'd treated her well and had never been shy with affection, but she'd never had his heart. Not really. That had always belonged to the girl from his past... Kat. He'd spoken of her endlessly, but had never actually uttered her name. She imagined it must have been too sacred for him. Kat... The ice queen with the attitude. She scowled and took another drink of wine.

A knock sounded on her door and she jumped up and ran to it, thinking it might be Van. He had been nicer to her after her confession in the dressing room.

She yanked the door open and frowned when she saw that it was a blond man she'd never seen before. He was very good-looking.

He smiled. "Nyah Densmoore," he said, his voice complete silk. "I was told you were here. I am, by far, your biggest fan." He flashed her an irresistible grin.

* * * *

Kat and Van were still hand in hand as they walked back to Kat and Rochelle's room. She felt like she had been reborn. She had never felt so free. It was nice to relenquish control for awhile and just allow herself to feel.

She was humming "In Joy and Sorrow" softly to herself as they walked, and Van grinned down at her.

"Tonight was heaven," he said with a rapturous grin.

She smiled and squeezed his hand. Heaven... Twenty-four hours ago, she never would have believed that the tainted and foul earth could hold anything even remotely close to heaven, but Van had proved her wrong. He was heaven, and everything he touched was magic.

Both of them jumped as they heard an unexpected scream.

Kat straightened and turned toward the closest door. "It sounded like it came from here," she said. "Whose room is this?"

Van blinked, thinking, then his eyes widened in horror. "Nyah's," he rasped.

Kat went to the door and knocked loudly on it. "Nyah!" she called. "Are you hurt?"

A cry for help sounded, but it was stifled. Kat tried the door, but it was useless without the key card. "Go downstairs and get help," she commanded.

Van frowned and looked torn for a moment. "What about you? I can't just—"

"Go!" she shouted.

Something in her voice demanded obedience and he nodded. He turned and bolted down the hallway.

Kat stared at the door for a minute. She stepped back and took off her shoes. She took a deep, calming breath, centered herself, and everything around her fell away. She heard her heartbeat, rhythmic and steady. She focused all of her energy, and with amazing force and lightning speed, she launched into action and kicked the door open.

It crashed against the wall with a clash of cacophonous noise. She barreled inside to see Nyah half-clothed with a man on top of her, holding her arms pinned above her head. Blood ran from the corner of her mouth and a swollen red mark marred her cheek.

Rage, blind rage, the kind of rage that makes people crazy, filled Kat and she charged at the stranger. He pulled a knife from his pocket and held it to Nyah's throat, as if doing so would keep Kat at bay.

Kat's lip curled into a malevolent sneer. "You think that a girl who just kicked a locked door down is going to be intimidated by that?" she snarled. Her fist was between his eyes before he could even think, and he fell backwards off the bed, dropping his weapon. Nyah scrambled to her feet, clutching the sheet around her half-naked frame.

Enraged, the man stood and glowered at Kat with cold hatred. She circled him slowly, like a great cat stalking its prey. She gave him another cold, wicked smile. She stepped aside as he charged at her in an attempt to knock her down and she drove her elbow down hard between his shoulder blades, causing him to collapse to the floor again. She waited.

He stood quickly and tried to take a swing at her. She dodged it with expertise and landed a right jab to his pretty face. As he staggered back, she delivered a roundhouse kick to his chest. He fell back against the wall, and Nyah screamed out of alarm. Kat took the moment and launched at her attacker, dealing blows that would have made her a champion in *Fight Club*. She had him in a headlock before he knew what was happening, and he clawed at Kat's arm, gasping for air against her relentless grip.

"Kat!" Rochelle's voice shouted. She flew into the room. "Kat, stop! You're killing him!"

"He deserves to die," she replied mechanically.

"Maybe so, but you don't deserve to go to prison! Kat, let go!"

Van trooped in behind her with several security guards, and Kat released the man, who fell choking and gasping to the floor. Nyah collapsed onto the bed and started to sob. Van rushed to her and gathered her in his arms as the guards slapped handcuffs on the bleeding and incoherent attacker.

"Good lord, what happened?" Rochelle breathed. "I heard the commotion all the way down the hall."

Kat straightened her hair placidly, ignoring the blood that dripped from her split knuckles. "That man tried to rape Nyah."

Rochelle blinked in bewilderment. "And you just happened to be here?"

She nodded. "We were on our way back when we heard her scream."

"How did you get in?"

"I kicked the door open," she replied.

Rochelle's eyes bulged. "In an evening gown?" she exclaimed.

Kat looked down at the dress she'd forgotten she was wearing. She shrugged and went over to Nyah. Van rocked her back and forth and soothed her by singing softly.

"Nyah, did he hurt you?" Kat asked.

She looked up at Kat and shook her head. "No, you got here just in time. It was my fault." Tears rolled out of her eyes and she sobbed. "I was drinking. I let him in because I was lonely."

Kat shook her head and sat down next to her. She pushed some of her hair off of her face. "It wasn't your fault," she assured her. The sound of her voice was strangely soft even to her own ears, and it contrasted with her steely absence of emotion. "I know it feels like it was, but it wasn't."

Nyah sniffed. "You saved my life." She shook her head. "You were amazing."

Kat smiled grimly.

"We'll have to get a report from you, ma'am," one of the guards said to Nyah as the other dragged the attacker out of the room. "You'll need to go down to the police station."

"I'll take you," Van said, pressing a comforting kiss to her forehead. He helped her up and ran his hands up and down her arms in an attempt to quell her awful shaking. "Let's get you cleaned up and into some clothes, okay?"

She nodded and let him guide her to the bathroom.

Rochelle sighed and ran a hand through her hair. "I'd better go let the others know." She glanced at Kat in concern. "Will you be okay?"

Kat gave a solemn nod.

"You'll have to come to the station as well," the guard said to Kat. "Give your report."

Kat nodded, so calm it was almost eerie. Van watched her as he waited outside the bathroom for Nyah to clean up. She stood poised and alert, like a predator. He couldn't believe that, in the two minutes it had taken him to find security, she had busted the door open and apprehended the attacker all by herself. A shiver went up his spine. He'd thought Rochelle had been exaggerating a little when she'd said Kat was like a *Kill Bill* assassin. He realized now that she hadn't been. His beautiful, caring, exuberant Kat was lethal.

He saw that her knuckles were bleeding and he stepped forward cautiously. He didn't want to startle her when she was in battle mode. He had made that mistake once, and his nose still hurt from it. He slowly reached out and took her injured hands. He ran his fingers over hers. "You're bleeding."

She glanced down at her knuckles. "I hadn't noticed."

He closed his eyes and kissed her fingers, then wiped the blood off tenderly with his sleeve.

Kat's cast-iron composure seemed to slip and her eyes softened as she looked up at him.

He smiled and touched her face, seeing her defenses relax. "Thank you for helping Nyah," he said.

She shook her head. "I couldn't let what happened to me happen to her." She averted her eyes.

Nyah reentered the room and Van went to her and put his arm around her. "Are you ready?"

She nodded, still visibly shaken.

Kat followed them out the door and to the police station.

Chapter Seventeen

Kat had horrid nightmares and woke up drenched in a cold sweat with lingering images in her mind of the terrible men she had known throughout her life. She sighed and sat up, running her shaking fingers through her hair. She let her mind slowly return to the present, and the events of the night flooded her. She may have been calm and composed during the attack, but that had been her training. She'd gone to the place in her mind that locked out all feeling so that she could focus on the job at hand. Now that it was over, her tumultuous emotions wouldn't leave her alone.

Nyah had been very quiet for the remainder of the evening, and she clung to Van like he was the only thing keeping her sane. When they had finished at the police station and returned to the hotel, the other band members and Hank had swarmed them, all wanting answers. Kat had explained to Hank so that Nyah could be ushered away by Jack and not bothered. Jack insisted that Nyah sleep in his room, and she didn't protest. Van had gone with them to make sure that she would be all right. Kat didn't mind. She understood completely, but some small part of her was disappointed that she hadn't even been able to tell him goodnight.

She swung her legs out of bed, her throat feeling dry and constricted. Her glance fell on her evening gown, which was lying across a chair, and she smiled. She would have to put it in the garment bag with her Bleeding Passion jacket. It would be a wonderful memory. At least she hadn't gotten any blood on it.

She stood and walked quietly into the kitchen to get a drink of water, grateful that they had been given their own two-bedroom suite. That way she didn't have to listen to Rochelle's incessant snoring all night long. She frowned as she saw something shift out of the corner of her eye, and she whirled, prepared. She relaxed her defenses almost immediately, but her frown deepened. She abandoned her water glass and went over to the sofa, where a familiar figure lay sleeping.

"Van?" she whispered, touching his shoulder.

His eyes opened slowly and he gave her a tired smile. "Hey."

"What are you doing on the couch?"

"I came in after you went to bed. I told Rochelle I wanted to be here in case you needed me."

Kat raised her eyebrows in surprise. "But Nyah was the one attacked. You should be with her."

"I stayed with her until she went to sleep. Jack is with her. You confronted an all too familiar situation tonight. I wanted to make sure that you were all right." He didn't mention that seeing her so steely had unnerved him like she wouldn't believe. That would only make her feel bad.

Kat had learned what she'd learned to survive, to never be a victim again. She had done what she'd thought was necessary and, because she had done it, she had been able to save Nyah. It would be wrong of him to burden her with his concerns when she had just rescued one of his closest friends.

Nevertheless, it had troubled him to see her so cold and unrelenting. It contrasted with everything he knew of her.

She stared at him for a moment, as if unable to comprehend someone thinking that much about her. She averted her eyes like she always did when she felt self-conscious and confused.

Van smiled. "Nyah was very impressed with you. All she kept saying was how you looked like Keanu Reeves in *The Matrix*."

She chuckled dryly and knelt down in front of the couch.

He touched her cheek and let his eyes appraise her beautiful face. "Hank was impressed too. Lance said he spent the whole night cursing our own security crew. They are supposed to keep fans out of the part of the hotel we stay in. He couldn't believe that you fought the attacker off all by yourself, in an evening gown no less, kicked a door down barefoot, and came out virtually unscathed. He was also impressed with how calm and composed you were when telling him what happened."

She shrugged, feeling flattered, but at the same time wishing she had never had to learn the things she had done earlier. There was a part of her that she could switch off, enabling her to feel nothing. She wondered if she would ever feel like a whole person while she possessed that ability.

"Thank you for what you did tonight, Kat," Van said. "All of us will be eternally grateful."

She met his eyes and smiled, but knew it came off rather forced.

He frowned thoughtfully. "Are you all right?" She nodded, but he sighed. "No you're not. Don't lie to me, Kat. Not after everything we shared tonight."

She let out a large sigh of surrender and looked down. How was it that he could still know her so well? After all the time they'd spent apart? She had a good front she hid behind, and he saw straight through it like it didn't even exist.

He sat up. "Come here," he invited. He pulled the blanket back and wrapped it around both of them as she came up to sit beside him on the sofa. "Your skin is cold," he observed, pulling her close to him. "Are you having trouble sleeping?" He rested his chin on her shoulder.

She nodded, attempting to swallow the lump that had risen in her throat. She couldn't handle how well he knew her, and she couldn't handle his gentleness. It always made her feel like she was spinning out of control. He ran a hand down her hair and pressed a tender kiss to her temple. She sighed, and he reached for the remote control while keeping her nestled in the sanctuary of his arms. The television flicked on and *VH-1's Insomniac Music Theater* was playing.

Van smiled. "Here, we can watch this while I tell you juicy facts about all the artists."

Kat's uneasiness vanished. He never pried, never pushed. He didn't ask her to talk about what was bothering her because he knew that, if she wanted to, she would. Some of the cold, tortured feeling she had been experiencing since the attack dissipated as Van's ever-present warmth seeped into her. It cradled her heart in that feeling of acceptance he had always given her. Suddenly, she wanted to cry. She glanced at Van as he mentioned something about one of the members of Velvet Revolver. "Van?" she whispered.

There must have been something strange in her tone because he stopped and stared at her in concern. "What is it, sweetheart?"

She let out a shaky breath and couldn't find her words. She reached out and took his face in her hands, pressing her lips full against his. He responded instantly and she wrapped her arms around his neck, wanting to take his beauty and passion into herself so that she could make herself whole again.

Van's heart pounded erratically and he let out a slow breath when she pulled away. "What was that for?" he murmured, his voice husky with emotion.

She touched his face with her fingertips and her lovely blue-gray eyes turned glassy. "I just..." She swallowed. "Your kisses...it's like they make me feel alive. *You* make me feel alive, and I've felt dead inside for so long."

He stared down at her. "Forever is what I want to give you," he whispered. "An eternity of all that you've been denied." He looked down shyly. "Hopefully, there is room in there for my kisses as well."

She grinned and snuggled against him, resting her head on his chest. "Denying me your kisses would be much worse than anything else I've missed out on."

He wrapped his arms around her securely and smiled. They lapsed into comfortable silence as they watched the music videos play, and he savored having her there with him. She claimed his kisses made her feel alive, but in truth, she was the one that kept him breathing. He didn't understand how he had lived without her for so long. The thought of ever being without her again was so painful it was unbearable. He had to be with her. It was not a want; it was a need. A need essential to his survival.

* * * *

Kat stretched her shoulders out and yawned as she waited in the lobby for Van and the others. They were heading out for the video shoot soon, which Rochelle was very excited about. She had been jabbering on all morning about how fascinating it would be to see how an actual music video was made. The bell on the elevator chimed and Kat glanced at it as Jack and Nyah stepped out. She sported a horrible purple bruise across her cheek and Jack had his arm protectively around her shoulders.

"How am I supposed to do a video like this?" she asked, tears making their way down her cheeks. "I look absolutely awful."

He squeezed her in an effort to comfort her. "They can take it out in post production. You know that. Don't even worry about it."

Kat gave him an understanding smile when he glanced in her direction.

"Let's just get you on the bus, okay?" he asked. "Try and relax and don't worry so much. Everything will be fine."

Kat decided that she would follow them out. She was tired of standing around in the lobby when she could be sitting on the bus. She didn't know what Van was doing anyway. He had gone back to his suite early that morning to "get ready." She had no idea what that entailed, but he was taking forever and she was suffering from her inability to sleep soundly the night before. "I'm going to go get on the bus too," she told Rochelle. Rochelle nodded and Kat turned toward the door, following after Jack and Nyah.

Kat stepped back in surprise as Jack opened the door and reporters swooped in from all directions. Lights flashed like fireworks and she blinked as the sheer obnoxiousness of it assaulted her eyes.

"Miss Densmoore, can we have a word?"

"Is it true that you were attacked last night by a crazed fan?"

"I hear it was Van Marshall that hit you. Is that true?"

Nyah looked shell-shocked and she tried in vain to hide behind her brother.

Kat scowled and pushed in front of Nyah and Jack. She grabbed a hold of Nyah's arm. "She has no comment," she stated, bullying her way through the hoard and guiding Nyah behind her. Jack brought up the rear, keeping the reporters from attacking from behind.

"Miss Densmoore! Miss Densmoore!"

"Please, just a minute! Is it true you let the man in willingly? That you were in a drunken stupor?"

Kat saw Nyah flinch as if she'd been slapped, and she shoved the meddling reporter aside. "I said no comment, you idiot," she growled.

"Miss, who are you? Did you see what happened? Tell us what you saw."

Kat turned and grasped the reporter by his collar. "You're going to be seeing the tread of my boot across your forehead in a second. I said no comment. Get out of the way." She shoved him backwards and continued to pull Nyah toward the bus. They stumbled in, Jack hurling every curse word in the English language.

Nyah flopped into the nearest chair, her head in her hands. "How did they find out?" she murmured.

"How do they ever find out?" Jack spat. "They have friggin' radar."

Kat noticed that Nyah's hands were shaking badly.

"That one man asked me if Van was the one who attacked me. Where would they come up with something like that? It's ridiculous! Van would never hurt me!"

"They just want dirt," Kat muttered.

Nyah looked up at Kat. "Thank you," she said meekly. Kat waved it away, but Nyah shook her head. "No, I mean it. I don't know what I would have done if you hadn't been there last night."

Kat met Nyah's sincere eyes and smiled a little.

"I'm going to get something to drink," Jack declared. "You guys want anything?"

Kat held up her hand to signal a no.

"Scotch on the rocks," Nyah stated.

Kat smirked and started toward the back of the bus.

"Kat?" Nyah called.

Kat looked at her over her shoulder.

"Come here for a minute?"

She sighed and went over to her. Nyah motioned for her to sit next to her, and she obeyed.

Nyah let out a long, drawn out breath. "Look, I know I've been horrible to you, but you need to understand something. It was never you I hated. It was the memory of you from Van's past." She met Kat's eyes. "Van's always loved you. I could never be you, no matter how hard I tried. I was jealous of you when you first came to our crew because I saw how Van looked at you. When I found out you were the woman I could never be, I knew my chances with Van were over. I loved Van. I really did. I know I'm the one that messed up our relationship. I wasn't there for him. I didn't treat him right. I realize that, but it doesn't make being second hurt any less, you know?"

Kat looked down, saying nothing. Van had really loved her all that time?

"What you did for me last night, I could never repay," Nyah continued. "You helped me when I have never been anything but awful to you."

"Nyah, I couldn't just stand there and do nothing."

She frowned. "You said something to me last night after the attack. You told me that you knew it felt like it was my fault, but it wasn't. What did you mean? How could you have known?"

Kat sighed. "I was raped once," she admitted. "And a few others have tried."

Nyah's eyes widened, and she stared at Kat. "That's terrible."

Kat smiled wryly. "Why do you think I know three different styles of martial arts?"

The door of the bus burst open and Rochelle, Lance, and Van flew in. "Good lord!" Lance exclaimed. "It's like a feeding frenzy out there!"

Van went to Nyah immediately. "Are you all right?" he asked in concern.

She smiled up at him. "I'm okay. Kat took care of me."

Van looked down at Kat and the expression in his eyes made her heart flip. Gratitude mixed with wonder. She averted her gaze, feeling her cheeks flush. She had learned everything she had in order to protect herself. It had been a relatively selfish decision. She hadn't thought that at some point, maybe her skills could also help others.

"Kat, you should have been in law enforcement, I swear," Rochelle said.

Jack brought Nyah her drink, and Van frowned. "Nyah, it's like seven in the morning."

She glanced up at him and scowled. "Ask me if I care." He chuckled.

"I'm buying drinks for Kat tonight," Jack said with a grin.

Kat shook her head. "Not necessary. I don't drink."

"Oh, come on, Kat," Rochelle urged. "One time won't hurt you. You went on a date and beat up a guy all in one night."

"And you attacked a reporter the next day," Nyah added.

Van frowned, and Kat rolled her eyes. "I did not attack

him. I just got him out of the way."

Lance and Van laughed.

"Needless to say, you've pretty much been protecting our band," Jack went on. "I think you deserve a night of free drinks."

Kat heaved a sigh. "I'll think about it."

"I am so holding you to that," Rochelle said with a grin.

Van chuckled and slipped his arm around Kat's waist. He pressed a kiss to the top of her head. "Be sure to stand in view at the video shoot today," he whispered. "I want to be able to see my inspiration while I perform."

Kat's cheeks burned with color and she bit her bottom lip shyly. She wondered if she would ever get used to him saying things like that to her. He chuckled and ran his hand down her hair before heading toward the kitchen. She watched him go and sighed to herself.

Her memory briefly conjured up his kisses and caresses from the night before. Her imagination took her thoughts further before she could stop it, and she felt a wave of heat sweep through her at the brazen images her mind conjured. She shook her head and decided to just sit down and stare at the fabric Rochelle's shirt was made of instead. She was not healthy for herself. She shouldn't be allowed alone with her own mind. It was becoming a dangerous thing.

Chapter Eighteen

The video shoot was at a place called The Cloisters, which was a branch of the Metropolitan Museum of Art. It was a medieval-style structure set high on a hilltop overlooking the Hudson River. Around a gorgeous courtyard filled with flowers, herbs, and a marble fountain sat chapels, monastic cloisters and other structures built in 12-15th century style. The band's performance was taking place right in the middle of the garden, but that was to be filmed last.

A table had been set up out of the way for the band members and crew to sit at when they weren't immediately needed. Lance and Erik were playing Slap Jack again, but they had come to the amazing conclusion that their band mate next to them, who was attempting to read over the itinerary, was named Jack, so they kept slapping him spontaneously.

Kat had brought her book along, but she couldn't keep her eyes off of what the crew was doing. She watched as the lighting was set up for some close-ups of Nyah. Nyah waited patiently by with her arms folded. It was unusual for her to be waiting so placidly. Usually, she would be acting completely irritated or put out at having to wait for any duration of time at all, but she seemed unperturbed.

Kat also noticed that she had opted out of her usual revealing outfits and was wearing a red and black corset top with a long, elegant black skirt. Her shining ebony hair fell around her shoulders like a blanket and Kat couldn't help but feel bad for her. The bruise on her cheek was still very apparent, despite the best attempts of the makeup artist. Digitally removing it would be the only option.

"What are you thinking about?" Rochelle asked, coming

to sit next to her. She opened up a cola that she had re-trieved from a nearby ice chest and took a drink.

Kat looked at her. "Oh, I was just watching everyone work. It's strange to be sitting here observing it instead of being part of it."

Rochelle smiled. "I know. I've been getting random foot-age, though. Seeing parts of how a music video is made will be interesting to viewers, don't you think?"

Kat nodded. "I was thinking about doing the same thing. There are a lot of other band DVDs out there that do that." She sighed as she glanced at Nyah again. "I feel bad for Nyah. She seems so not herself. I mean, granted, her usual self is far from pleasant, but I would rather her be subdued because of something other than what happened to her last night. I wouldn't wish that on anyone."

"It's just a good thing you walked by when you did. She could be a lot worse off."

"It scares me how I can just turn my emotions off and go into attack mode," Kat admitted quietly. "It felt danger-ous...deadly."

Rochelle looked over at her. "We all possess the ability to tap into our dark side. Some people are just forced, by cir-cumstance, to learn how to live in both worlds. Unfortunate-ly, that's what you had to do, Kat."

"I don't like feeling dark, though. I miss feeling free and light like I used to." She smiled to herself. "The only time I feel like that is when I'm with Van."

Rochelle grinned and leaned over to whisper mischie-vously, "Then let him be the light to your darkness."

Kat couldn't help but snicker. "That sounds so romance novel."

"Don't knock it till you try it. You deserve a romance nov-el relationship."

Kat laughed. "Romance novels are nothing but smut."

Rochelle raised her eyebrows playfully. "You could defi-nitely use a bit of that too."

Kat averted her gaze as she felt her cheeks turn hot. She didn't really need to be encouraged in that department. She was tending, against her own will, to have smutty enough thoughts without Rochelle helping her out. She glanced over at Van, who was across the courtyard getting his makeup done. She gave a soft sigh.

He wore a pair of low-riding, black pants and a dark blue shirt unbuttoned three buttons down. He had a black necktie hanging loosely around his neck and the makeup artist was making his eyes very black. It made sense. The song they were doing the video for was a dark, melodic ballad. Kat looked down at her own outfit and she frowned in distaste. Geez, had she always been so boring? All she had on was a pair of blue jeans and a white, short-sleeved shirt. She looked so plain in the midst of all this gothic beauty.

The director started calling out directions for Nyah's close-up shots and Kat focused her attention back to her. She watched them progress through the series of shots and briefly thought that Nyah, bruise and all, was a very beautiful woman. It was unreal to think that she felt threatened by the mere memory of Kat. She had never thought that she'd made such an enormous impression on Van. He had told her that he'd loved her his whole life. She didn't even know what to say to that.

"Dude! Would you knock it off!" Jack shouted.

Kat looked over just in time to see him wallop Lance in the back of the head with the flat of his hand.

Lance looked stunned. "What the crap?" he cried.

"How do you like it?" Jack asked in irritation. "Maybe you should play Slap Lance instead. That sounds like a great game to me."

Erik snorted. "Jack, don't be an idiot. There are no cards in a deck called a Lance."

Lance started to laugh, and Jack scowled.

Kat smirked and looked back over to the shoot. Nyah was standing at the marble fountain, trailing her fingers absently in the water as she sang along with her own voice. The director then had her change into a different dress she had brought, this one simple and black with spaghetti straps. When she returned, he ushered her over to a tree and had her sit underneath it, singing the same verse she had just sung over again. As the shots finished, the lighting crew moved on and started to set up for Van's close-up shots.

Nyah walked over to Van as she finished, and he smiled at her. He pulled her into his arms and held her close for a moment, pressing a kiss to the top of her head. He murmured something to her that must have been just what she needed to hear because she wrapped her arms around him and squeezed him hard.

The day progressed slowly. Kat continued to watch the shoot, paying rapt attention to whatever happened to be going on with Van. His close-up shots were done with him walking down a corridor around the courtyard, which was surrounded by stone pillars, and standing in an ornately carved stone archway leading into an abbey. He had performed that shot shirtless, much to Kat's enjoyment.

Van was no body builder by any means. He was thin by nature, but his body had enough lithe muscle to make her want to stare for the rest of her life. Everything about him was pure decadence. The unsure, lanky boy from her past had grown into the very embodiment of sex. It made her smile, made her burn, but most of all, made her proud. Proud of the man he had become.

He could have done like so many others similar to him, retreated into the darkness and let his issues become his crutch. He could have given up on all of his dreams, but he had pushed himself beyond his limits. He had achieved so much more than most people. Her heart swelled with pride when she looked at him.

The director changed his mind halfway through the day and decided that they would go ahead and shoot the band's performance anyway. This greatly agitated all members of the crew as they had to clear out all of the equipment and tables they had set up in the courtyard and move everything helter-skelter around in obscure locations.

Kat helped the crew move the table they had all been sitting at, then stood back to observe some more. She had been recording things off and on all day, but was letting Rochelle do most of it. She was enjoying just being an onlooker for once. Suddenly, an arm snaked around her waist and she was pulled up against someone's chest. She looked down at the hand on her side and saw familiar black nail polish. She smiled.

"Ugh, I haven't seen you all day. This is torturous," Van murmured. He nuzzled his nose against her neck.

Kat smiled and closed her eyes as she leaned back against him. "What do you mean you haven't seen me? I've been right here."

"Yes, but I've only been able to gaze at you from afar, and that is just not good enough." He turned her around so that he could look into her eyes. He was back in his blue shirt, and the color, along with his dark eye makeup, made his eyes look pale.

"So you're going to do the performance after all?"

He snorted. "Apparently so, which, if you ask me, is completely ridiculous. We only have about four hours of daylight left. It will take a million years just to get the location lit correctly. They have to do close-up shots of all the band members before we do the entire performance and the only way we're going to get it all done in time is if absolutely nothing goes wrong and, inevitably, something always does."

She tried to give him a comforting smile. "How is Nyah?"

"As well as can be expected, I guess. She's very quiet."

Kat nodded, then smiled in hopes of lightening the mood. "It's been fun watching you guys all day. Usually I'm behind the camera. It's nice to just be able to watch."

"Well I'm glad you're having a good time because you're about to witness pure chaos and pandemonium as soon as we start trying to get this stupid performance done."

She gave him a hug just as she heard the director start yelling for him. He gave her a wearied expression and she giggled. "See you sometime in the future," she teased.

"Sometime before I'm dead, I hope." He gave her a quick kiss and swaggered back out into the courtyard.

The performance did indeed take forever. They managed to get it done right as the sun was setting, which gave everyone momentary hope, but then the director announced that he wanted to take several shots of the band members in the dark. This was not met with happy responses, but everyone grudgingly obliged. Hank came up to Kat and Rochelle and told them that he was heading back to the hotel if they wanted to go with him. Rochelle wanted to stay and record more, but an idea struck Kat as she glanced over at Van and saw him run his fingers through his hair, looking utterly exhausted. She took Hank up on his offer and left the set without saying anything, a sly smile on her lips.

* * * *

Van left the elevator tired and confused. He didn't understand why Kat had just disappeared. She hadn't even said goodbye. One second she had been there, watching him, and the next she had vanished without saying anything at all. It didn't make sense to him, and he wasn't going to pretend that it didn't bother him. He'd asked Rochelle, but all she'd said was that Kat had decided to go back to the hotel because there was no point in her staying there anymore. What did *that* mean? Had he upset her in some way without even knowing it?

With a heavy sigh, Van reached into his pocket and pulled out his key card. He slid it through the slot on the door of his room and entered slowly. He closed the door behind him and gave a startled shout as he looked up. His entire room was filled with candles of all sizes and colors, flickering and glimmering in the dark of the room.

He blinked and raised an eyebrow. "Hello?" he called tentatively. He stepped into the middle of the room with caution and frowned. Did he smell incense? "Um...hello?" he called again. Suddenly, the first strains of "It's Been Awhile" started to play and his eyes widened. He jumped as someone lunged at him out of nowhere and arms wrapped around his neck.

Before he could even think, he had soft lips pressing against his, and his eyes drifted closed in bliss as the taste of chocolate filled his mouth. He let out a groan as he reached up and tangled his fingers in Kat's hair. He rested his forehead against hers and sighed. "That was, by far, the most erotic thing I've ever experienced," he whispered.

"I was attempting to recreate our first kiss." Her smile was playful in the candlelight and much more reminiscent of the girl he had once known.

"I remember it being slightly less...forceful," he said with a chuckle.

"Well, I'm older...and deprived."

He wrapped his arms around her and dipped her dramatically. She let out a shriek and giggled. He grinned and gazed into her eyes. "And you're even more beautiful." He lowered his lips to hers with slow deliberateness. She wrapped one arm around his neck and let her other hand rest on his shoulder. She giggled again, obviously pleased with her success.

Suddenly, the door burst open, sending blinding light spilling into the dark room. Van winced at the unexpected entry and assault on his eyes, and he let go of Kat without thinking. She gave a shout and tightened her grip around his neck as she fell, bringing him down on top of her.

"Hey Van, have you seen Kat? I—whoa...." Jack stopped in mid-sentence and his eyes widened as he looked down at the two of them. "Aw man, my bad." He turned away quickly. "I thought, 'cause the door wasn't closed all the way and everything..." He pointed to the door. "I'll just go and you can call me when you're finished. I owe Kat a round of free drinks and all..." He grumbled something unintelligible as he all but fled from the room.

Van started laughing and he looked down at Kat, who was sprawled beneath him. She laughed too and his heart melted. He eased himself down so that he was lying next to her on his side, propping his head up with his elbow. He watched her laugh, taking in all of her infinite beauty.

"Well that wasn't part of my plan." Kat sniggered.

He grinned. "Your plan," he muttered. "I thought you were mad at me or something. I couldn't figure out why you had left the set without even saying goodbye."

She turned her eyes to meet his. "I wanted to surprise you. Toward the end there, you looked so exhausted. Hank came over to Rochelle and me and offered to take us back to the hotel." She shrugged. "You've been so sweet to me through all this. I just wanted to repay you in some small way."

He reached out and ran his fingers across her cheek and down her jaw. "Rochelle told me that you'd said there was no point in staying at the shoot anymore."

She chuckled and shook her head. "She's so evil." She groaned. "I think I ate about half a bag of those stupid chocolates waiting for you. I didn't know when you were coming back, so I just kept popping them in. I think I made myself sick."

"It was worth it." He leaned in to give her another soft kiss. "Thank you for the surprise. It was very thoughtful."

She bit her bottom lip, suddenly feeling embarrassed. "I just wanted to do something nice for you. I wanted to make you smile."

He kissed down her jaw to her neck. "You always make me smile."

Kat closed her eyes and tilted her head so that he could kiss his fill. A soft sigh escaped her lips. He smelled divine, even after a hard day of working on the video.

"I love you," he whispered against her ear.

Her stomach flopped like it enjoyed doing, and she could do nothing but hold him tighter. She didn't know what to say when he told her that. Love. Love from a man like Van. Love for her. It was almost unbelievable. He was the sexiest gothic rocker in the entire country, and yet, he claimed to love a girl in blue jeans and a white shirt who had severe issues and had almost killed a man the night before. It totally didn't make sense to her. If she was him, she would be running far, far away from her and all her infinite baggage.

She couldn't say it back to him. She never could. It would lodge in her throat right behind a looming wall of paralyzing fear. She hated that she couldn't express what she so obviously felt, and she hated that he had to always be left out in the cold when he made his confession.

"Are you going to let Jack buy you drinks tonight?" he asked with a playful twinkle in his eyes.

She appreciated how he never pressed, and how he always changed the subject with ease right when she started to feel like she would suffocate. "I don't know. What's the big deal anyway? Who cares if I drink?"

"I think he's just trying to tell you thank you for helping his sister. We should go. It'll be fun. Just get one beer. That will appease him, and one won't bother you that bad."

She smiled up at him and nodded.

He stood and offered her his hand. He helped her into a standing position and they blew out the candles before heading over to Jack's room.

Kat did order a beer that night and allowed herself to relax for the first time in too long. Before she knew it, one beer had turned into four beers, a margarita, and a few shots of something back at the hotel Lance had made that he liked to call Pimp Juice.

She woke up the next morning with a massive headache, her stomach roiling like an angry ocean, and a vague memory of dancing on a table and a game of darts wearing only her bra. She groaned, knowing she had made a complete fool out of herself and that Rochelle would have left the camera on all night. She vowed to never, ever drink again.

Chapter Nineteen

A week went by with very little disturbance. The reporters gradually faded and Nyah's incident was forgotten by most of the public. Kat, however, had made the front page of one tabloid. It had a picture of her holding the reporter by the collar with the headline: *Feminine Fury- One Member of Bleeding Passion Takes Matters Into Her Own Hands*. That had been a great source of amusement for everyone and Kat had kept a copy. It wasn't every day your wrath made headlines.

They had finished the video shoot and made their way around the East Coast, now finding themselves in Florida. Kat was sitting in Van's dressing room reading her Edgar Alan Poe book while he got ready for that night's performance. He glanced over at her in the mirror and smiled to himself.

"What are you looking at?" Kat teased.

"The most beautiful woman in the world." He turned away from the mirror and stood, going over to her. "I can't concentrate when you're around. You drive me to distraction."

She reached up to touch his face as he lowered his lips to hers. She threaded her fingers through his soft hair and sighed. "I don't think I'm going to tape anything tonight," she said when she pulled away. "I have enough concert footage to last my entire life. I think I'm just going to watch you perform." She grinned. "I love to watch you. Your passion amazes me. You truly do bleed passion, Van."

He framed her face with his gentle hands and his expression grew serious. "You are my passion, Katrina."

She raised her eyebrows. "No one's ever called me Katrina unless I was in trouble."

He smiled. "Your name is extraordinary. Just like you." He kissed her again.

Kat wanted to crawl inside of him and live there forever. His lips moved over hers with such tenderness. His gentle seduction made her feel like her blood was on fire. It made her hunger for things she had thought dead to her. She knotted her fingers in his hair and tugged slightly, drawing a surprised sound of pleasure from him. He wrapped his arms around her shoulders and held her close as he painstakingly explored her mouth.

"Kat!" Rochelle cried, barreling into the room. Her eyes widened and she stopped. "Whoa there! Sorry."

Van pulled away, and Kat blinked, trying to remember where she was and what was going on. She frowned playfully at Rochelle. "What is it?"

A worried frown creased Rochelle's brow. "We're being sent home," she stated sadly.

Kat stared at her, uncomprehending. "What? Why? We have a week and a half left."

Rochelle snorted. "I guess Paul and Arnie are being sent on some huge assignment and they need us back there to pick up their slack. They said we should have ample footage by now and a week and a half won't matter."

Kat continued to stare forward, her chest feeling like someone was squeezing her heart.

"We leave in the morning," Rochelle concluded.

Kat looked down. She had known that she would have to go home, but she had planned on having a week and a half more with Van first. She didn't want to return to L.A. She hated L.A. She knew it was stupid, but that city was a symbol for everything bad that had happened in her life. Tears stung her eyes. She suddenly felt all kinds of twisted up inside and couldn't make heads ot tails of any of it.

Rochelle sighed and glanced at Van. "I'm sorry, Kat." She turned and left them to one another.

Van felt like he had just been dealt a nasty and unexpected blow that left him numb and disoriented. He slipped his arm around Kat, pressing a kiss to her temple.

"This sucks," Kat whispered, sounding feeble.

"Why don't you stay?" He hated that his voice carried a slight pleading note. He wanted to be strong for her, but the thought of not having her by his side was so painful that he couldn't help it.

"I can't stay, Van," she murmured. "I have a job I need to do. I can't leave Rochelle with the entire load. That wouldn't be fair. Besides." She forced a smile. "I want to know I was the chief editor of your DVD."

He gave a small smile and touched her cheek.

"How much longer are you on tour?" she asked.

"About a month," he replied. "I promise to come see you when we're finished."

She nodded, tears still burning behind her eyes. She tried to swallow the lump in her throat, but it only made her want to choke. His words of ages ago, *"I promise I'll call you,"* echoed through her mind, and she felt sick. This felt too familiar, and she couldn't help but think the outcome would be the same. He was a famous musician. How could he not get wrapped up and distracted by his life? She would be naive to believe differently.

"Van, you guys are on in fifteen," one of the roadies announced, popping his head in the door.

Kat stood. "I'd better go find a good place to stand. We can talk more afterward."

He took her hand and pressed a kiss to her palm, but could offer no words. She forced another smile and left. He sighed and went to his mirror. He stared at his reflection for a moment, then scowled and started to apply black eye makeup almost savagely, his artistic attempt to reflect his sudden dark mood.

* * * *

Kat's hands were shaking as she packed up her last suitcase. She had an oppressive weight crushing her, and she had been fighting tears all morning. She silently cursed herself, wondering what had happened to her strong resolve. Now she just felt like an emotional fool. She sat down on her bed with a sigh and waited. She had already said goodbye to the rest of the band, and Lance was helping Rochelle get all of the equipment in order.

The band was supposed to leave that afternoon for their next stop, making it impossible for Van to go with Kat to the airport. Lance had told her that he would be stopping by her room shortly. Now, she waited, staring blankly down at her hands in her lap. She felt someone's presence, and she glanced up to see Van standing in the doorway. He was swathed entirely in black, with even an ankle length black trench coat hugging his elegant body.

His eyes were shaded with thick, black eyeliner and dark shadow, a look that she hadn't seen him wear in everyday life since high school. He wore his makeup on stage and during the video shoots. The only thing she had ever seen him wear in day-to-day life was sometimes a thin smudge of eyeliner. Her heart twisted painfully as he met her eyes, his dark hair falling gently around his beautiful shoulders.

Van let out a small sigh. "Forgive my dreary appearance," he said softly. "It's the only way I know how to express what I feel right now."

She forced a smile. "You look like a vampire," she tried to tease.

He gave her a smile, just as forced. "You'd better watch your neck then."

She snorted. "You can bite me any day."

His smile remained strained and he sat next to her. He took her hands in his and caressed her fingers. He closed his eyes, trying to memorize the softness of her skin. "Stay," he whispered.

Van was careful with the world. He only ever let them see so much of him—the confident, poised rock star. It was only when he played and when he was with Kat that he was completely open, holding nothing back, vulnerable to assault and not caring about it. He wondered if she knew just how much he belonged to her. He would do anything for her, lie down and die for her if she asked him to. His life had been hers for many years.

"You know I can't," she replied dismally.

He continued to look down, unable to meet her eyes. He felt tears and let them come. He had never been one who could stifle his emotions easily. He felt too much. His emotions had always been like a volatile tempest, careening this way and that.

"But how can I lose you once I've found you again?" he whispered. "You don't understand. I hated myself for so long for letting you go. I got a second chance, to make it right. To make right all of the pain that you suffered at my expense."

She frowned. "Van—"

He shook his head. "I wasn't there. I should have been there. I should have protected you. How am I supposed to protect you when you're so far away from me? I never want you away from me." He squeezed his eyes shut. "Kat, I am basically just a selfish man." He braved a look up into her eyes. "I ache without you." He always had.

The emptiness he had suffered for so long was because of her absence. Only she had ever made him feel like a whole person, even with his awful anxiety and his bizarre symbolism and his overly intense emotions. There was no way he could ever express the loss he felt when she was not with him. Nothing could ever replace it or make it lessen. That emptiness he had felt for years, it was the space in his heart he kept solely for her. She had bought that piece of his heart along with six guitar strings nine years ago.

Kat couldn't deal with his pain. It was her one weakness. He was her weakness and her strength, and she knew that didn't make sense, but she was tired of trying to make sense of things.

She was beginning to realize that some of the best things in life may not have to make complete sense all of the time. She could not plot out her course and control every step she took. It was impossible and unhealthy to even try. She realized Rochelle had been trying to get her to see that for some time, but it took Van to make her understand.

She stared at his beautiful face. His tears ran unheeded through his black eye makeup, leaving trails down his cheeks. His gray eyes were somber and she briefly thought that he looked like a rainstorm. All grays and blacks, raining tears. She wrapped her arms around him and held him close. "You said yourself that we'd see one another in a month," she stated, attempting to be cheerful. In the back of her mind, though, even as she tried to silence them, her meddlesome defenses were screaming not to count on it. He was a rock star. One month could turn into six, six to a year. They could grow apart. He could find someone else. He could...

She firmly told herself to shut up.

"Torture," he stated.

She sighed and nuzzled against his neck. She breathed in his patchouli smell and her eyes drifted closed. She fought a shiver. His voice. So melodic and pure, the tool of his craft; it

always sounded like a caress. Hearing pain beneath its resonance made her heart ache in a way she was unfamiliar with.

His hands were caressing her back, soft and tender like
always. The tightness around her heart increased until it hurt
acutely, then it fell away like a knot uncoiling as realization
and acceptance washed over her. The hopes and the maybes
and the what-ifs didn't matter. If nothing else came from all
of this, she knew Van was alive, and he had made her remember what it was like to enjoy life again, to allow herself
to feel again. That was a gift. *He* was a gift. And, suddenly, it
wasn't such a scary thing to admit. "Van," she murmured. "I
love you."

Van didn't breathe for several heartbeats. Then, he slowly moved away to look at her. He cupped her face in his
hands, his eyes reflecting both surprise and passion. "Oh,
Kat. I could never tell you in a thousand lifetimes how much
I love you."

He pressed his lips to hers softly, but with a deep intensity that could only belong to Van. His kisses were like the music he played, tantalizing and seductive with a dark sensuality that always made Kat want more of him.

A soft knock sounded on the door. "Kat?" Rochelle's voice
called tentatively. "I'm sorry, but we have to go."

Kat sighed and pulled away from Van. She looked up into
his sad eyes and wanted to burst into tears, but she was determined to stay strong. She could cry later when she was on
the plane. She reached up and caressed his cheek. "I love
you," she whispered. "I think I always have."

He closed his eyes at her touch and a small smile graced
his lips. "I'll call you tonight and every night until you're back
in my arms again. Unless I start to drive you insane."

She laughed a little.

"You still have my CDs, don't you?"

She nodded. He had given her a multitude of music to listen to of his favorite bands, and she had the CDs in the case
in her backpack. "I can give them back. I just forgot—"

He shook his head. "No. On the HIM album, Razorblade
Romance, listen to track number four."

"Okay." She stood and gathered her things, steeling her
resolve to be strong. Hank escorted them to the parking lot
where a cab waited to take them to the airport. Kat looked
up instinctively to the window of her hotel room and saw Van

standing there, like living art, dark and strong and so very exquisite. He reminded her of Brandon Lee in *The Crow* with the way his makeup had streaked, and she had to look away to fight back an overwhelming wave of grief that she hadn't expected. She got in the car and stared straight ahead as the driver slowly put distance between her and the man she had thought lost to her. Her best friend, her dark poet and musician, the man she loved. The only man she'd ever loved.

She swallowed and opened up her backpack. She removed her CD player and popped in the one Van had instructed her to listen to. She turned it to track four and the lyrics assaulted her ears with their words of love and devotion. Kat didn't make it to the plane without crying. She burst into tears halfway to the airport and cried like a lunatic all the way back to L.A, the place she hated. Her prison.

Chapter Twenty

Four months later

It was torture putting the Bleeding Passion DVD togeth-er. The wonderful kind of torture that nearly drove a person crazy. Kat sat in the editing room all hours of the day, cut-ting and splicing and re-living those sweet weeks of her life.

Bushman Productions had delayed Kat and Rochelle's project for several months to send them on a ridiculous as-signment shooting footage of lake trout. Hours upon hours of lake trout. They had spent the better part of two weeks holed up in a cabin with a half-crazed hillbilly who apparently had tons of money and a passion for fishing. He had enlisted Bushman to help make his documentary. It was not a very glamorous job after being on tour with a rock band.

Finally, after satisfying the man's eccentric wishes, Kat and Rochelle had been allowed to return to the Bleeding Pas-sion DVD. That had been three months ago. Three months wasted of splicing shots on fish.

Kat had been disappointed, but not surprised when Van had told her he would not be able to see her after the tour. The band had been trying to schedule a European tour for the better part of the year and finally succeeded. Unfortu-nately, that meant they had to launch into it right away. Kat didn't blame him. It was his job and his life. True to his word, he did call her every night. She missed him, but she couldn't say she was surprised. He was a rock star. Romance took a back seat to that.

So, she busied herself with her martial arts training, as it was the only consistent thing she really had, and filled her days with footage from the road.

For all intents and purposes, she should be close to finished by now, but she kept re-doing her work, never satisfied. No one knew the real reason why she kept going over it
again and again. No one but Rochelle, who always knew. She
couldn't bear to let go of it. It was still real when she
watched it, the magic of falling in love and feeling free from
the oppression of life. If she let that go, her life would return
to what it had always been and she couldn't bear that. She
just couldn't. So instead, she made up excuses, telling her
boss that she'd made a mistake, had been sloppy, or the film
hadn't edited properly. And she watched the man she loved
over and over, like a depraved, obsessed fan, longing for just
one more second of his gentle touch.

* * * *

Van stood backstage listening to the roar of the crowd
before the final encore. Germany. It wasn't so much different from London, or New York, or any other place for that
matter. A small smile touched his lips. The only performance
that had ever really been different had been that one in
Turnbeck, Arizona. Ozzy Osbaum and his crazy, big-busted
mother. He grinned, remembering Kat as she sat by the
stage at sunset. He sighed and his smile faded.

She plagued him constantly. He wished with all his heart
that she could be with him. He would love to show her Europe. He knew she would like foggy London at night, and he
wanted to take her Notre Dame Cathedral in Paris. She was a
fan of beautiful things, and there were so many beautiful
things in Europe. He had no desire to visit them alone.

He had many friends on this side of the world that he
would love to introduce her to. Just two days ago, he had
met up with some good friends of his in Finland. All he had
been able to think about was how much fun Kat would have
with all of them. There was never a second that ticked by
that he wasn't thinking about her. He felt like half a person.

"Van?"

Van glanced up at Lance, who gave him a questioning
look.

"Are you all right? Panic bothering you?"

He shook his head, dispelling his thoughts. "No, I'm fine."
He threw his shoulders back and went out on stage, forcing

himself to think of his music and not his beautiful Kat. It was not easy to do.

* * * *

Kat had been sitting in the editing room for the better part of an hour, just staring. She was two seconds away from being finished and she couldn't bring herself to do it. She had run out of excuses, but she still couldn't do it.

"Kat?" Rochelle's voice called as she came into the room. "What are you still doing in here? Are we going out tonight or what?"

Kat turned in her chair and met Rochelle's eyes. "I'm finished," she murmured.

Rochelle raised her eyebrows. "Seriously?"

She looked down. "Well, almost. I have one scene to add and I can't bring myself to do it."

"Which one?" Rochelle went to stand behind Kat's chair.

Kat turned back to the computer and played the scene. It was one of the final ones Rochelle had gotten before they had left. She had filmed everyone filing backstage after the show, and they, one by one, looked at the camera and waved or smiled. Van was the last in line and seeing Rochelle standing there with a camera in his face had caught him off guard. He gave the camera a somewhat bashful smile that melted Kat's heart every time she watched it.

Rochelle grinned. "That was so Jake," she commented.

"That's why I like it so much."

Rochelle glanced down at her. "It's not symbolic, you know?"

Kat looked up at her with a frown.

"Just because you're finished with the DVD doesn't mean that you and Van are finished."

She sighed in defeat. It was useless trying to hide anything from Rochelle. "How can we even work?" she murmured. "This isn't how relationships are."

"And how are they supposed to be? Last time I checked, there wasn't a set criteria. Every relationship is unique to the couple. Van's a celebrity. It would be the same if you were dating Brad Pitt."

Kat raised an eyebrow. "No, if I was dating Brad Pitt I would have died from shock, and there wouldn't even be a relationship."

Rochelle giggled. "Just don't forget who Van is, Kat. He's so loyal. He pined for you for years. He couldn't even be with Nyah because of you! He's not going to just leave you." She placed her hands on Kat's shoulders. "Finish the DVD, Kat. I'll wait for you outside."

Kat sighed and watched the scene one more time. She paused it on Van's face and stared at him for somewhere around a whole minute before she managed to add the scene to the rest of the footage and finalize it. She stared at the completed prototype in her hand for the longest time, then put it in her bag. She would drop it off to her boss on the way out.

* * * *

Nyah walked through the bus and frowned as she saw Van at the table surrounded by chocolates of all sorts. He was dumping chocolate syrup into a glass of milk by the bucket loads. She raised an eyebrow and slid into the booth across from him. "You know, most people drown their sorrows in alcohol."

He glanced up at her, sullen, and said nothing.

Nyah sighed heavily. "Van," she blurted, "you suck."

He frowned and looked up at her. "Well, thanks," he muttered.

She shook her head. "I mean, you always sound wonderful because you're talented, but you're gutless."

"I'm...gutless?"

"You have no soul, no passion. Your hundreds of millions of fans don't notice because they adore you, but I notice. I know you, Van, and so does everyone else in this band, but no one else has the guts to say anything to you. You haven't been the same since Kat left." She hated that she had to be the one to say this to him. She hated that she even cared. In the past, she would have jumped at the opportunity and tried to use it to her advantage, but she knew that would be stupid and selfish. Van loved Kat. He always had and, because Nyah loved Van, she would surrender him to Kat so he could be happy.

"I haven't seen you perform with the kind of passion that you had when she was here," she continued. "Since she's been gone it's been like watching a shadow of you perform. You go through the motions, but you're heart's not there. You wear your black eye makeup every day, which is so not like you."

He snorted. "You told me you liked my black eye makeup. Maybe I was doing it for you."

She gave him a pointed glare. "Oh get off it, Van! You're trying to get drunk off of chocolate!"

"Well what do you want me to do?" he snarled. "I'm so sorry! I just won't think about her anymore! Will that make you happy?"

"No!" she exclaimed. It wouldn't make her happy. It should, but it wouldn't. She couldn't stand to see him so miserable. "You can't keep doing this! You need to be with her, Van."

He looked a little bit puzzled. He was probably surprised that she wasn't being sarcastic or snide. He sighed. "How am I supposed to accomplish that?"

"Postpone the tour."

"I can't postpone the tour. All of our fans are counting on us."

She huffed in frustration. "You are a rock god. Those people idolize you. Some of them even idolize the rest of us, but most of them idolize you. They're not going to go away. They'll just scream louder when you come back. You forget, we call the shots here, Van. Don't let yourself lose your passion for this life. If you do, it'll just become a job to you, and you know that's not what music is about."

Van sighed, close to surrender. "Well, I'm not deciding anything on my own. It has to be unanimous, like always."

"We already voted," she stated.

He stared at her in surprise.

She reached across the table and took his hands in hers. "Don't make the same mistake I did," she said. "Don't let the best thing in your life get so far out of your reach that when you go to grasp for it, it's gone."

He met her eyes, then turned his hands in hers so that he was holding them. "I just wish I could bring her with me somehow."

The smallest of smiles touched Nyah's lips. "Oh, that reminds me, Hank needs to discuss something with you."

* * * *

There were certain times when Kat dearly loved her best friend. They had made plans to go to a club Rochelle had been dying to go to, but Rochelle had let the opportunity go so that she could reminisce with Kat instead. They were sitting in the living room of their apartment, Rochelle with a quarter pounder and Kat with a gyro, watching their senior class video.

"You are in, like, every one of these scenes!" Rochelle laughed as she stuffed a french fry in her mouth.

Kat rolled her eyes. "That's not my fault. I didn't do the editing. Vince Carpenter did."

"Oh man! That dude was obsessed with you!"

"Tell me about it," she muttered.

Rochelle pointed to the TV in sudden excitement. "Look!" she cried. "It's Van!"

The camera focused on the young Van Marshall sitting in the quad, writing in a notebook. He glanced up at the camera and put his fingers in the "rock on" sign, then stuck his tongue out like a serpent. Afterward, he gave a shy laugh and hunched back over his notebook, looking embarrassed.

Kat laughed. "I shot that. He was writing a song."

"Oh look! It's Greg Carlyle!" Rochelle pointed out.

"Ugh," Kat made a face. "That guy made me sick. He was such a perv. What kind of jerk tears off someone's guitar strings?"

There were several shots of prom where Rochelle nearly died of laughter, crying, "why did I wear that?" over and over again. At the end, there was a shot of the entire class standing behind the banner of their graduating year. Kat was toward the front between Rochelle and Van, or Jake, rather. Her hair was long, past her shoulders, and Van was skinny and awkward. He had his hands in his pockets and his shoulders were hunched. She had one of her arms around him and she kept saying something to him that made him smile in his bashful way. She sighed, remembering those happy moments of her life.

The video ended and Kat looked away sadly, fighting the lump of emotion that clogged her throat.

Rochelle got up and took the tape out, replacing it with something else and giving Kat a mischievous grin.

Kat frowned as she looked up at the television and her eyes widened as five teenage girls, including her and Rochelle, started dancing to "You Drive Me Crazy" by Britney Spears. Kat cried out in surprise. The Senior Show! "Oh gosh! Why, *why* do you have this?" she asked.

Rochelle laughed. "My dad taped it, remember?"

Kat grimaced. "Why am I dancing to Britney Spears?"

"Because the rest of us were."

She made a face. "This is not a historical moment I am proud of."

Rochelle laughed again, and the song ended. There were several more skits that had them rolling on the floor in hysterics before Van's came on.

"Why did your dad tape Van?" Kat asked.

"Because I told him to." Rochelle smiled. "I thought maybe you'd want to watch this someday." She glanced at Kat. "I knew you loved him back then, even though you hadn't realized it yet."

Kat watched him play his song, feeling as if she had been transported back in time. It had been that song that started it all. It caught her attention and she had seen him, really seen him, for the first time. She sighed and watched the rest of the video in silence, disappointed that Rochelle's dad had not taped Van's impromptu performance of the original he had written.

After the Senior Show was their graduation, which Kat and Rochelle also laughed their way through. There were lots of shots of Kat and Rochelle being silly, and there was one of them both bombarding Van with hugs. He was laughing, but looked very embarrassed. It was strange for Kat to watch. It seemed like so long ago. She barely knew the person in that video. Who had she become? A stranger even to herself.

When the tape finished, they both sat back in silence. "Thanks, Rochelle," Kat said. "I needed that."

Rochelle grinned. "Any time." She made a face as she looked at what was left of Kat's gyro. "That thing looks sick. You need a bite of my burger."

Kat grimaced. "Do you know how much fat—"

"Come on!" Rochelle exclaimed. "One bite! I dare ya!"

Kat sighed and looked up at her friend.

Rochelle handed her a beer also.

"Oh gosh, no," Kat protested. "Did you see that embarrassing footage you shot of me?"

Rochelle giggled. "Come on, Kat. Let's celebrate. Our first big project is completed and you're in love. I think you can drink to that."

Kat smiled and surrendered. She took a bite of Rochelle's greasy burger and chased it with a swallow of beer. She sighed. Fat, carbs, carbonation, and nameless other things that are bad for you.

It was divine.

Chapter Twenty-One

Kat wandered into the apartment at about nine o'clock in the morning sweating and out of breath.

"How was jogging?" Rochelle asked.

Kat made a face. "As refreshing as jogging in L.A. can be. My lungs are full of carbon monoxide."

"I made breakfast. French toast and bacon!"

Kat raised an eyebrow. "Thanks."

"Oh, Van called," Rochelle said nonchalantly. "He wants to make sure we watch *Regis and Kelly*."

Kat frowned as she grabbed a water bottle from the fridge. "Why?"

"I guess they're performing."

"Aren't they supposed to be in Europe?"

Rochelle shrugged. "Go get cleaned up so we can eat and watch."

Kat nodded and went to shower quickly. She dried her hair without bothering to curl it and she didn't bother to put on her usual foundation, eyeliner, and mascara either. She headed into the living room and sat down on the couch, taking the plate Rochelle offered her. She turned on the TV and they proceeded to watch an interview with John Corbett and one with Keira Knightley before Bleeding Passion was announced.

Kat grinned as she looked at all of the members, but her eyes riveted on Van. He was dressed in an untucked, burgundy button-down shirt and black slacks. She noticed a new tattoo around his wrist and she frowned. "When did he get that tattoo?"

Rochelle shrugged as she inhaled her breakfast.

Kat discarded the small moment of disappointment she had over the things she would miss while he was doing what he did and she was living in mundane-land, and she continued to study him. His hair was tied back, revealing his defined features, and he wasn't wearing anything but a little bit of eyeliner. She smiled as he turned to say something to Lance while Regis and Kelly continued their introduction of the band. Lance grinned and nodded at whatever he was saying, and Van's face lit up with a breathtaking smile. Kat briefly remembered that it was his gorgeous smile that had first caught her attention. The entire world was illuminated when he smiled.

"Here to perform their new song, Bleeding Passion!" Kelly finished saying.

Van smiled at the audience and approached the microphone. "This song is special to me," he said softly. "It's going to be our new single. It comes straight from my heart." He flashed another shy smile and they launched into their song.

Kat's heart plummeted into her stomach while her stomach plummeted into her feet. She stopped eating and just stared at the television. Nyah was playing guitar instead of Van and he was just singing, singing a song that was all too familiar to her. A song that she had not listened to in years, one that she had locked away in a box to keep safe and protected, untarnished like the memory of when she'd first heard it.

Rochelle raised her eyebrows and glanced at Kat.

Kat watched him perform and felt like she was back in high school, watching the Senior Show all over again. Only this time, it wasn't a somewhat geeky, brooding boy singing it to her. It was a very sensual and artistic man with a voice of complete sinful resonance. She suddenly felt very lightheaded.

"Geez, Kat," Rochelle breathed. "What do you make of that? They totally turned that song he wrote for you all those years ago into their next single."

Kat opened her mouth to speak, but no words came out. She had no words. All she could do was stare. A knock sounded on the door just as the song ended and Kat nearly jumped up to the ceiling. She scowled and stood, irritated that someone would interrupt her right now. She wanted to see the interview also.

Agitated, she jerked the door open, fully expecting it to be their annoying neighbor or the maintenance guy finally come to fix their leaky faucet. She felt all of the color drain from her face, joining her already plummeted heart and stomach. "Van?" she croaked, sounding feeble and tiny.

He smiled, leaning nonchalantly against the doorframe, his hands in his pockets.

"But—But, you're on there." She pointed back into the apartment and over to the television.

He grinned. "That was recorded yesterday."

"But you're wearing the same thing." She was still unable to comprehend that he was actually there.

He glanced self-consciously down at the same burgundy shirt and black slacks. "I was in a hurry," he explained. He glanced up at her. "They're clean."

"Aren't you supposed to be on tour?" She was fully and thoroughly confused.

"Postponed," he replied, trying not to laugh at the completely perplexed look she must have had on her face.

"Postponed? Why?" She touched her hair in disdain. It was lying all limp and flat. It probably looked awful.

"My band mates were tired of seeing me mope around. We only postponed for a month."

She stared at him, in all his regal glory, feeling frozen to the floor. He had haunted her dreams at night and all of her waking thoughts. Could it be possible that he was actually there? That he had postponed his tour just to come and see her? Could she actually mean that much to another person?

Van chuckled and stood up straight. "I came to see the woman I love. Is she here somewhere? I see someone who looks like her, but she has this vacant look in her eyes that's frightening me."

She shook her head and blushed furiously. Sense returned to her and she let out a loud laugh, flinging her arms around him and holding him close. "I'm sorry! I was just so flabbergasted to see you! I just got home from jogging and Rochelle shoves French toast in my face while telling me that you commanded me to watch this interview. Then, of course, I was completely stunned by hearing that song you wrote for me so long ago. I haven't heard it since then. You caught me so off guard!" His warmth enveloped her as he held her tight against him. She closed her eyes as she breathed in his scent. "You smell so good," she murmured. "You feel divine."

She felt like she was home for the first time in months. She sighed and relaxed her body against his strong frame, melting into him. Her hips nestled against his and she felt a jolt of heat and electricity course through her.

Van clutched her to him, and she could feel the furious pounding of his heart. He tangled his fingers in her hair. "I missed you so much," he whispered.

She smiled and pulled away enough to look up at him, but not far enough to leave his arms. He met her eyes and leaned in to kiss her in the slow, tantalizing way that they both loved. She clung to him, not realizing how incomplete she had felt without him. Being back in L.A. had felt like normal life to her. It depressed her to realize that her normal life had apparently been so incomplete. She ran her hands up Van's chest, feeling all of his lithe muscles, and wrapped her arms around his neck, pressing her body even more intimately to his.

Van moaned into her mouth and grasped her hips, pulling her closer. He kissed her savagely, showing her how passionate she made him, how much he wanted and needed her. He pushed her back a little too far as he leaned over her, causing her to lose her footing. She stumbled backwards into the apartment and he followed, staggering into the room, his lips still fused to hers. Kat held onto him, not wanting to relinquish one minute of the succulence of his mouth.

"Ugh, you two. Get a room," Rochelle muttered.

Van finally pulled away from Kat, out of breath and grinning. He looked over at Rochelle and chuckled. Rochelle grinned and ran over to him, giving him a hard hug.

Kat stood back, trying to compose herself. She could barely believe how she was acting. She was not the type of person to give such a wanton display. Van awoke a passion in her that she had never even known existed.

"It's so good to see you!" Rochelle exclaimed. "Is your tour over?"

"No, we postponed it for a month."

"What for? Is everything all right?"

"With any luck," he said quickly. He cleared his throat and looked at Kat. "Kat, darling, could you go get your purse? If you don't have anything planned today, I'd like to show you something."

Kat smiled. "As if I would let something trivial stand in the way of plans with you. Give me just a second." She went to fetch her purse and make herself look more presentable. She was so excited that she barely even registered how Van turned to Rochelle with an almost pained expression and put his arm around her in a conspiratorial way.

Kat was curling her hair when Rochelle came blowing into the room. "You have to get out of your sweat pants," she declared.

Kat frowned. "You think?"

"Put on something cute."

She turned and looked at Rochelle in exasperation. "What is your obsession with my wardrobe?"

Rochelle gave her a fixed stare. "Just trust me, okay? Your rock star boyfriend shows up out of nowhere after four months of you being miserable and you ask me what my obsession is? You're the one who should be fretting about it."

Kat snorted. "For your information, I already picked out what I'm going to wear. It's sitting on the bed."

Rochelle groaned. "Of course it's going to be something sensible and boring and..." Her eyes bulged as she looked down at the outfit Kat had laid out. It was a black camisole-style tank top that was deep burgundy across the breasts with a tiny black satin bow. She had also chosen a black skirt with the bottom slashed in all different jagged lengths of cloth. "Holy cow, where did you get this?" she asked.

Kat smirked to herself. "I bought it about a month ago. I just didn't know where I was going to wear it yet. I got the shirt at Hot Topic and the skirt at some family owned novelty shop."

"It's all gothic-looking!"

Kat's smirk grew. "I know," she stated.

Rochelle gaped at her. "Why didn't you show me?"

She shrugged. "Didn't think about it."

"You'll match Van." Rochelle pointed to the burgundy in the shirt.

"Well, that wasn't really my intent when I bought it." She turned away from the mirror and quickly dressed in the outfit she had laid out. She applied a light amount of makeup that consisted of foundation, eyeliner, mascara, and lip gloss, and she turned to Rochelle. "Acceptable?"

Rochelle could only stare. She shook her head. "Van is going to crap his pants."

Kat laughed. "Let's hope not." She strode out of her room and back into the living room where Van waited. She couldn't help but smile at the completely stunned look on his face. It

felt good to not be so boring for a change. She knew the outfit showed off her toned frame and it made her feel sexy and
confident.

Van held his arms out to her and she went willingly into
them, closing her eyes in bliss. She had missed him more
than she'd even realized.

"You look gorgeous," he murmured. "Are you ready?"

She nodded, smiling up at him.

He looked at Rochelle and she winked at him. He smiled
and guided Kat out the door. He shook his head and chuckled. "Really, Kat, you look amazing."

"So do you. Europe agrees with you."

"Europe was nothing without you. Nothing is beautiful
without you." He stopped and turned toward her. He took
her face in his hands and let his eyes roam over her. "I felt
so empty without you." He shook his head. "Now I finally feel
whole again." He let his fingers trail across her cheek and he
lowered his lips to hers slowly. "You complete me in so many
ways."

Van's kiss and the way he held her made Kat's head spin.
He held her like she was so cherished, so protected.

"I missed you so much, sweetheart," he murmured. "I
nearly drove everyone crazy. Nyah was the one who finally
convinced me to postpone the tour."

Kat raised an eyebrow in surprise.

He chuckled. "Come on, we'd better get going." He took
her hand and led her out of the apartment building.

* * * *

Kat studied Van's wrist as he drove and traced her finger
across the new tattoo. It was a simple band of some elegant
Celtic pattern. "When did you get this?"

He glanced down at his wrist. "Oh, last month. I saw the
design and really liked it."

She turned to stare out the window at the hilly terrain.
They had been driving for almost two hours, talking about
the tour and listening to music. She had given him a run-
down of the DVD and he had told her all about the things in
Europe that he wanted to show her. She glanced over at him
and sighed.

This action made her want to giggle as Shakespeare's

words suddenly filled her memory, dredged up from some college course from the past. "*...And then the lover, sighing like furnace, with a woeful ballad.*" That was not a phrase she would have ever associated with herself. She was not the type of person to be sighing over anything. She wasn't fanciful. She was practical. It was nice to know that she did, indeed, have a little bit of a romantic underneath all that hard practicality.

She glanced back over at Van's magnificent face and studied the angles and contours of his profile. His hair was tied back, giving her free rein to inspect.

He grinned. "You're staring at me," he stated. "You're going to make me go right off the road."

She smiled. "I just can't believe you're here." She sobered and looked down as if ashamed. "I really missed you, Van." She felt his hand on her hair and she looked up at him.

"Kat," he said, "that is not something you should feel guilty for. I nearly died without you."

She looked at him, still amazed at the things he said to her, then glanced out the window again. Poetry was as natrual to Van as everyday speech. She frowned as she spotted a road sign stating that Cambria was only ten miles away. "Van, where are we going?" she asked, feeling excited.

He glanced at her and grinned. "You'll see."

"Please tell me," she urged.

He chuckled. "I thought we would have a nice day out together. Maybe wine tasting around Cambria, some antique shopping. I thought we could get lunch in San Luis Obispo, explore around there a little. How does that sound?"

She stared at him in complete adoration. "That sounds divine."

"I have plans for dinner, and afterwards, there's a party with some friends of mine I want to take you to. It's in a cove on the beach about a half hour away from Cambria. Will you go with me?"

She nodded. "Of course. Where are we going to stay?"

His smile was sly and secretive. "I already made reservations somewhere."

She raised an eyebrow. "Aren't you full of surprises?"

"Just relax and enjoy," he said. "Today is your day."

Chapter Twenty-Two

The day was sunny and warm and the vineyards were lush and expansive. Kat had seen them from the road before, but she had never been to any.

Van took them up a remote country road where many wineries were hidden from the view of the main highway. They took their time at each one, admiring the scenery and tasting wines here and there. What Kat loved most was how they laughed together. Van made her feel carefree and jubilant, and time melted away when she was with him.

She had always felt so comfortable around him. She could show him all sides of her. She could even show him the one that she kept carefully hidden away. The one that had prompted her to wear the outfit she had on, the side of her that was passionate and crazy. The one he remembered from long ago.

She never showed that side to anyone anymore, not even Rochelle. She had thought she had squashed it, but she found that it resurfaced around Van. Perhaps it came with feeling safe.

After they'd had their fill of wine and had spent a relaxing couple hours wandering the beautiful countryside hand in hand, they headed to San Luis Obispo where they ate a late lunch and shopped. Or rather, Kat shopped while Van watched her with a permanent smile on his lips.

He loved seeing the walls she had placed around herself demolished when they were together. He remembered the girl he had known in high school. She had been popular because she had been so friendly and social. She had laughed and teased and played.

The Kat he had met in the hotel lobby had been much

different, solemn and subdued with a sadness in her eyes that had pained him. It was marvelous to see her laughing and happy again. To know that he had been the one to bring that back to life astounded him.

Van remembered all too well how he had reacted when he'd first seen Kat all those years ago. His heart had stopped just for a second. It was freshman year and he'd seen her walking down the hall with Rochelle. She laughed and he'd heard music. He knew he had. His life was music, and she had inspired it. In that moment, her laugh was the most beautiful song in the world.

He had spent the next three years silently watching her. He had never even thought of speaking to her. In high school, everything had been status. She was on the highest rung of the ladder and he wasn't even on a rung. He wasn't even fit to breathe the same air as her, let alone speak to her. It would have been like Quasimodo trying to speak to Aphrodite.

By some freak accident, he had been granted the chance to sit in front of her in art class their senior year. He would have been content with that, but he would never forget how his heart slammed against his chest at the sound of his name on her lips as she ran backstage after the guitar string incident. She had known his name. And she had liked his music. And she had invited herself over to his house. And she had kissed him. The freak. The goth. The guy voted most likely to either kill himself or blow up the school. The quiet musician with panic disorder. She had given her beauty to him.

Not having the courage to tell her how he felt about her before going to college had been the biggest regret of his life. The fact that he had been given a second chance meant everything to him, and he would never not tell her how he felt again. She was all to him.

"Van?"

He blinked and snapped out of his thoughts. How long had he been standing there? He glanced down at Kat, who was giving him a questioning look.

She frowned in curiosity. "What in the world were you thinking about?"

"You...old times. I was just remembering high school."

She smiled and wrapped her arms around his waist. "Anything in particular?"

He sighed and ran his fingers through her hair. "A thousand little things all centered around a beautiful woman I know." He gazed into her eyes and lost himself there. "Are you finished with your shopping? I want to show you something."

She nodded.

He smiled and took her hand, leading her back to where he had parked the car.

* * * *

Kat frowned as she stood in front of a two-story house in Cambria. Van had driven all the way back here to show her a house?

"What do you think?" he asked.

"This is what you wanted to show me?"

He nodded.

"Well...it's beautiful, but..." She looked up at him. "Van, why am I staring at a house?"

He held up his hand and let a key dangle from his fingers. "Because it's yours," he said, looking all too pleased with himself.

Kat stared at him for a minute, uncomprehending. She blinked. "It's...what?"

"Yours," he repeated.

She felt all of the color drain from her face for the second time that day. "What crazy nonsense is coming out of your mouth?" she breathed.

He grinned. "I remember you telling me you wanted to live here. I want to make all your dreams a reality, Kat." He held the key out to her. "Here, take it."

She shook her head and backed away. "No, no, no, wait a second. Van, are you out of your mind? I can't afford this!"

"You don't have to—"

She continued to shake her head, her mind still spinning. "There's no way I can afford this! I mean, it's insane! You're insane!"

He chuckled. "You don't have to pay for it, Kat. I wasn't planning on having you pay for it."

"No," she stated. "I can't allow it. I will not have you making payments on a house for me. Have you lost it completely?"

"Kat!" he exclaimed. "Listen to me. As humble as I might be, I'm not even going to pretend I don't know the obvious. I'm loaded, Kat. What else am I going to do with my money? I have everything I want. No one's making payments on anything. It was paid in full. Your name is on the deed."

She stared at him in complete and utter shock. This couldn't be happening. Was this really happening? "You bought this house for me just because?" she murmured.

He pulled her into his arms and smiled down at her. "Because I love you. You hate L.A. It's the source of all your suffering. You can start over here, be at peace. No bad memories."

Kat couldn't believe him. She had never had someone listen to her so completely. "But my job," she sputtered. "My job is in L.A."

He sighed and bit his bottom lip. "How would you like a different job?" She frowned and he continued. "Hank spoke to me right before we postponed the tour. He still hasn't gotten over what happened with Nyah. He can't believe how lax our security was or how you handled the situation." He took a deep breath. "Kat, he would like you to be the band's head of security."

Kat's eyes bulged. "Are you serious?"

He smiled and nodded. "He thinks you're incredible."

Kat was completely unable to process all of this information at once. "So I would go on tour with the band?"

"You would go everywhere with the band."

She met his eyes. "I would be with you?"

He laughed. "You would be guarding me. How many girlfriends can claim that?"

She giggled, and then frowned. "Wait, what about Rochelle? I haven't been apart from her in all these years. We have plans to be old ladies together cleaning one another's dentures."

He arched an eyebrow and chuckled. "Hank has an offer for her too. He wants her to be in charge of wardrobe for everyone. I don't know if you're aware of it, but Rochelle organized all of our clothing and accessories on numerous occasions."

"Sounds like Rochelle."

"And we thought it was time Nyah had a real personal hair dresser. Both of you made an impression on Hank. He said the tour went smoother with you guys there than it ever did."

She frowned. "You mean getting lost, stuck in the airport and having a band member almost raped was smooth for you?"

He shrugged. "We always have setbacks, but Nyah *wasn't* raped because of you, and the other things were made much more enjoyable by your presence. Rochelle makes an entire room light up, you know that. She was like good medicine for everyone. Please, Kat, say you'll do it. I can't bear to be away from you. I've been tortured for years because of my own idiocy." He pulled her close against him. "Please don't make me do penance it any longer."

His voice was hushed and his mouth was close to hers, whispering his words over her lips. She closed her eyes for a moment and sighed. She waited for her stone cold logic to scream at her that this idea was irrational and ridiculous, but for once, it didn't interfere. She actually couldn't think of one good reason why she should not take the job. She loved Van, and she enjoyed the other band members. She had been happier on tour than she had been in ages. Besides, she was very good at defense. Why not make a career out of it? She would see and experience much more on tour with a rock band than she would staying holed up in a city she hated.

She smiled to herself. Months ago, she would have thought the idea to be a huge no-no. It would have been out of her safe zone, dangerous territory. Now, with Van, that suddenly didn't seem like such a horrible thing. Nothing was out of her safe zone because he was her safe zone. "I'll take the job," she whispered without hesitation.

He smiled and nuzzled his nose against hers. "And you'll take the house?"

She nodded with a small sigh, her head still reeling from that one.

He grinned like a little boy who had just been given a long coveted toy. "Let's go look at it," he said, taking her arm and pulling her along.

Kat giggled and marveled at the house as they walked up the few steps to the door. Van pressed the key in her hand and stood back, waiting for her to unlock it. She looked at the key, then glanced at Van and grinned. Overcome by sudden enthusiasm, she laughed and turned the key in the lock.

She stepped inside and gasped. It was spectacular! The bottom floor alone was bigger than her entire apartment! It had an expansive front room with hardwood floors and an enormous kitchen. The dining room had huge windows all the way around it and a patio outside a pair of French doors.

"Look," Van said, pulling her down a hallway off to the left. "There's a bedroom and bathroom down here, and—" he opened a door "—a wine cellar."

She laughed. "For all that alcohol I don't drink."

He raised an eyebrow. "I don't know. You were going to town on Lance's Pimp Juice that one night."

She scowled playfully and slugged him in the arm. That entire sentence just sounded really wrong.

Van winced and rubbed at his bicep. "Geez," he muttered. "Even your play punches are brutal."

She blushed.

"Come on, let's go upstairs." He led her to the second story where there was another room that looked like a den, two other bedrooms, an office, and a fireplace.

"Oh my gosh," Kat breathed. "What am I going to do with all this space? I could live quite comfortably in the master bathroom alone!"

He smiled. "Well, Rochelle can stay with you if you want. I'm sure she'll have the place decorated in no time."

Kat laughed.

"Here, look at this," he invited. "This is why I bought this for you." He went over to a sliding glass door off to the side of the den and opened it.

Kat stepped outside and gasped. It was a balcony that overlooked the ocean! She could even hear the surf! Tears filled her eyes and her hands flew to her mouth. "Oh, Van," she whispered.

He smiled and ran his hand down her back. "All the peace and solitude you could ever want. I knew this was it when I saw the balcony. I could picture you sitting out here reading your books and I just had to buy it."

She turned to him. "This is incredible. I can't even think of any words."

He took her in his arms. "Then don't speak." He lowered his lips to hers softly. "Are you happy, love?"

"Happy?" She shook her head as she heard seagulls crying in the distance. "Happy doesn't even begin to describe it."

He grinned. "I have another surprise."

"I don't think I can take anymore!"

He took her hand. "Come with me." He led her around to the other side of the balcony as it wrapped around the house. There he had a table and chairs set up with a picnic basket on the table.

Kat grinned. "Dinner?"

He nodded. "Would you like to eat it here or down on the beach?"

"On the beach!"

He chuckled. "All right, then. Let's go." He picked up the basket and they left the house, heading down to the shore.

Van had packed sandwiches, as well as strawberries and chocolate, which they got great enjoyment out of feeding to one another. Chocolate kisses were, after all, their favorite. Around sunset Van started to glance at his watch. "We should head down to the cove soon," he said. "I want to get there before it's too dark to find."

"All right, let's go then."

They packed the picnic basket in the car and drove for about twenty minutes in almost complete silence. Van hadn't so much as said two words the entire time, and he looked almost ill. It made Kat worry a little. "Van, are you okay?"

He nodded gravely.

"Is your anxiety bothering you?"

He swallowed and slid a glance over to her. "Just a little."

She nodded and reached over to rest her hand over the one he wasn't driving with. She turned on the radio, hoping the music would calm him somewhat.

He smiled at her care.

When Van finally parked the car, it was in a recreation area surrounded by thick, dangerous-looking trees. "We have to walk up the beach a little ways," he said as they started toward the shore.

She nodded, then asked, "What is this party for any-way?"

"It's an engagement party."

She raised an eyebrow and smiled. "Oh, for who?"

"Us," he stated. He stopped walking and turned to her.

Kat blinked. Had he just...? She felt very nauseous all of a sudden, and her legs wobbled in a threatening manner.

"That is, if you want me." He let out a very large and shaky breath. He looked down as if trying to get a grip on his emotions, then met her eyes again.

She continued to stare, feeling like she'd been hit by a truck. The house, that had been a shock. But this, this was...leveling.

Van let out another ragged breath. "Will you...marry me, Kat?"

All she'd ever thought she'd known exploded. Married? Married to Van? She looked at him. He looked horrified. Probably because she wasn't saying anything, but she couldn't find her words. How could she tell him that in the last four months she had imagined being his wife? That she'd dreamed of sharing a bed with him and giving all of herself to him the way she would never be able to with another man? How could she tell him that he owned her heart? That she was his for all eternity? That he had brought her back to life? Somehow, she just couldn't find the words. They all tried to come out at once and stuck together at the base of her throat, making her mute.

"Kat?" he prodded.

She blinked and shook her head. She cleared her throat about three times and tried to regain some semblance of sanity. She finally succeeded in giggling nervously. "I'm sorry, I think I went into a coma."

He smiled, let out a nervous laugh of his own, and shook his head. "Well..." He cleared his throat and ran a hand through his hair. "Considering I just unceremoniously blurted that out like an idiot, I guess I can at least do it right." He knelt down in the sand and pulled a box from his pocket. "Marry me, Kat." He opened the box to reveal a simple band of white gold with three small diamonds.

"Oh..." It came out more like a breath than an actual word. "Van, it's beautiful."

"Simple and elegant," he whispered. "Like you."

Kat's world continued to spin, and she felt a tear slip down her cheek. She still couldn't speak past the lump in her throat, but she held her hand out to him. It was trembling horribly. Van smiled and kissed her hand before slipping the ring on her finger with his own shaking hands.Kat shook her head and looked down at the ring as he stood. "I'm sorry, Van. I just can't think of anything to say."

He smiled softly and touched her face. "Then don't speak."

She met his eyes and sighed. Passion unlike anything she had ever known bombarded her and she launched at him, attacking his mouth with the kind of kiss she had been saving her whole life for the man she would marry, the man she'd never thought she'd find. She kissed him deeply and thoroughly, wanting him to know how she desired him, how he fulfilled every part of her.

Van held her fiercely against him as if to meld them into one person. He wanted to cry out in rapture. He finally had her. Finally, after so long, the woman who haunted all of his fantasies and thoughts would be his wife.

"I love you," she whispered as she broke the intense kiss.

He smiled, caressing his hands down her shoulders and back. "You are my blood and my breath," he murmured.

She smiled in return.

He touched her cheek. "We'll have to get married before we go back on tour. Otherwise, things will get too crazy and I don't want to wait any longer. I know it doesn't give us much time, but—"

She kissed him again. "It's fine."

He breathed an audible sigh of relief.

She laughed.

"Come on," he said, "our friends are waiting."

"Just out of curiosity," she said as they started hand-in-hand down the beach, "what would you have done about this party if I'd said no?"

"It was rigged to go either way. Depending on your answer it was either going to be an engagement party, or a rejection consolation drunken orgy." She laughed and he chuckled. "I just hoped really hard that you'd say yes."

She squeezed his hand. "Honestly, Van, how could I ever say no to you?"

He looked up at the night sky as a soft breeze touched his face. Even the heavens seemed dull compared to Kat's beauty. He sighed. He was the luckiest man in all creation.

Chapter Twenty-Three

There was very little time to get everything that needed to be done accomplished. Kat was hurled into a swirling cauldron of chaos and felt like she was going to lose her mind. She and Rochelle had quit their job at Bushman, as Rochelle had been more than willing to accept Hank's offer of employment.

Van and Kat had decided to have their wedding on the beach and spend their first night as husband and wife in their new home. Van had been disappointed that he could not offer her a romantic honeymoon right away, but she had insisted that Europe would serve as a fine honeymoon for her.

She had no idea how many people Van was inviting, but they had decided on a relatively small wedding so that they wouldn't have to stress over all the preparations and the media wouldn't have a field day. The only person Kat had invited from her side had been Rochelle. She had no desire to have her parents there, and they wouldn't come anyway, considering she was marrying the "gothic freak." In all honesty, she had been estranged from her parents for years. Rochelle was her family, and all of the people she would consider friends were Van's friends.

Rochelle and she had spent the first week taking care of work related issues and paying out of their lease, and they had spent the past few days moving all of their stuff into Kat's new home. Since Van had his things shipped from his apartment in Washington, Kat was trying to figure out where to put everything.

She had given Rochelle the bottom floor bedroom, and they had managed to decorate the front room and upstairs den nicely. Van had helped them with a lot of that, for which

Kat was grateful. It turned out that he had very good taste.

"There is too much space here," Kat muttered as she looked around the top floor. "I have no idea what to do with any of it. I don't even have a dining room table. The bottom floor looks barren." She gave a short laugh. "And look at the poor office." She indicated the room where only a desk with a computer and printer sat like a lonely island in the middle.

Rochelle grinned. "Well, since Van's a millionaire, I'm sure you'll have no problem finding a dining room table, or anything else for that matter."

"Yeah, he already has plans for our bedroom. He told me I had to put my bed in the spare guest room because he had a bed already picked out, but he won't tell me what it looks like."

Rochelle glanced at Kat and raised her eyebrows playfully. Kat blushed and looked away.

"I can't believe you're actually getting married," Rochelle said.

"Neither can I." She smiled. "I never saw this in the cards for myself."

"We still have to find you a wedding dress. That's kind of important."

There was a knock on the door and Kat frowned. She went downstairs and opened it to see Jack and Nyah standing there. "What are you guys doing here?" she asked with a puzzled look. "I didn't think you were due in till next week."

"We were at Lance's up in Washington and some of the stuff Van was shipping got sent there by mistake. Probably because Van and Lance used to be roommates or something and the stupid UPS people got confused," Jack explained. "It's a bunch of music stuff. Do you want me to bring it in?"

Kat nodded and took a guarded glance at Nyah. They had both been at the party in the cove before flying to Washington so that they could get some things from Lance's apartment for the wedding. Nyah hadn't been rude at the party, but that might have been because she hadn't said much of anything at all. "Do you want to come in?" she invited.

Nyah smiled a tiny bit and nodded as Jack went back to the car to fetch the boxes. "The house is nice," she remarked.

"I love it. I just don't know what to do with it."

There was an uncomfortable silence and then Nyah

sighed. "Look, Kat, I want to say something."

Kat tensed. Oh, great.

"Van's heart has always been yours, even when he didn't know where you were. I watched him on tour after you and Rochelle left and it was the most depressing thing I've ever seen. I've never seen him like that. I had to do something about it, especially since I've been such a jerk. I felt like I owed it to him, you know? So, I called the band together and we voted to postpone the tour. Everyone else was thinking the same thing anyway. The truth is, I'm glad you guys are doing this. Van deserves to be happy. He's been miserable for too long."

Kat smiled. "Thanks, Nyah." She ran her hand through her hair self-consciously and took a deep breath. "I know you care a lot about Van, and I know you mean very much to him. I think it would mean a great deal to him if you were in the wedding party so," she cleared her throat, "do you want to be my bridesmaid?"

Nyah blinked as if she hadn't completely comprehended what Kat had just said. She frowned in confusion. "I beg your pardon?"

Kat laughed. "You're going to actually make me ask you twice?"

Nyah giggled. "That's very nice of you, Kat. Of course I will."

Kat smiled and stepped aside as Jack started carting in a bunch of hard travel cases and boxes. She raised an eyebrow. "Good lord, what is all this stuff?"

"The hard cases are his guitars," Nyah said. "I don't know what's in the boxes."

Kat bent down to one of them and pulled the tape off. She opened it up and looked inside. She raised her eyebrows. It was full of pictures and laminates from different venues and tours. There were also several video tapes. "Do you know what these are?" she asked Jack as he came puffing in with the last box.

He looked down at the tape and smiled. "Those are videos we made of our early stages as a band. All of our first gigs and a bunch of stupid home video stuff."

Kat grinned. She glanced at the other boxes that were full of music, guitar books, posters, CDs etc., and tried to think of where she was going to put it all. Her eyes widened as an idea struck her. "Hey, Rochelle, Van's out all day, right?" she shouted up the stairs.

"How should I know? He's your fiancé!"

Kat rolled her eyes. "I think he's out all day with Lance. He went shopping for a tux and wedding bands. Then they have some sort of press thing they're doing." She looked up at Jack and Nyah. "Can I enlist your help for a couple of hours? I want to surprise Van with something, but I can't possibly get it done by myself."

Jack and Nyah exchanged glances, then shrugged indifferently and nodded.

Kat grinned. "Great. Rochelle!" she shouted. "Come on! We need to get my bed out of the spare bedroom! We have work to do!"

* * * *

The four of them worked all day, finally finishing around six, an hour before Van was due home. He and Lance decided to go to dinner, and then he would be on his way.

Kat, Rochelle, Nyah, and Jack were sprawled all around the front room downstairs, sweaty and exhausted.

"I can't move," Rochelle groaned.

"I reek," Nyah stated, taking a whiff of her own armpit. "That is so gross."

"Yeah, you smell worse than me," Jack remarked.

Nyah scowled at him.

"Thanks for your help," Kat said with a satisfied smile. "Van is going to be surprised."

"Let's watch some of that old video footage," Jack suggested. "I'd love to see our awkward beginning stages again."

Kat smiled and crawled over to where she had set them next to the TV, DVD player, and VCR. She popped one of them in and sat back. A much younger-looking Van appeared and Kat's heart flipped.

"This was right when we started the band," Jack said. "Van had just dropped out of college."

He looked so much like she remembered. His hair was still short, streaked with blue and purple, and he was more the skinny boy that he had once been.

They were in somebody's garage, practicing an early

song. Lance was wearing a hat that looked like Slash's from Guns N Roses. Nyah's hair was shoulder-length and her face was rounder. Erik had huge-framed glasses and Jack's hair was a strange orange-yellow color.

"What is up with your hair?" Rochelle laughed.

Jack chuckled. "An attempt to bleach black hair."

Kat watched them continue to play their practice set and a smile crept across her lips. "Rochelle, can I ask a favor?"

Rochelle glanced at her. "If it has anything to do with moving anymore furniture, no."

"No, I just want you to tape everything that goes on with the wedding, okay? I mean, if I don't happen to tape it myself."

Rochelle smiled and nodded.

* * * *

The next several days, Bleeding Passion was supposed to be doing signings, and they were booked on almost every late night show to perform their new single, so Jack and Nyah had decided to head out early. Nyah started complaining that she needed to take a hot bath or all her muscles would cramp up and she needed her beauty sleep. Jack muttered something about the gargantuan bags under her eyes when they left.

Rochelle and Kat were discussing where they were going to go shopping for wedding dresses when Van walked in the door. As his lean, sexy frame filled the foyer and he closed the door behind him, a tremor went through Kat. She would be watching him enter that door for many years to come. This was their home, hers and Van's. He was going to be her husband. The reality of that suddenly hit her very hard.

Van met Kat's eyes and grinned. He crossed the room and bent to kiss her on the top of the head. "Hey, gorgeous," he greeted.

She smiled up at him from her place on the sofa. "Hey. How was your day?"

He shrugged. "Long. You would not believe the ordeal I went through at the tux shop. It was ridiculous. The girl who was taking my measurements was some giggly teenager who was a huge fan and she took forever to get the job done because her hands were shaking and she kept dropping the measuring tape. Plus, whenever she touched me at all she burst into a fit of giggles and blushed."

Kat smiled.

"I got our wedding bands, though," he said with a grin. He sat down next to her on the couch as Rochelle scooted over. He pulled a box out of his pocket and opened it. There sat two simple white gold bands. "I decided simple would be best. I know you're not the flashy type."

Kat ran her fingers over them lightly. "They're perfect," she murmured.

He smiled slyly and pulled hers out of the box. "Yours has one minor difference." He held it out to her. "Look at the inside of the band."

She took the ring and squinted at something she saw engraved in it. *You are the music of my soul.* She stared at it for a moment, then turned to him and buried her face against his neck.

Van chuckled and ran his hand down the back of her hair. "You like it?"

"I love it. Thank you so much." She pressed a kiss to his jaw, then stood. "I have a surprise for you too." She grabbed his hand and pulled him to his feet. "Follow me." She led him up the stairs and into what was once the spare bedroom. "Close your eyes," she instructed as they reached the door. He did so with a smile and she opened it, guiding him inside. "Okay, open."

Van opened his eyes and gasped in amazement. His guitars lined one of the walls, and several amps were sitting in the corner. On another wall, all of his laminates had been put up in a sort of collage, and there were various pictures of him and his band mates interspersed around a Bleeding Passion T-Shirt with the symbol of the band showing prominently.

In between the pictures and the laminates were newspaper clippings, magazine articles, and pictures from photo shoots. All of the things he had kept as keepsakes were now gracing the wall in a sort of shrine. On the floor, one of the hard travel cases he had shipped his guitars in was lying open with all of his sheet music and guitar books in it. He turned and saw Kat's old double bed against the other wall. He frowned and pointed to it.

Kat shrugged. "We tried to take it out, but there was nowhere else to put it. We decided we would just leave it in here. That way, if you're working really late on a song or something, you can be comfortable."

He grinned. On the wall above the bed were all of his band posters. But what he saw on the last wall was what caught his attention the most. His eyes widened. There was a mahogany desk with all of his lyrics notebooks stacked on it, and above it, his red electric guitar from high school hung on the wall next to a framed picture. He went over to take a closer look and saw it was the one of him and Kat that had been taken in high school. His mother had taken it, he remembered.

Kat had been over at the house and he had been showing her a new song he was writing. He was sitting on his bed, his guitar in his lap. Kat was next to him. She had her head on his shoulder and she was grinning broadly. His smile was shy. He couldn't believe she had found that. He had looked at that picture so much over the years he had almost worn it out.

He glanced above the picture to where the lyrics of the song he had written for Kat were posted. They were written in his own hand, and at the bottom, like a silly teenage girl, he had drawn a heart around Kat's initials. He blushed and looked at her. "That is humiliating." He pointed to the heart.

She smiled and shook her head. "No, that is adorable."

He rolled his eyes and looked back up at the last picture on the wall. It was above the lyrics and it was a recent picture of the two of them. It must have been taken candidly because neither one of them were looking at the camera. Kat was sitting on his lap, laughing about something, and he was pressing a kiss to her head, his smile apparent. He reached out and touched it as if doing so could recapture the moment.

He shook his head. "I don't even know what to say. This is so amazing. You did all this?" He turned to her.

She shrugged. "I had some help, but it was my idea. You need a music room, a room that is all yours. Your creative domain."

"Look at this desk! Where did it come from?" He ran his hand over the smooth surface.

"We picked it up somewhere," she said enigmatically.

He smiled and turned to her. "This is amazing. Kat, thank you so much...wait." His eyes fell on something by the door he hadn't noticed earlier. "Is that a mini fridge?"

She giggled. "Nyah said that when inspiration struck, sometimes you'd go at it for hours and write an entire album in one night. I didn't want you to starve or dehydrate, and it would just be wrong to make you go *all* the way into the kitchen." She grinned at him playfully.

He laughed, then frowned. "Wait, did you say Nyah told you?"

"Yeah, she helped me today. She and Jack brought this stuff over. It was delivered to Lance's apartment instead and they brought it down."

"She helped you?" He couldn't mask his surprise.

She nodded. "I asked her to be a bridesmaid also."

His eyes bulged. "You what?"

"Well, she's one of your closest friends. It didn't seem right to just exclude her."

Van stared at her in shocked adoration. "And she was okay with that?"

Kat shrugged. "She seemed fine. She was actually really nice."

He arched an eyebrow and sighed. "Man, I don't even know who she is lately. She's been so considerate."

"Not having second thoughts, are you?" Kat prodded.

He frowned at her.

"You're not wanting to ditch me and go back to her because she's being less heinous?" She gave him a sly smile.

He scowled playfully and all but tackled her, pulling her into his arms. She let out a startled shriek and laughed as she fell against his chest. He tangled his fingers in her hair and smiled, holding her close. He took a quick look around his new music room again and smiled, squeezing her tighter. "I've never had a music room all to myself before," he said. "This is the best present I have ever gotten."

She looked up at him and met his eyes, which he knew were reflecting an overabundance of joy and worship. "I love you," she said simply.

He grinned and his heart jolted. He wondered if he would ever get used to hearing her say that. Every time those words left her mouth, he wanted to fall down on his knees before her and tell her he was her slave to command. That was melodramatic, he knew, but he didn't care. He felt that all the way into the very depth of his soul. He sighed softly and caressed his knuckles down her cheek, making both of them smile. He lowered his lips to hers and was swept away once again by the virtual tsunami of love that washed over him. She was so perfect. Every touch was a gift. Every kiss made him want to cry.

His entire body tensed when he felt her fingers slip underneath his shirt to lightly caress the skin on his stomach. He shivered and his tender kiss turned fiery.

Kat had no idea what she was doing. She just knew that she had to touch him. It wasn't something she really had control over. She needed to feel his skin. She ran both of her hands up his chest and frowned in irritation when his shirt halted her progress. Still kissing him, she pulled her hands back out and began deftly unbuttoning his shirt until it was open and his upper body was free for her inspection.

She lightly drew her fingers down his chest, relishing in how he felt. She hadn't really been able to touch him since the night they had been stranded in Phoenix, and she felt as if she had been denied far too long. She broke away from his lips and began trailing kisses along his jaw line to his neck and throat, wanting to sample as much of his soft skin as possible.

Van's eyes rolled back in ecstasy and he tipped his head to allow her better access. She slipped the fabric of his shirt off his shoulders and nibbled along his collarbone before returning her lips to his in a ferocious kiss. He grasped her face in his hands as their tongues tangled with one another, and she ran her fingernails lightly down his chest in a way that caused him to shudder.

He groaned and took her by the shoulders, pushing her back a little. He fixed her with a stare. "Are you trying to kill me, vixen?"

She grinned. Vixen. Now there was a word she never would have put next to a picture of herself. She blushed horribly and averted her eyes. What was she doing anyway? Had she lost her mind completely? "Sorry," she mumbled.

He smiled and lifted her chin so he could look into her eyes. "I don't want to stop you," he admitted, "but if I don't stop you now, I won't stop at all, and you deserve better than that. I have waited my whole life to give myself to someone completely. I feel so honored that I can give that gift to you on our wedding night."

She blinked, completely shocked. Had she just heard him right? She frowned. "Wait...what?"

He grinned. "That's right. I've never been with a woman intimately. Does that surprise you?"

Surprise? She was beyond surprised. She was baffled beyond all logical thought! He was Van Marshall, for crying out loud! "You're kidding me, right?" she asked. "I mean, you're a famous rock star who exudes charisma and sex appeal. Half the women in the world would sell their souls just to have one look from you. Everyone wants you."

He grinned even broader. "They can want all they like. Doesn't mean they're going to get anything."

Kat raised her eyebrows, remembering how she had said something similar to that years ago when he had been surprised about her never having been kissed before.

She frowned again. "But, what about Nyah?"

He shrugged. "I don't know. It just never felt right with Nyah. Call me old fashioned if you want, but I wanted it to be perfect. I always felt like I would know without a doubt when that moment was." He gazed down at her and sighed. "It's perfect with you. Everything's perfect with you."

She couldn't speak. What could she say? She was touched, and admired him much more than she had five minutes ago, but then the tears came. They coursed down her cheeks like someone had suddenly turned on a faucet and she looked down.

Van frowned in concern. "Kat?" he murmured. "Sweetheart, what's wrong? Why are you crying?"

She shook her head. "Because I'm not perfect," she whimpered. "I'm not pure. I'm spoiled, tarnished. I don't deserve to be your first."

He stared at her for a moment, then wrapped his arms around her and held her close. He sighed. "My beautiful Kat, how can you say that about yourself? How could you think that I would think that of you? Did you have a choice in the matter?"

She winced at the memory and shook her head, burying her face against the still exposed warm flesh of his chest.

"Did you willingly give yourself to that man?"

She shook her head again and let out a little sob.

He held her out and looked down at her. "Do you willingly want to give yourself to me?"

His voice brushed over her so soft and tender that she had to look up into his eyes. She let out a shaky breath. He was looking at her with such warmth and love. It was still so overwhelming. "Yes," she whispered. "You're the only man I've ever thought that way about."

He smiled gently and wiped away her tears. "Then, if I'm the only man you've ever thought that way about, I will be your first as well. That man stole something from you. You didn't give it to him. You will be giving me your love in every way and I will be giving the same to you." He pressed a light kiss to her lips. "It fits, don't you think? We were each other's firsts in every other way."

She smiled tremulously and sniffed. "I think you stole that kiss from me in your bedroom, if I remember correctly."

He grinned. "The first one, yes." He snorted. "I don't even know what possessed me to do that. I thought I'd lost my mind."

She laughed a little.

He held her closer and sobered. "Please, love, don't ever think you are not good enough for me. I could never get any better than you. Someone better doesn't exist in this world or any other. I've only ever wanted you."

Kat sighed and rested her head on his shoulder as his hands caressed her back. She smiled to herself. She and Van would only ever know each other. That was very romantic to her. He would be hers completely, and she, his. The dynamic, sensual, stunning Van Marshall would be all hers. It made her feel so special to know that, in a way, he always had been.

She closed her eyes and snuggled closer to him. She never would have thought that anything could feel this fantastic, but then again, Van had always made her feel amazing. Now, she would spend the rest of her life feeling that way. Like herself. Not hiding, not running, not frightened. She could just be Kat. To her, that was the greatest gift of all.

Chapter Twenty-Four

Kat tried to ignore the fluttery feeling in her chest when she glanced at her wedding dress, which was currently hanging up in the music room. She had been commanded to sleep in there until the wedding night, as Van wouldn't allow her to see whatever it was he was doing to the bedroom. She sighed heavily and sat down on the bed, staring at the garment.

In less than twenty-four hours, she would be wearing it and walking down the aisle to become Van's wife. The fact that she was becoming the wife of one of the most famous rock stars of the decade somehow didn't seem that big of a deal to her, but the fact that she was marrying the boy from her past seemed enormous.

She thought of what people would say and think at their ten-year class reunion. Most people probably wouldn't have made the connection that Van was really Jake. She smiled as she imagined the looks on the faces of people like Greg Carlyle and the others who had been so cruel to him as he walked in, suave and seductive, more successful than possibly half of the graduating class...and she would be on his arm. She would be at his side. She, the girl who had been so popular, would be married to the boy who had been anything but. Except the tables had turned. He was now more popular than half the people in the world, and she was relatively unknown. Life had a funny way of working things out.

She stood again and went over to her dress to examine it. Rochelle had managed to find it for her after a long and arduous day of searching with no results. She touched it lightly and smiled. They had managed to find Rochelle and Nyah bridesmaid's dresses also. They were simple, black gowns, long and elegant.

Van's parents were due in at any second for the rehearsal dinner. Kat technically didn't know what they were having a rehearsal for. They were getting married on the beach. It wasn't like they would be confused as to which direction they were going. It seemed silly to her, but Rochelle was having a grand time organizing it, so she kept her mouth shut.

Rochelle had thrown Kat a horribly naughty bachelorette party. Nyah had been there, as well as Alana from Thrill My Koi and a few people from Kat and Rochelle's job. Lance had been the stripper, which had made Kat blush so horribly that she thought she would be red for months. She thought that might have been more for Rochelle's enjoyment than her own, but she couldn't deny that she'd had a fun time. Embarrassing, but fun.

She heard the doorbell, but paid no attention to it. Rochelle would get it. It would just be Van's family anyway. She would go down in a second after she had cleared her mind. Right now, it was racing like crazy, and she didn't feel like facing Van's father with anything less than a clear mind. She was sure Van had told him about the misunderstanding, and even though it was technically his fault, she felt embarrassed.

She continued to stare blankly at her dress, still unable to comprehend that it was really the eve of her wedding. After the rape, she had thought she would never even let another man touch her, let alone marry her. She had always pictured Rochelle getting married and having a family while she lived by herself forever. She made a face. How could she have convinced herself so thoroughly that she enjoyed being alone? Now that she had Van, that thought seemed ridiculous. She could no longer picture her life alone. Not after Van. He had brought beauty back into her world.

"Kat?" Rochelle came in the room with a quizzical expression on her face.

She glanced at her.

"Bam Margera is in your living room, Kat," she said nonchalantly.

Kat's eyes bulged and her mouth dropped open. "What?" she cried.

"Along with some other really, really, *really* hot guy."

Kat pushed past Rochelle and went over to a part of the house where the bottom floor could be seen from the top over a railing. She glanced down into the front room and her eyes widened in complete shock. She stepped back from the railing and pulled Rochelle back into the music room. "That's Ville Valo!" she exclaimed.

Rochelle frowned. "Who?"

"Ville Valo! He's the singer from HIM. You know, Van's favorite band?"

Rochelle arched an eyebrow. "Is he single?"

Kat ignored her and tangled her fingers in her hair. "Holy crap, what are they doing here?"

"They're here for the wedding tomorrow. They wanted to stop by and see Van before they went to their hotel."

Kat stared at Rochelle, completely dumbfounded.

Rochelle laughed. "Why are you looking at me like someone just shot you? It's not really that strange that they're here. Van loves Bam Margera."

Kat stared at her friend. "I didn't know he actually knew Bam Margera!"

Rochelle laughed again. "Well, he's kind of famous, Kat. Does it really surprise you that he would have famous people at his wedding?"

"He just never mentioned it. All the times we were watching *Viva La Bam* together he never once slipped in 'Oh, by the way, I know Bam Margera.' And all the times he told me to listen to various HIM CDs he never informed me that he knew Ville Valo either! What am I supposed to do? Where is Van anyway? He's supposed to be here!"

"He's over at the hotel where the rest of the band is staying. You know that. He'll be home in about a half an hour."

"So I have to entertain them for a half an hour?" She threw her hands up in the air in exasperation. "This is nuts!"

Rochelle grinned and shook her head. "Kat, they're not aliens. They're just people."

Kat fixed Rochelle with a stare. "Well I'm glad this is all so easy for you."

She giggled. "Look, Kat, you're marrying Van Marshall. You understand that? Not Jake Marsallis. *Van Marshall*. He's famous. Therefore, I would imagine a lot of his friends are famous also. You're going to have to get used to that." She smiled. "They're just Van's friends, Kat. That means they're going to be your friends too. Just ignore the fact that they're famous and act like you're any other bride that has to meet her fiancé's friends."

Kat huffed. "What in the world am I supposed to talk to them about? I don't want to tell Bam how funny I think he is, or tell Ville how much I love his music. Then I'll just sound like a groupie." She let out a frustrated growl. "I just wish Van was here. I don't like being in the spotlight. He's the performer. He should be the one doing this. Not me. And he really should have told me who he invited to the wedding because I was really not prepared for this!"

Rochelle took Kat by the shoulders and giggled again. "Kat, you are stressing something major. Take a deep breath, go down there and say hello. I'll go with you. If you get stuck or start to look like a deer in the headlights, I'll take over." She offered Kat her arm with a grin.

Kat sighed. She linked her arm with Rochelle's. "I don't know what I'd do without you," she said seriously. "You've been there with me through the worst of my life. I never could have made it without you."

"I'm just looking forward to being there with you through the best of your life." She nudged her playfully. "Now come on. Let's get you on the road to being a rock star's wife."

Kat smiled and nodded, feeling momentarily better.

* * * *

The half hour Kat spent entertaining Bam Margera and Ville Valo seemed like an eternity. She had never been so happy to see Van walk through the door in all her life. Her nerves were completely shot. After all, she was getting married in the morning. She didn't need to add entertaining celebrities to her "to do" list. She escaped into the kitchen as soon as humanly possible and started helping Rochelle make the dinner for the rehearsal. The rest of the wedding party was coming over in about an hour and she wanted everything to be ready to go. The sooner everything was prepared, the faster everything would be over and Kat could escape into a corner for awhile.

This was not her forte. Rochelle was the party planner. Maybe back in high school, Kat had organized assemblies and school functions and prom, but she had been a virtual recluse for years and this was not how she wanted to be re-inducted into the world of socialization.

The doorbell rang, and Kat turned from where she had been chopping carrots almost frantically to go answer it. She whirled so quickly that she almost plowed right into Bam, who had been coming into the kitchen. She let out a shout and jumped back, then looked down, feeling horribly embarrassed.

Rochelle looked at Kat and started to laugh. "Did you need something?" she asked Bam, who was laughing also.

Kat squeezed past him through the entryway and darted to the door as quickly as possible. What was the matter with her? She felt like a complete idiot. She shook her head and opened the door only to see Torrey, Taegen, and three other complete strangers standing there. She blinked in bewilderment and looked up at Torrey. "Hi," she greeted feebly.

Torrey grinned. "Hey, Kat! Congratulations!" He lunged forward and caught her in a hug, which she returned somewhat stiffly.

"Van said we could come by for the rehearsal if we wanted to," Taegen said.

Kat forced a smile. *Did he? Oh how nice of him.* She looked over the other three people. Two guys and a girl. One guy was blond and looked like everyone's All American jock, and the girl was slender and lovely with a bright smile and black hair. But it was the third guy that caught her attention. He had black-framed glasses and had his hands stuffed into his pockets. He looked uncomfortable, like he didn't really enjoy being around a lot of strange people. He looked just like Jake.

"Kat, these are our friends," Torrey said suddenly. "Javan, Maxim, and Alyx. Remember, the night we had dinner was the night Maxim proposed to Alyx?"

Maxim turned a faint shade of red and Kat smiled. "That's right. You're Van's friends from Oregon that he met at the concert last year." She stepped aside and motioned them in. "Come on in, make yourselves comfortable. Glad you could make it."

She recited the required pleasantries even while her mind was spinning eighty miles an hour. What was she going to do with all of these people? Van hadn't told her anything about celebrities randomly showing up on her doorstep and he certainly hadn't told her that his friends from Oregon were coming. A little bit of a heads up would have been nice considering Rochelle and she had only planned on making dinner for Van's family and the members of the wedding party.

"Hey! You guys made it!" Van's voice shouted as he spotted Torrey, Taegen, and the others.

"Holy crap!" the blond guy named Javan exclaimed. "Bam friggin' Margera is here!"

Kat sighed and closed the door. As soon as she'd taken two steps into the room, the doorbell rang again. She stopped, squeezed her eyes shut, and whined pitifully for a second before turning back and opening the door. Van's parents were standing there. Somehow, that didn't make her feel any better. She sighed again and plastered a smile on her face.

"Kat?" Van's mother questioned. "Is that you?" She grinned. "Oh you look fabulous!" She held her arms out in an embrace.

Kat couldn't help but give a genuine smile. Van's mother had always been so warm. She returned the hug. "It's good to see you. You look good too!" She was a tall, slender woman with dark hair like Van's and soft-looking skin. She had always been beautiful to Kat, but that might have been greatly due to the fact that she had always been so nice. Kat turned to Van's father, who was also very tall and dark, and gave him a small smile.

He shook his head and grinned. "Care to give an old idiot a hug?"

She smirked as the tension broke, and she hugged him as well. "Come in, both of you," she invited.

"Is this your house?" Van's mother breathed. "It's so beautiful!"

Kat smiled. "Van," she called. "Your parents are here."

Van practically leapt up from where he had been talking to his friends on the couch and he ran to his parents where he doled out hugs. Kat smiled and stepped back, unsure of what to do. She knew nothing about being "wifely," or really anything about being a hostess.

She took a careful glance into the kitchen to see if Bam was still in there. She frowned in agitation. He was. And now Ville was too. Crap, where was she supposed to go? She looked over at Van, who was laughing with his parents, and she felt tremendous sorrow well up inside of her. Everyone there was Van's family and friends of Van's. All but Rochelle.

Rochelle was the only person Kat had.

Her family should have been there. Her mother should be the one telling her what to do and not to be nervous. Her father should be the one telling her how beautiful she looked and how he was so happy for her, the way Van's father was telling him how happy he was.

Tears filled her eyes and she turned to walk purposefully up the stairs. She went into the music room and locked the door, then sat down on the bed and cried. Within minutes, there was a knock on the door and she bristled. She let out a huge sigh and tried to calm herself. "If you're one of the famous people in my living room, I'll be with you in a second when I'm finished losing my mind," she said. "If you're Rochelle, I'm losing my mind. I'll be out in a second. Finish dinner without me."

"And if I'm your fiancé?" came the soft voice behind the door.

Kat sighed again and stood. She unlocked the door, then sat back on the bed. "Then come in, I suppose."

Van poked his head in tentatively. His eyes widened in concern when he saw her tear-streaked cheeks and red eyes. "Honey, what's wrong?" he asked. He came into the room and closed the door behind him. He sat down next to Kat and took her hands in his.

She looked down into her lap as more tears cascaded down her cheeks. "Why didn't you ever tell me you knew Bam Margera?" she cried.

"It just never came up." He frowned. "You're crying because I know Bam?"

She sniffed. "No, I just... I don't know how to do any of this, Van. I don't know how to entertain famous people. I've forgotten how to throw any kind of social event. I don't want to make you look like a fool, and yet, I don't know how a wife of a famous musician is supposed to act. You should have married Rochelle because she's in there talking to Bam like she's known him for years, while I feel like I'm going to lose it."

To Van's credit, he tried to fight his smile. She saw the momentary struggle, but the smile won out in the end. She couldn't blame him really. She was rambling again, her signature telltale sign that she was stressed. For some reason, he thought that was cute.

He smoothed her hair in a loving gesture. "You don't have to behave a certain way, Kat. Just be yourself. You're very likable. Ask any of my band mates and any of the roadies. Everyone loves you."

She sighed. "Yeah, well, roadies are a lot less intimidating than Bam Margera and Ville Valo." She looked up at him. "Who else famous have you got coming anyway?"

He frowned thoughtfully. "I think Davey Havok from AFI, Darren Hayes and the guys from Fat Stinky, and Steven Tyler."

Kat's eyes bulged. "Steven Tyler? As in from Aerosmith?" She groaned and put her head in her hands. "You've got to be kidding me! I don't want to do this anymore."

Van chuckled and rubbed her back consolingly. "You'll be fine, sweetheart. Torrey and Taegen are here. You know them. And Torrey knows Darren so that will take some of the pressure off."

She looked up at him and scowled. "Yeah, that's another thing. You might have told me that your friends from Oregon were just going to randomly show up. I don't have enough food for everyone, Van! I wasn't prepared for any of this!" She felt more out of control in that moment than she had in years. She knew it was all really stupid, but for some reason, the fact that she didn't have enough wieners in wraps for everyone seemed like a huge deal.

Van smiled. "Kat, it's okay. Torrey and the others didn't show up to eat your food. They just want to be good friends and show their support."

She met his eyes. "But they're you're friends, Van. All of them are your friends." She looked down as her voice cracked, and she felt tears again.

He frowned. "Is that what this is about?"

"It just hurts to watch your parents shower you with love and warm words of encouragement when mine could care less what is happening with me. I mean, if I called them up to tell them, all they would do is yell at me for marrying someone who was a freak. I have no one here. No one but Rochelle. A girl shouldn't have to be all alone on her wedding day." Another soft knock sounded on the door and Kat sighed. "Come in."

Van's father came in slowly. "Am I interrupting?"

She looked up at him and shook her head.

He glanced at Van and gave him an understanding smile. "I couldn't help but overhear when I was coming up here," he said, going to Kat. "Which is actually what I wanted to talk to you about." He knelt in front of her and looked at her with gentle eyes that reflected warmth, like Van's did.

"I know your family was never really there for you, and I know I ended up making a real mess of things for you because of a stupid misunderstanding, but you've always been like family to us, Kat. I remember back when you used to come over and you and Van would stay in his room all hours of the day listening to music and helping one another with homework. I remember hearing such laughter from him when you were there, and happiness was something we rarely saw out of Van back then."

Kat glanced up at Van; he smiled shyly. She laced her fingers with his.

"The truth is...you were always a ray of light in our family, making things sunny and beautiful wherever you went. We could never find anyone better for Van than you. He has loved you for such a long time. I'm truly sorry for what I said to make you think Van was dead. I would never have knowingly hurt you. I hope you can forgive me because I agree that no girl should have to be alone on her wedding day and, if you'd let me, I'd like to walk my new daughter down the aisle."

Kat stared at him for a moment, uncomprehending. Then, fresh tears filled her eyes and she flung her arms around his neck.

He smiled and held her gently. "You're not alone anymore. You're part of our family."

She cried harder, feeling like the entire life she had built around herself was crumbling down in ruins at her feet. She didn't have to hold onto everything that had been hurting her for so long. None of it mattered anymore. Her awful family didn't matter because she had Van's family. The horrible fear she had of men taking advantage of her didn't matter because she had a beautiful and wonderful man to stand by her and protect her. Her life, which had been shrouded by shadow for such a long time, was suddenly filled with amazing possibilities that she had never thought would be available to her. Van had liberated her. He had set her free from the prison she had placed herself in and let her remember what it was like to feel happiness. She could never, in all her life, repay him for that.

"Kat?" Rochelle's voice called. She poked her head in. "Oh... I'm sorry. It's just...the rest of the band just showed up, and that Fat Stinky guy is here too."

Kat pulled away from Van's father and heaved a sigh.

He grinned and wiped at Kat's tears. "Now you don't worry about all those famous people," he said. "They weren't always famous. They were all, at one time, just like Jake."

She met his eyes, and he winked at her. He stood and smiled at his son before walking out with Rochelle, leaving Kat alone with Van. A strange calm came over her at his departing words. That was true. They had all been nobodies at one point. She didn't know why that knowledge made her feel better, but it did, or maybe it was just that she had needed to hear it from someone other than Rochelle, who was virtually unflappable. She looked up at Van and smiled tremulously. "Thank you," she murmured.

He cupped her cheek in his hand. "For what, sweetheart?"

She wrapped her arms around him and rested her head against his chest. "For being what you are."

He smiled as he stroked her hair. "And what is that?"

"Everything to me."

He held her close to him and sighed. "I am merely a reflection of the beauty you show me," he whispered.

Her heart melted, just like it did every time she looked at him. Everything was all right when he was with her. She was sane when he was with her. The world made sense.

"Now, do you think you're feeling up to coming downstairs for the rehearsal? Or am I going to have to get Lance to stand in for you?"

She giggled. "No, I think I can do it."

"You're not going to flip out when you see any of my friends? Not going to scream at Bam?"

She blushed, feeling embarrassed that he had apparently caught her doing that. She shook her head. "I think I'll be okay... I'm just a little stressed, Van. I'm kind of getting married tomorrow. Everything seemed very overwhelming all of a sudden."

He pressed a kiss to her forehead. "You don't need to explain yourself to me. I understand completely." He stood and took her hand, pulling her up against him. She giggled and he kissed her. She marveled over the fact that she would be able to kiss his lips every day for the rest of her life.

Kat felt empowered as she left the room with Van. She felt like she could brave the living room full of people now. She could do anything when Van was with her. She knew it sounded silly and romantic, but it was true. Plus, she was finding that being silly and romantic was a much more pleasant alternative to being sullen and cold. For the first time in too long, she felt like she was actually living her life instead of just existing. She wanted to hold onto that feeling forever.

Chapter Twenty-Five

Silence. All was silence except for the cry of seagulls and the lapping of the waves on the shore. Kat let out a slow breath and closed her eyes. Rochelle, Nyah, Lance, Erik, Jack and Van's parents had gone down at the crack of dawn to set up the chairs for the wedding, and the tents and tables for the reception. Thus, Kat had been able to eat her breakfast in peace and quiet.

That fleeting moment of peace, however, was destroyed when all of them trooped back in talking at once, trying to command one another. Kat was all but bodily removed from her chair and taken back up to the music room where Rochelle and Nyah proceeded to gather all of her things and take them down to the tent they were supposed to change in. They demanded that Kat get in the shower and be out with dried hair by the time they got back. She figured it would be better to comply than fight, so she obeyed.

Nyah was given the task of doing Kat's hair while Rochelle recorded the random goings on of the others like Kat had asked her to do. It amazed Kat that she was actually trusting Nyah, but she had been very helpful over the past three weeks, and she figured it wouldn't hurt to give her a second chance. She had, after all, apologized more or less.

Nyah left her hair straight and parted it on the side. She placed an elegant rhinestone headband on her that sparkled and glittered like a thousand tiny diamonds. After the hair had been finished, Rochelle was called in to do makeup. Kat tried to protest that she could do her own makeup, but she was overruled yet again, so she just shut up.

Kat was actually impressed by what Rochelle did with her. She had gone for a subtle, natural look, which Kat always preferred anyway, but she had managed to make it look like her skin was glowing. She had just a hint of rosy-colored eye shadow on and a subtle rosy lipstick that was covered in shimmery gloss.

Rochelle stood back with a satisfied grin. "There," she stated. "How do you like it?"

Kat stared at her reflection a little longer and sighed. "I like it." She met Rochelle's eyes in the mirror and swallowed hard. "I'm horrified," she said bluntly.

Rochelle smiled and helped Kat out of the chair. "No time to be horrified," she teased. "We have to get you down to the beach and changed. Nyah and I have to get ready too, you know."

The next hour or so went by so quickly and was accompanied by so much insanity that Kat felt like she was running on high speed. Lance kept popping in and out of the tent for the sole purpose of trying to drive Nyah and Rochelle crazy, and Van's mother kept coming in to see if she could do anything to help. Kat felt a familiar knot form in her stomach when she began to hear the chatter of guests arriving. Not being able to help herself, she poked her head out of the tent to see who was there. It didn't make her feel any better.

"Kat!" Rochelle scolded. "What are you doing? What if Van sees you?"

"He won't," she replied mechanically. "He's over there talking to Steven Tyler." She moved back from the tent flap and gave Rochelle a stunned, yet vacant look. "Steven Tyler is at my wedding."

Rochelle laughed and went to her friend. "Kat, you look like you're about to go to your execution."

Kat met her eyes.

"Breathe," Rochelle commanded.

Kat took a deep breath and closed her eyes, trying to relax. "Why do I feel so terrified?"

"Because you're treading on unfamiliar territory. You're taking a leap and that's not something you like doing. However," she offered a comforting smile, "at least you know that Van will catch you if you fall."

Kat stared at her for a minute, then grinned as she slowly felt her fear being replaced by a tingling warmth at the thought of Van always being by her side.

"Is the bride almost ready?" Van's father's voice came

suddenly.

"Just about," Rochelle replied.

He poked his head inside the tent and grinned at Kat. "You look so beautiful. You will take Van's breath away even more than you already do."

She blushed and looked down, briefly wondering if he felt as anxious as she did.

* * * *

Van took a deep, calming breath and tried to will his hands to stop shaking. He felt like a fool. Why was he even nervous? It's not like he was having doubts about marrying Kat. He supposed it just had something to do with the fact that marriage was such a huge commitment, and he was hoping that he would always be able to be what Kat needed. He wanted his marriage to be forever. Especially considering he could never love another woman on the planet like he loved Kat.

"You gonna survive?"

Van turned to the entryway of his tent and saw Maxim standing there. He smiled. It wasn't like he knew Maxim that well; he hadn't known him that long. Their friendship consisted of intermittent emails sent when Van had a spare second, but at that moment, Maxim was just who he needed to see.

He reminded Van of himself. The brooding artist. Maxim wrote books while Van wrote music, and both of them did it with a rare kind of passion. When Van had first met Maxim, he'd felt an instant bond with him. They were two eccentrics living in a world of ignorant people who didn't understand them. Their souls were the same, and they probably understood one another on a level that no one else would be able to comprehend.

Maxim grinned and approached Van slowly. "I'm asking because I figure that, if you can survive, so can I."

Van chuckled and shook his head. "Yeah, your day is coming," he teased. He looked at his friend and sighed. "Look at us, Max," he said. "Look how far we've come. When I met you, I was sitting in a club in Vegas, aching with jealousy over the fact that you had found a once in a lifetime love with Alyx. You were still reeling over the fact that she cared for you at all, and now, here you are, engaged to her."

"And here you are, marrying the one you let get away. Life is weird sometimes."

Van sobered and nodded in agreement.

"Are you nervous?" Maxim questioned.

"To marry her? No. I'm just hoping I can always be what she needs. I left her behind when she needed me the most because I was too afraid to tell her how I felt. I want to spend the rest of my life making that up to her and I just hope that I can be the man she deserves."

Maxim grinned and put his hand on Van's shoulder, gripping it purposefully. He looked him right in the eye. "I know exactly how you feel."

Van laughed, causing Maxim to chuckle as well. "Thanks for being here, Maxim. It means a lot."

"Hey, come on. You gave me that little extra push I needed to write my novel. You were the one that showed me I had a purpose." He grinned. "You were the one that made me realize I wasn't the only freak out there."

"Brothers in oddness always."

"Amen, brother," he said, quoting what Van had said to him once before.

Van grinned.

"You doing okay?" Lance asked suddenly, coming into the tent.

Van looked at him and nodded. "Yeah, I think I'm ready." He took a deep breath and smiled.

Lance grinned. "Well, we're all ready. You want to go take your place? It's now or never."

This information made his stomach flip dramatically and he swallowed hard. This was the defining moment of his life. He took another deep breath and closed his eyes. He nodded again.

Lance chuckled and patted him on the back. "All right."

Van watched Lance start off to the tent where the others waited, and he walked outside and up the aisle. He turned stiffly toward where the minister stood and briefly glanced over the small crowd, grateful that no one had managed to spill the beans to someone who knew someone in the media. So far, they were devoid of reporters, but he didn't know how long that would last. It was, after all, a public beach.

He walked up the sandy aisle and took his place, playing

with his fingers nervously. Feeling silly, he clasped his hands behind his back so at least he could play with them out of everyone's view. None of the guests needed to know how nervous he was.

Suddenly, Erik, who had been put in charge of music, started playing a soft instrumental song on his acoustic guitar, and Lance and Rochelle started to walk down the aisle. He smiled as Rochelle caught his eye and winked. Next was Jack and Nyah. He felt a tiny bit of consolation knowing his friends stood up there with him, but he stopped breathing when Erik switched to playing a Bleeding Passion song intro that Kat had really wanted to walk down to. His eyes riveted to the tent she would be stepping out of at any second.

* * * *

Kat took another deep breath in an attempt to calm her wildly beating heart as she heard Erik start playing the song she was supposed to walk to. Van's father patted her on the hand and smiled down at her. She looked up at him. His warmth made her ease a little. He gave her a questioning look, as if to ask her if she was ready, and she nodded. He guided her out of the tent and she briefly scanned the area until her eyes fell on Van.

He looked so stunning in his tux with red rose boutonniere. He had his hair down and it fell around his shoulders, framing his handsome face in the way that she loved. She sighed and her nervousness abated just a little. How could she feel apprehensive when she was marrying the most beautiful man in the world?

Van's heart stopped in just the way it had when he had first seen Kat walking down the hallway his freshman year. She was wearing a simple, elegant two-piece gown that had tiny, shimmery white flowers on the bodice and cap sleeves made of the same material. Her hair was straight, which he rarely saw, and he liked the way it had been parted. The layers she had in it framed her face and the headband she was wearing made her look like a princess. She was carrying a bouquet of white calla lilies. He grinned as she started walking slowly toward him. She looked like a goddess. His goddess. The one who had enchanted him so long ago.

As Kat reached Van, she handed Rochelle her bouquet

and took his outstretched hand. Her fingers were trembling and he placed them to his lips briefly, offering her an encouraging smile. He didn't hear what the minister was saying. His voice just sounded like a droning hum. All he could hear was his own heartbeat and all he could see were Kat's beautiful eyes. He saw his entire life in those eyes, his past, present, and future.

Kat felt like she was standing up there for an exceedingly long time before they finally got to the exchanging of rings and the vows. Her hands still had not ceased trembling when Van had to place the ring on her finger, and she felt a curious churning in her stomach when she placed the ring on his. With such a simple gesture, she had bound herself to the man in front of her for all eternity. She looked up into his eyes as she heard the minister ask her the most important question she would ever answer.

"Katrina Erin Vauss, do you take Van Jacob Marshall to be your lawfully wedded husband, to love and stand beside through all the days of your life?"

Kat smiled. She hadn't known that when he'd changed his name he had kept Jacob as his middle name. "I do," she murmured without hesitation.

Van grinned warmly at her.

"Do you Van Jacob Marshall take Katrina Erin Vauss to be your lawfully wedded wife, to love and protect through all the days of your life?"

Van couldn't tear his gaze away from Kat. Love and protect her. He would protect her from any kind of harm until time stopped. And nothing could ever make his love for her cease. It would endure for all eternity. "With all of my heart," he breathed.

Neither one of them heard the minister ramble off the last few lines of the ceremony. All they heard was when he told them they could kiss one another. Van smiled softly and stepped closer to her. He cupped her cheek in his hand and gazed at her for one long, glorious second before he lowered his lips gently to hers. When he pulled away, he had tears in his eyes that he didn't bother trying to hide. He rested his forehead against hers and sighed. "My life, my whole world, is complete now," he whispered.

Kat closed her eyes and wished that they could just disappear. Even though she was looking forward to the reception, she wished she could have escaped in that moment with him and stayed there forever. Unfortunately, they had a bunch of guests sitting there waiting. Reluctantly, they pulled apart and turned to face the crowd.

"It gives me great pleasure to introduce Mr. and Mrs. Van Marshall," the minister finished.

Erik began to play the wedding march on his guitar, and Kat and Van made their way back down the aisle. Van grinned and scooped Kat up into his arms once they reached the back, drawing a startled shout from her. He laughed and yanked back the flap on one of the tents, then set her down on her feet. He took her face in his hands and kissed her all over, making her giggle. "My wife," he breathed. "My beautiful, perfect wife."

Kat blushed. She wrapped her arms around his waist and held onto him. She looked up into his eyes and lifted her lips to meet his in a hungry kiss. He tangled his fingers in her hair; her knees went weak at the magic of his lips. She leaned into him, pressing her body into his, never wanting to be apart from him again. "Van," she rasped, pulling away just enough so that she could speak.

"Yes, darling?" he whispered, smoothing her hair and gazing deeply into her eyes.

"I love you so much..." She smiled impishly. "Couldn't we just skip the reception?"

His grin was wolfish and he chuckled. "As tempting as that sounds, I think our guests would be sorely disappointed." She gave a playful pout, and the fire in his eyes that blazed to life at her expression let her know just how much he wanted her at that moment. He trailed his knuckles absently down her cheek. "I have waited this long. I suppose a few more hours won't kill me." Even as he said it, he didn't look very convincing.

She frowned. "And what about me? Aren't you supposed to honor your wife's wishes?"

He raised an eyebrow. "I think there may be a side of you I am unfamiliar with," he laughed.

"There is a side of me that's always been lurking, dying to get out. It's a side of me that only you will ever know." She trailed her fingers through his hair. "A side that I've never wanted to share with anyone but you."

He kissed her forehead tenderly. "I am looking very forward to spending the rest of my life getting to know every-thing about you." He sighed. "But, right now, I think we had better go greet our guests before the tongues start wagging."

She laughed and nodded. She laced her fingers with his and they left the privacy of the tent to go and greet their friends as man and wife.

Chapter Twenty-Six

Kat remembered the day before Jake had gone away to college. She'd snuck into his room late at night. She remembered how barren his room had looked with all of his things packed and how he had kept looking at her as if there was something very important he wanted to tell her. Kat hadn't told him, but she had felt like part of her world was crashing down around her that day. She'd had an awful feeling that she would never see him again. And then, when she had thought he was gone forever...

She sighed, smiling to herself as she heard him saying his goodbyes to Rochelle, who had come to get her things. She was staying at the hotel with the other band members for a few days. Kat watched as Van came back into the room and she couldn't believe that he was all hers, forever. She had thought him lost to her, and now, he was her husband.

Van met Kat's eyes and grinned. "Alone at last," he teased.

She smiled.

"Just one second. You wait here. I desperately want to kiss you, but I don't want to do it with dinner still in my teeth."

Kat giggled and sat on the arm of the couch, waiting. It had been a long day. The wedding had been at noon and it was six o'clock already. She had begun to think that she was never going to get out of there. The pictures alone had taken a good hour and a half, and then, of course, there was dinner and dancing and the cake cutting. The day couldn't have gone more perfectly, but she was exhausted. She was grateful that she would only have to get married once.

Van emerged grinning from the bathroom, and she

laughed as he swooped her up into his arms and began to carry her up the staircase. She wrapped her arms around his neck and rested her head on his shoulder.

When they reached the door to the bedroom, Van stopped. "I really hope you like this," he said. "I'm not entirely sure how you like to decorate, but I wanted it to be a surprise."

She smiled. "Just open the door."

He turned the knob. He stepped inside and Kat gasped. The bed alone was enormous. It was a king-sized four-poster that looked like something out of the middle ages. There was black velvet draped across the top like a canopy and wrapped around the posts, and the comforter was a deep burgundy color. Several pillows of alternating black and burgundy decorated the bed. The curtains were the same burgundy and there was an oak vanity and chest of drawers on the far wall. There was also a rather large entertainment center with all of the essential electronic devices.

Candles were placed all around the room, mostly deep red and deep purple ones, and there was a black fluffy throw rug right before the entrance to the master bathroom. "I hope it's not too dreary for you," he said.

She smiled. "Too dreary? It's totally you. How could I not like something that has you written all over it?"

"You like it then?"

"I love it." She turned her face so she could look at him and their eyes met. She leaned in to kiss him. He tightened his arms around her and carried her over to the bed. He set her down gently, breaking their kiss. She searched his eyes, feeling horribly awkward all of a sudden. She had no idea how she was supposed to go about any of this. He smiled softly and caressed her cheek, pressing his lips to hers again.

Van made sure his kisses were slow and gentle. The last thing he wanted was for Kat to feel like she was being rushed. He wanted her, yes, but he wanted to experience and savor all of her. He wanted to show her what intimacy was supposed to be and erase all of the horrible memories she had of the unwanted experience from her past.

He pulled away again and smiled at her. He sat down on the edge of the bed next to her and reached down to pull off his shoes. He flopped down onto his back afterward and let out an enormous sigh.

Kat giggled and lay down next to him, her head propped up on her elbow. "Today has been so surreal," she said, toying with his fingers. "I felt like I was dreaming all day, like it wasn't really happening." She shook her head. "I guess I just never imagined myself married."

He smiled. "How do you like it so far?"

"Being your wife?" She sighed. "The wife of the ever-desirable Van Marshall. I don't know how I'm going to like beating women off of you with a stick all the time, but..." She shrugged. "Considering I am going to be head of security, I can get away with it."

He chuckled and reached up to touch her face. His fingers trailed softly across her jaw and down her neck. He watched her close her eyes and felt her shiver as he traced one finger along the neckline of her dress, aching to see the rest of her smooth skin. He smiled and reached behind her neck, gently guiding her down to his lips once again. He kissed her slowly, teasing her lips with his, savoring the silken softness that now belonged only to him.

She had always had such power over him, with her intoxicating kisses and radiant soul. He always felt a measure of vulnerability when he was with Kat. He didn't know if it was because she was the goddess of all his fantasies and he had never truly felt he deserved her beauty, or if it was because he knew she had always been able to see right into him as if she had known him always. Whatever it was, he knew he would never be able to keep anything from her. She knew all of his strengths and all of his weaknesses. Every pulse of his heart beat only for her, the vibrantly gentle woman who had altered his entire existence.

It was easy for Kat to lose herself in Van's kiss. He did something to her she would never rightly be able to explain. He bewitched her with his seductive sensuality and she didn't even think he knew he did it. She wondered if he truly knew how desirable he was, how sexy and perfect. She believed that part of Van would never be able to see himself that way, no matter how famous or how good-looking he had become. There was a piece of his heart that was still very much that boy in her art class.

She sighed, and her body went pliant against Van's as he delicately explored her mouth, taking his time, making her melt with his warm gentleness. Her fingers slipped deftly underneath his tux coat, which had been unbuttoned for a good portion of the day, and she ran her hand up his chest, savoring the feel of his muscles beneath his shirt and dying to feel his skin. She attempted to slip the coat off his shoulder, but that was made greatly impossible considering he was lying down. She pulled away from his lips and frowned, irritated at the fact that her progress had been halted.

Van chuckled as he looked up into her disgruntled face. He sat up and removed his tux coat, sending it sailing haphazardly to the floor. She laughed and he grinned, wrapping his arms around her and pulling her close to him again. He tilted her chin sideways and began pressing tender kisses along her jaw line and down her throat. He feathered his fingers down her neck and along her shoulder, taking the cap sleeve with them.

He bent his head to her exposed shoulder and placed a slow, soft kiss to it, wanting to memorize the supple texture of her skin. His heart hammered in his throat and he felt like he was seventeen all over again, kissing her for the first time. Never in his life had he thought he would be touching Kat this way. It had always been a vision from one of his torturous dreams, not a reality. But now, she was with him. She was his.

He trailed his kisses down her arm all the way to her fingers, where he pressed a kiss to her palm. She reached her hand up to cup his cheek and he closed his eyes, leaning into her touch. Her other hand came up to thread through his hair and his heart jolted when he felt her lips on his face, kissing his forehead, his nose, his chin. Her lips traveled down to where his pulse pounded against the hollow of his throat and she kissed him there, making him draw in a shuddering breath. He tilted her face upwards, needing to sample the heaven of her mouth again.

Kat complied willingly, allowing his sweet seduction to overtake her yet again. Everything about him was so tender. She had never felt safer than when she was with Van. He touched her as if she was something delicate, something fragile and precious that could be broken easily.His fingers brushed up her back briefly and stop at the top of her zipper. She drew in a shaky breath as he slowly slid it down, exposing her back to him. She shrugged her arms out of the sleeves and threw the bodice to the floor. She kept her mouth on his so she wouldn't have to think about the fact that she was only in her bra now.

She knew she was safe and with the man she loved, but undressing herself in front of him still made her feel vulnerable, and she didn't need her mind going where it didn't need to. There was no reason for her to remember the shadows of her past. This was her wedding day. This was the beginning of her life with Van. He would never hurt her; he would never take advantage of her. He was the source of her joy and her passion and a quickly growing desire that she wanted to explore.

She busied herself with his mouth and wrapped her arms around his neck, pressing herself close up against him. He made a small noise in his throat and held her tighter, his hands languidly caressing her back and shoulders. Her own hands reached up to the top button of his shirt, thinking it was unfair that he could touch her bare skin and she didn't have the same luxury.

Her fingers fumbled on the last button and she had to pull away from him to look down. She tugged the shirt free from his pants and opened it, slipping her hands inside and caressing his chest in much the same way she had that night in the music room. Her fingers lingered on the music notes tattooed over his heart and she smiled. She pulled his shirt off the rest of the way and swallowed as she gazed at him. Her hands started to tremble without warning and she looked down, letting out a slow breath.

Van opened his eyes and frowned in concern. "Kat?" he murmured, touching her face. "What is it, baby?"

"You're just so beautiful," she whispered. She stole a look up at him and shook her head. "It's intimidating."

He blinked in confusion. "Intimidating?"

She nodded. What if she didn't please him? What if she let him down and was just a disappointment? It's not like she had any experience to draw on. Okay, true, neither did he, but the art of seduction just seemed to come naturally to him. She felt so awkward.

Van gave a soft smile. "You're thinking too much again," he teased.

She smiled tremulously. Maybe she was. She needed to just chill out. What was the matter with her? Why did she always have to overanalyze everything? This was her wedding night, for crying out loud. She only got this once.

He tilted her chin up so he could look into her eyes. "We don't have to do anything if you don't want to," he said softly. "I could spend the rest of my life just holding you in my arms and be perfectly content."

She stared at him, shocked and touched beyond all comprehension. The fact that he could love her so selflessly was overwhelming. Any thoughts she had been having suddenly fled her mind and all she saw was the man in front of her. She wrapped her arms around his neck and attacked his mouth with another one of those wanton kisses that seemed to come out of nowhere. A million different visions of him flashed through her mind, memories that made her heart melt every time she thought of them. Their entire history played out for her in several seconds until it ended right where they were, husband and wife, together for all of eternity. They were no longer two separate people. She was him and he was her.

Van's body ignited at her sudden onslaught of passion. He laid her back against the bed and blanketed her body with his, turning the attention of his lips to her neck again. He kissed and nipped playfully, running his tongue up the line of her neck to her earlobe and nibbling. He felt her fingers trace up his arms and dig gently into his shoulders. He trailed fiery kisses along her collarbone and all the way down to her flat stomach where he paused for a moment. He took the time to trace the subtle lines of muscle, letting out a sigh.

Kat frowned and opened her eyes. Why had he stopped? Stopping wasn't allowed. "What's wrong?" she asked.

"Your stomach is more ripped than mine, Kat," he teased. "I feel inadequate. I don't know if I can get around that."

She snorted and rolled her eyes. "Oh shut up," she snarled. She sat up and fused her lips to his again, stifling his playful laughter. His fingers knotted in her hair and he laid her back down.

He took control of the kiss, pouring his very essence into it, wanting her to feel how she set him ablaze with passion for her. He kissed her deeply, teasing and taunting until she was breathless. He ran his hand down her side to her hip and she arched her back, allowing him to unzip the back of her skirt. The contact of her body pressed full against his nearly undid him and he pulled the garment off hastily, bending down to press a kiss to her stomach as he did so.

Van slowed his progress as he caught sight of her long, slender legs. He let his breath out steadily and caressed his hand up the length of one of them. How could any one person be so perfect? How could such a perfect creature belong to him? He felt tears behind his eyes and he moved up to look at her.

She was so exquisite in every way. He let his eyes roam over her radiant figure and he cradled her cheek tenderly. He was shaking and not just with his want for her. He was shaking from the overpowering emotion he felt, the love for her that dwarfed the sun with its intensity.

His eyes traveled over her body and his heart lurched in a way that made him feel sick and delighted all at once. Who was he really? No one. Maybe a famous rock star to the world, but he was really nothing more than a stoic musician. A wandering bard who told stories in verse.

So he had an anxiety problem and he'd been made fun of in school. So what? His family had loved and supported him. He'd had friends stand by him through the hardest times in his life. Kat's family had never supported her. Her uncle had tried to molest her for years. She'd enrolled in every school activity known to man so that she wouldn't have to go home. She'd been raped and brutalized and had taught herself not to feel anything at all to keep herself safe. She was a warrior, the kind of invincible force that people told stories about... And she was offering herself to him.

She was proud of her body. It had become her weapon. It was everything in her world that mattered. And she was giving it over to him, letting him look his fill, touch where he wanted...trusting him. It was almost too overwhelming.

He swallowed and ran his hands in an unhurried caress up her legs again, worshipping every inch of toned perfection. His fingers came to rest on her hips and he tucked them underneath the waistband of her panties, slipping the fabric down her body in a torturously slow path. She unhooked her bra and he gazed down at her as if he was staring right at heaven. His heart hurt with the amount of love and adoration he felt.

He quickly rid himself of his remaining clothing and came to lie beside her, his entire body shivering and burning all at once as his bare skin made contact with hers.

"Kat?" he rasped.

She smiled at him and wrapped her arms around him, pulling him up so that he was lying on top of her. Nothing in her life had ever felt as right and perfect as this moment. There were no doubts in her mind, no frightening remnants of old terrors. Just love. She loved the man before her so acutely that she knew it would be the end of her. The end of everything she had forced herself to believe. Van was her destruction and her salvation.

She sighed and trailed her fingers back and forth across his spine. "Yes?" His eyes were smoldering, full of passion and hidden messages. It made her want to lose herself in them, lose herself in him, for all time.

He sighed and gazed deep into her eyes. "I want to make love to you like I play my music," he breathed.

A tremor went through Kat's body. His voice, so power-ful, so velvet soft, caressed over her, and his words... Those words would live in her heart for all time. She reached her arms around his neck and pulled him back down to her, of-fering all of herself to him, wanting all of him for herself, and drowning in the maelstrom of his perfect love.

* * * *

Van somehow managed to wake himself up around seven in the morning, even though he really wanted to sleep much longer. He rolled over in irritation at waking up and frowned when he saw that the space on the bed next to him was empty. That's what had been wrong. He'd woke up because Kat was missing.

He swung his legs out of bed and went to the closet where he grabbed a black robe and hastily wrapped it around himself. He checked the bathroom, but when he didn't find her there, he left the bedroom and went into the den. He frowned as he noticed that the sliding glass door to the bal-cony was open and he went over to it. He poked his head out, shivering with the morning fog that was blanketing eve-rything in white vapor, and he stopped breathing altogether.

Standing there, like some sort of mythical siren of old, Kat was completely nude, the wisping fog licking along her supple skin as if it was caressing her. She was living art, the most beautiful thing ever created. "Kat," he murmured.

She turned and grinned when she saw him. She went to him and slipped her arms inside his half-open robe, wrapping them around his waist.

Van closed his eyes and let out a small, satisfied groan as her body came in contact with his. He untied his robe and wrapped it around the both of them, pulling her securely against him. She raised her lips to his and he kissed her gently as he sighed in rapture. "I'm the luckiest man in the world," he whispered.

She giggled. "Why? Because you have a wife who stands naked on the balcony?"

He chuckled and held her tighter, tucking her head beneath his chin. "I have to say, I was not expecting to see that."

"I just wanted to feel the fog on my skin. I've felt nothing for so long and I feel alive again for the first time in ages." She shrugged. "That probably sounds stupid."

He smiled softly. "Not at all." He shivered. "It's cold out here!"

She laughed and snuggled closer to him. "I don't even feel the cold. My heart is too warm." She looked up at him, loving how the fog made everything disappear, made everything silent. It made her feel like she and Van were the only two people on the planet, that they existed within their own world of fantasy.

Making love with Van had been more than she could ever have imagined. Having no pleasurable sexual experience of any sort to draw on, she had been completely in the dark as to what to do or what she was supposed to feel. None of that had mattered. Only Van had mattered, and the dance of love they had partaken in that was as old as time.

For as long as she lived, she would remember the gentle way he had treated her. The way his warm hands caressed her skin with such adoration, and the way he'd gone so slow, ensuring her comfort. He'd been so patient, so meticulously caring. It had made it impossible for her to think of painful memories. She would be forever grateful for that. He had the part of her that no one else would ever have. She belonged to him and only him, forever.

"I love you," she murmured as she gazed up into his gentle gray eyes.

He smiled softly and kissed her again. "I love you too, sweetheart. Come on, let's go inside before the fog wears off and you give the neighbors a show."

She grinned. "If we go inside, I'm bound to give you a show."

He arched an eyebrow and made a purring noise low in his throat. "That had better be a promise," he whispered as he kissed his way across her throat.

She laughed and let him guide her inside, so happy that she didn't know what to do with herself. She had never imagined that she could feel so content and at peace. She'd never imagined that she could feel so alive. Van had given everything to her. He was all she ever needed or wanted.

As Van closed the sliding glass door, Kat went into the bedroom to grab a robe for herself. She was hungry and thought she might make some breakfast, but when she re-entered the den, she stopped upon seeing that Van had started a blazing fire in the fireplace. He looked up at her and smiled. She grinned as she recalled all of the wicked fantasies she'd had about being with him in front of a fireplace...

Deciding that breakfast could wait, she went to join him, pulling him close and kissing him with all of the passion that he had given back to her soul.

Chapter Twenty-Seven

The roar of the crowd was more deafening than usual as Kat stood backstage, waiting. They were in London, and she figured it was time. She had been putting it off for the last month. Waiting for the perfect time, the perfect crowd. Tonight was it. Van was on fire and the audience was amazing. She took a deep breath and gave a decisive nod as she began making her way through the backstage area and down the corridor that would take her out to the back of the auditorium.

"Are we doing this tonight?" the light technician asked through Kat's earpiece.

Kat smiled. He had been asking her that during every show. The poor man had been on edge forever, just waiting to see when he would have to unveil Kat's well-kept secret. "Yeah, tonight. In about five," she replied.

"Holy crap, are you serious?"

Kat laughed. "Yeah, cue everything up." Her mind was a blur as she threaded through the crowd and tried to find a place that was not crawling, where she could stand and still see the stage fairly well. The last month and a half... She couldn't even describe it. The only thing better than being loved by Van was loving him in return. Every single moment was radiant when she was with him.

Van finished up the song he was singing and stabbed his arm up in the air, giving the "rock on" sign to the audience. They screamed, and the lights suddenly went very dim. Van blinked in confusion. He exchanged glances with his band mates, but they all looked as confused as him. The soft opening notes of HIM's "Beautiful" started to play, and a glow began to emanate from the screen behind the stage that they showed images on during the show. Van turned very slowly so he could face it, bewildered.

Suddenly, as the song became louder and more powerful, an old video clip of Kat and him at graduation was projected across the screen. She was laughing, as she had so often done back then, and she had her arm around his shoulders, hugging him. He had his eyes downcast, a shy smile on his lips, looking for all the world like he might invert at any given moment.

As the lyrics began, more images of high school times played across the screen. Him playing at the Senior Show; him writing a song in the quad and being silly while Kat recorded him; him and her standing together for the senior class picture; them walking across the stage at graduation. Then there were images of him in present day, playing and singing on stage; him and Kat standing and talking while Rochelle recorded; him walking off the stage and giving the camera a somewhat shy smile; Kat waving with a half-amused, half-bored expression to the camera.

There were more various shots of Van playing at different venues, him at the signing, a shot of all of them in Turnbeck, Arizona talking to Ozzy and laughing, Kat dancing on a table while intoxicated. He chuckled to himself, then sobered as the series of images changed to him and Lance loading furniture into their new house; Kat and Rochelle preparing the rehearsal dinner; Kat standing inside the music room and showing it off; him and Kat sitting on the couch together looking through a *Modern Bride* magazine; the two of them exchanging a personal look in the hall.

Van swallowed as the music became softer and shots of various wedding guests started flashing across the screen. Then it showed him, standing up by the minister, waiting. He looked deep in thought. Then, slowly, he turned toward the aisle just as the lyrics struck up again and Kat started walking down. His heart flipped just like he was experiencing it all over again.

Images of them exchanging rings, sharing their first kiss as husband and wife, turning to face the audience as they were announced Mr. and Mrs. Van Marshall. There were shots of them dancing, of Kat throwing her bouquet, of them feeding cake to one another, of Van looping his arm around her waist and spinning her as she laughed.

Then, as the chorus repeated one more time, it showed Kat standing backstage with her earpiece in, watching a show, her and him sitting on a couch together backstage, his arm around her and her head resting on his chest. They were both reading and he was absently playing with her hair. It showed her shoving him playfully and laughing about something, then a shot of the two of them standing together backstage, looking at the camera and smiling. As the music began to fade, the opening shot of them at graduation flashed again briefly before showing Kat standing by herself, facing the camera, her hand over her chest with her fingers formed into the American Sign Language sign for "I love you."

It stayed like that until the song faded out completely.

When the video was over, Van stood there, in complete silence, trying hard to contain himself. Tears sat behind his eyes, just waiting to come out. He couldn't believe what he had just witnessed. She had done that for him? Their whole relationship played out before him to one of the most beautiful songs ever written by his favorite band of all time. He couldn't deal with the surge of emotion he felt.

Slowly, he turned back toward the crowd, who was also silent, save the few screams and hollers of encouragement from various audience members. He walked up to the mic as if in a trance and cleared his throat. "I'm-uh—sorry for the interruption," he said, his voice still raspy. He frowned. "I—I think I'm going to need a little assistance from all of you guys," he said.

He knew Kat was in the back. She had to be. He couldn't see her from where he was standing, but he knew she was back there. She wouldn't create something like that and not watch it. She would want to see his reaction and, since it was what she used to do for a living, she would want to know it had turned out the way she planned.

"You see," he continued, "I'm standing up here and my wife is all the way back there and I need to get to her as soon as possible, so if you could all help me out I'd appreciate it." He rushed through the last part of his speech, not able to wait any longer. Then, without any thought at all, he leapt off the stage and dove down into the crowd below.

Kat let out a little shout as Van was caught by his fans, all screaming now. He had never been the crowd surfing type. She laughed as the fans guided him toward the back and, as he caught sight of her, he pointed in the direction he needed to go. When he was finally set down beside her, she could barely get out a thought before his lips were on hers. He kissed her with savage intensity, and she held onto him for fear she might fall over at any moment. When he pulled away, she looked up into his eyes, breathless and disoriented. "You're insane," she breathed.

He held her face in his hands and stared down into her eyes. "You are the one who is beautiful," he murmured.

She shook her head. "Don't you understand? All this time you have been claiming that I made you beautiful. You have always been beautiful. It was you who brought beauty to my life. I would be nothing without you. My life was a wasteland before you. I had forgotten what beauty was. All that I am now is because of you."

He squeezed his eyes shut as his emotions threatened to overtake him and make him look like a blubbering fool in front of all of his fans. He rested his forehead against hers and whispered the most important words in his world. "I love you."

Kat looked up into his face. She touched his cheek tenderly. He had never really changed. Not really. He had grown up, but not changed. His eyes were smudged with heavy eyeliner and he had some crazy-colored red eye shadow on. She smiled. He was still the eccentric artist, the gothic poet, the boy who had given her her first kiss and her first taste of love. He was hers for all time. She giggled. "Go finish your show. I'll be here when you finish." She sobered. "I'll always be here."

He gazed into her eyes for a long moment, then his lips split into a spectacular grin. He turned back to the crowd and began to run back through them up to the stage. A spotlight had followed him all the way back to Kat and had stayed on them for their whole personal moment. Now, it followed him back through the crowd, the fans screaming the entire time. He jumped back up on stage and turned to the microphone, shouting the title of the next song they were going to play. The band exploded into a fast, hard song. Kat watched him and smiled, a tear streaking down her cheek. She imagined she would always be amazed by him.

"Kat, what are you doing? Are you going to stay back

there all night? We need you up in the front."

Kat jumped as she heard one of the security guards in her earpiece. She had totally forgotten she was working! She shook her head. "Be there in a sec," she said. She moved back through the crowd to the backstage door and headed toward the stage.

Later, when she wasn't working, and Van wasn't performing, they could cease being Van, the mega-star sex symbol and Kat, the head of security. They could curl up together and be Katrina and Jake, who they had always been, who they always would be.

About the Author

I have been telling stories since I was able to comprehend words. While most kids in the first grade were playing tag, I was the one all by myself in the corner of the soccer field pretending it was a gateway to a different world. For as long as I can remember, there have always been people in my head begging to have their stories told.

I write love stories. Contemporary and fantasy. The world we live in is greatly devoid of love and true friendship. I write stories that revolve around these themes, as well as the overall message to be true to yourself. We were created as individuals. We should strive to be just that.